ONCE UPON A TIME MACHINE

VOLUME 2

To Pete,

Yo Joe!

Chis -- 19

CHRIS

For my mother, Denise, who worked so
hard to allow a little boy to dream, and
still found time to listen.

ANDREW

For my family—past, present, and future.

AT DARK HORSE BOOKS:

Mike Richardson, President and Publisher | Lin Huang, Designer |
Randy Stradley and Freddye Lins, Editors | Kevin Burkhalter, Assistant Editor

Neil Hankerson, Executive Vice President | Tom Weddle, Chief Financial Officer | Randy Stradley, Vice President of Publishing | Nick McWhorter, Chief Business Development Officer | Matt Parkinson, Vice President of Marketing | David Scroggy, Vice President of Product Development | Dale LaFountain, Vice President of Information Technology | Cara Niece, Vice President of Production and Scheduling | Mark Bernardi, Vice President of Book Trade and Digital Sales | Ken Lizzi, General Counsel | Dave Marshall, Editor in Chief | Davey Estrada, Editorial Director | Scott Allie, Executive Senior Editor | Chris Warner, Senior Books Editor | Cary Grazzini, Director of Specialty Projects | Lia Ribacchi, Art Director | Vanessa Todd, Director of Print Purchasing | Matt Dryer, Director of Digital Art and Prepress | Michael Gombos, Director of International Publishing and Licensing

Published by Dark Horse Books | A division of Dark Horse Comics, Inc. | 10956 SE Main Street | Milwaukie, OR 97222

DarkHorse.com

To find a comics shop in your area, visit comicshoplocator.com.

First edition: April 2018

ISBN 978-1-61655-666-2

1 3 5 7 9 10 8 6 4 2

Printed in China

ONCE UPON A TIME MACHINE

VOLUME 2

Edited by

ANDREW CARL

and

CHRIS STEVENS

Cover and Title Pages:

FAREL DALRYMPLE

Back Cover:

AARON CONLEY
JOSEPH BERGIN III

Associate Editor:

JOSH O'NEILL

Visit OnceUponaTimeMachine.com for more information and insight into the gods, legends, and the creative process behind the book.

DARK HORSE BOOKS

CONTENTS

"ICARUS"

written by
ANDREW CARL

illustrated and lettered by
GIDEON KENDALL

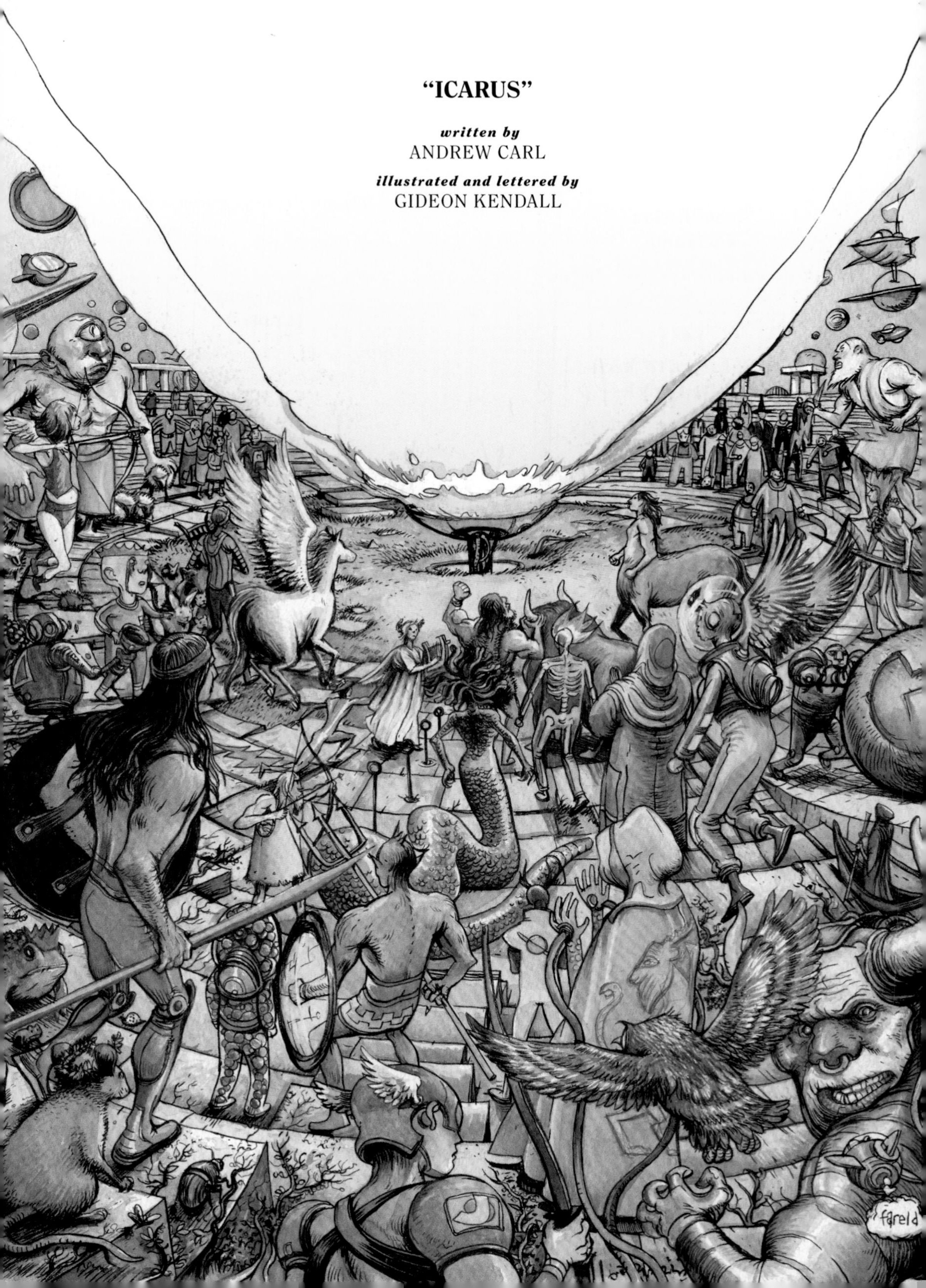

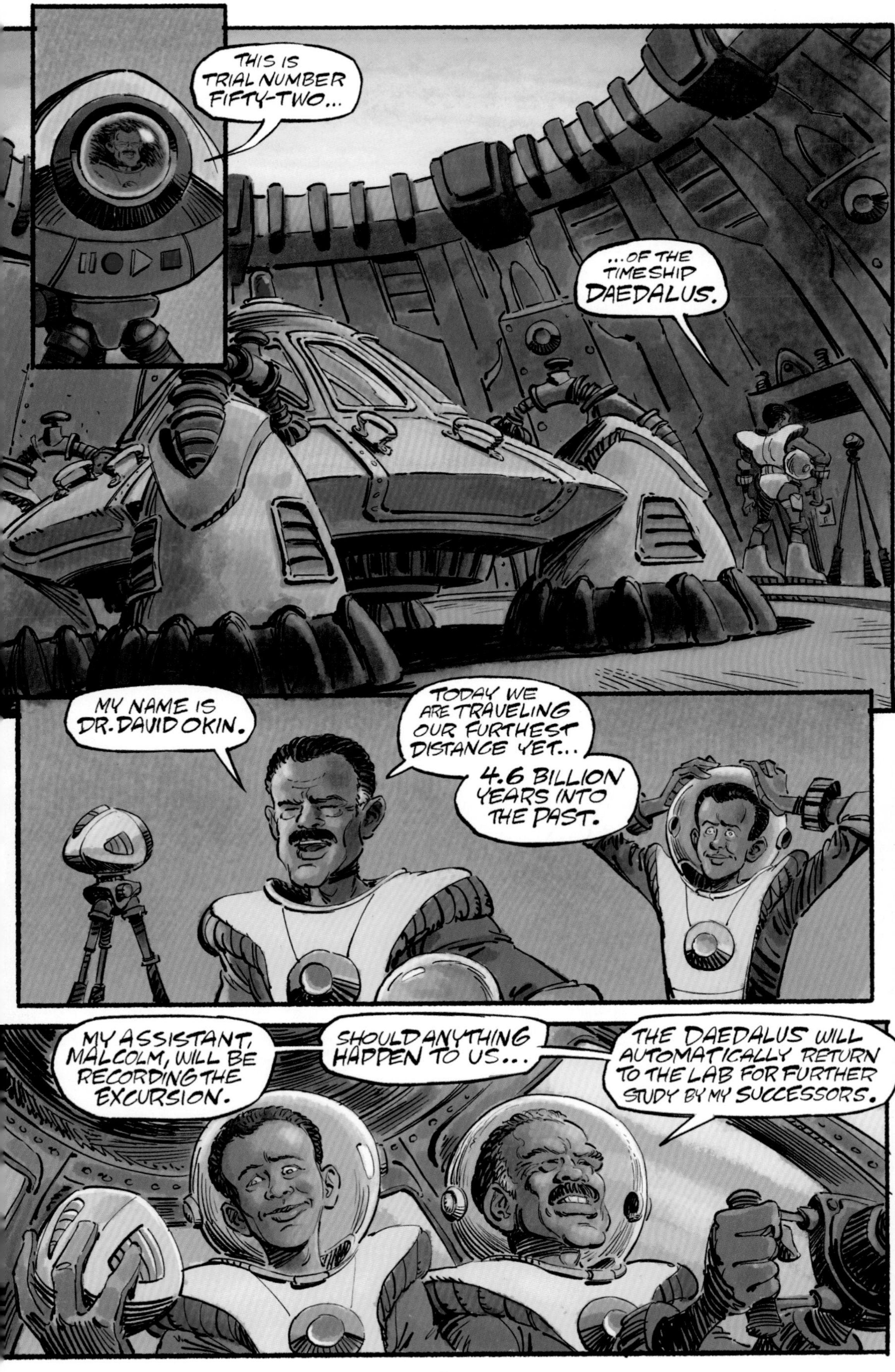
THIS IS TRIAL NUMBER FIFTY-TWO...
...OF THE TIMESHIP DAEDALUS.
MY NAME IS DR. DAVID OKIN.
TODAY WE ARE TRAVELING OUR FURTHEST DISTANCE YET...
4.6 BILLION YEARS INTO THE PAST.
MY ASSISTANT, MALCOLM, WILL BE RECORDING THE EXCURSION.
SHOULD ANYTHING HAPPEN TO US...
THE DAEDALUS WILL AUTOMATICALLY RETURN TO THE LAB FOR FURTHER STUDY BY MY SUCCESSORS.

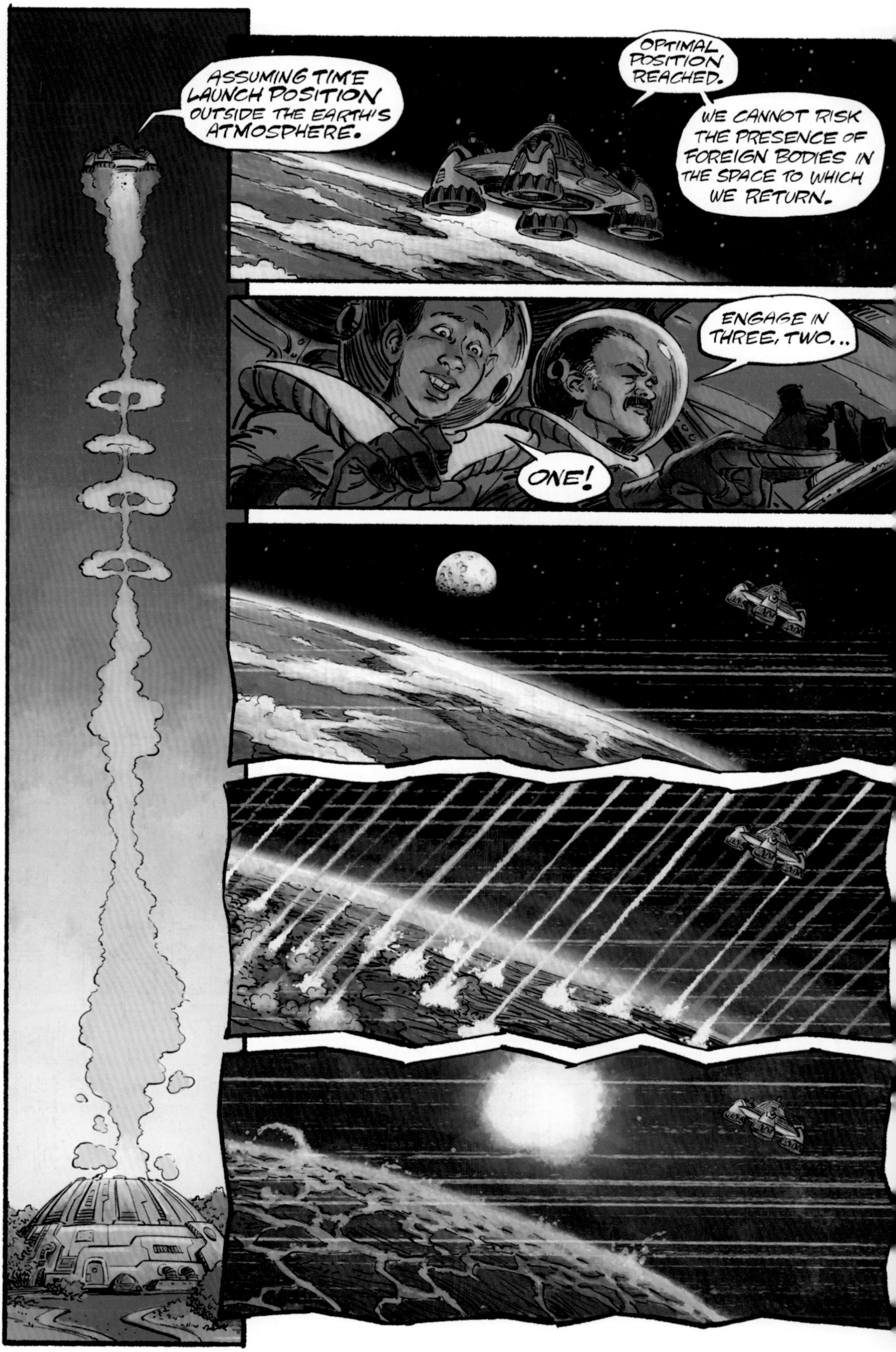
ASSUMING TIME LAUNCH POSITION OUTSIDE THE EARTH'S ATMOSPHERE.
OPTIMAL POSITION REACHED.
WE CANNOT RISK THE PRESENCE OF FOREIGN BODIES IN THE SPACE TO WHICH WE RETURN.
ENGAGE IN THREE, TWO...
ONE!

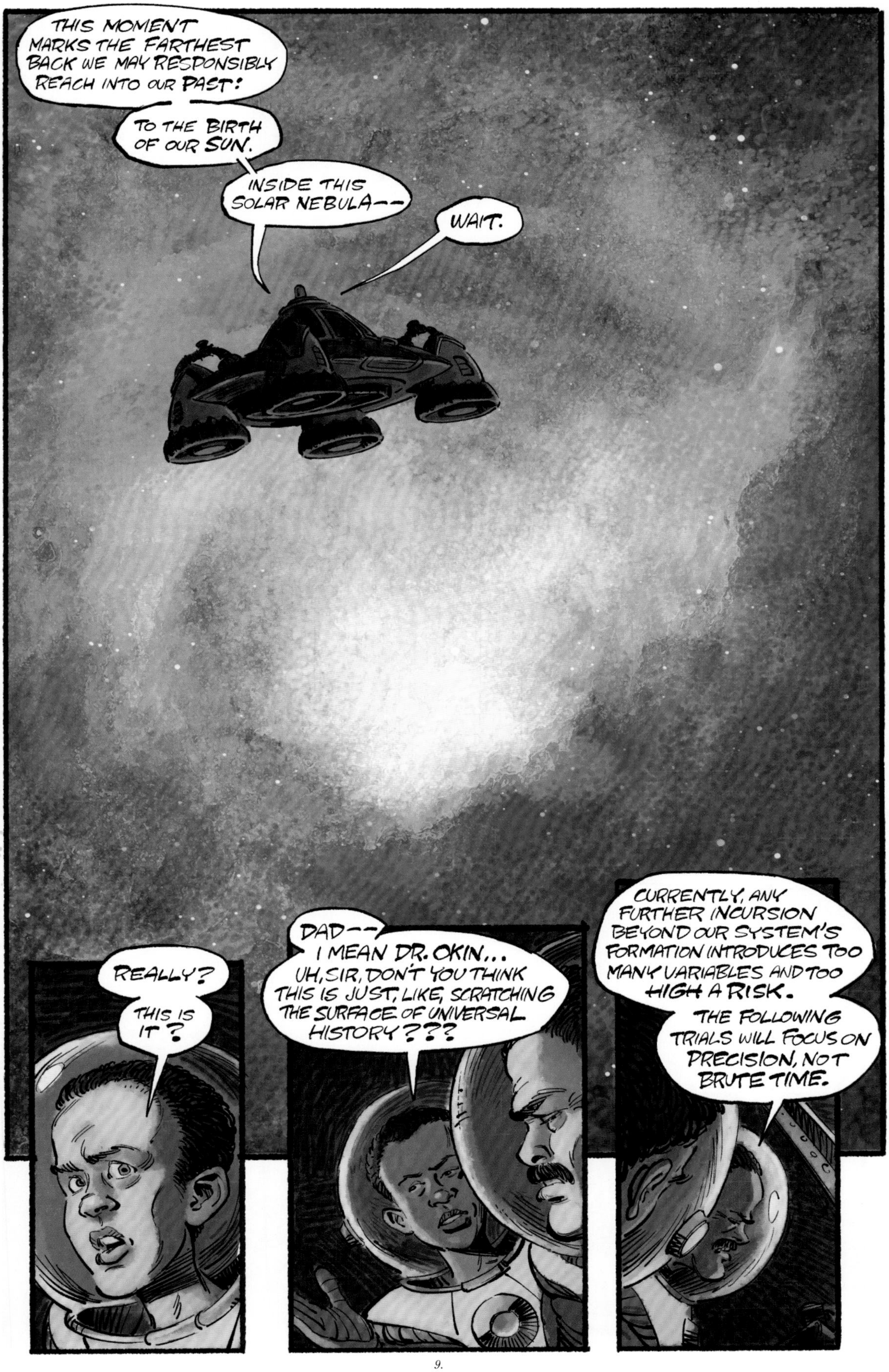
THIS MOMENT MARKS THE FARTHEST BACK WE MAY RESPONSIBLY REACH INTO OUR PAST:
TO THE BIRTH OF OUR SUN.
INSIDE THIS SOLAR NEBULA--
WAIT.
REALLY?
THIS IS IT?
DAD-- I MEAN DR. OKIN... UH, SIR, DON'T YOU THINK THIS IS JUST, LIKE, SCRATCHING THE SURFACE OF UNIVERSAL HISTORY???
CURRENTLY, ANY FURTHER INCURSION BEYOND OUR SYSTEM'S FORMATION INTRODUCES TOO MANY VARIABLES AND TOO HIGH A RISK.
THE FOLLOWING TRIALS WILL FOCUS ON PRECISION, NOT BRUTE TIME.

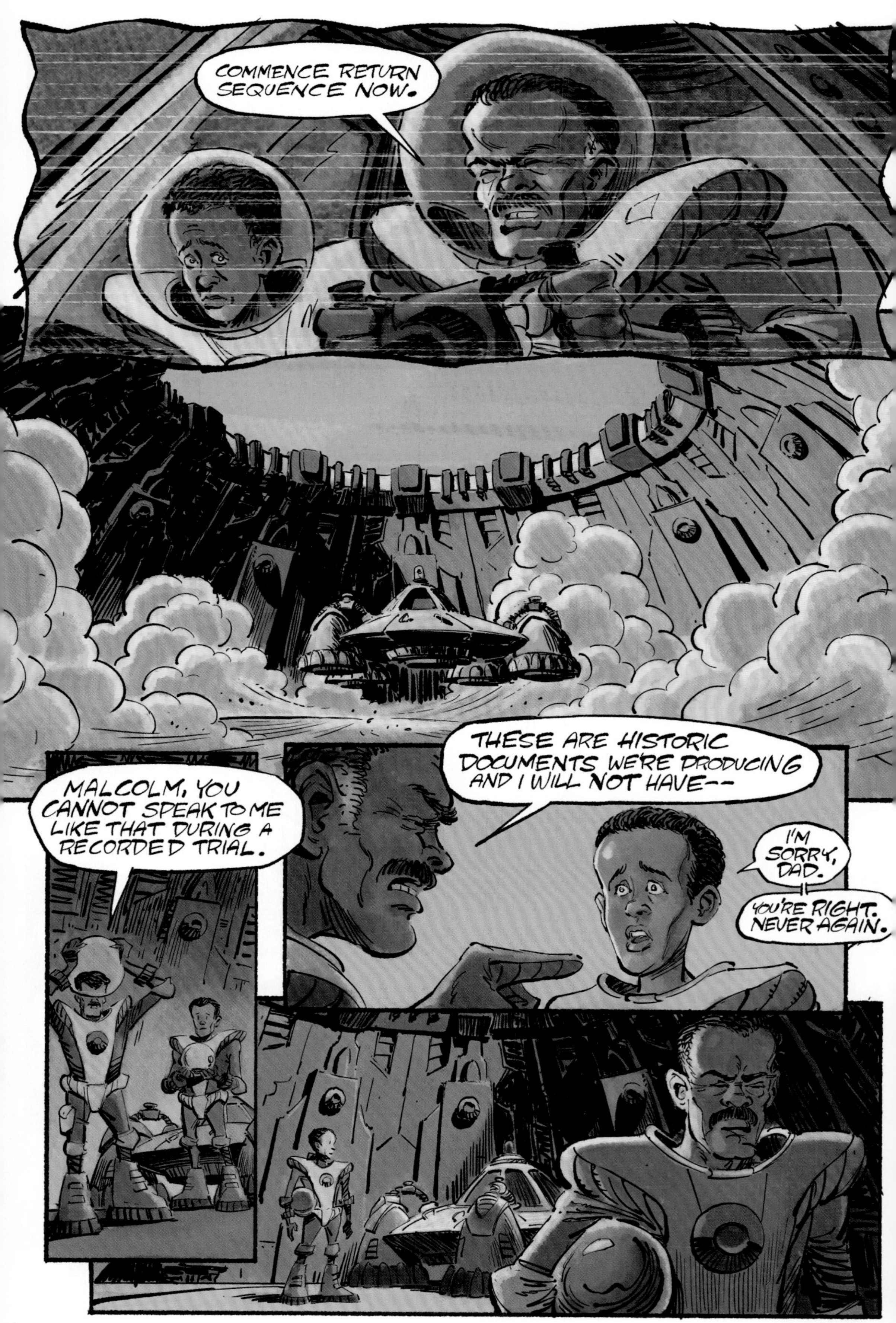
COMMENCE RETURN SEQUENCE NOW.
MALCOLM, YOU CANNOT SPEAK TO ME LIKE THAT DURING A RECORDED TRIAL.
THESE ARE HISTORIC DOCUMENTS WE'RE PRODUCING AND I WILL NOT HAVE--
I'M SORRY, DAD.
YOU'RE RIGHT. NEVER AGAIN.

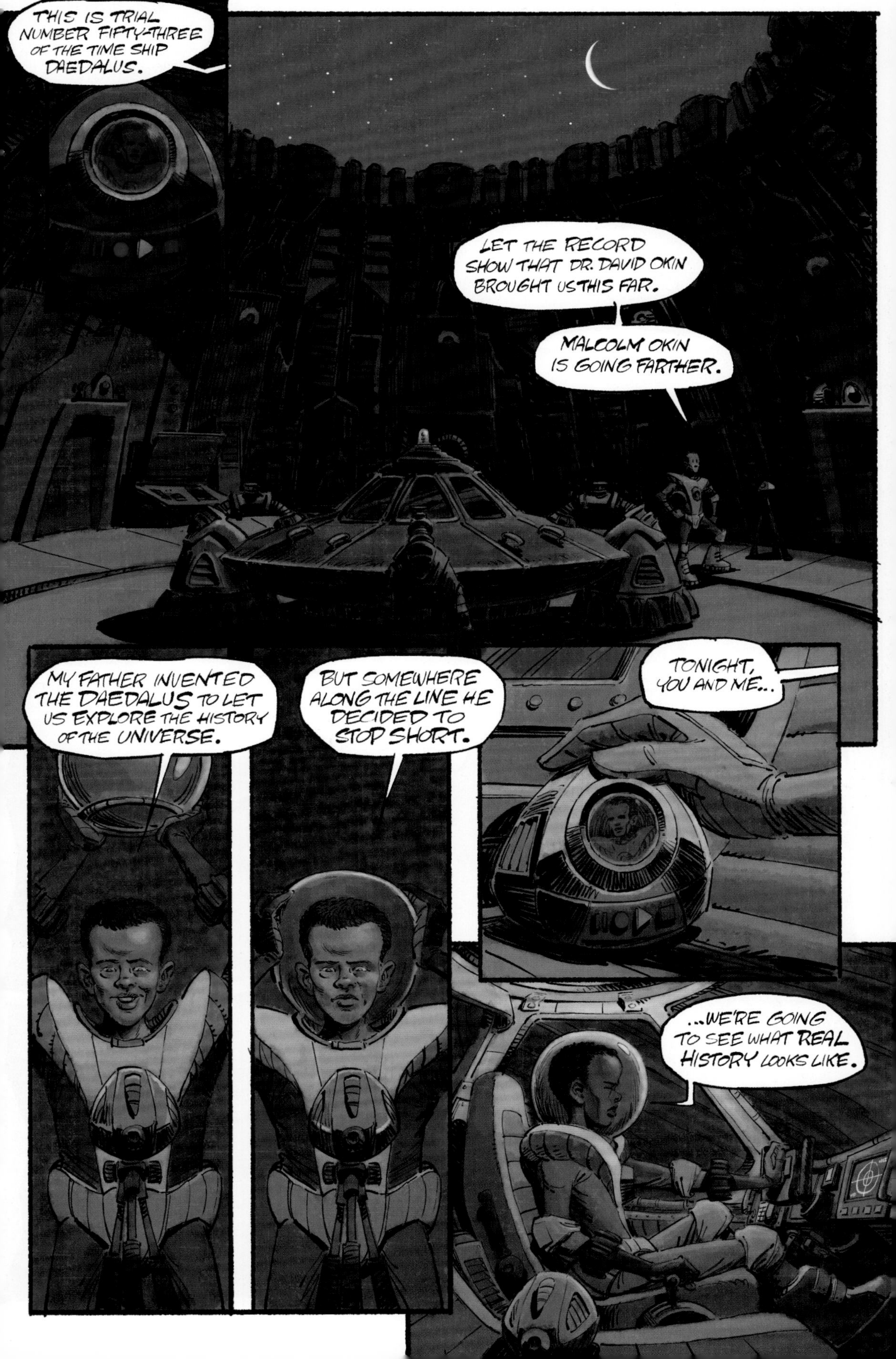
THIS IS TRIAL NUMBER FIFTY-THREE OF THE TIME SHIP DAEDALUS.
LET THE RECORD SHOW THAT DR. DAVID OKIN BROUGHT US THIS FAR.
MALCOLM OKIN IS GOING FARTHER.
MY FATHER INVENTED THE DAEDALUS TO LET US EXPLORE THE HISTORY OF THE UNIVERSE.
BUT SOMEWHERE ALONG THE LINE HE DECIDED TO STOP SHORT.
TONIGHT, YOU AND ME...
...WE'RE GOING TO SEE WHAT REAL HISTORY LOOKS LIKE.

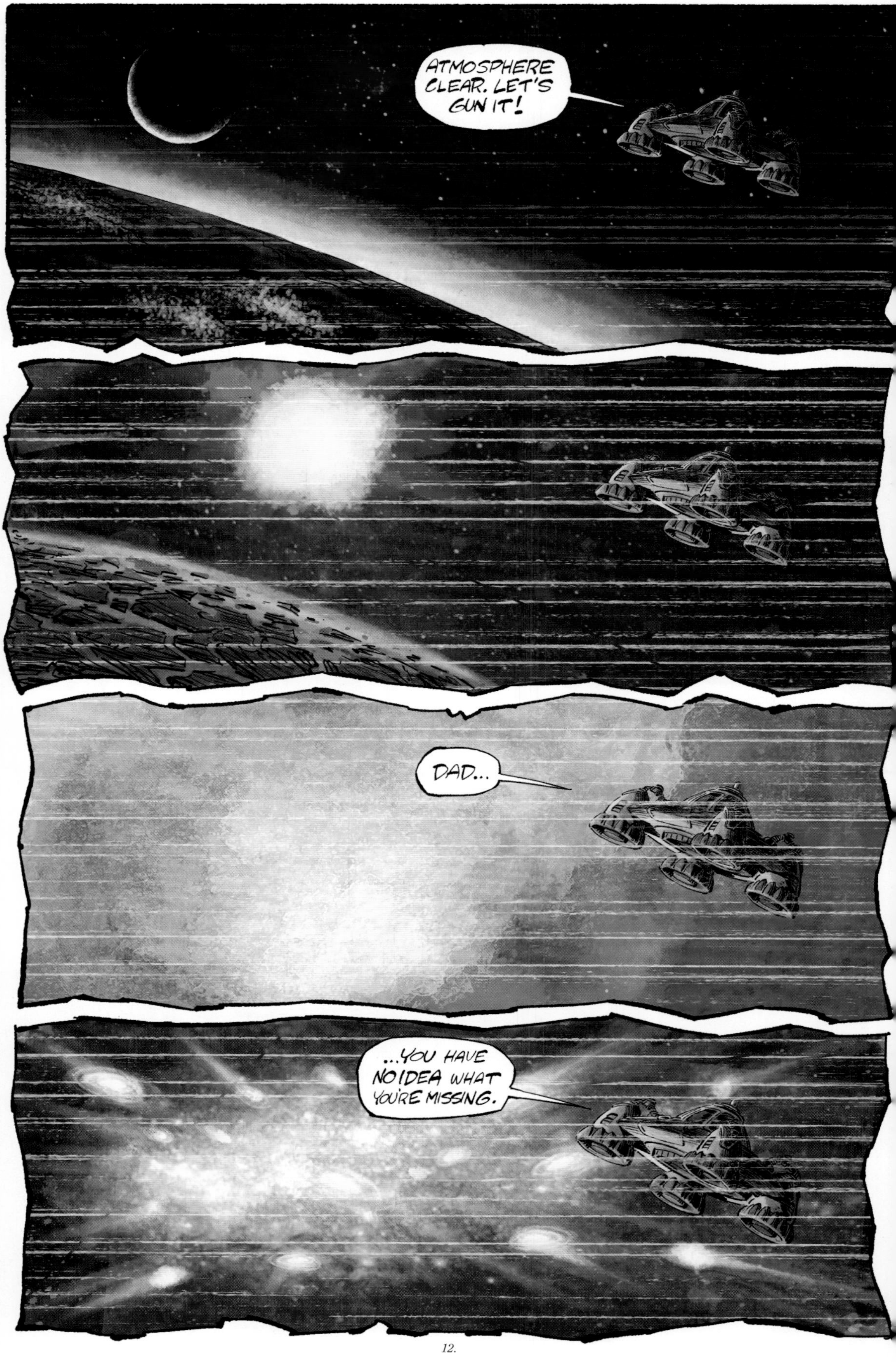
ATMOSPHERE CLEAR. LET'S GUN IT!
DAD...
...YOU HAVE NO IDEA WHAT YOU'RE MISSING.

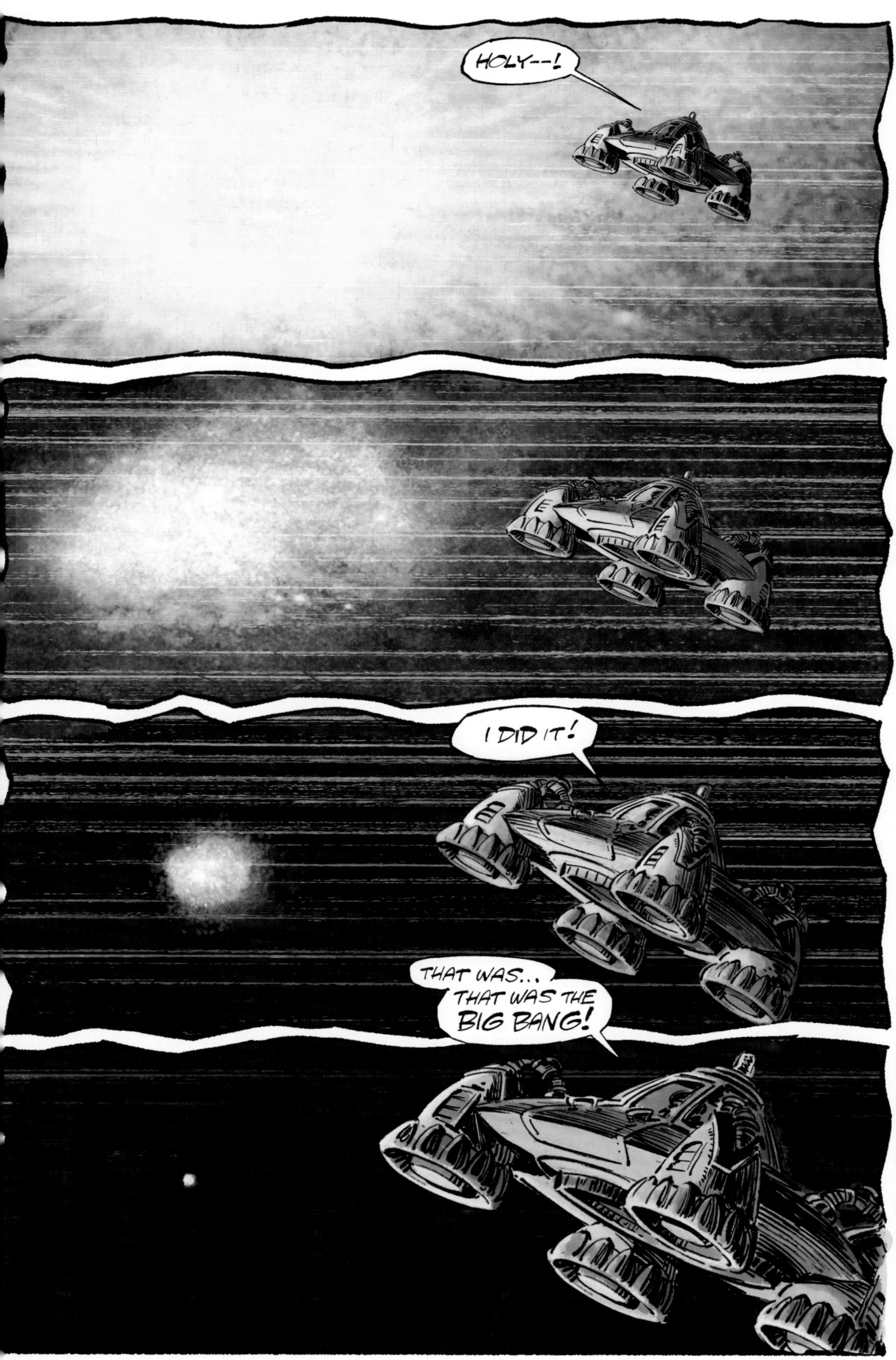
HOLY--!
I DID IT!
THAT WAS... THAT WAS THE BIG BANG!

AND THIS...

THIS RIGHT HERE IS EVERYTHING THAT'S EVER GONNA BE...

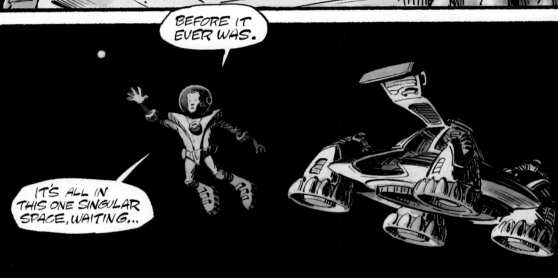

BEFORE IT EVER WAS.

IT'S ALL IN THIS ONE SINGULAR SPACE, WAITING...

WAITING FOR JUST THE RIGHT MOMENT TO...

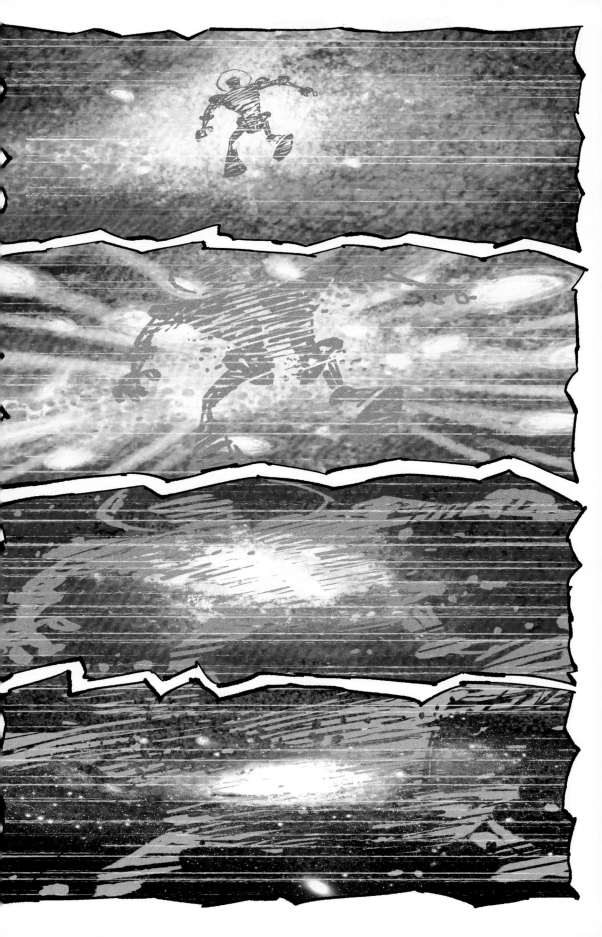

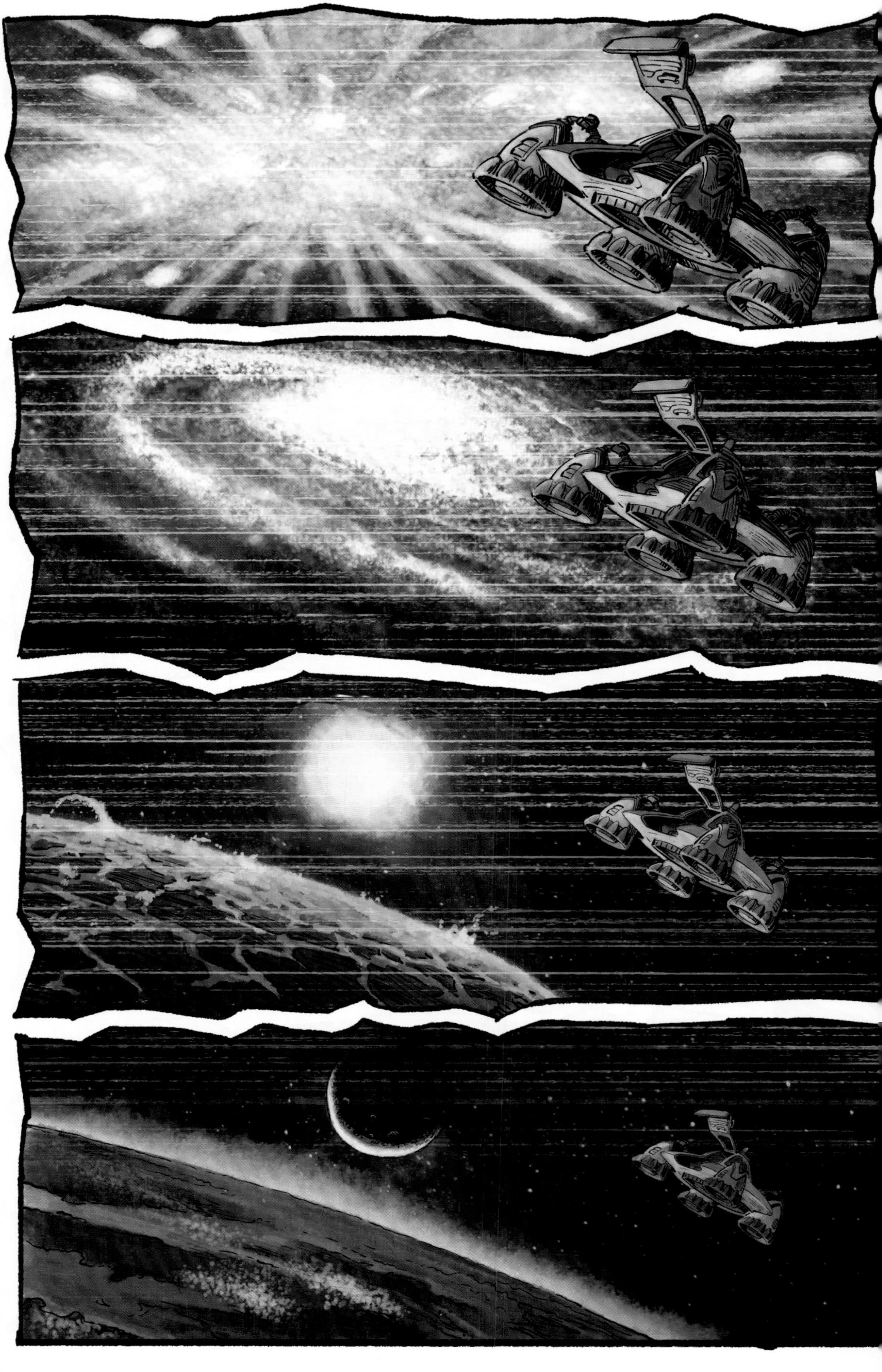

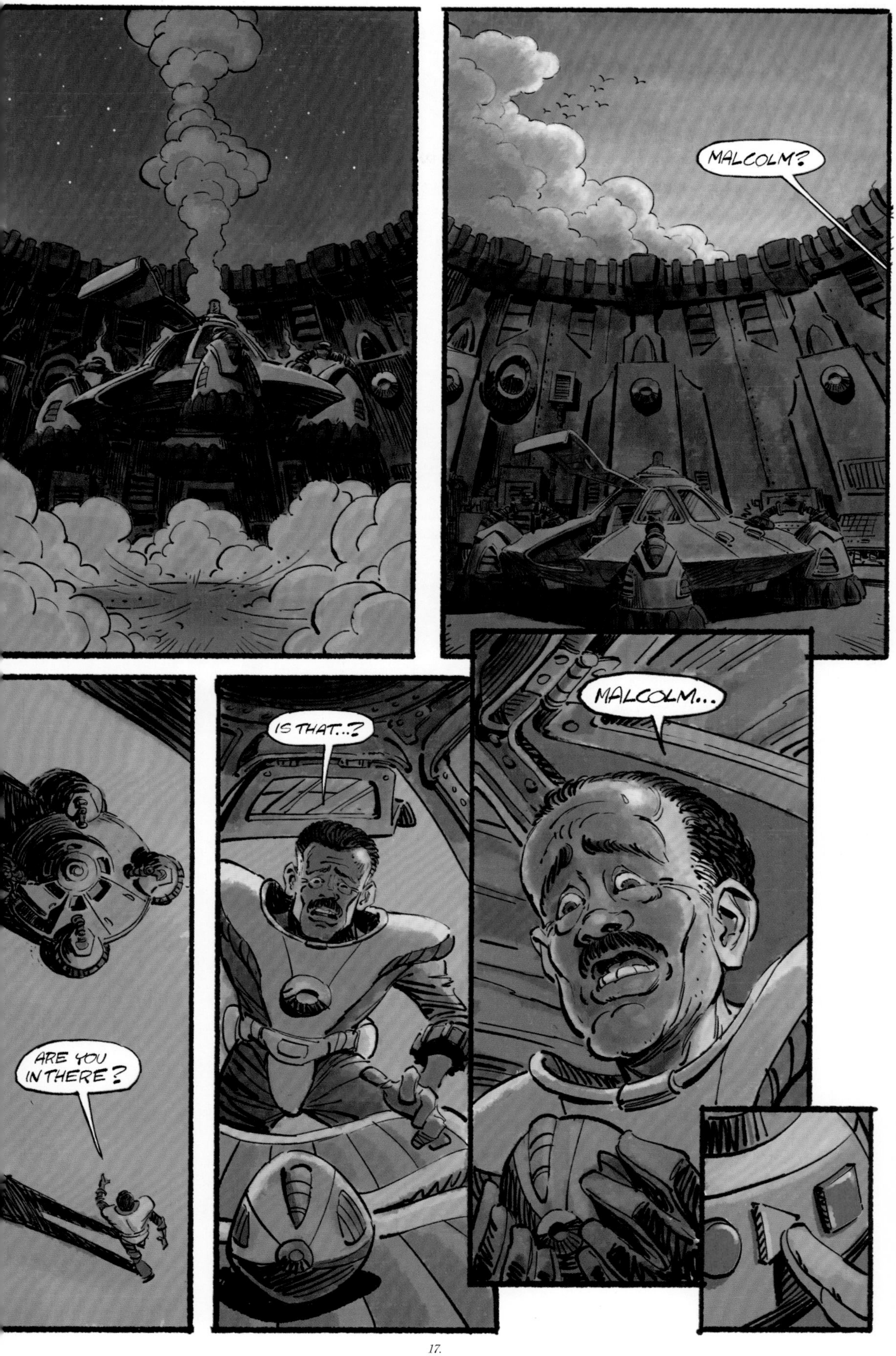
MALCOLM?
ARE YOU IN THERE?
IS THAT...?
MALCOLM...

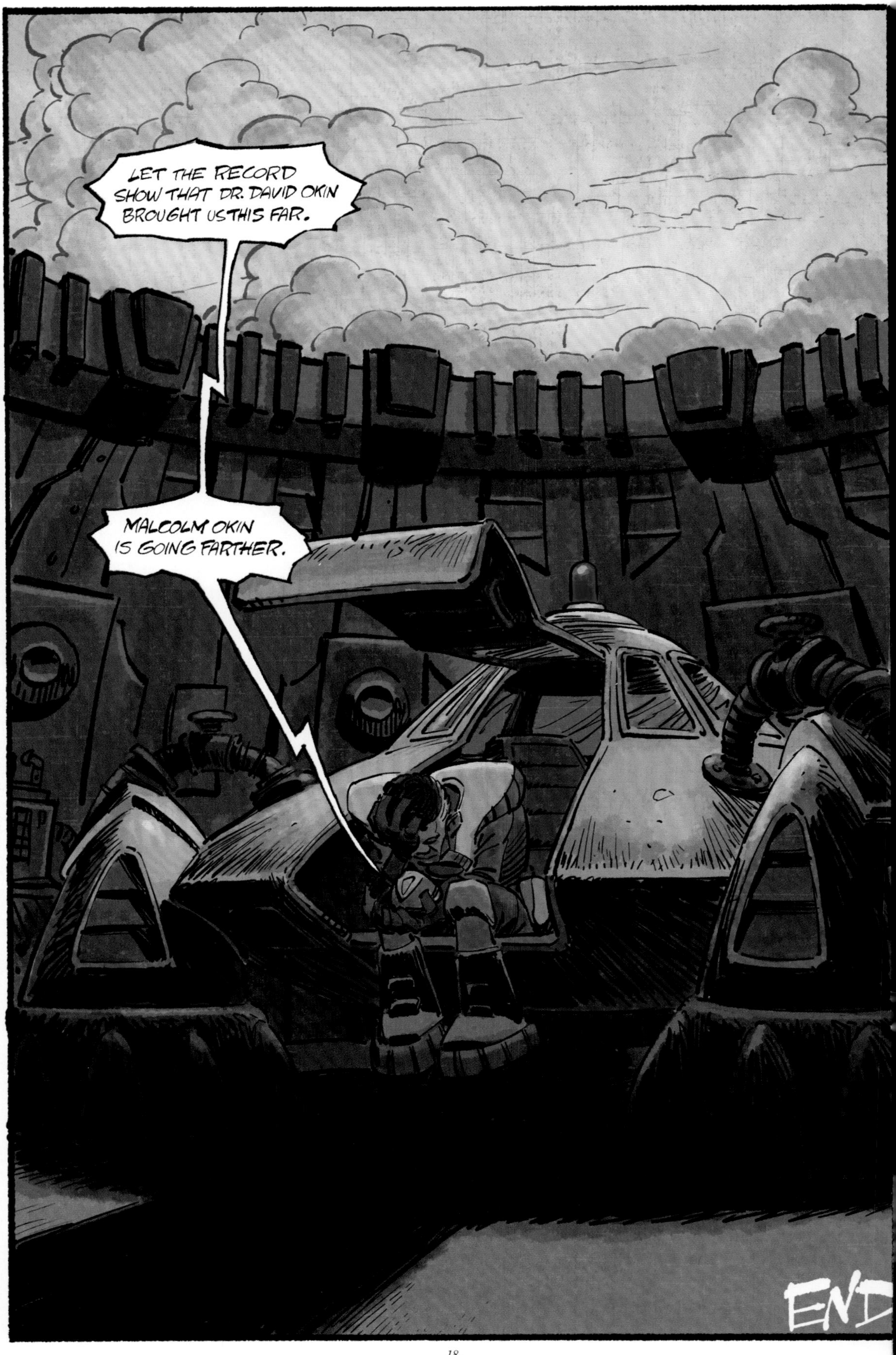
LET THE RECORD SHOW THAT DR. DAVID OKIN BROUGHT US THIS FAR.
MALCOLM OKIN IS GOING FARTHER.
END

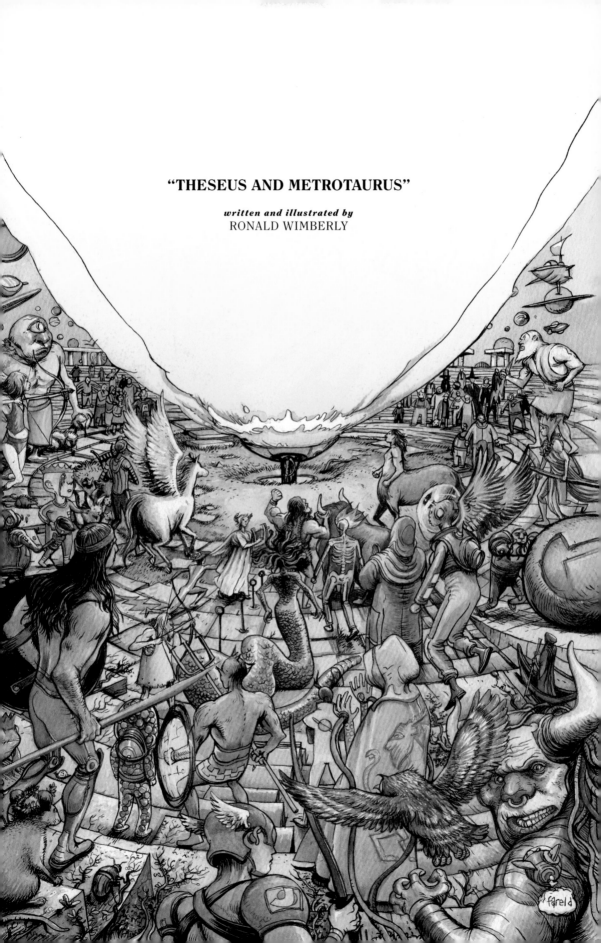

"THESEUS AND METROTAURUS"

written and illustrated by
RONALD WIMBERLY

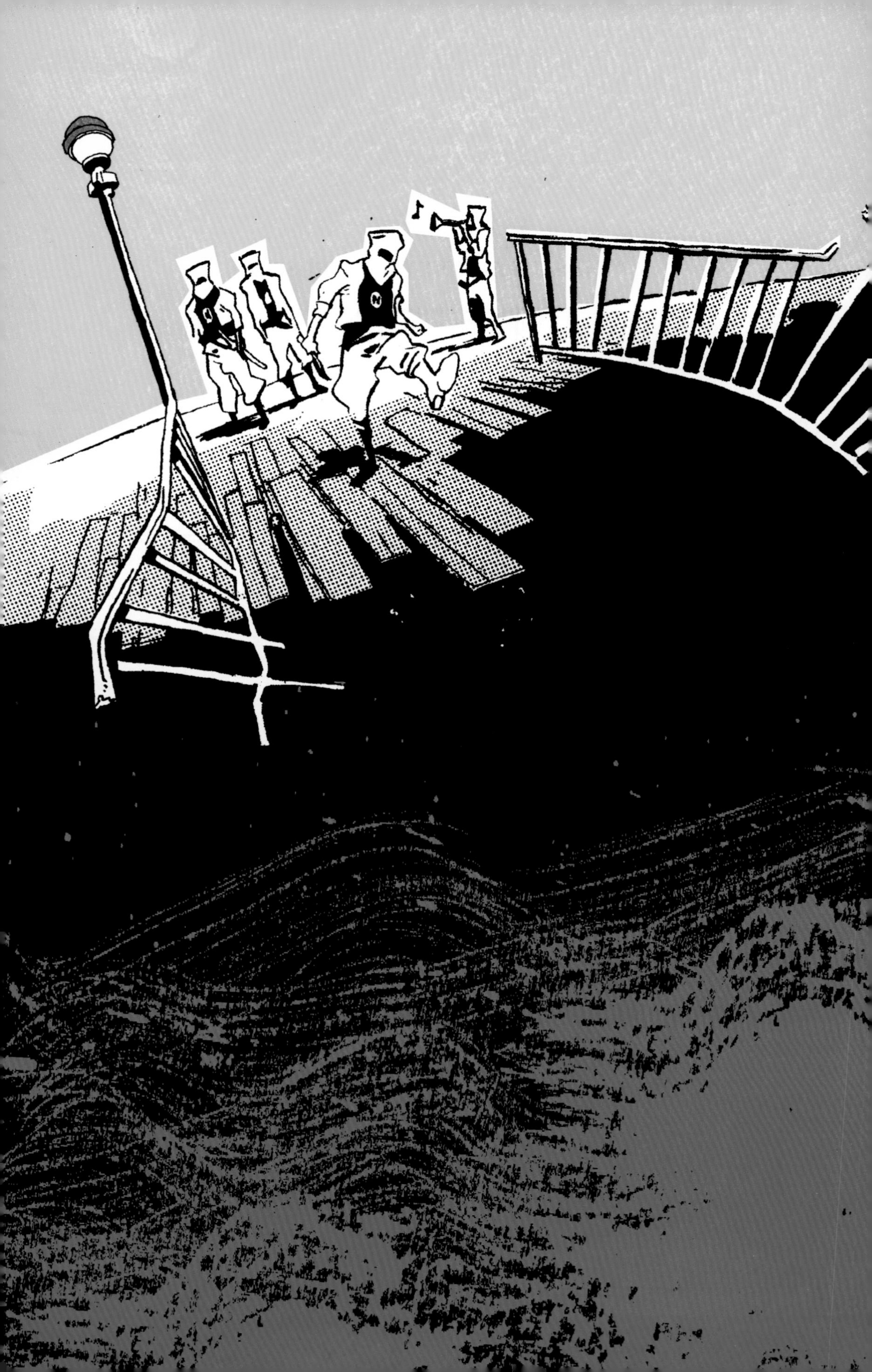

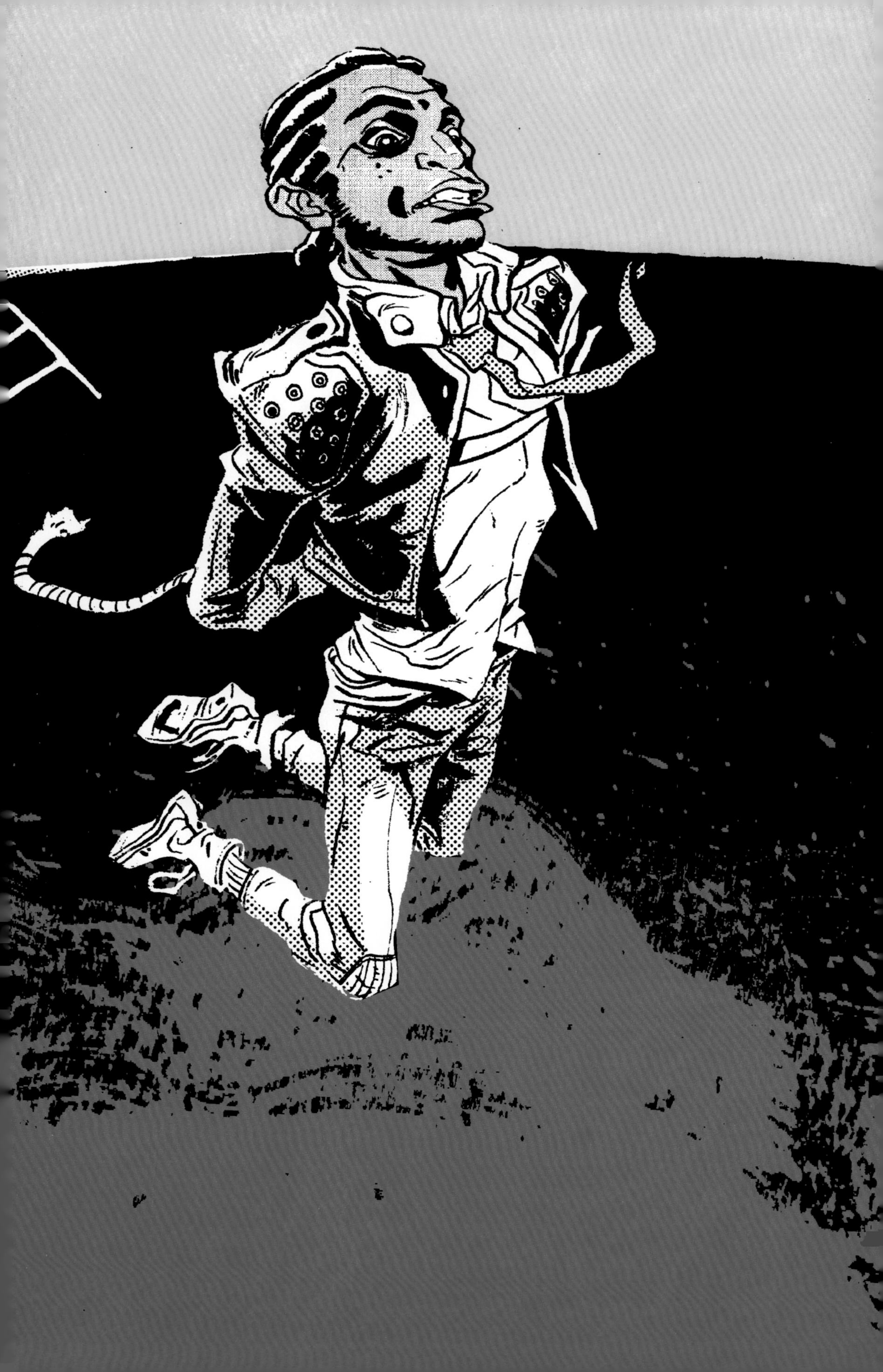

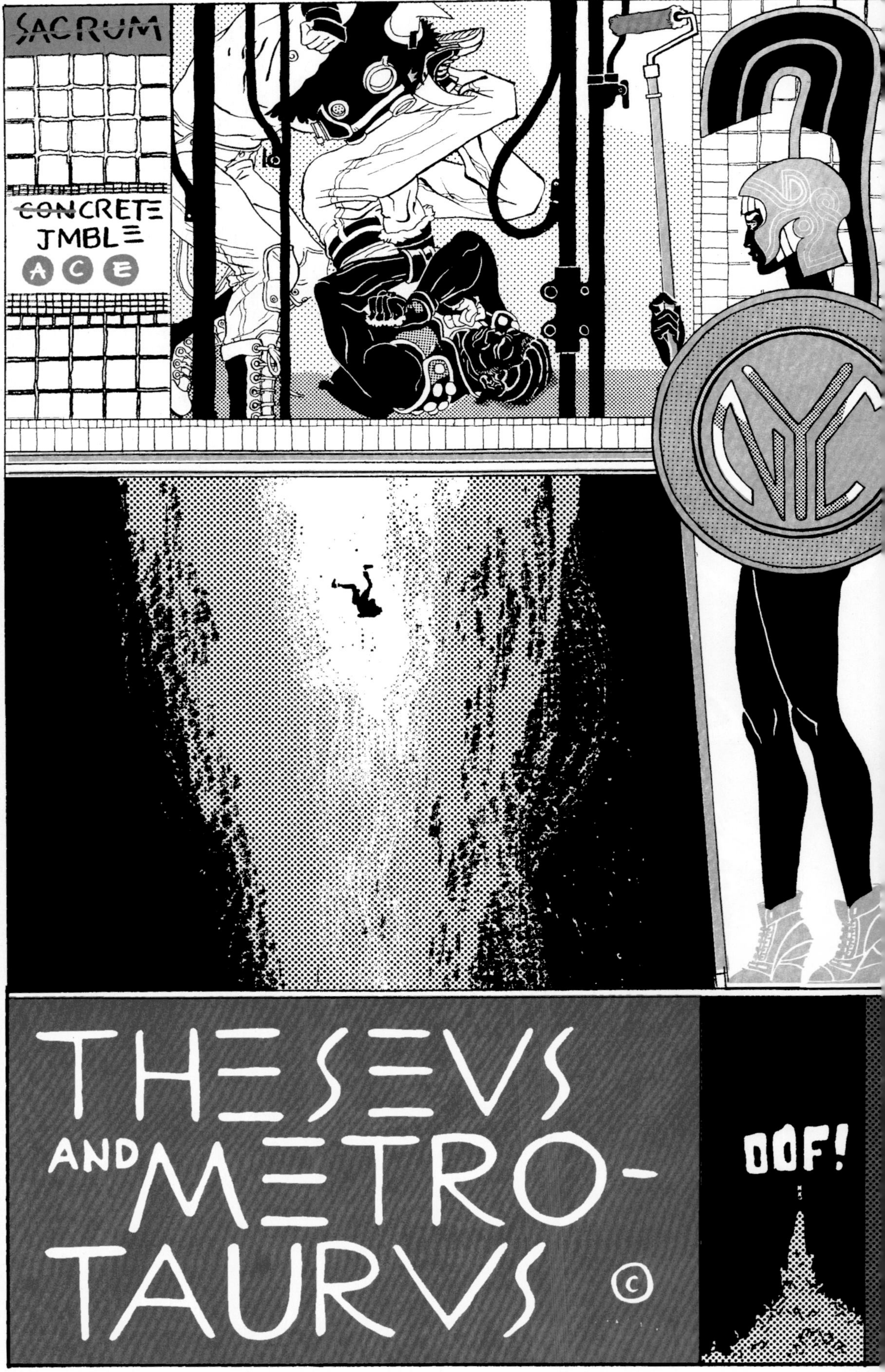
SACRUM
CONCRETE
JMBLE
A C E
THESEVS
AND METRO-
TAURVS
©
OOF!

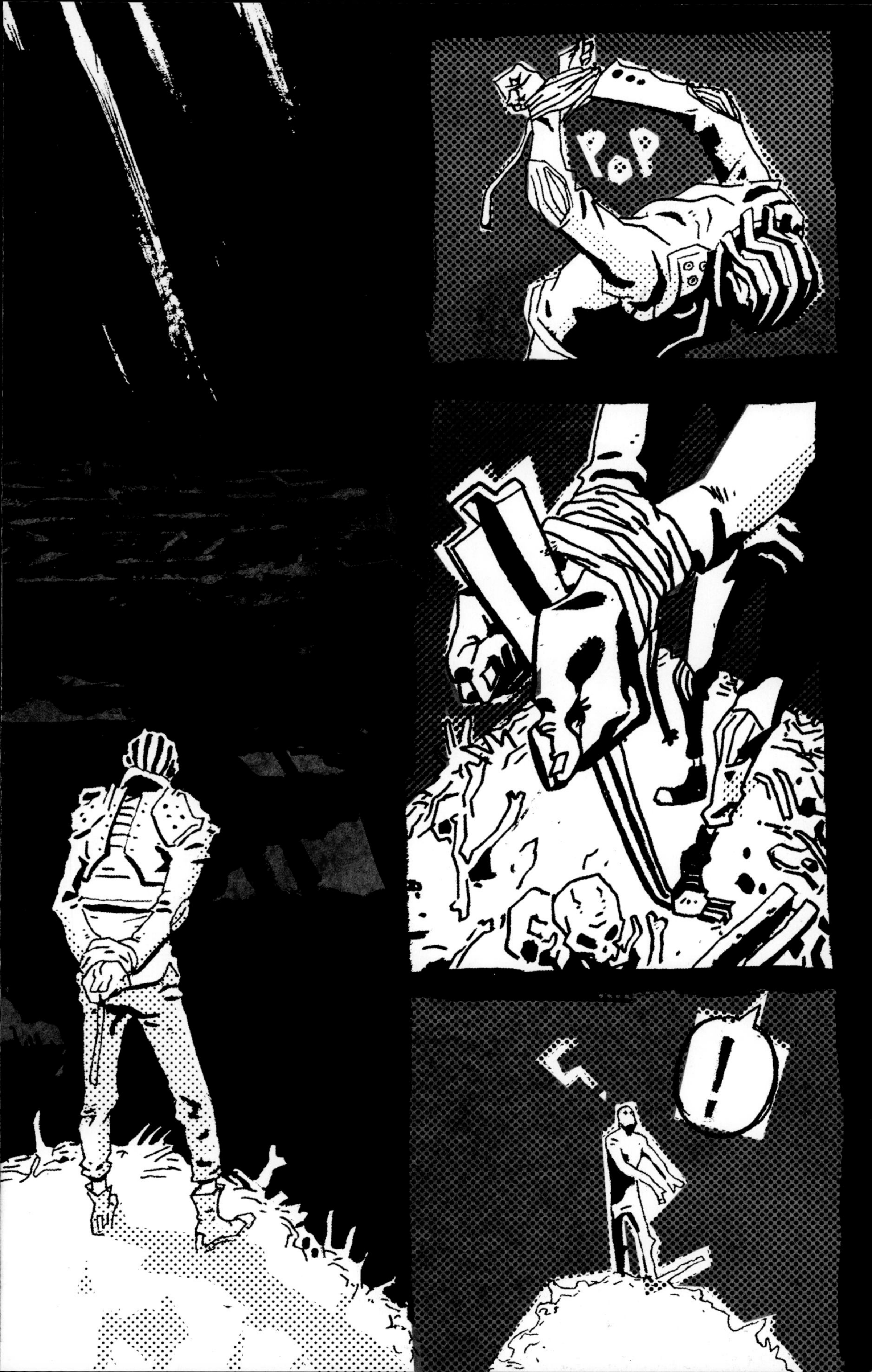
POP
!

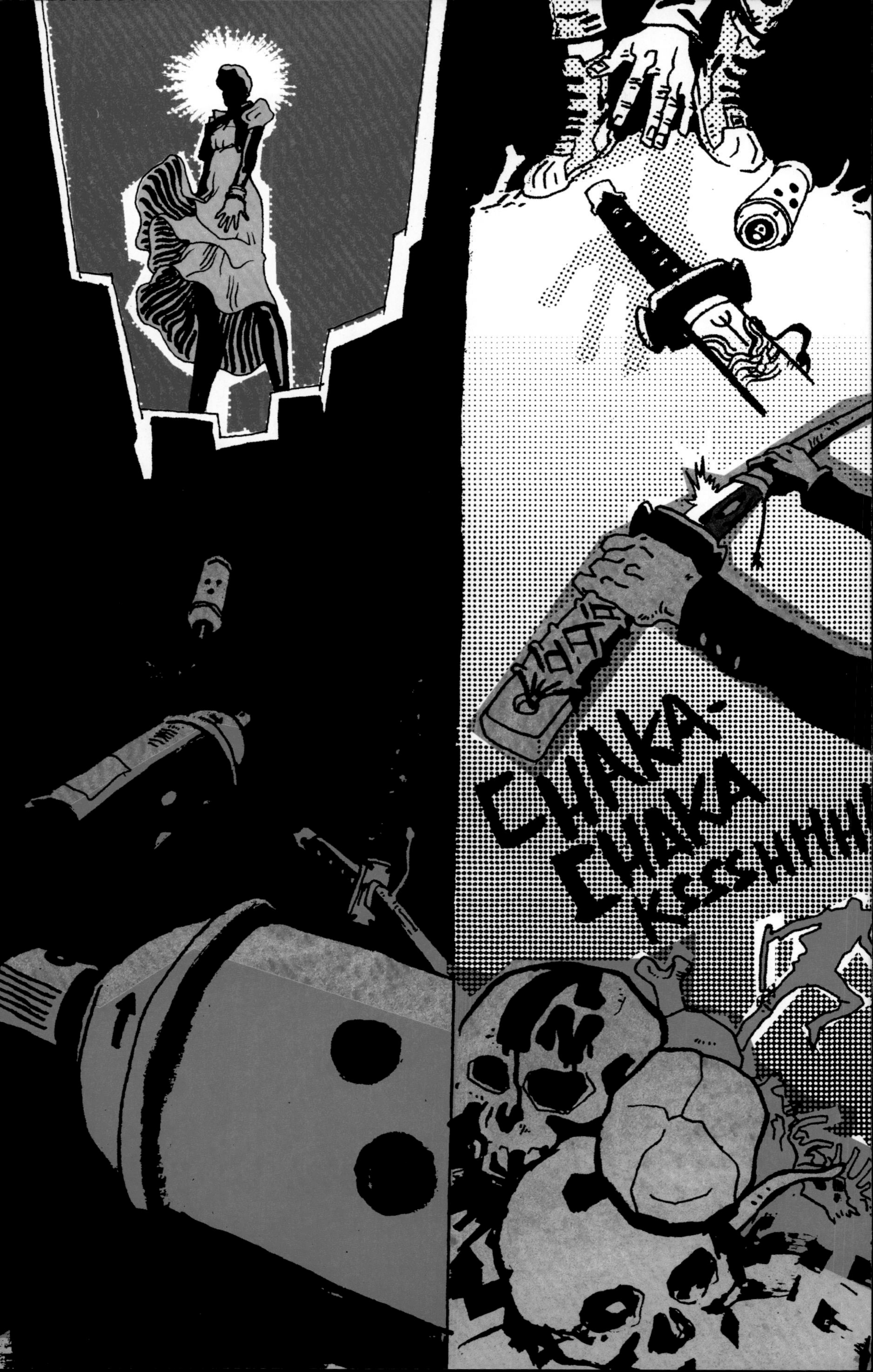
CHAKA-
CHAKA
KSSSHHH

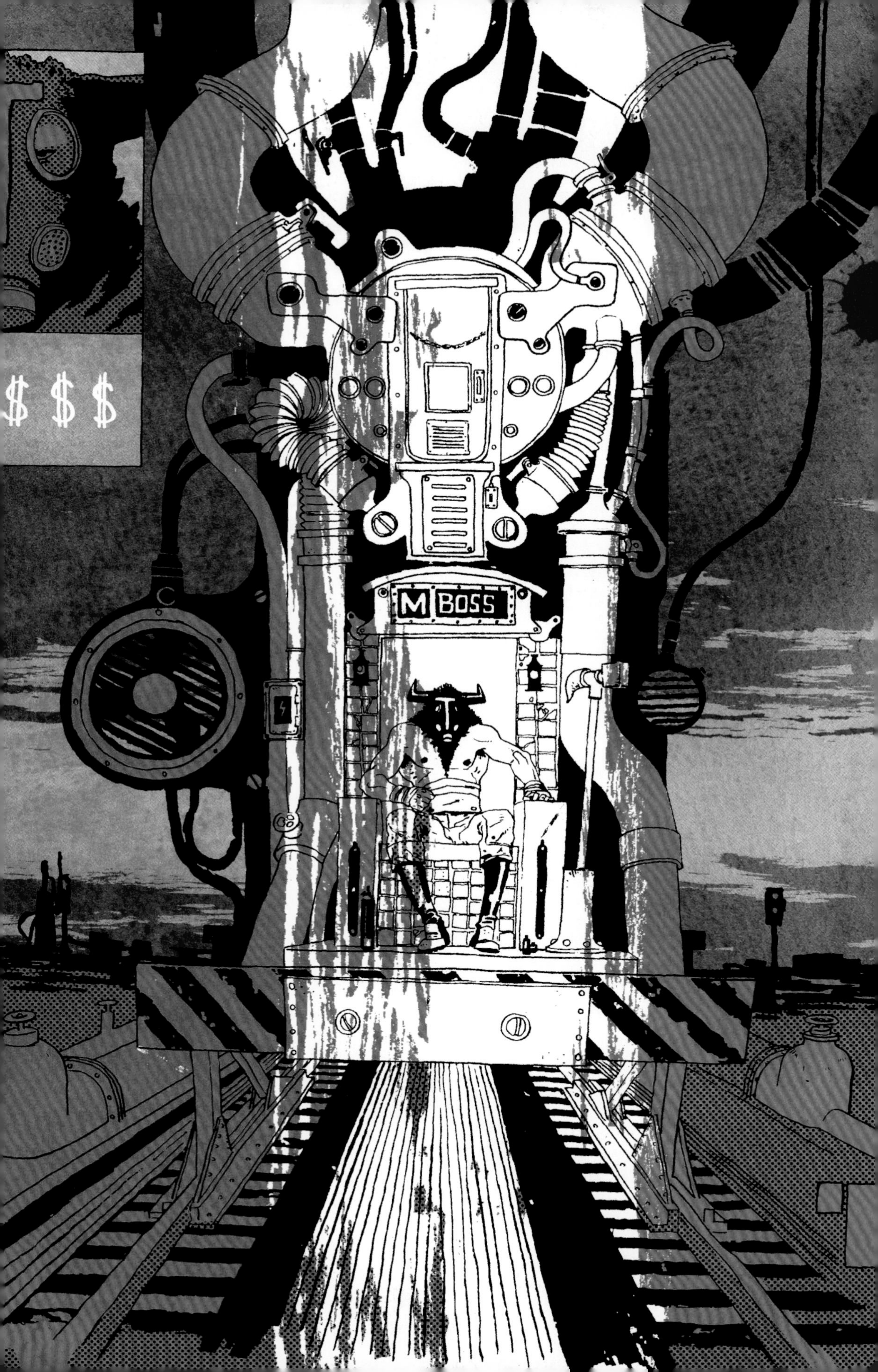
$ $ $
M BOSS

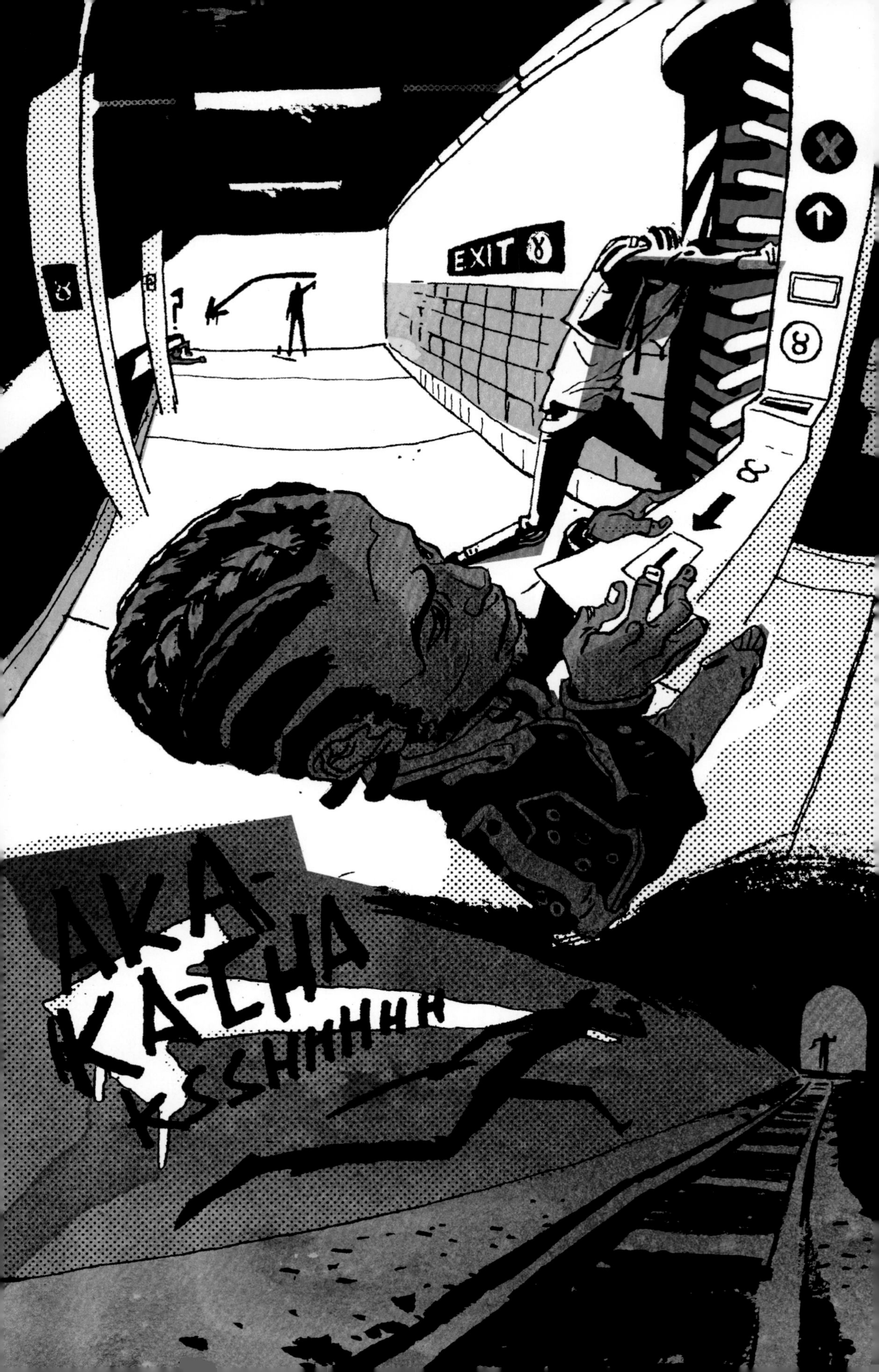
EXIT
AKA-
KA-CHA
KSSHHHHH

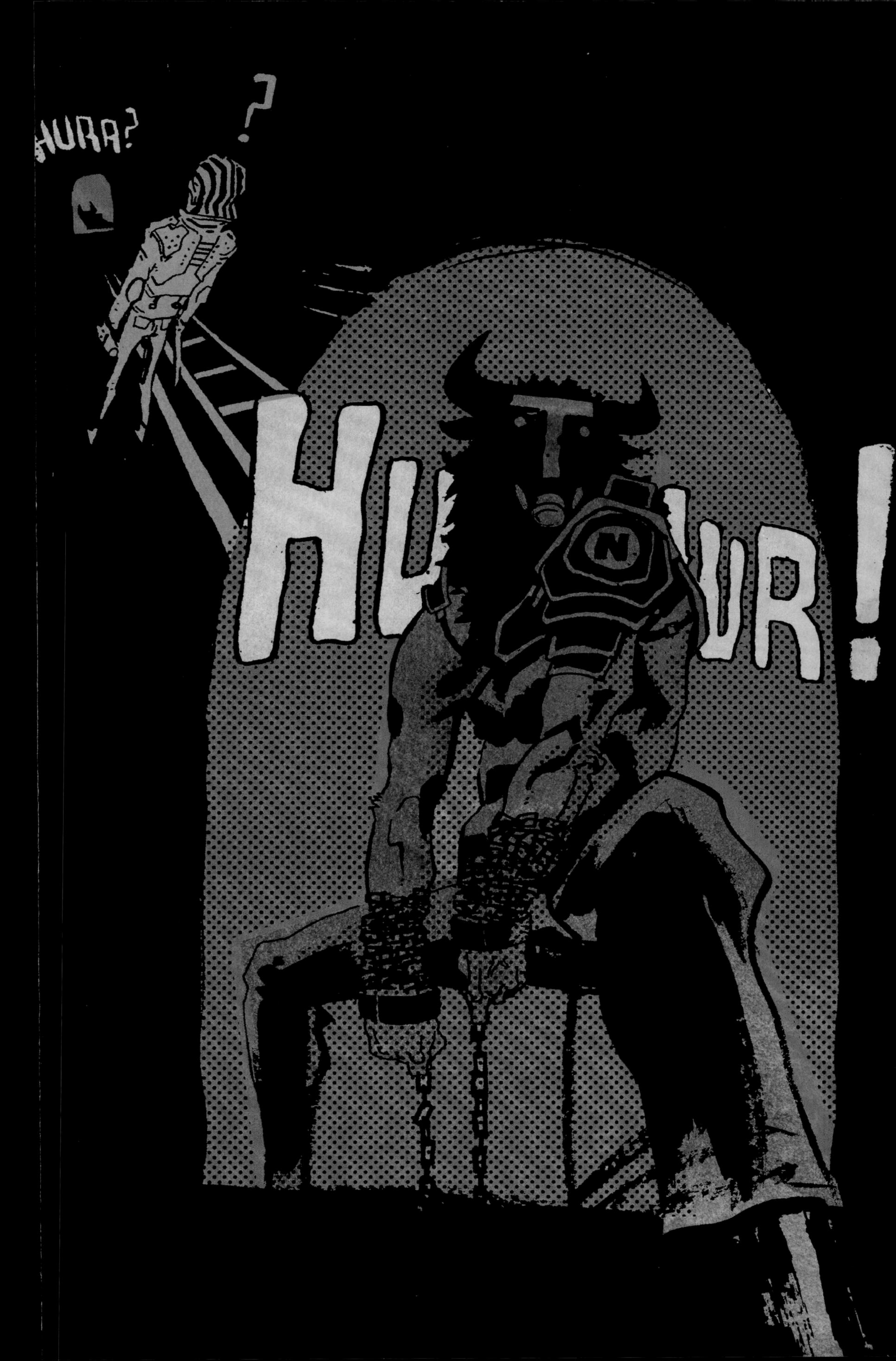
HURA?
?
HU
UR!

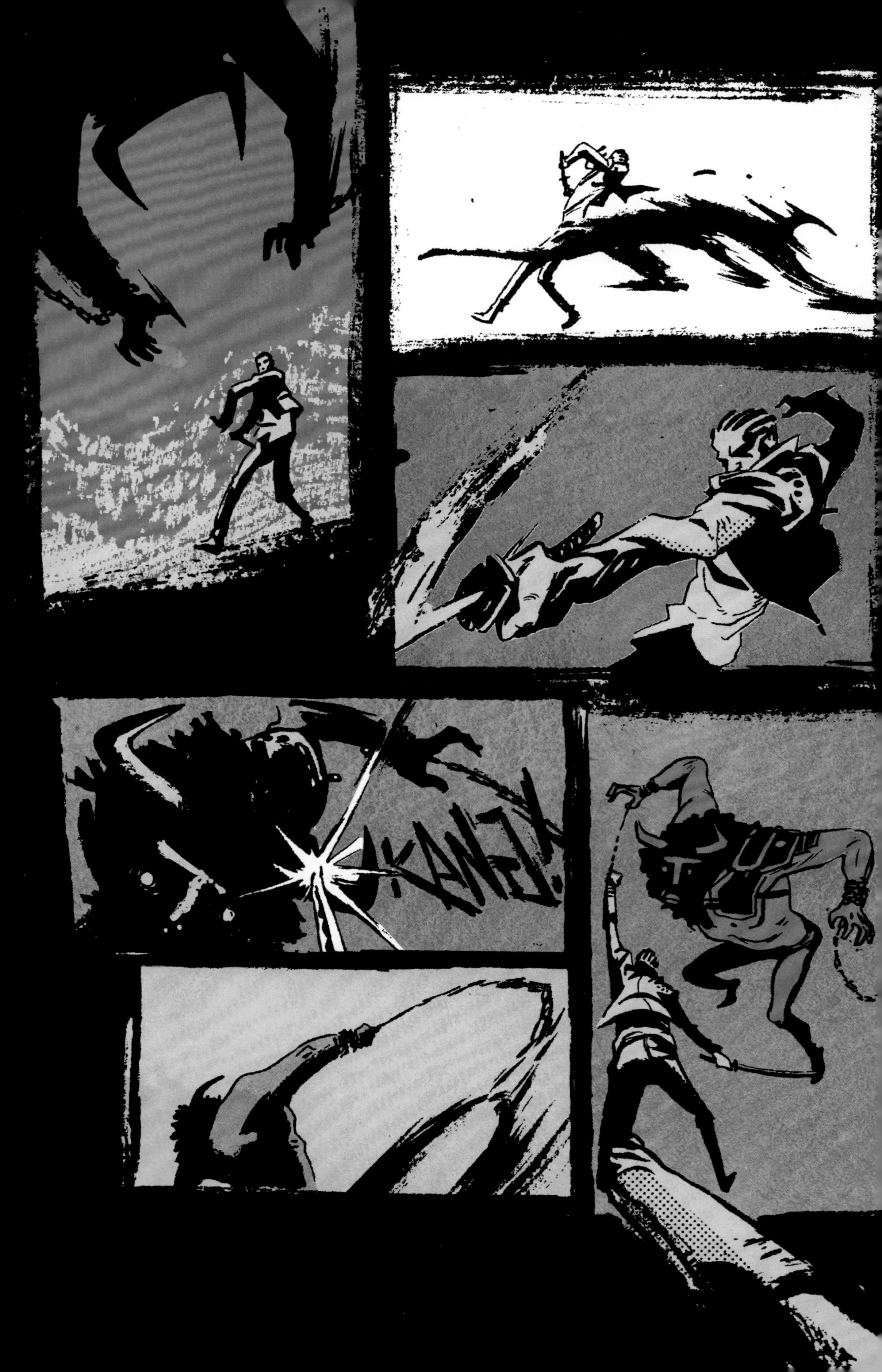

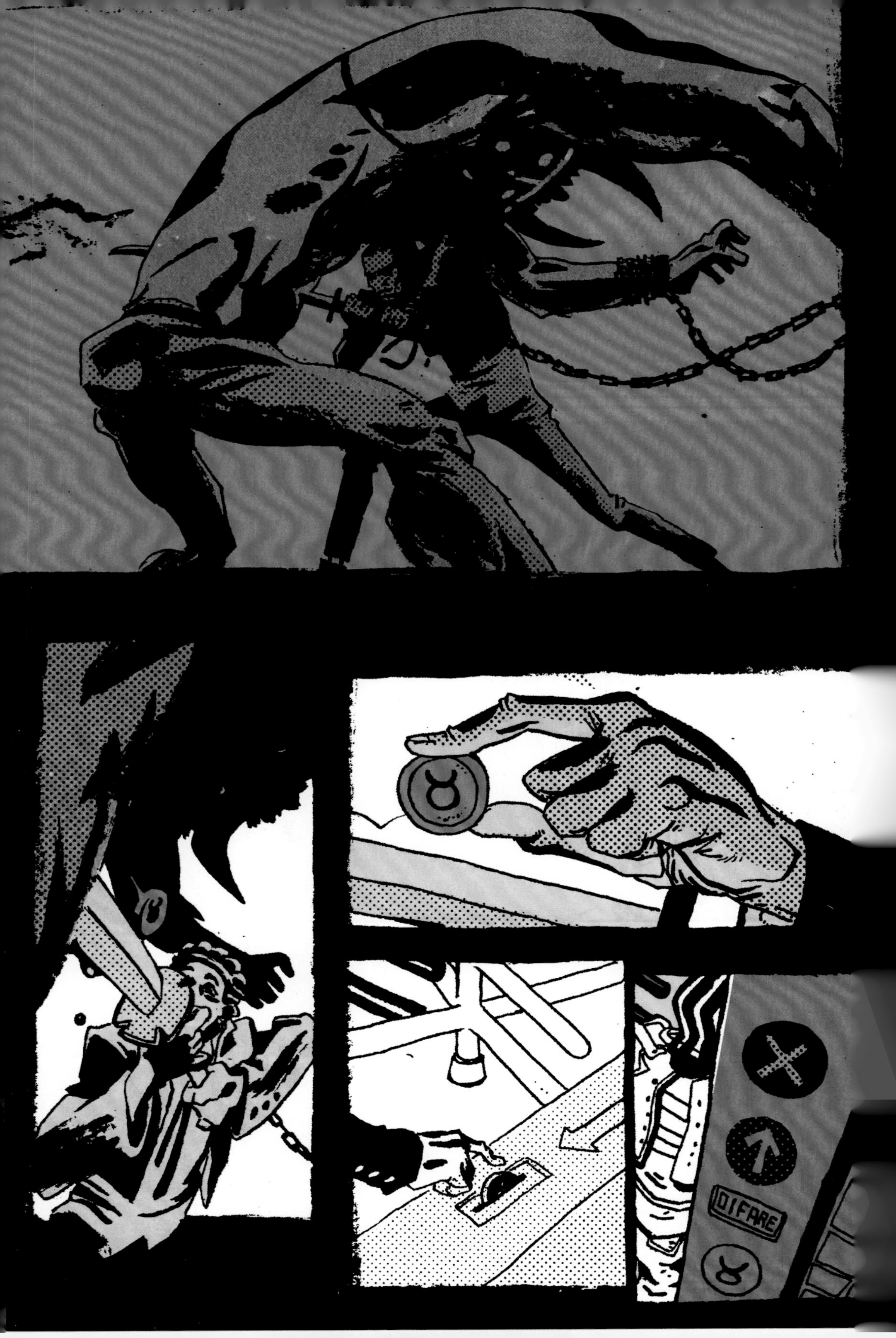
DI FARE

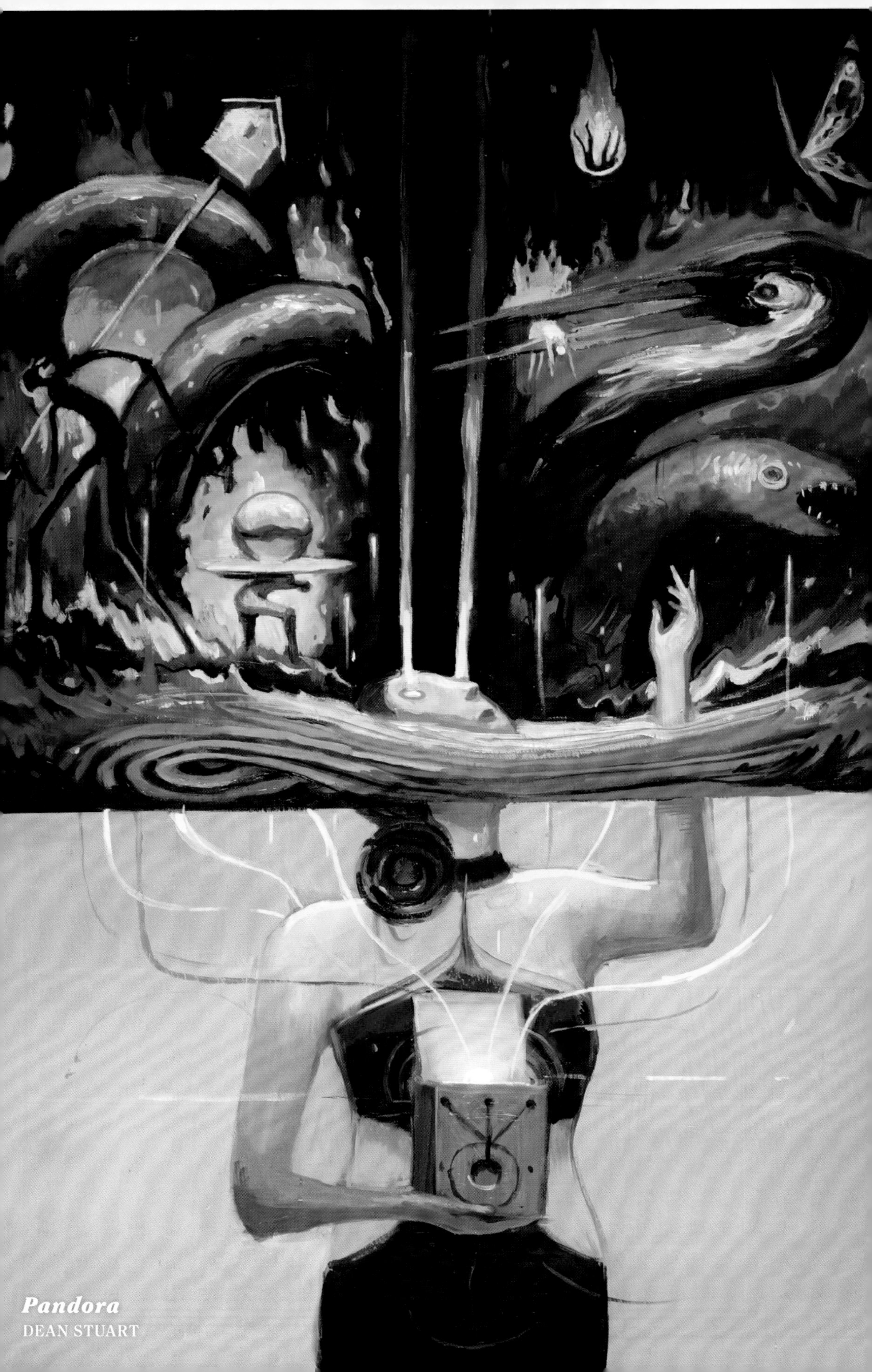

Pandora
DEAN STUART

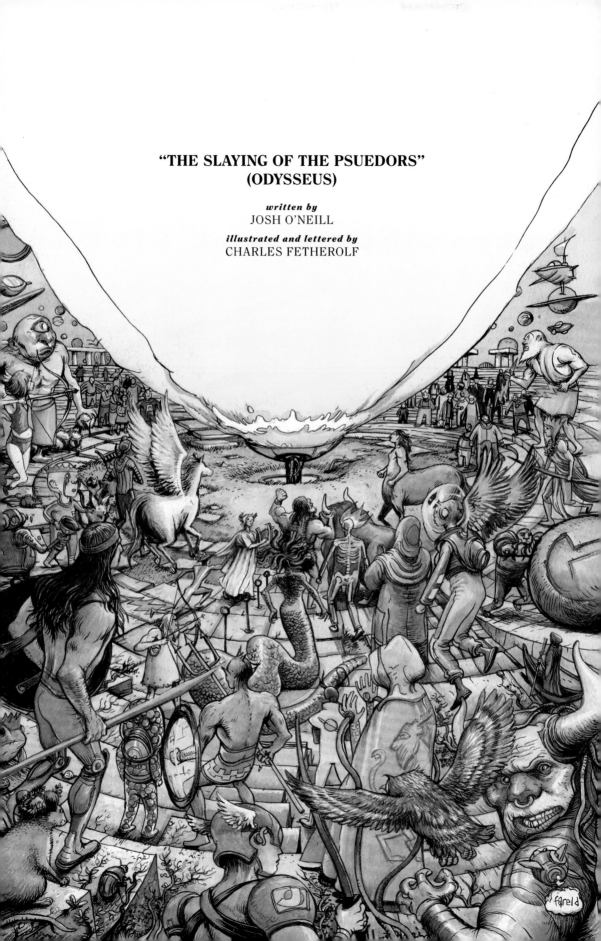

"THE SLAYING OF THE PSUEDORS"
(ODYSSEUS)

written by
JOSH O'NEILL

illustrated and lettered by
CHARLES FETHEROLF

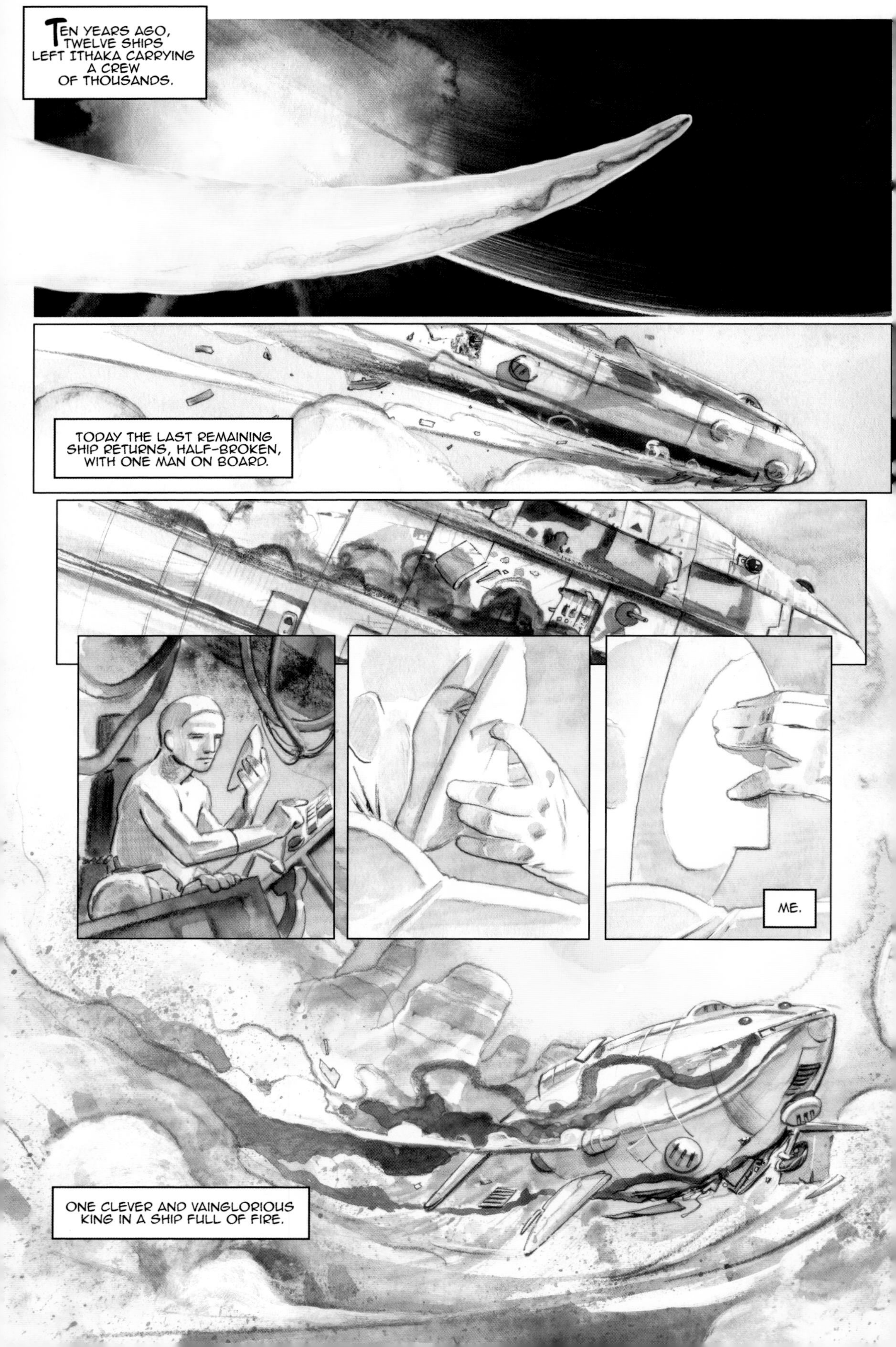
TEN YEARS AGO, TWELVE SHIPS LEFT ITHAKA CARRYING A CREW OF THOUSANDS.
TODAY THE LAST REMAINING SHIP RETURNS, HALF-BROKEN, WITH ONE MAN ON BOARD.
ME.
ONE CLEVER AND VAINGLORIOUS KING IN A SHIP FULL OF FIRE.

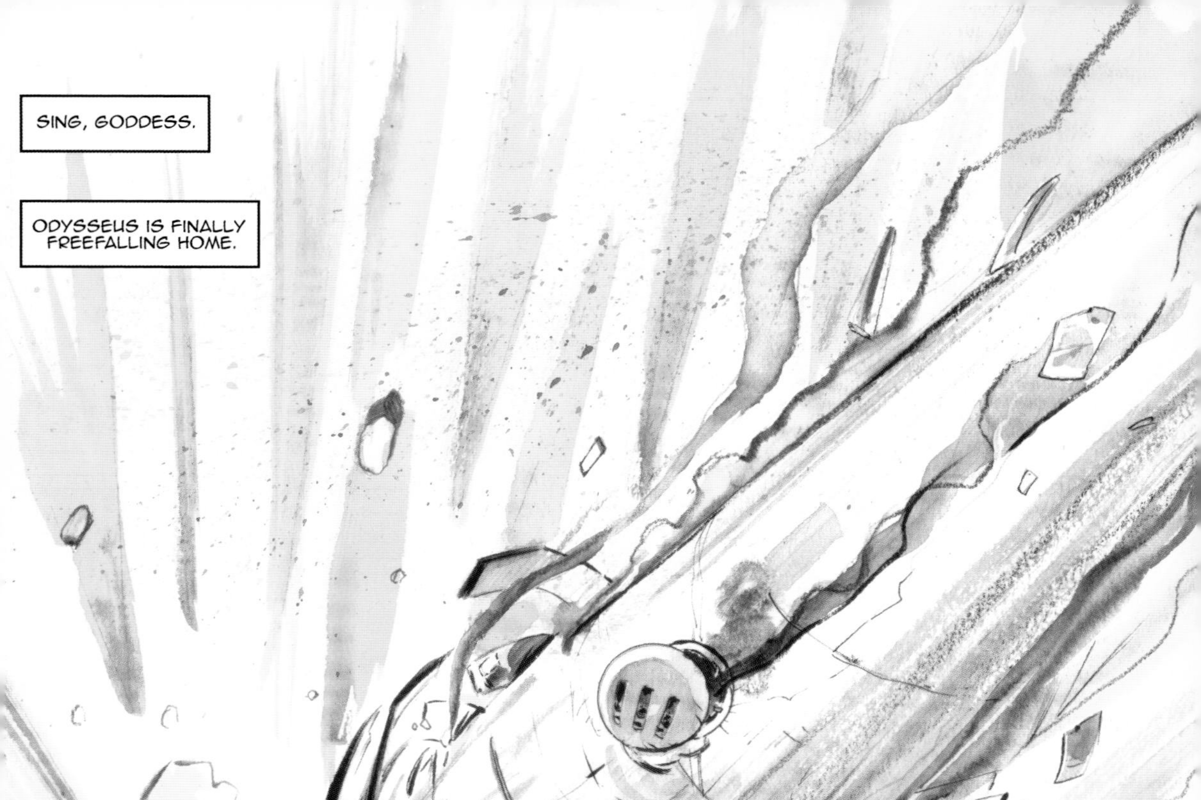
SING, GODDESS.
ODYSSEUS IS FINALLY FREEFALLING HOME.

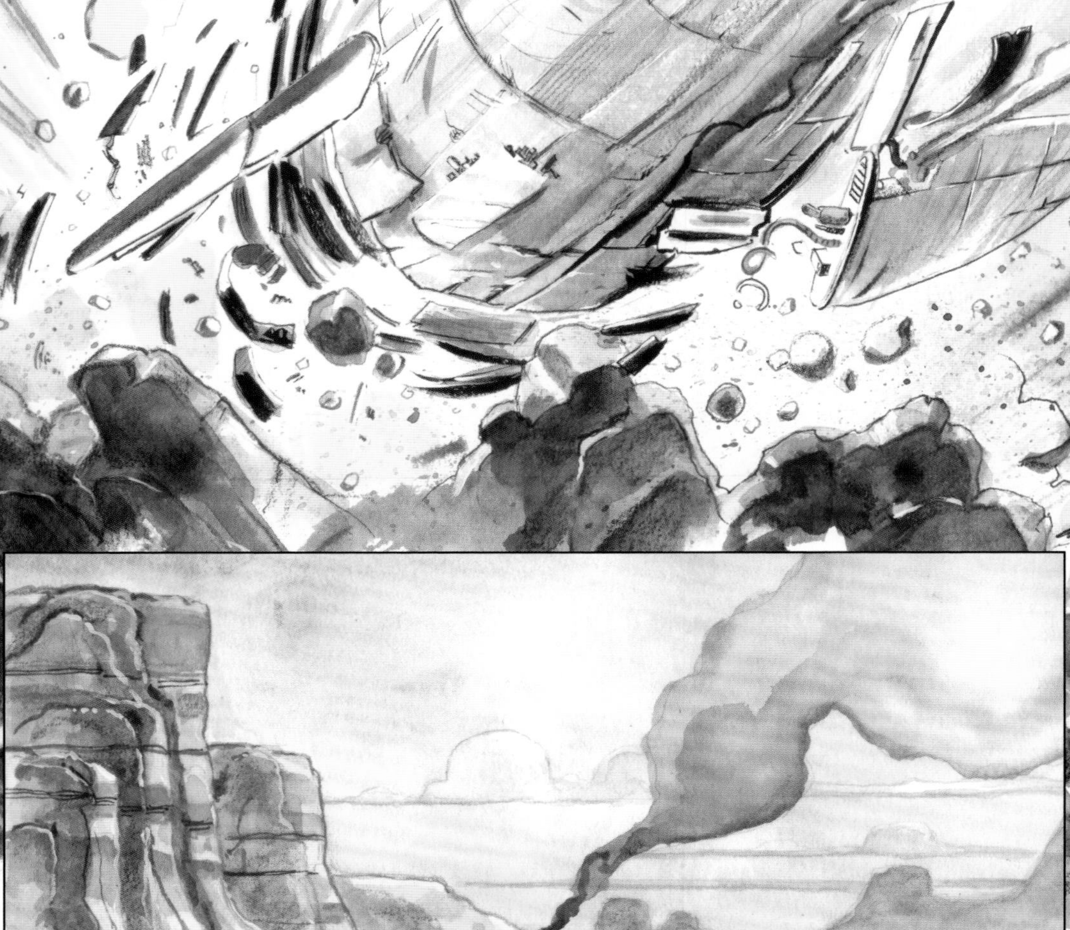

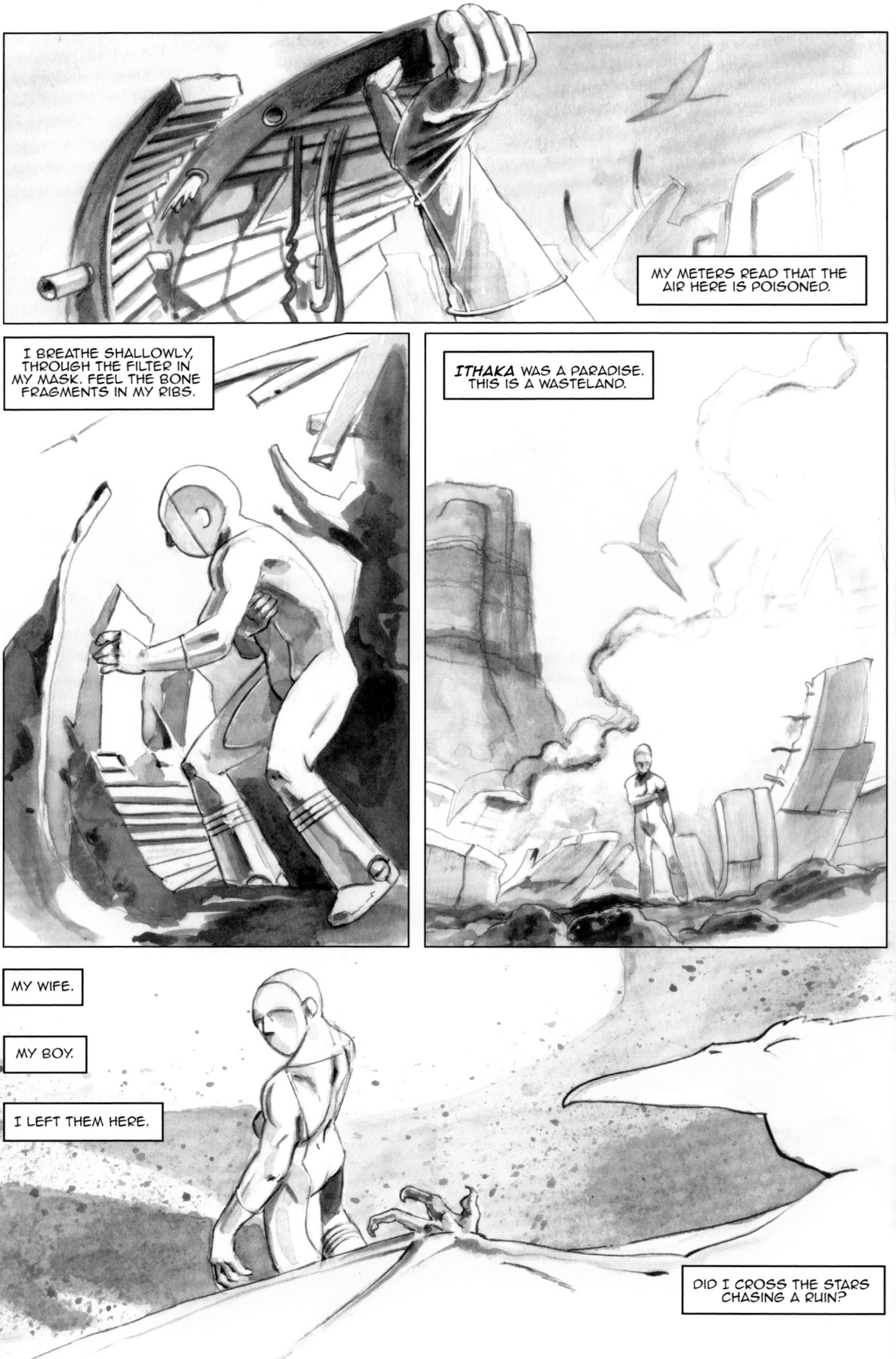
MY METERS READ THAT THE AIR HERE IS POISONED.
I BREATHE SHALLOWLY, THROUGH THE FILTER IN MY MASK. FEEL THE BONE FRAGMENTS IN MY RIBS.
ITHAKA WAS A PARADISE. THIS IS A WASTELAND.
MY WIFE.
MY BOY.
I LEFT THEM HERE.
DID I CROSS THE STARS CHASING A RUIN?

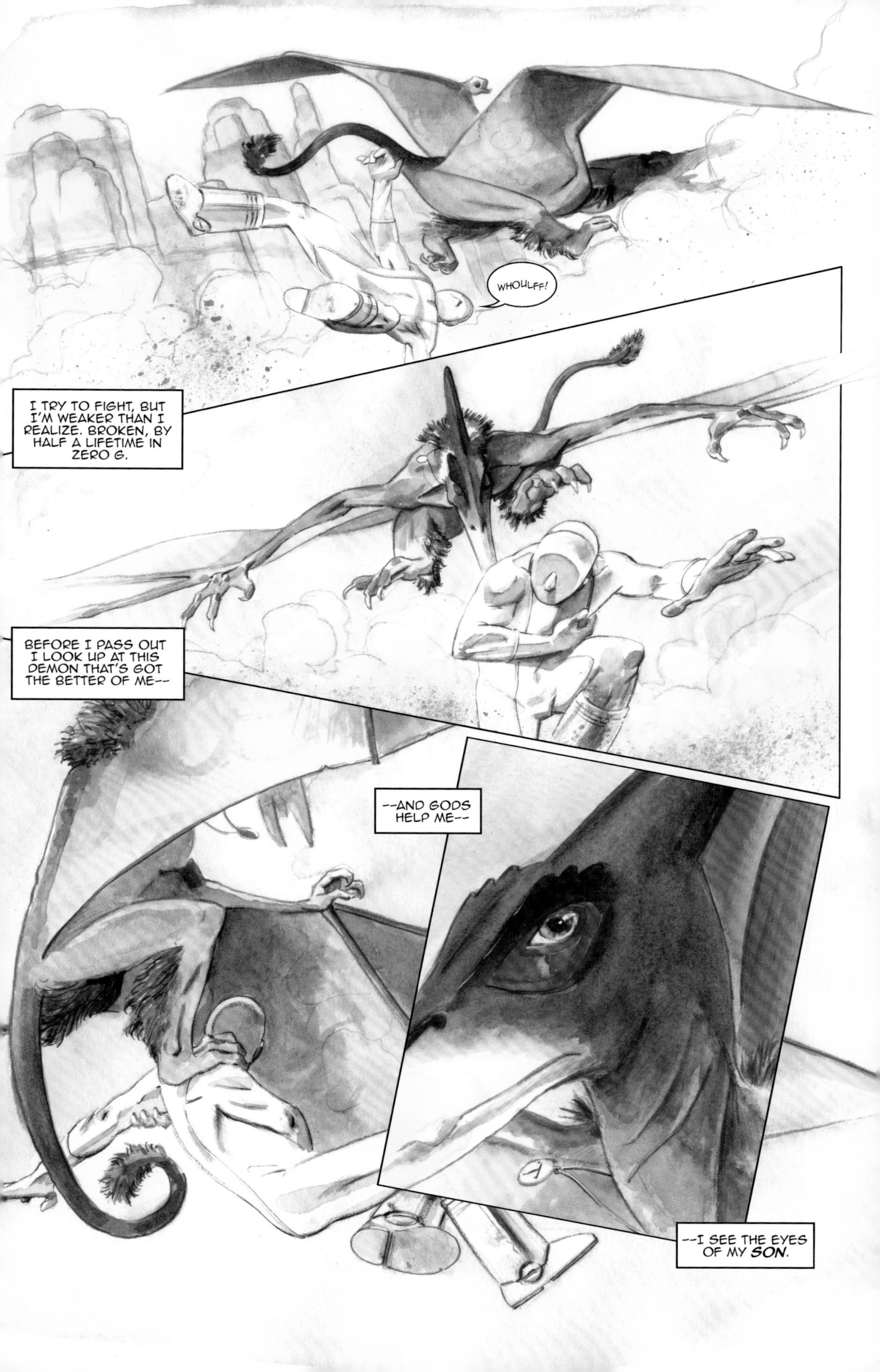
WHOULFF!
I TRY TO FIGHT, BUT I'M WEAKER THAN I REALIZE. BROKEN, BY HALF A LIFETIME IN ZERO G.
BEFORE I PASS OUT I LOOK UP AT THIS DEMON THAT'S GOT THE BETTER OF ME--
--AND GODS HELP ME--
--I SEE THE EYES OF MY *SON*.

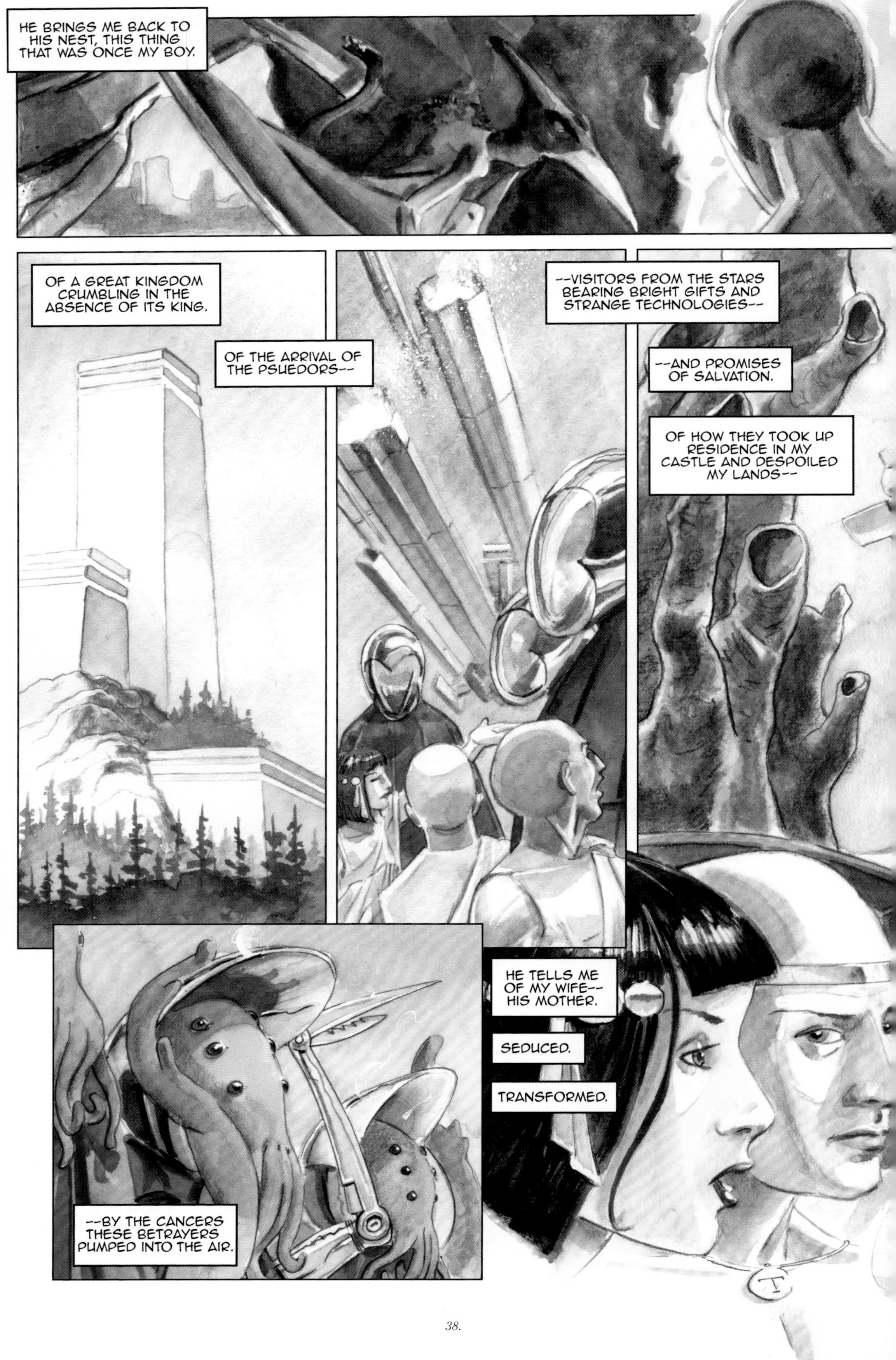
HE BRINGS ME BACK TO HIS NEST, THIS THING THAT WAS ONCE MY BOY.
OF A GREAT KINGDOM CRUMBLING IN THE ABSENCE OF ITS KING.
OF THE ARRIVAL OF THE PSUEDORS--
--VISITORS FROM THE STARS BEARING BRIGHT GIFTS AND STRANGE TECHNOLOGIES--
--AND PROMISES OF SALVATION.
OF HOW THEY TOOK UP RESIDENCE IN MY CASTLE AND DESPOILED MY LANDS--
HE TELLS ME OF MY WIFE-- HIS MOTHER.
SEDUCED.
TRANSFORMED.
--BY THE CANCERS THESE BETRAYERS PUMPED INTO THE AIR.

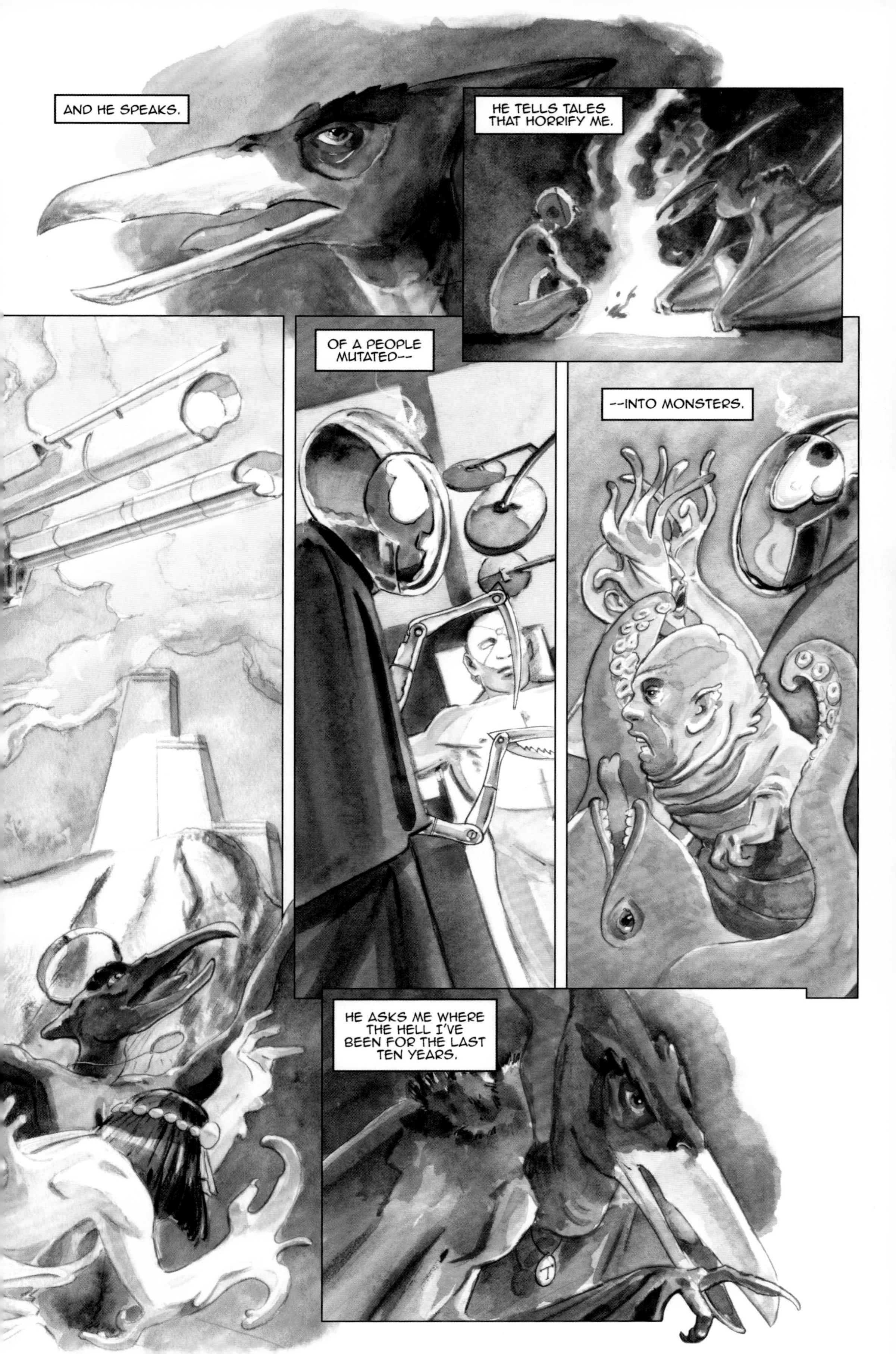
AND HE SPEAKS.
HE TELLS TALES THAT HORRIFY ME.
OF A PEOPLE MUTATED--
--INTO MONSTERS.
HE ASKS ME WHERE THE HELL I'VE BEEN FOR THE LAST TEN YEARS.

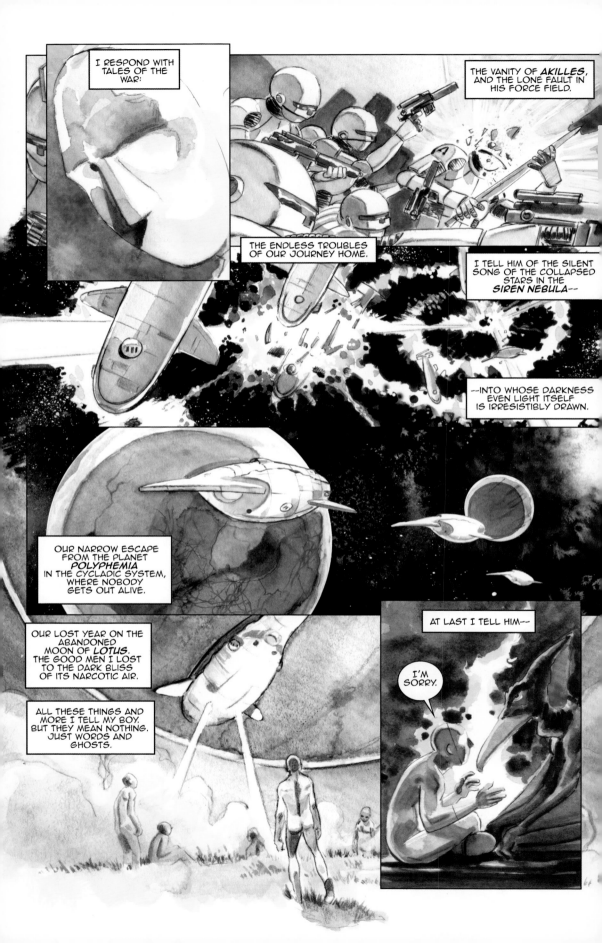

I RESPOND WITH TALES OF THE WAR:

THE VANITY OF *AKILLES*, AND THE LONE FAULT IN HIS FORCE FIELD.

THE ENDLESS TROUBLES OF OUR JOURNEY HOME.

I TELL HIM OF THE SILENT SONG OF THE COLLAPSED STARS IN THE *SIREN NEBULA*--

--INTO WHOSE DARKNESS EVEN LIGHT ITSELF IS IRRESISTIBLY DRAWN.

OUR NARROW ESCAPE FROM THE PLANET *POLYPHEMIA* IN THE *CYCLADIC* SYSTEM, WHERE NOBODY GETS OUT ALIVE.

OUR LOST YEAR ON THE ABANDONED MOON OF *LOTUS*. THE GOOD MEN I LOST TO THE DARK BLISS OF ITS NARCOTIC AIR.

ALL THESE THINGS AND MORE I TELL MY BOY. BUT THEY MEAN NOTHING. JUST WORDS AND GHOSTS.

AT LAST I TELL HIM--

I'M SORRY.

66

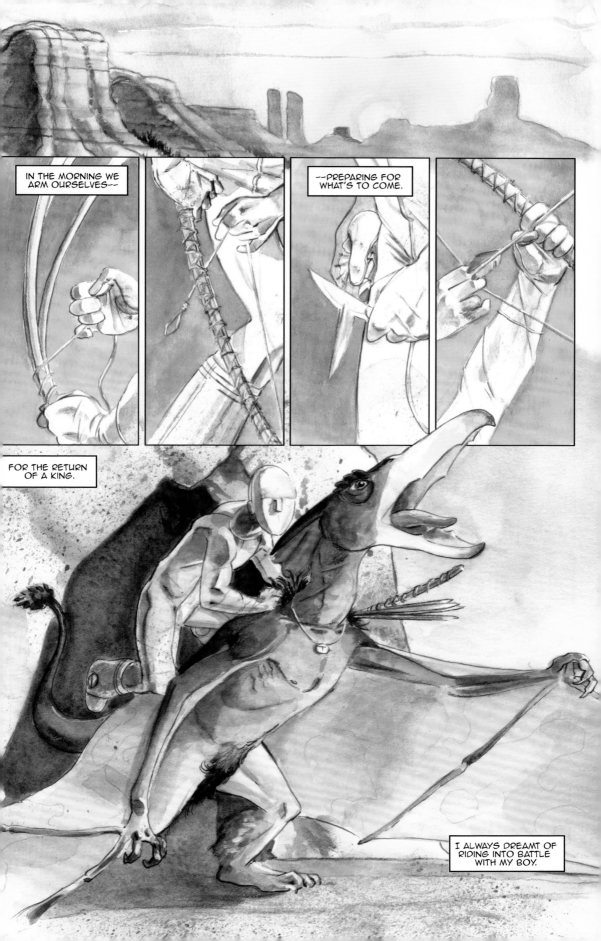

IN THE MORNING WE ARM OURSELVES--

--PREPARING FOR WHAT'S TO COME.

FOR THE RETURN OF A KING.

I ALWAYS DREAMT OF RIDING INTO BATTLE WITH MY BOY.

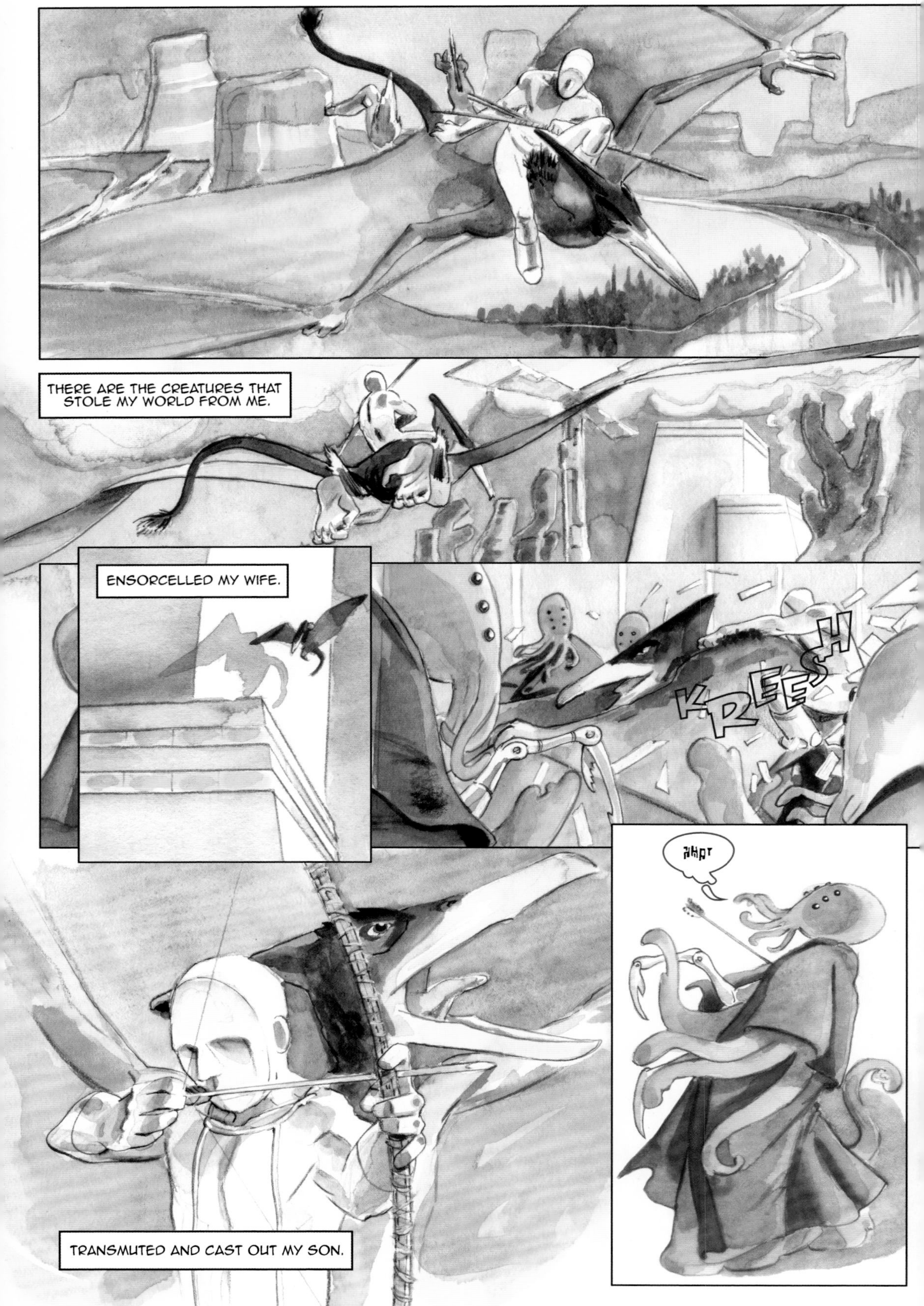
THERE ARE THE CREATURES THAT STOLE MY WORLD FROM ME.
ENSORCELLED MY WIFE.
KREESH
TRANSMUTED AND CAST OUT MY SON.

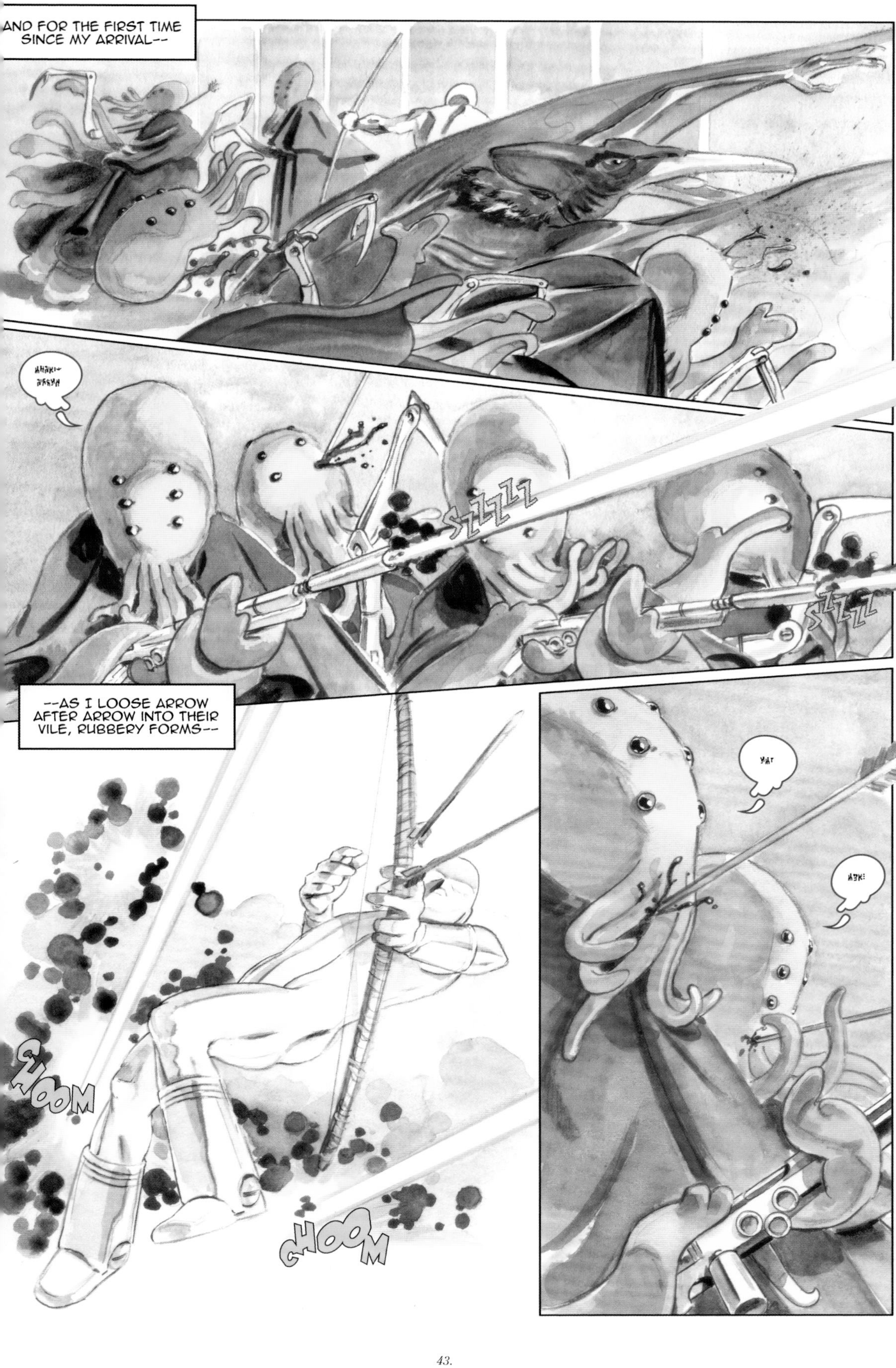
AND FOR THE FIRST TIME SINCE MY ARRIVAL--
--AS I LOOSE ARROW AFTER ARROW INTO THEIR VILE, RUBBERY FORMS--
CHOOM
CHOOM

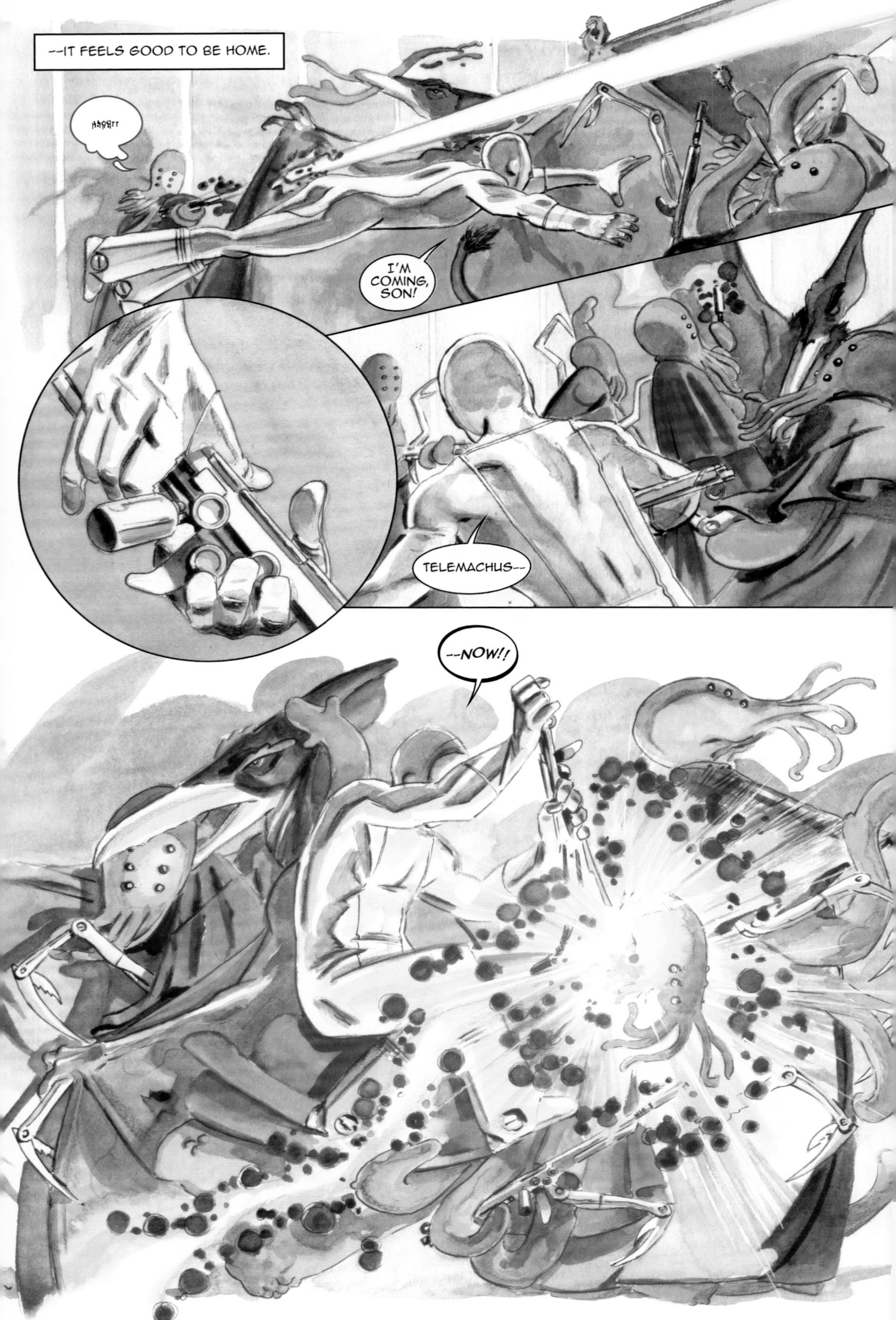
--IT FEELS GOOD TO BE HOME.
I'M COMING, SON!
TELEMACHUS--
--NOW!!

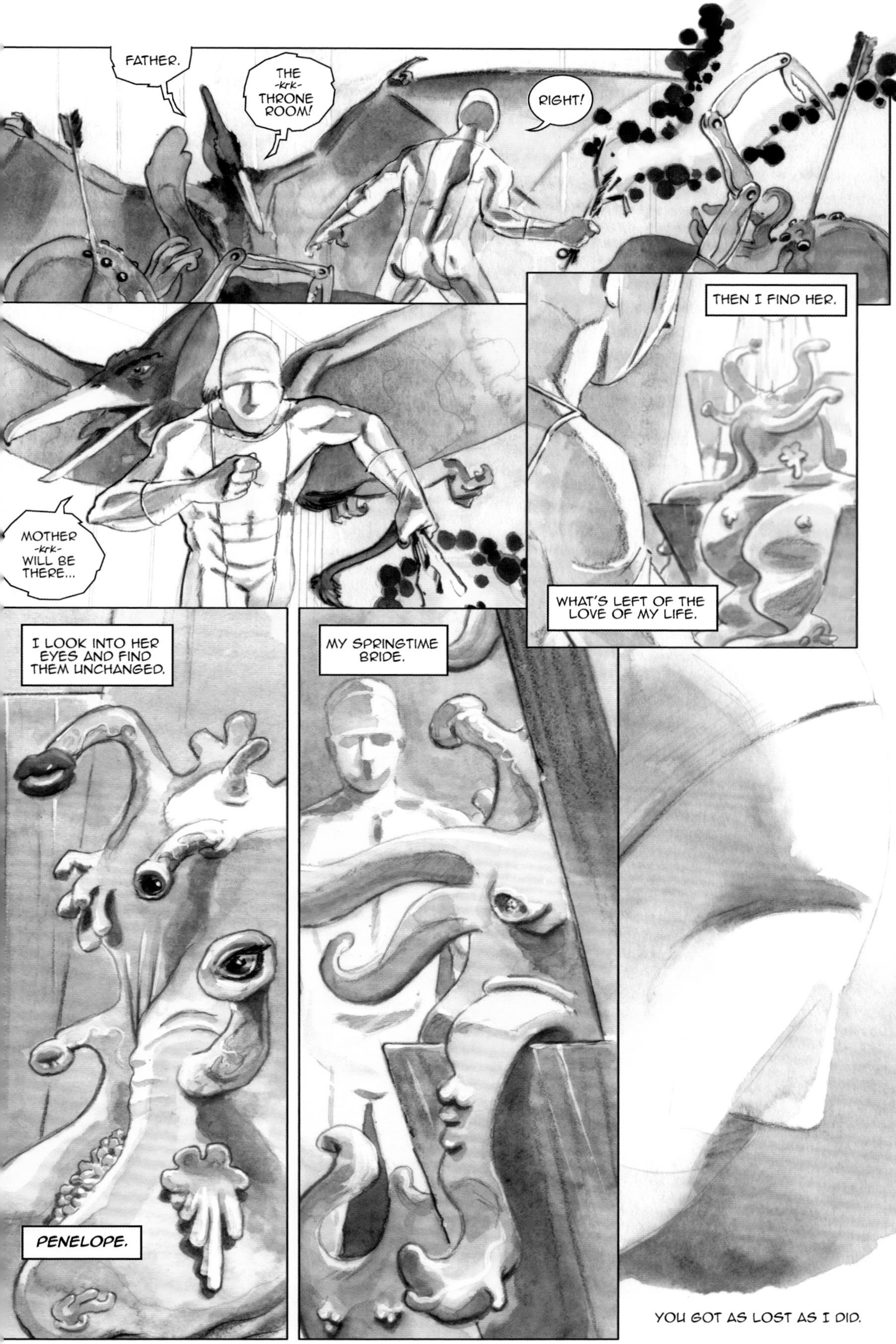
FATHER.
THE -krk- THRONE ROOM!
RIGHT!
MOTHER -krk- WILL BE THERE...
THEN I FIND HER.
WHAT'S LEFT OF THE LOVE OF MY LIFE.
I LOOK INTO HER EYES AND FIND THEM UNCHANGED.
PENELOPE.
MY SPRINGTIME BRIDE.
YOU GOT AS LOST AS I DID.

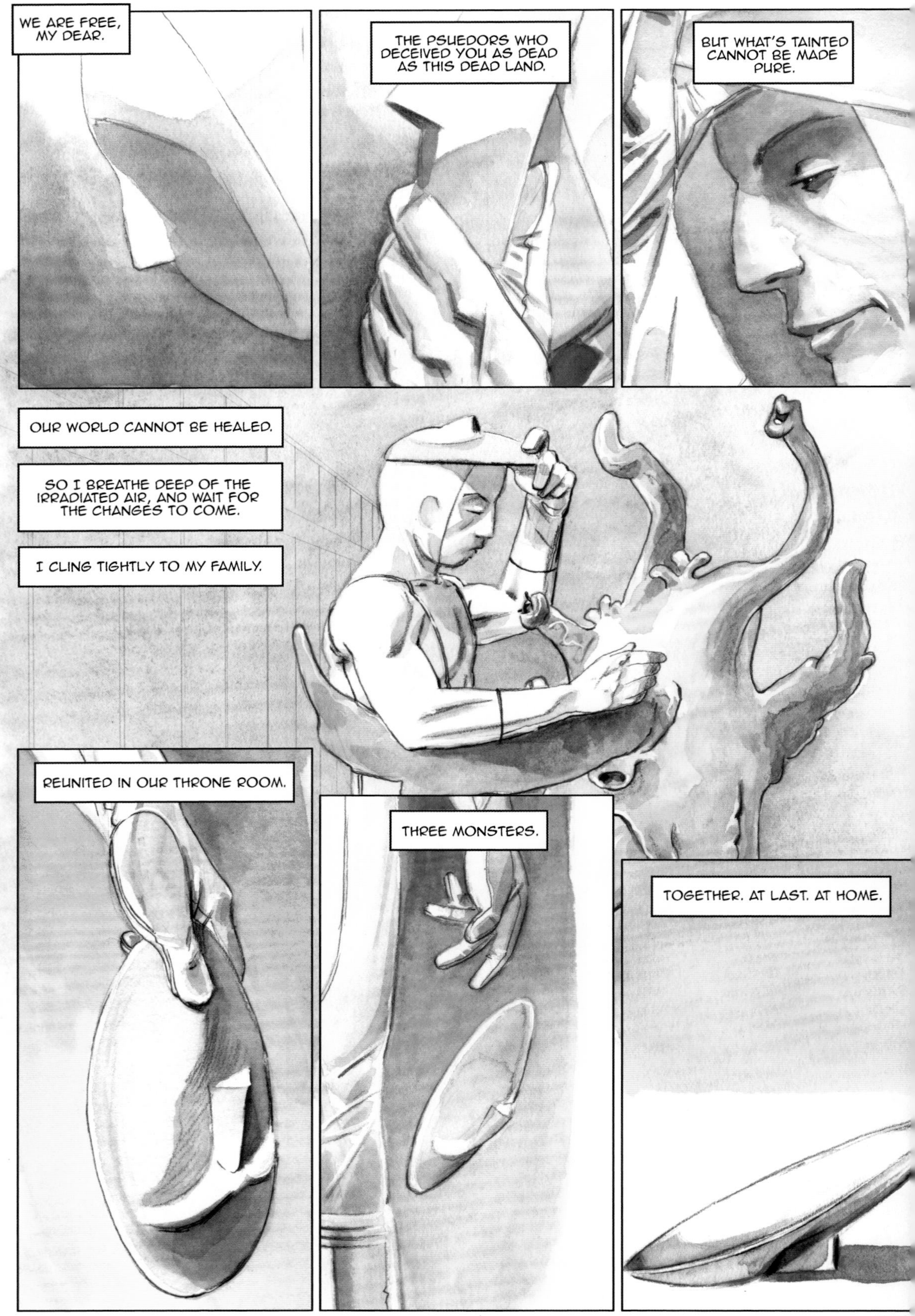
WE ARE FREE, MY DEAR.
THE PSUEDORS WHO DECEIVED YOU AS DEAD AS THIS DEAD LAND.
BUT WHAT'S TAINTED CANNOT BE MADE PURE.
OUR WORLD CANNOT BE HEALED.
SO I BREATHE DEEP OF THE IRRADIATED AIR, AND WAIT FOR THE CHANGES TO COME.
I CLING TIGHTLY TO MY FAMILY.
REUNITED IN OUR THRONE ROOM.
THREE MONSTERS.
TOGETHER. AT LAST. AT HOME.

END.

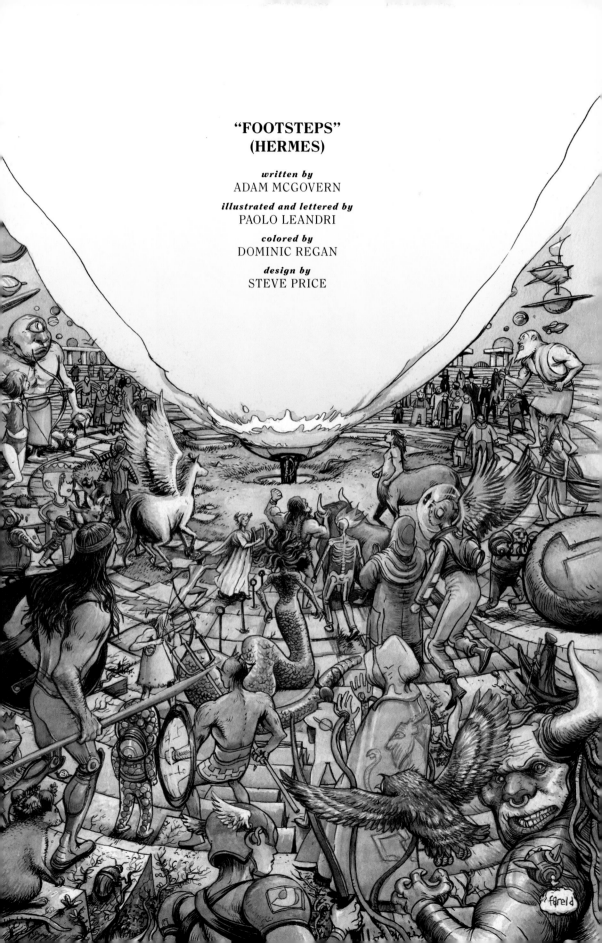

"FOOTSTEPS"
(HERMES)

written by
ADAM MCGOVERN

illustrated and lettered by
PAOLO LEANDRI

colored by
DOMINIC REGAN

design by
STEVE PRICE

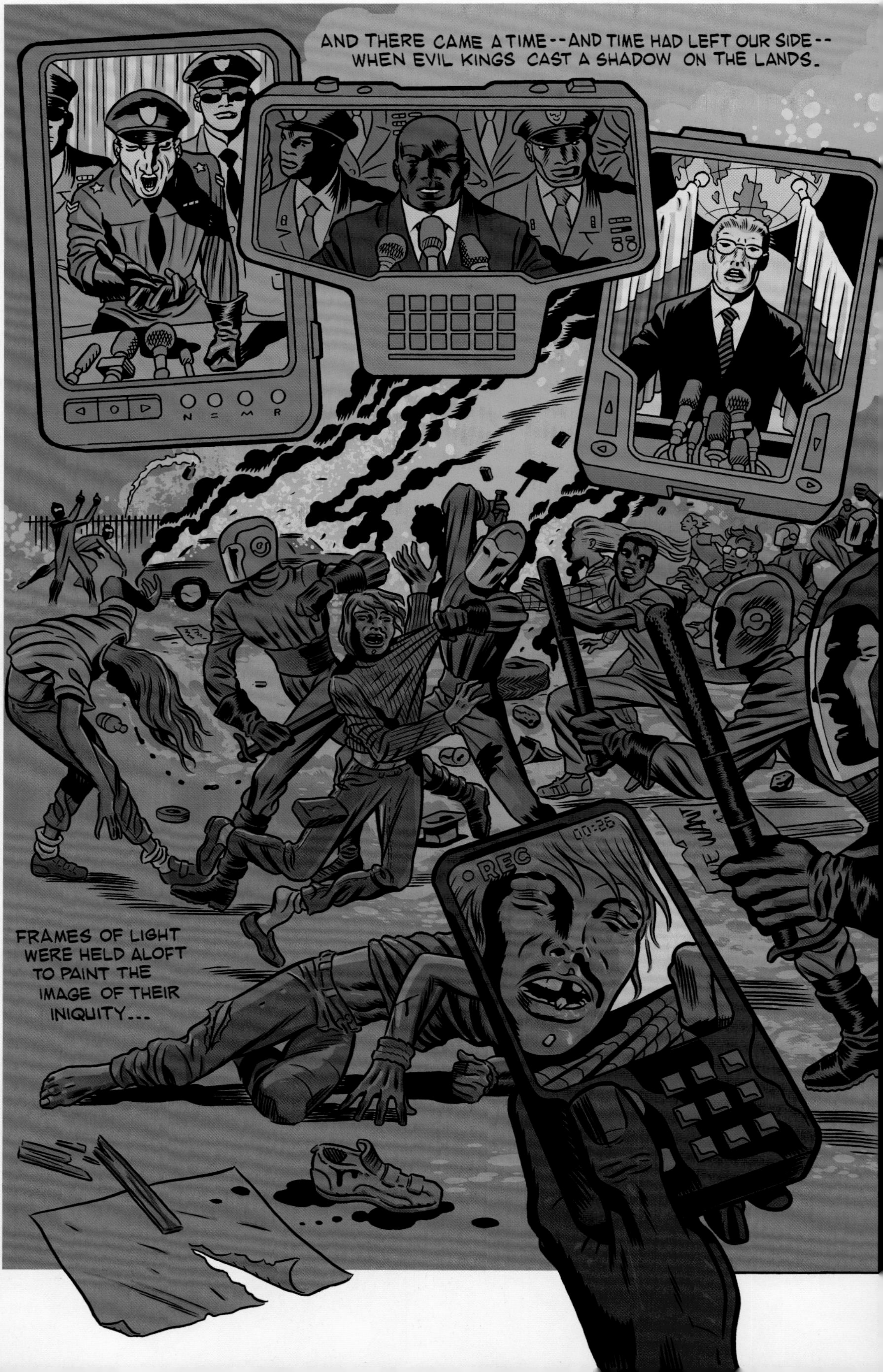
AND THERE CAME A TIME--AND TIME HAD LEFT OUR SIDE--
WHEN EVIL KINGS CAST A SHADOW ON THE LANDS.
FRAMES OF LIGHT
WERE HELD ALOFT
TO PAINT THE
IMAGE OF THEIR
INIQUITY...
REC
00:26
WE WANT

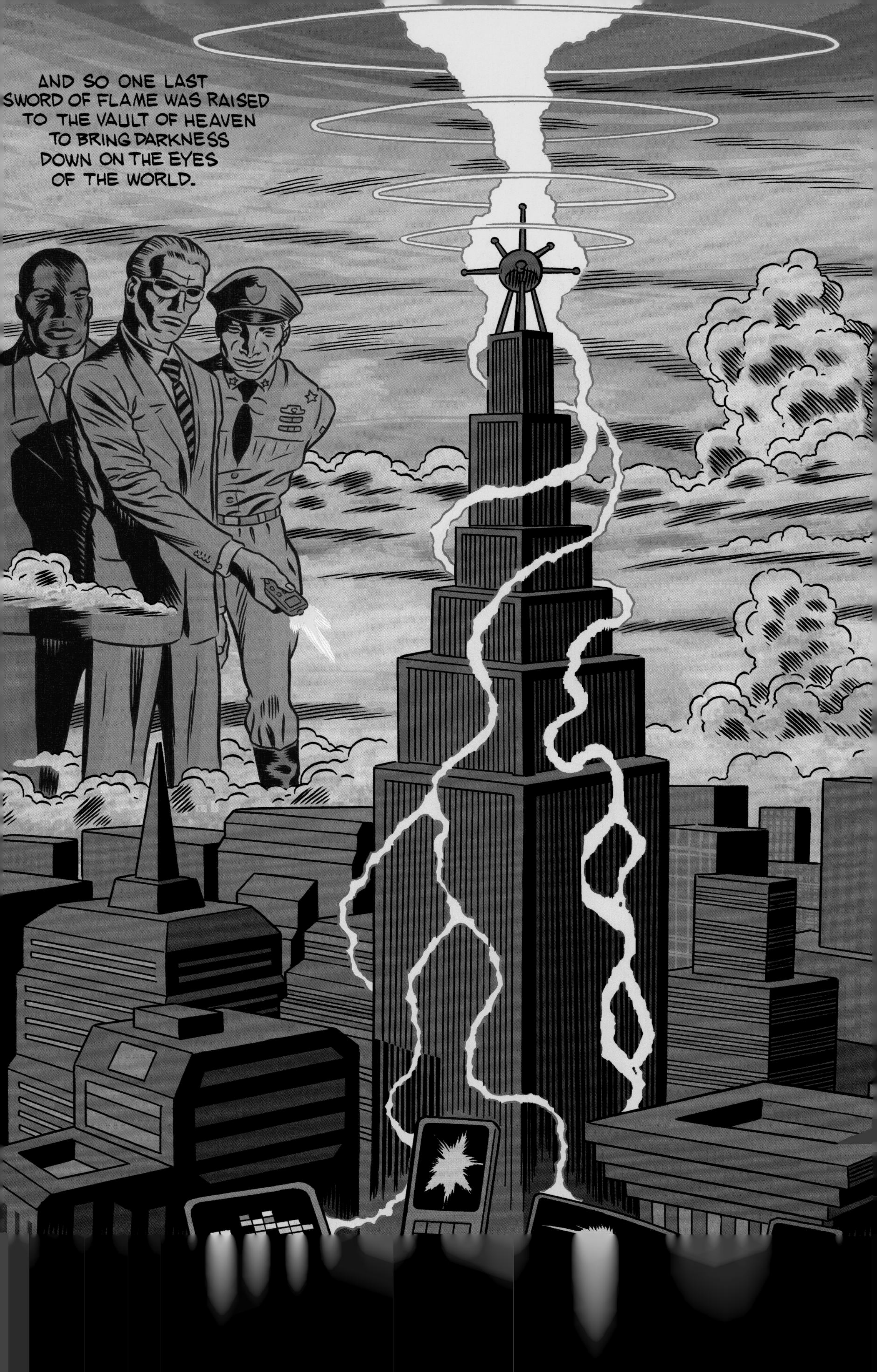
AND SO ONE LAST SWORD OF FLAME WAS RAISED TO THE VAULT OF HEAVEN TO BRING DARKNESS DOWN ON THE EYES OF THE WORLD.

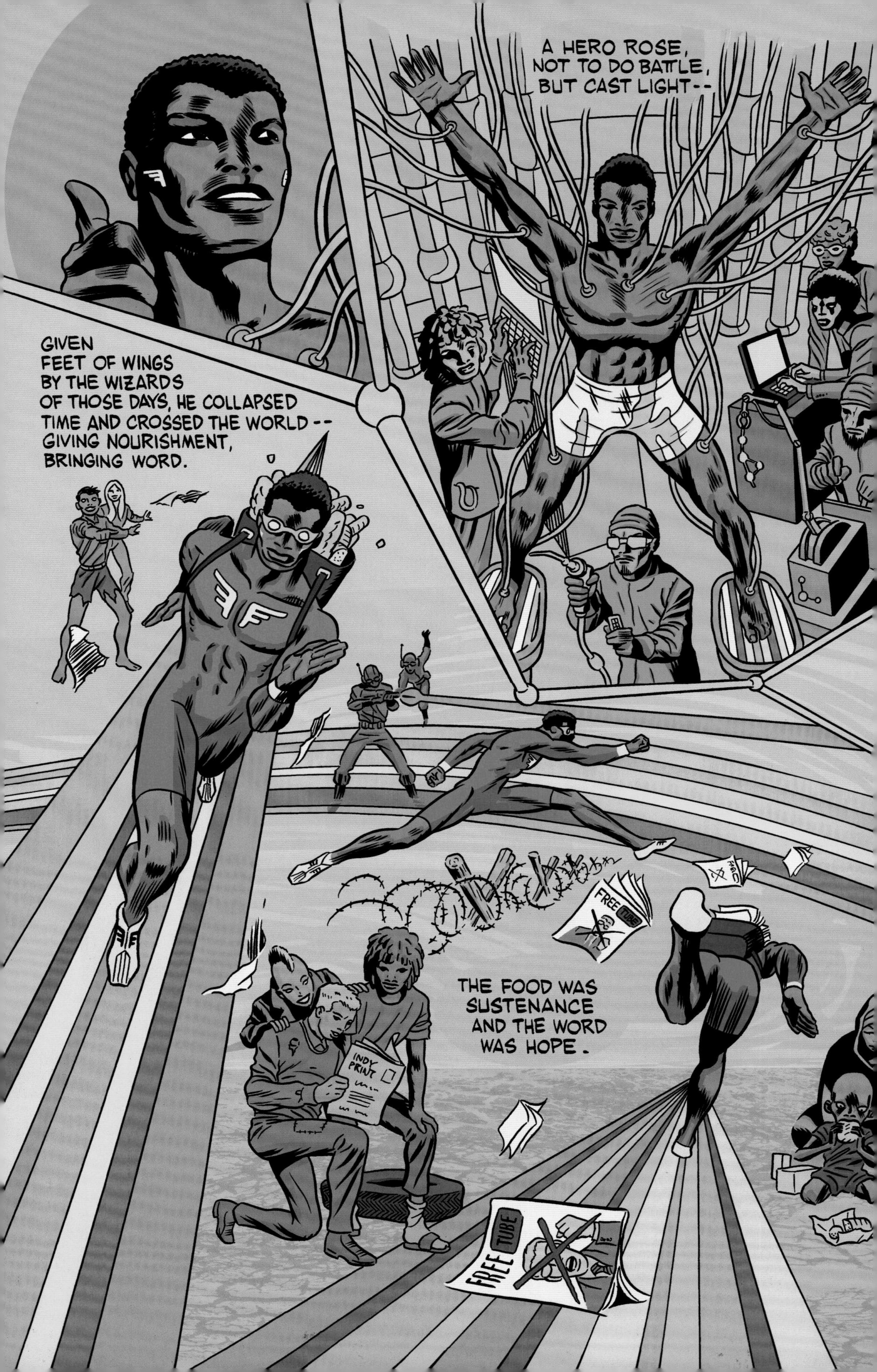
A HERO ROSE, NOT TO DO BATTLE, BUT CAST LIGHT--
GIVEN FEET OF WINGS BY THE WIZARDS OF THOSE DAYS, HE COLLAPSED TIME AND CROSSED THE WORLD-- GIVING NOURISHMENT, BRINGING WORD.
FREE TUBE
INDY PRINT
THE FOOD WAS SUSTENANCE AND THE WORD WAS HOPE.
FREE TUBE

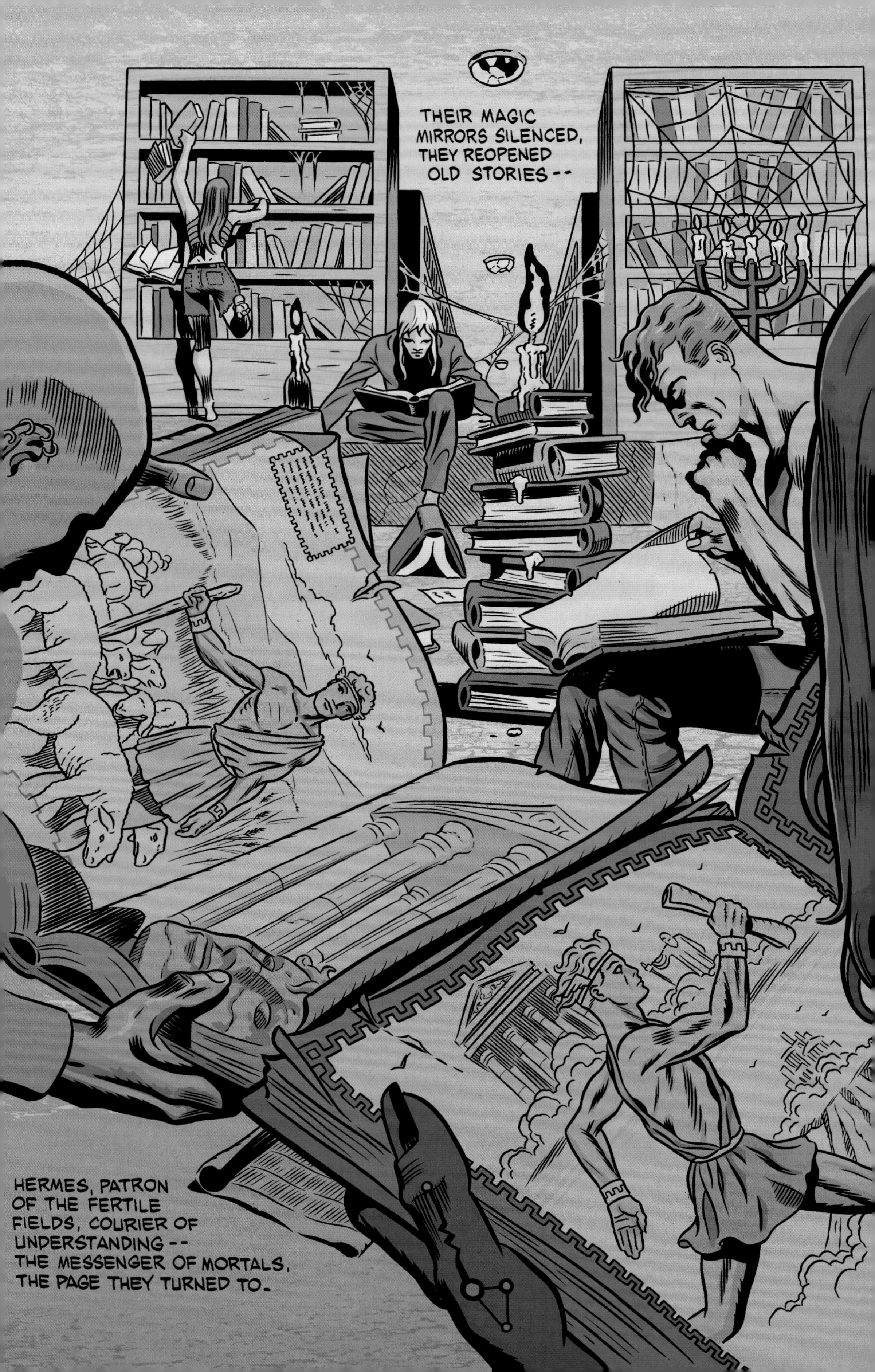
THEIR MAGIC MIRRORS SILENCED, THEY REOPENED OLD STORIES --
HERMES, PATRON OF THE FERTILE FIELDS, COURIER OF UNDERSTANDING -- THE MESSENGER OF MORTALS. THE PAGE THEY TURNED TO.

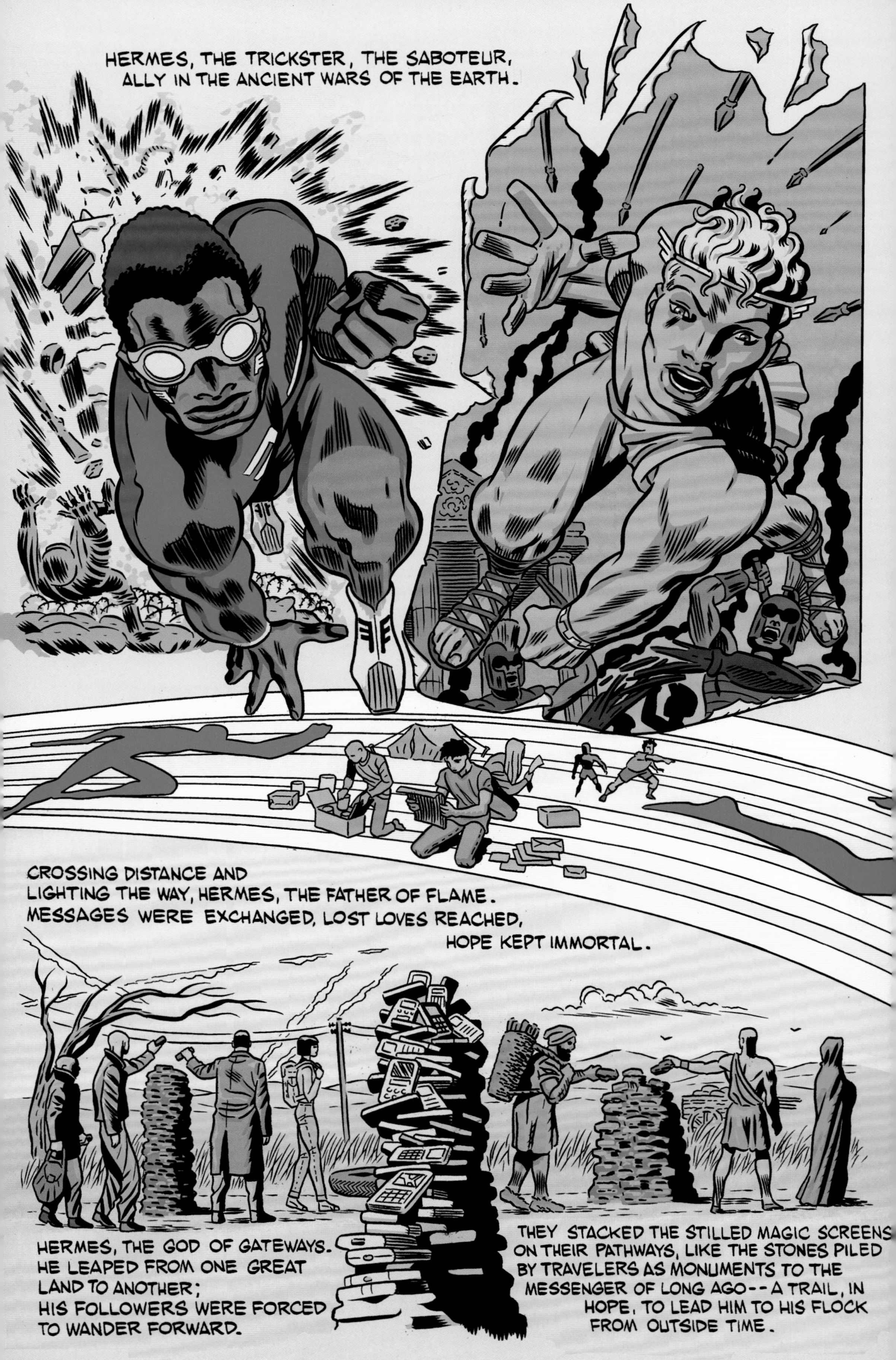
HERMES, THE TRICKSTER, THE SABOTEUR, ALLY IN THE ANCIENT WARS OF THE EARTH.
CROSSING DISTANCE AND LIGHTING THE WAY, HERMES, THE FATHER OF FLAME. MESSAGES WERE EXCHANGED, LOST LOVES REACHED, HOPE KEPT IMMORTAL.
HERMES, THE GOD OF GATEWAYS. HE LEAPED FROM ONE GREAT LAND TO ANOTHER; HIS FOLLOWERS WERE FORCED TO WANDER FORWARD.
THEY STACKED THE STILLED MAGIC SCREENS ON THEIR PATHWAYS, LIKE THE STONES PILED BY TRAVELERS AS MONUMENTS TO THE MESSENGER OF LONG AGO--A TRAIL, IN HOPE, TO LEAD HIM TO HIS FLOCK FROM OUTSIDE TIME.

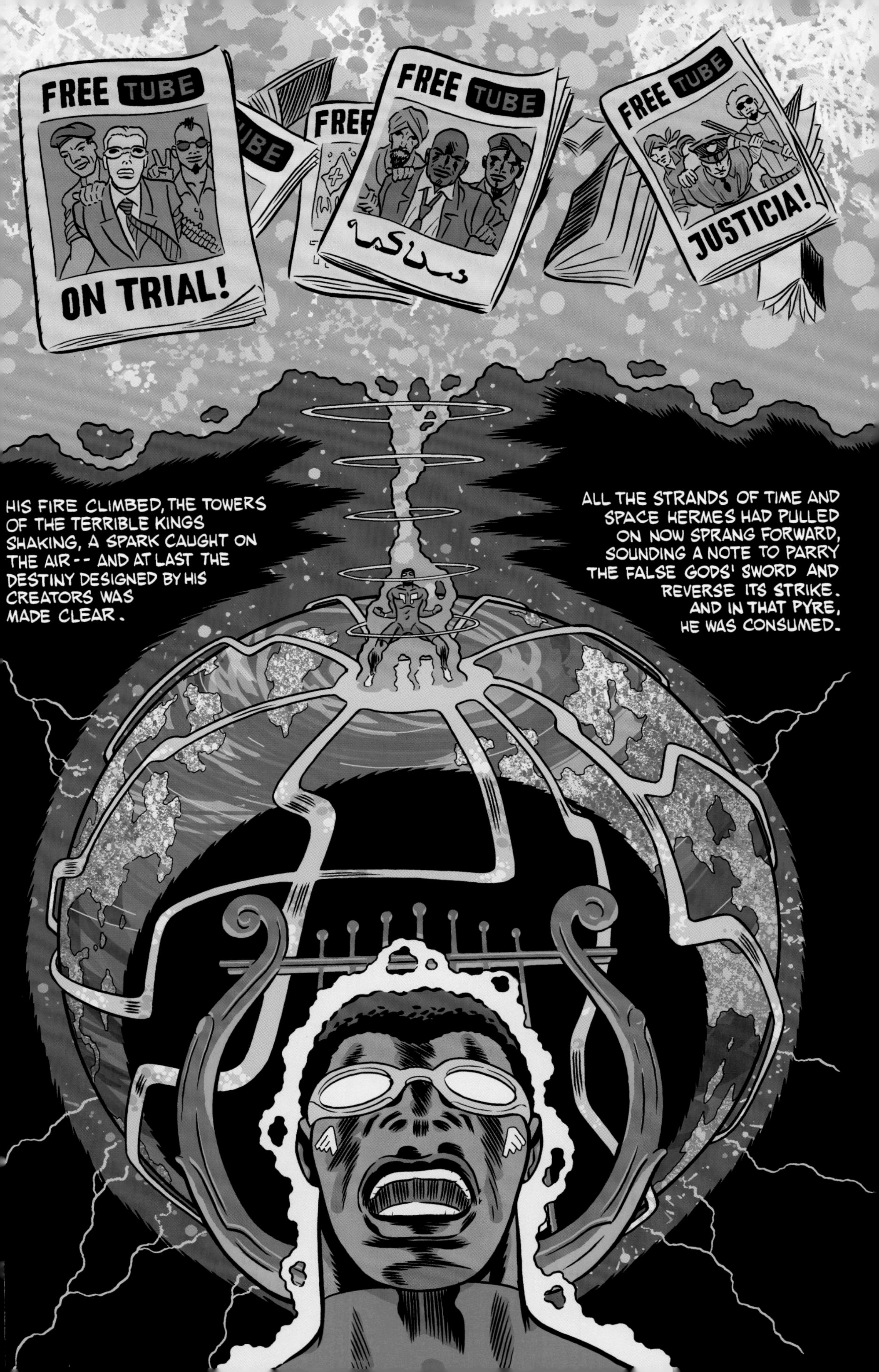
FREE TUBE
ON TRIAL!
FREE TUBE
FREE TUBE
JUSTICIA!
HIS FIRE CLIMBED, THE TOWERS OF THE TERRIBLE KINGS SHAKING, A SPARK CAUGHT ON THE AIR-- AND AT LAST THE DESTINY DESIGNED BY HIS CREATORS WAS MADE CLEAR.
ALL THE STRANDS OF TIME AND SPACE HERMES HAD PULLED ON NOW SPRANG FORWARD, SOUNDING A NOTE TO PARRY THE FALSE GODS' SWORD AND REVERSE ITS STRIKE. AND IN THAT PYRE, HE WAS CONSUMED.

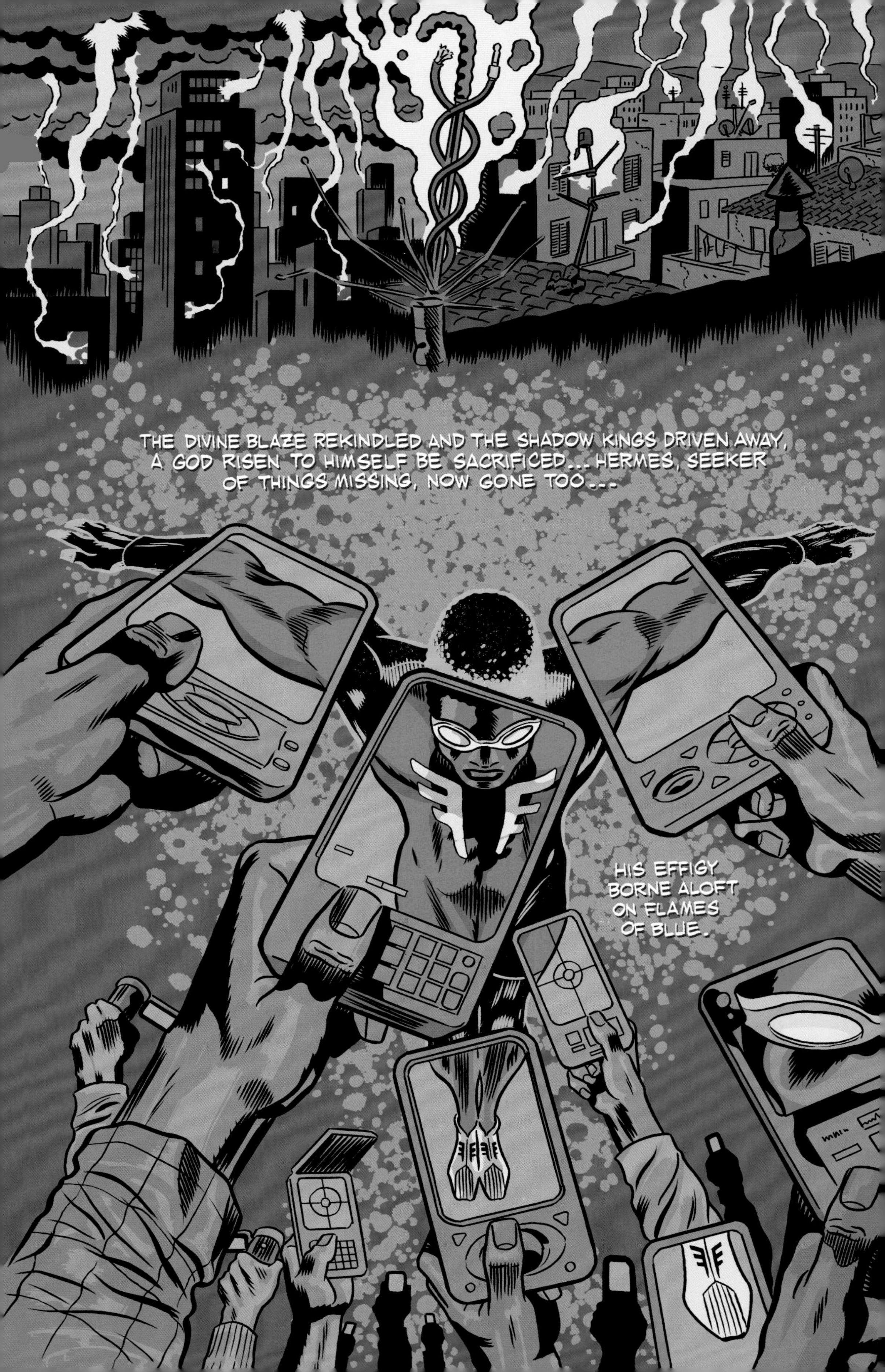
THE DIVINE BLAZE REKINDLED AND THE SHADOW KINGS DRIVEN AWAY, A GOD RISEN TO HIMSELF BE SACRIFICED... HERMES, SEEKER OF THINGS MISSING, NOW GONE TOO...
HIS EFFIGY BORNE ALOFT ON FLAMES OF BLUE.

THIS HAPPENED MANY TURNINGS OF THE EARTH FROM NOW, MY SCHOLARS, TO YOUR CHILDREN'S CHILDREN LONG GONE TO THE VOID.

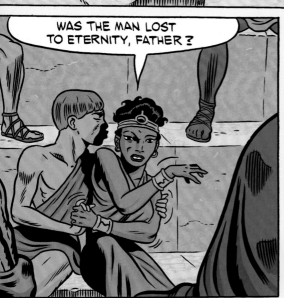

WAS THE MAN LOST TO ETERNITY, FATHER?

HE VANISHED ON THE AIR THAT EVER SEEMED TO CARRY HIM, BUT HIS STORY WRITES OUR WILL TO STAY ALIVE.

ARE WE DOOMED TO LIVE THIS TRIAL, FATHER?

WE ARE FATED TO ENDURE!

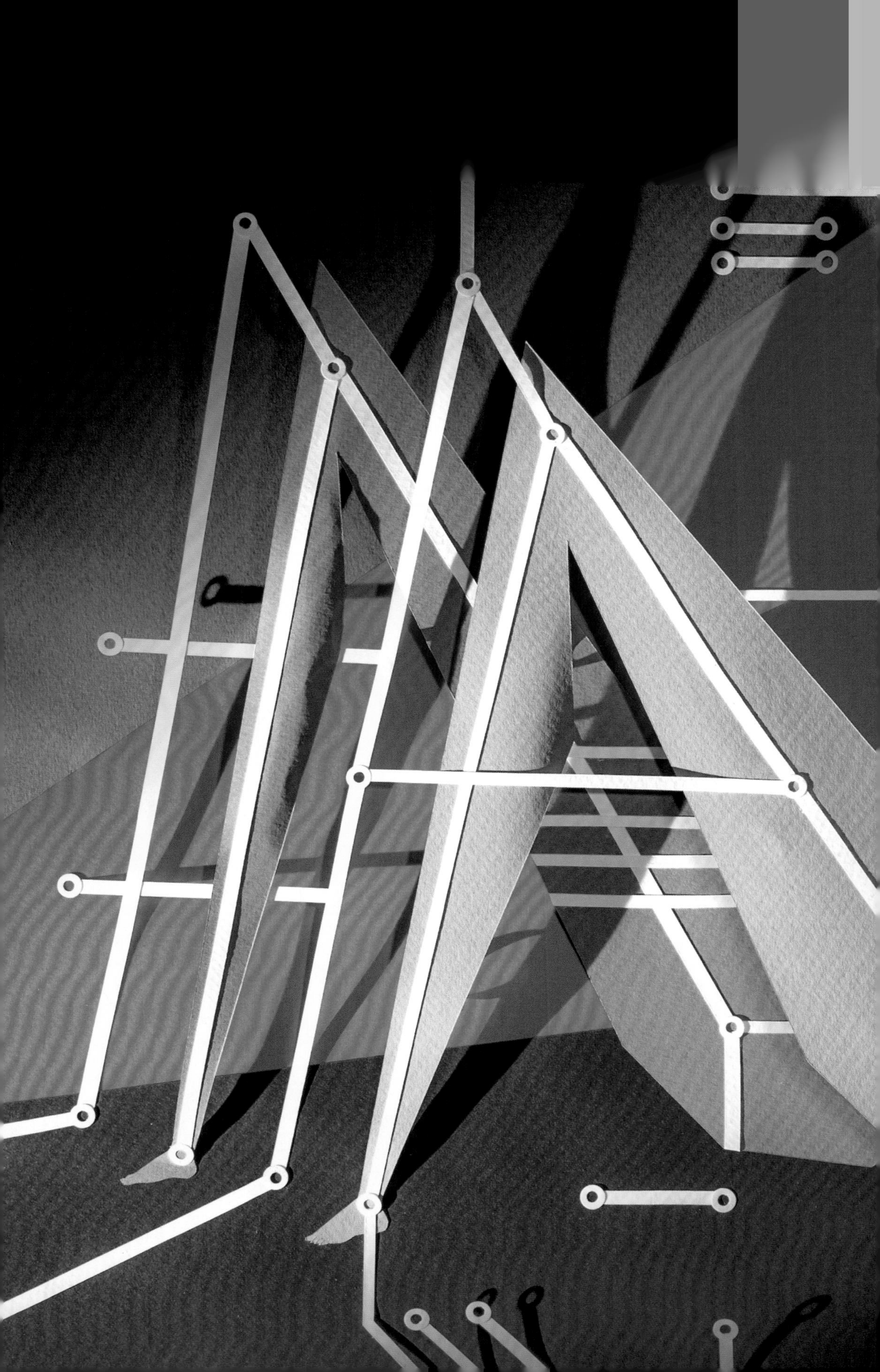

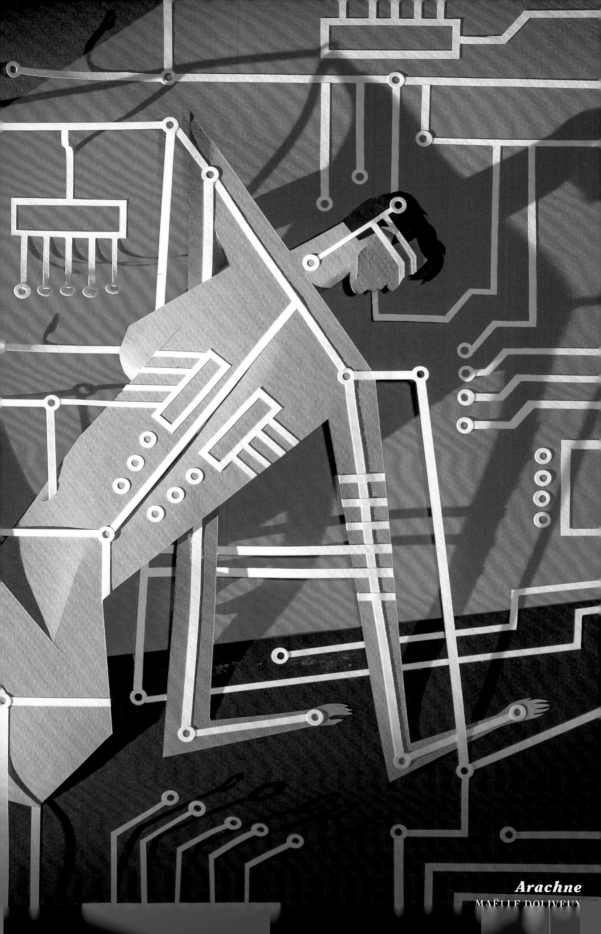

Arachne

MAËLLE DOLIVEUX

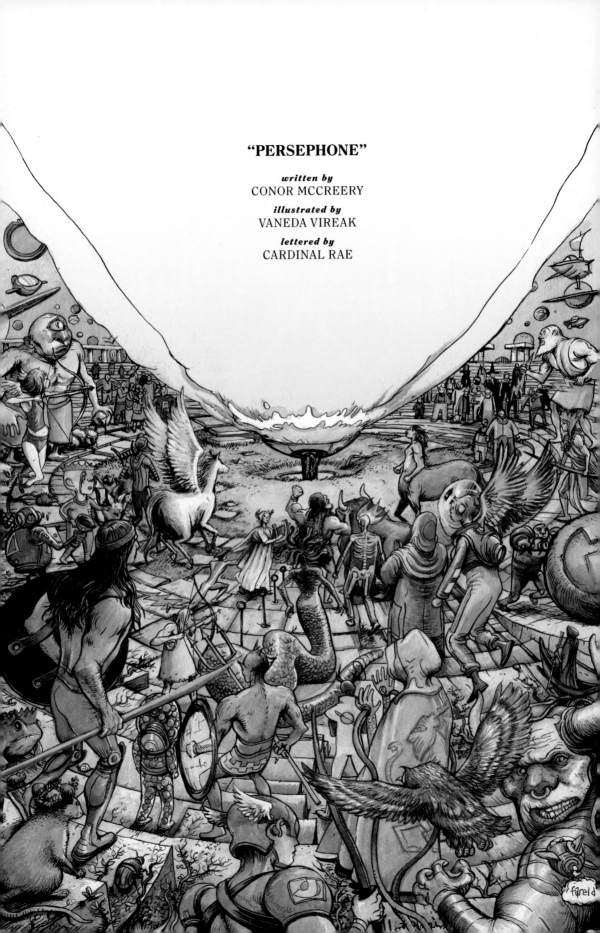

"PERSEPHONE"

written by
CONOR MCCREERY

illustrated by
VANEDA VIREAK

lettered by
CARDINAL RAE

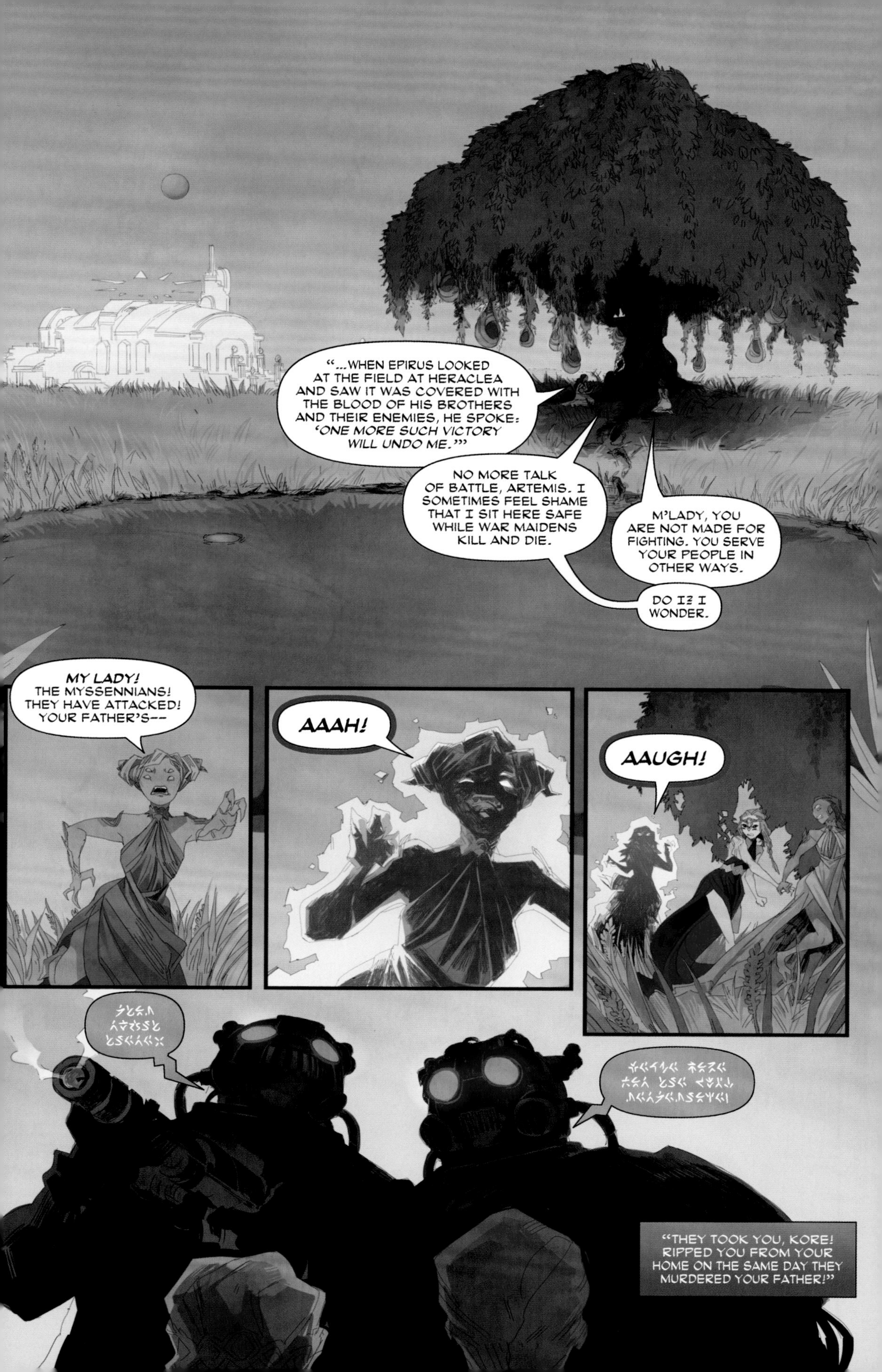
"...WHEN EPIRUS LOOKED AT THE FIELD AT HERACLEA AND SAW IT WAS COVERED WITH THE BLOOD OF HIS BROTHERS AND THEIR ENEMIES, HE SPOKE: 'ONE MORE SUCH VICTORY WILL UNDO ME.'"
NO MORE TALK OF BATTLE, ARTEMIS. I SOMETIMES FEEL SHAME THAT I SIT HERE SAFE WHILE WAR MAIDENS KILL AND DIE.
M'LADY, YOU ARE NOT MADE FOR FIGHTING. YOU SERVE YOUR PEOPLE IN OTHER WAYS.
DO I? I WONDER.
MY LADY! THE MYSSENNIANS! THEY HAVE ATTACKED! YOUR FATHER'S--
AAAH!
AAUGH!
"THEY TOOK YOU, KORE! RIPPED YOU FROM YOUR HOME ON THE SAME DAY THEY MURDERED YOUR FATHER!"

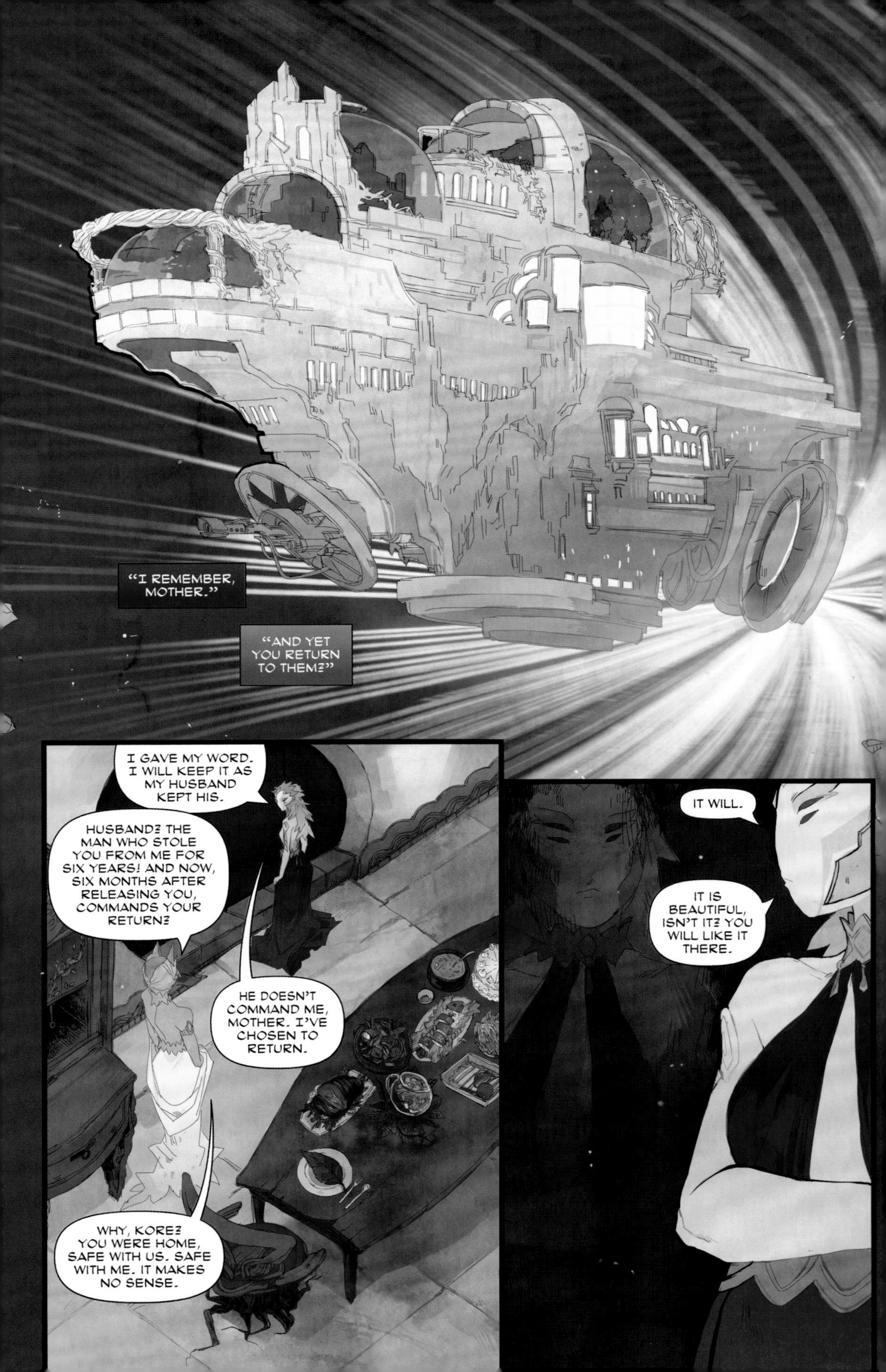
"I REMEMBER, MOTHER."
"AND YET YOU RETURN TO THEM?"
I GAVE MY WORD. I WILL KEEP IT AS MY HUSBAND KEPT HIS.
HUSBAND? THE MAN WHO STOLE YOU FROM ME FOR SIX YEARS! AND NOW, SIX MONTHS AFTER RELEASING YOU, COMMANDS YOUR RETURN?
HE DOESN'T COMMAND ME, MOTHER. I'VE CHOSEN TO RETURN.
WHY, KORE? YOU WERE HOME, SAFE WITH US. SAFE WITH ME. IT MAKES NO SENSE.
IT WILL.
IT IS BEAUTIFUL, ISN'T IT? YOU WILL LIKE IT THERE.

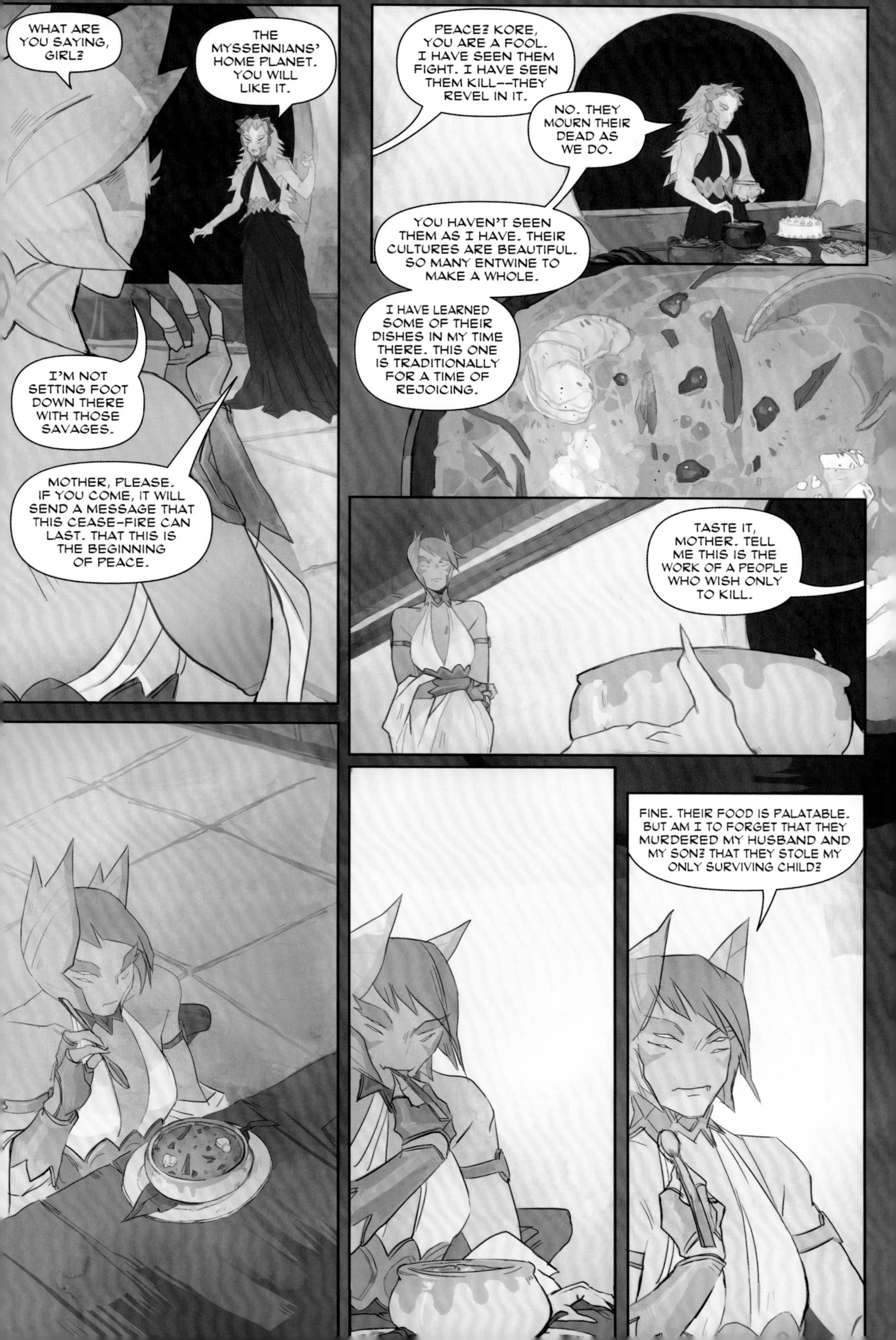
WHAT ARE YOU SAYING, GIRL?
THE MYSSENNIANS' HOME PLANET. YOU WILL LIKE IT.
I'M NOT SETTING FOOT DOWN THERE WITH THOSE SAVAGES.
MOTHER, PLEASE. IF YOU COME, IT WILL SEND A MESSAGE THAT THIS CEASE-FIRE CAN LAST. THAT THIS IS THE BEGINNING OF PEACE.
PEACE? KORE, YOU ARE A FOOL. I HAVE SEEN THEM FIGHT. I HAVE SEEN THEM KILL--THEY REVEL IN IT.
NO. THEY MOURN THEIR DEAD AS WE DO.
YOU HAVEN'T SEEN THEM AS I HAVE. THEIR CULTURES ARE BEAUTIFUL. SO MANY ENTWINE TO MAKE A WHOLE.
I HAVE LEARNED SOME OF THEIR DISHES IN MY TIME THERE. THIS ONE IS TRADITIONALLY FOR A TIME OF REJOICING.
TASTE IT, MOTHER. TELL ME THIS IS THE WORK OF A PEOPLE WHO WISH ONLY TO KILL.
FINE. THEIR FOOD IS PALATABLE. BUT AM I TO FORGET THAT THEY MURDERED MY HUSBAND AND MY SON? THAT THEY STOLE MY ONLY SURVIVING CHILD?

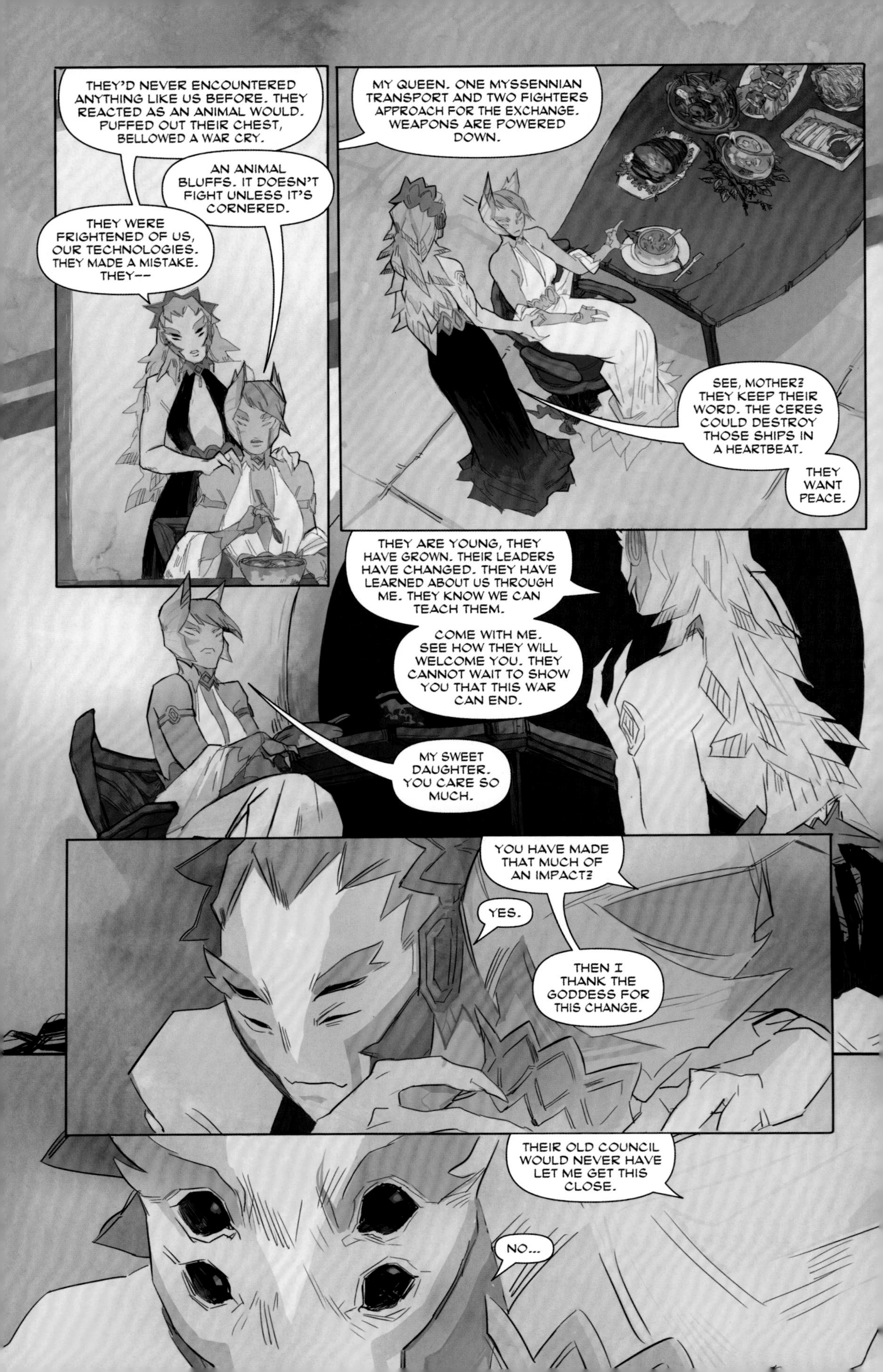
THEY'D NEVER ENCOUNTERED ANYTHING LIKE US BEFORE. THEY REACTED AS AN ANIMAL WOULD. PUFFED OUT THEIR CHEST, BELLOWED A WAR CRY.
AN ANIMAL BLUFFS. IT DOESN'T FIGHT UNLESS IT'S CORNERED.
THEY WERE FRIGHTENED OF US, OUR TECHNOLOGIES. THEY MADE A MISTAKE. THEY--
MY QUEEN. ONE MYSSENNIAN TRANSPORT AND TWO FIGHTERS APPROACH FOR THE EXCHANGE. WEAPONS ARE POWERED DOWN.
SEE, MOTHER? THEY KEEP THEIR WORD. THE CERES COULD DESTROY THOSE SHIPS IN A HEARTBEAT.
THEY WANT PEACE.
THEY ARE YOUNG, THEY HAVE GROWN. THEIR LEADERS HAVE CHANGED. THEY HAVE LEARNED ABOUT US THROUGH ME. THEY KNOW WE CAN TEACH THEM.
COME WITH ME. SEE HOW THEY WILL WELCOME YOU. THEY CANNOT WAIT TO SHOW YOU THAT THIS WAR CAN END.
MY SWEET DAUGHTER. YOU CARE SO MUCH.
YOU HAVE MADE THAT MUCH OF AN IMPACT?
YES.
THEN I THANK THE GODDESS FOR THIS CHANGE.
THEIR OLD COUNCIL WOULD NEVER HAVE LET ME GET THIS CLOSE.
NO...

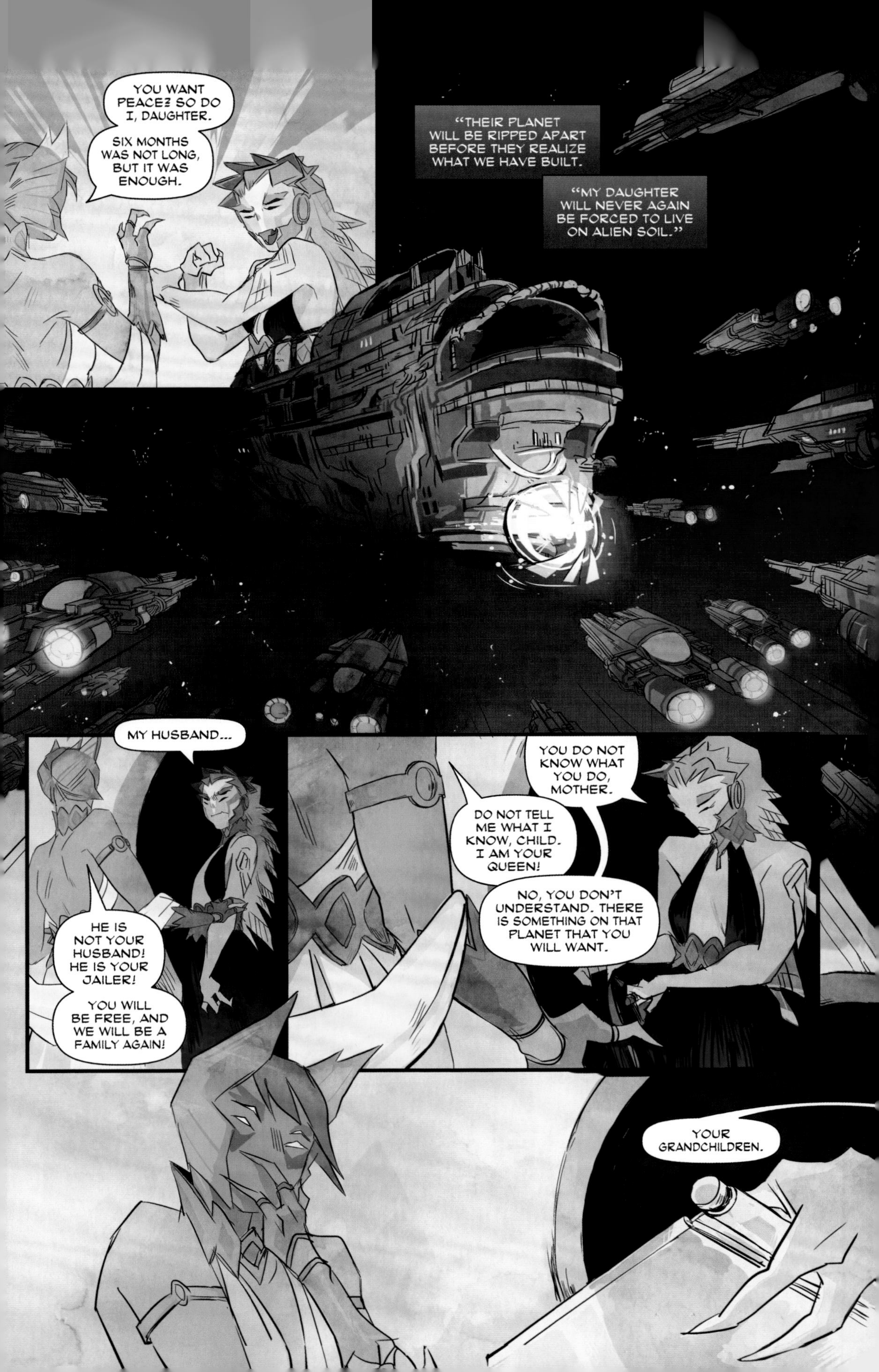
YOU WANT PEACE? SO DO I, DAUGHTER.
SIX MONTHS WAS NOT LONG, BUT IT WAS ENOUGH.
"THEIR PLANET WILL BE RIPPED APART BEFORE THEY REALIZE WHAT WE HAVE BUILT.
"MY DAUGHTER WILL NEVER AGAIN BE FORCED TO LIVE ON ALIEN SOIL."
MY HUSBAND...
HE IS NOT YOUR HUSBAND! HE IS YOUR JAILER!
YOU WILL BE FREE, AND WE WILL BE A FAMILY AGAIN!
YOU DO NOT KNOW WHAT YOU DO, MOTHER.
DO NOT TELL ME WHAT I KNOW, CHILD. I AM YOUR QUEEN!
NO, YOU DON'T UNDERSTAND. THERE IS SOMETHING ON THAT PLANET THAT YOU WILL WANT.
YOUR GRANDCHILDREN.

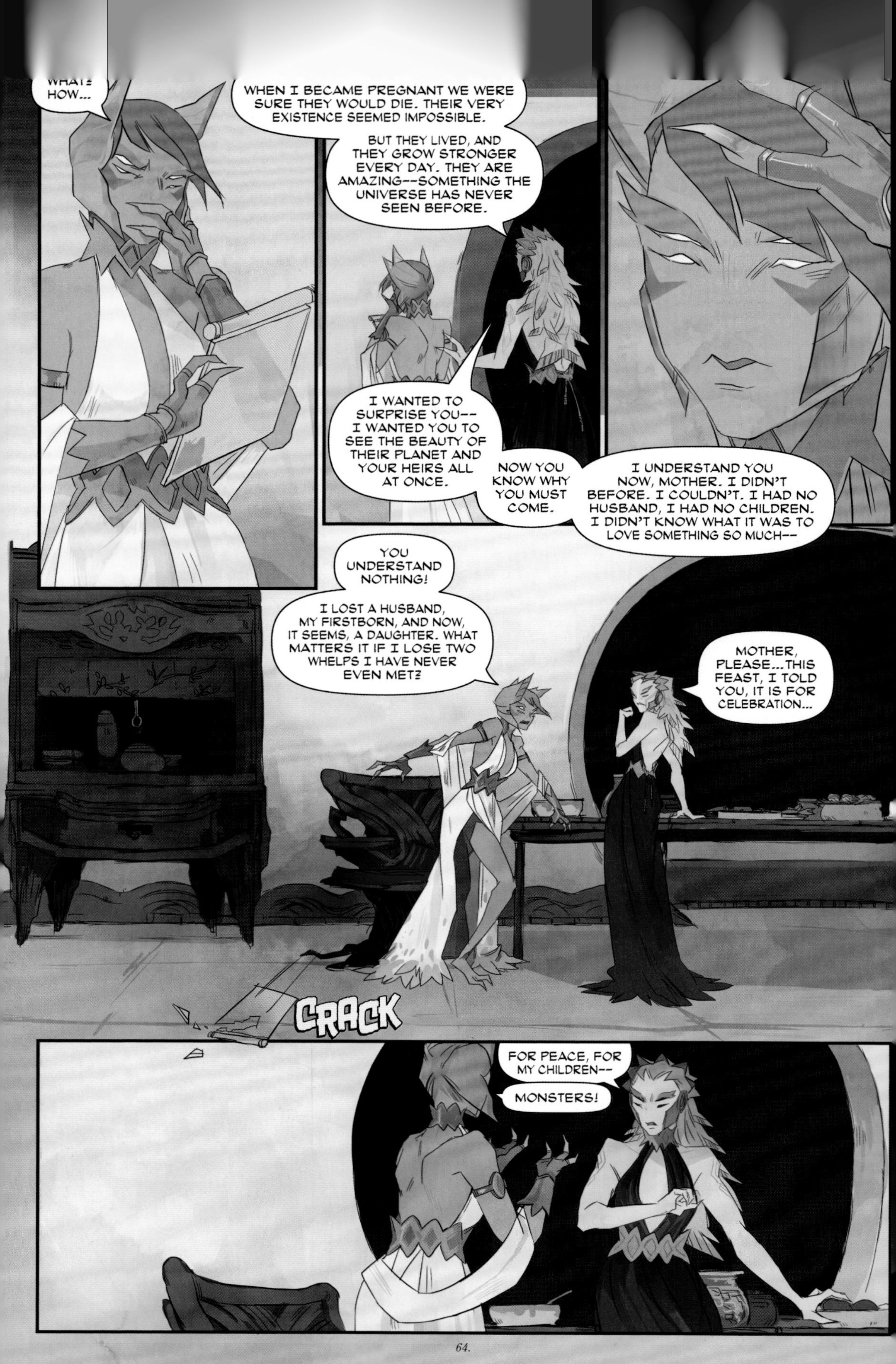
WHAT? HOW...
WHEN I BECAME PREGNANT WE WERE SURE THEY WOULD DIE. THEIR VERY EXISTENCE SEEMED IMPOSSIBLE.
BUT THEY LIVED, AND THEY GROW STRONGER EVERY DAY. THEY ARE AMAZING--SOMETHING THE UNIVERSE HAS NEVER SEEN BEFORE.
I WANTED TO SURPRISE YOU--I WANTED YOU TO SEE THE BEAUTY OF THEIR PLANET AND YOUR HEIRS ALL AT ONCE.
NOW YOU KNOW WHY YOU MUST COME.
I UNDERSTAND YOU NOW, MOTHER. I DIDN'T BEFORE. I COULDN'T. I HAD NO HUSBAND, I HAD NO CHILDREN. I DIDN'T KNOW WHAT IT WAS TO LOVE SOMETHING SO MUCH--
YOU UNDERSTAND NOTHING!
I LOST A HUSBAND, MY FIRSTBORN, AND NOW, IT SEEMS, A DAUGHTER. WHAT MATTERS IT IF I LOSE TWO WHELPS I HAVE NEVER EVEN MET?
MOTHER, PLEASE...THIS FEAST, I TOLD YOU, IT IS FOR CELEBRATION...
CRACK
FOR PEACE, FOR MY CHILDREN--
MONSTERS!

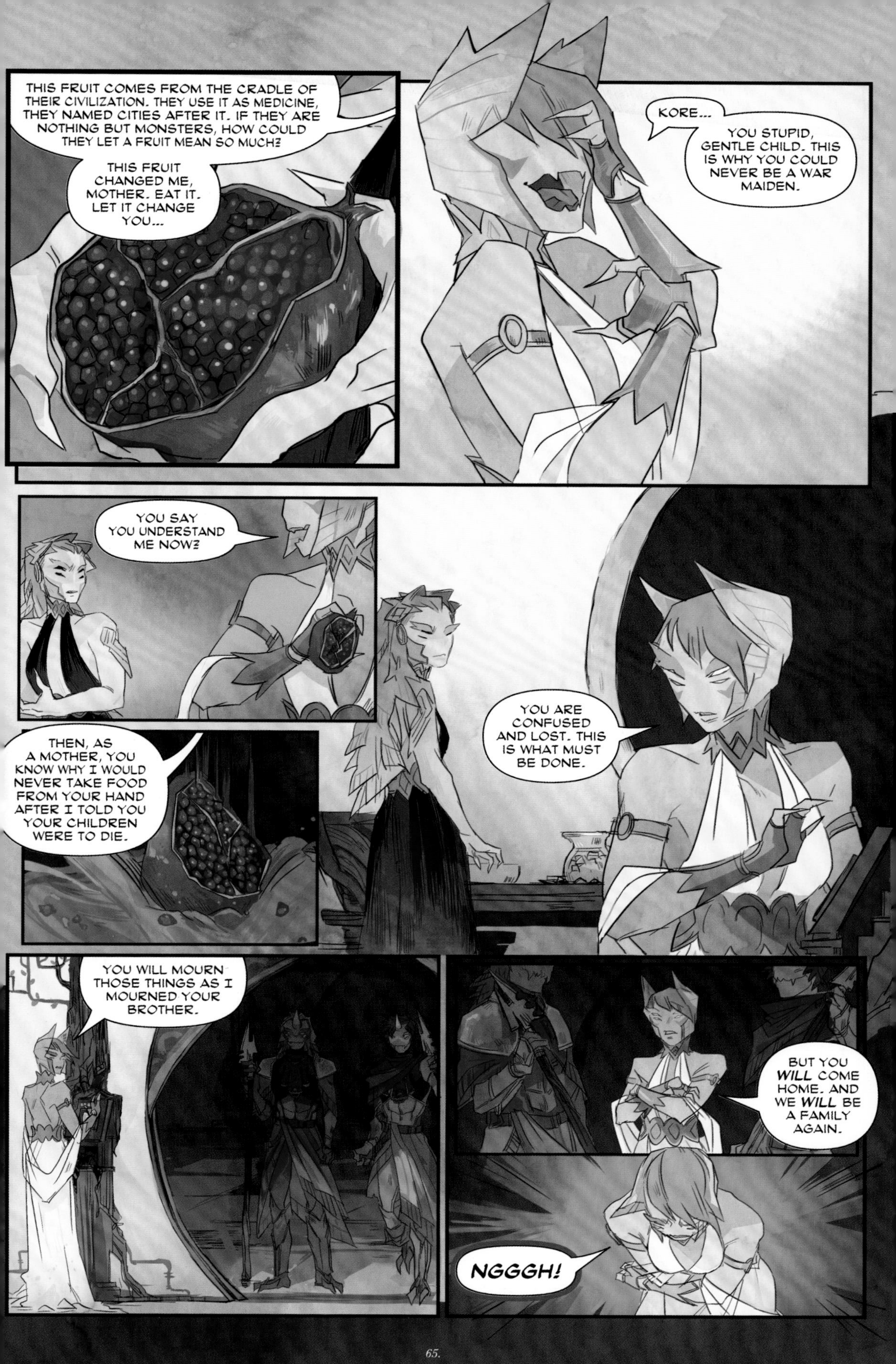
THIS FRUIT COMES FROM THE CRADLE OF THEIR CIVILIZATION. THEY USE IT AS MEDICINE, THEY NAMED CITIES AFTER IT. IF THEY ARE NOTHING BUT MONSTERS, HOW COULD THEY LET A FRUIT MEAN SO MUCH?
THIS FRUIT CHANGED ME, MOTHER. EAT IT. LET IT CHANGE YOU...
KORE...
YOU STUPID, GENTLE CHILD. THIS IS WHY YOU COULD NEVER BE A WAR MAIDEN.
YOU SAY YOU UNDERSTAND ME NOW?
THEN, AS A MOTHER, YOU KNOW WHY I WOULD NEVER TAKE FOOD FROM YOUR HAND AFTER I TOLD YOU YOUR CHILDREN WERE TO DIE.
YOU ARE CONFUSED AND LOST. THIS IS WHAT MUST BE DONE.
YOU WILL MOURN THOSE THINGS AS I MOURNED YOUR BROTHER.
BUT YOU WILL COME HOME. AND WE WILL BE A FAMILY AGAIN.
NGGGH!

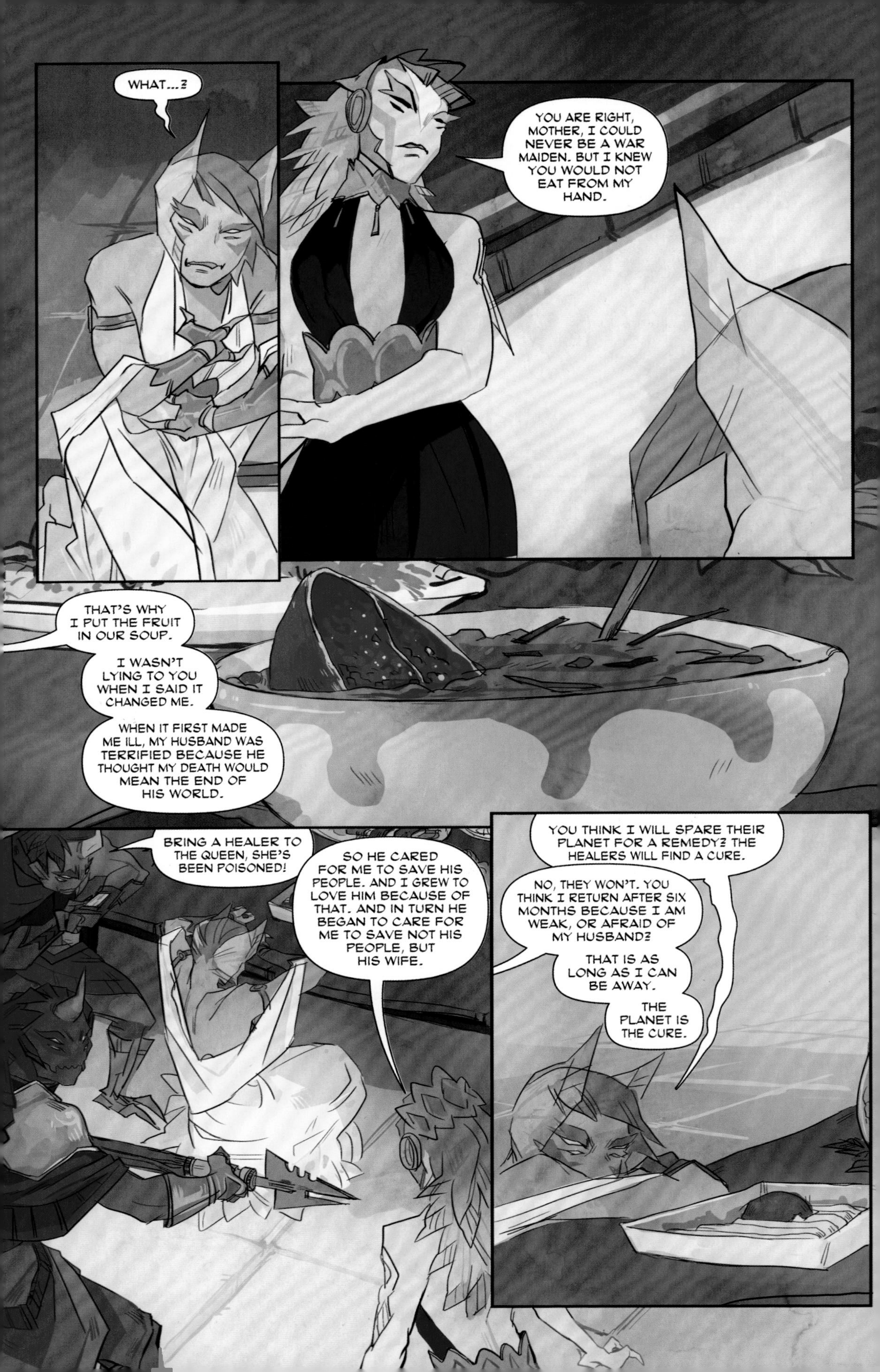
WHAT...?
YOU ARE RIGHT, MOTHER, I COULD NEVER BE A WAR MAIDEN. BUT I KNEW YOU WOULD NOT EAT FROM MY HAND.
THAT'S WHY I PUT THE FRUIT IN OUR SOUP.
I WASN'T LYING TO YOU WHEN I SAID IT CHANGED ME.
WHEN IT FIRST MADE ME ILL, MY HUSBAND WAS TERRIFIED BECAUSE HE THOUGHT MY DEATH WOULD MEAN THE END OF HIS WORLD.
BRING A HEALER TO THE QUEEN, SHE'S BEEN POISONED!
SO HE CARED FOR ME TO SAVE HIS PEOPLE. AND I GREW TO LOVE HIM BECAUSE OF THAT. AND IN TURN HE BEGAN TO CARE FOR ME TO SAVE NOT HIS PEOPLE, BUT HIS WIFE.
YOU THINK I WILL SPARE THEIR PLANET FOR A REMEDY? THE HEALERS WILL FIND A CURE.
NO, THEY WON'T. YOU THINK I RETURN AFTER SIX MONTHS BECAUSE I AM WEAK, OR AFRAID OF MY HUSBAND?
THAT IS AS LONG AS I CAN BE AWAY.
THE PLANET IS THE CURE.

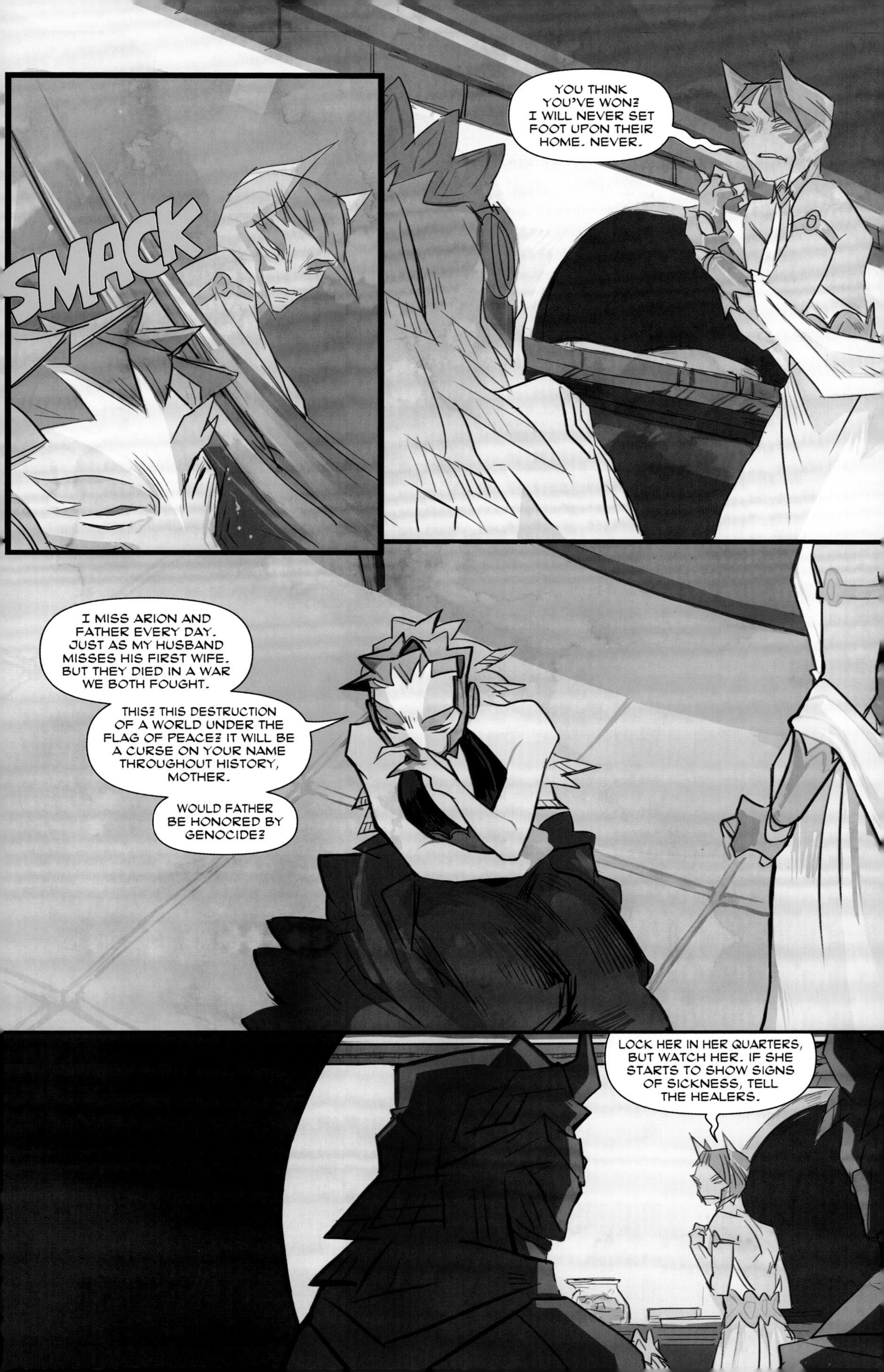
SMACK
YOU THINK YOU'VE WON? I WILL NEVER SET FOOT UPON THEIR HOME. NEVER.
I MISS ARION AND FATHER EVERY DAY. JUST AS MY HUSBAND MISSES HIS FIRST WIFE. BUT THEY DIED IN A WAR WE BOTH FOUGHT.
THIS? THIS DESTRUCTION OF A WORLD UNDER THE FLAG OF PEACE? IT WILL BE A CURSE ON YOUR NAME THROUGHOUT HISTORY, MOTHER.
WOULD FATHER BE HONORED BY GENOCIDE?
LOCK HER IN HER QUARTERS, BUT WATCH HER. IF SHE STARTS TO SHOW SIGNS OF SICKNESS, TELL THE HEALERS.

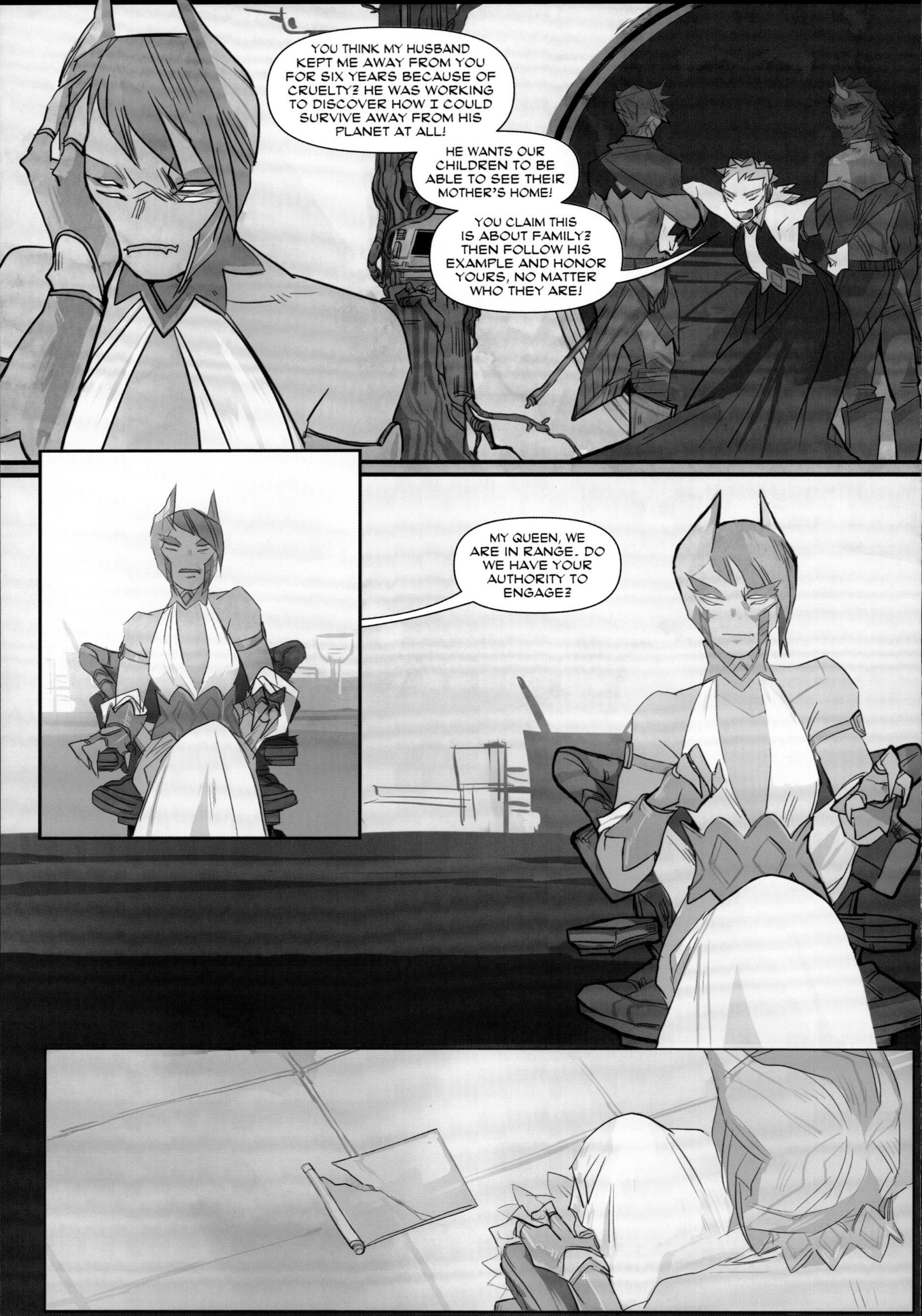
YOU THINK MY HUSBAND KEPT ME AWAY FROM YOU FOR SIX YEARS BECAUSE OF CRUELTY? HE WAS WORKING TO DISCOVER HOW I COULD SURVIVE AWAY FROM HIS PLANET AT ALL!
HE WANTS OUR CHILDREN TO BE ABLE TO SEE THEIR MOTHER'S HOME!
YOU CLAIM THIS IS ABOUT FAMILY? THEN FOLLOW HIS EXAMPLE AND HONOR YOURS, NO MATTER WHO THEY ARE!
MY QUEEN, WE ARE IN RANGE. DO WE HAVE YOUR AUTHORITY TO ENGAGE?

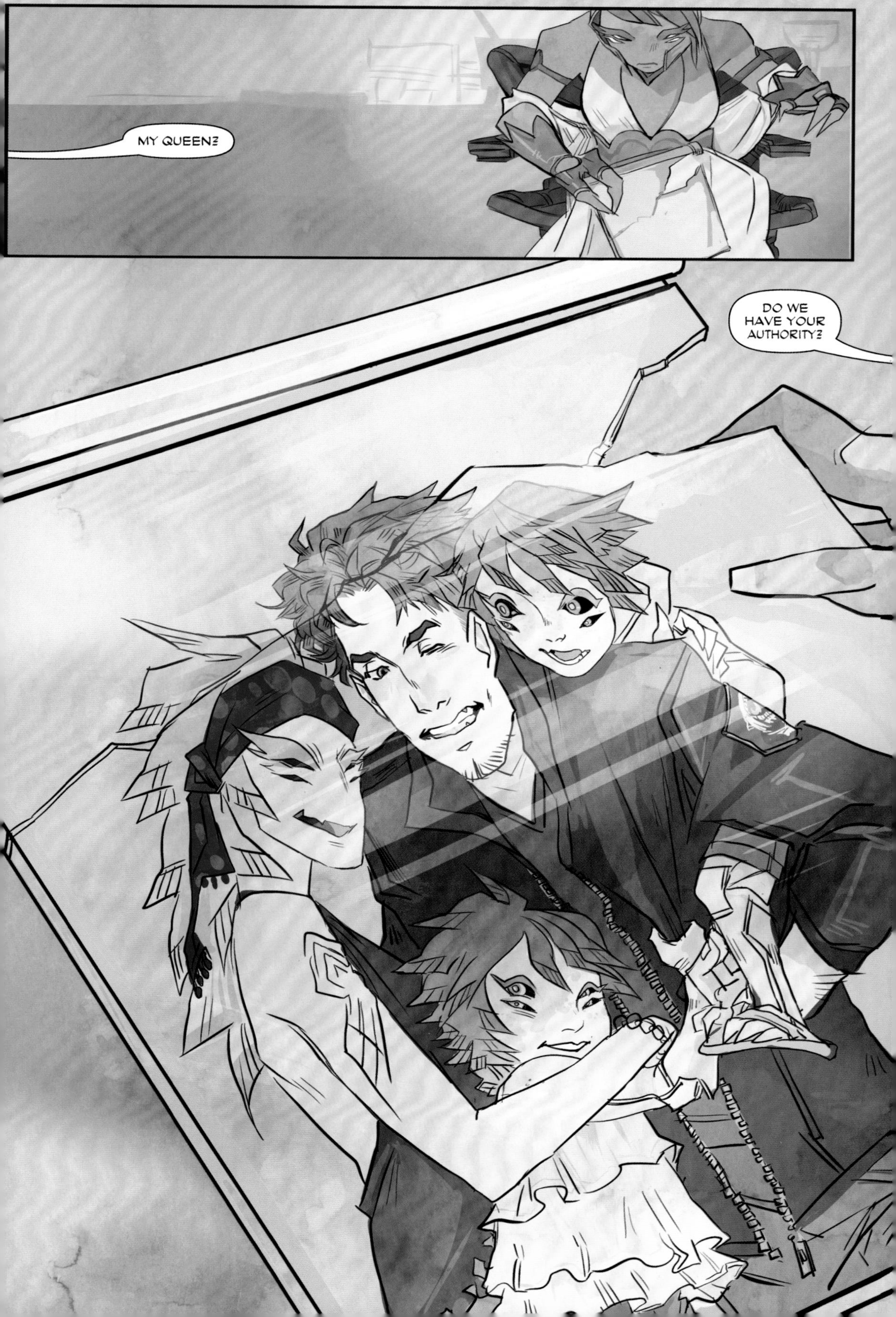
MY QUEEN?
DO WE HAVE YOUR AUTHORITY?

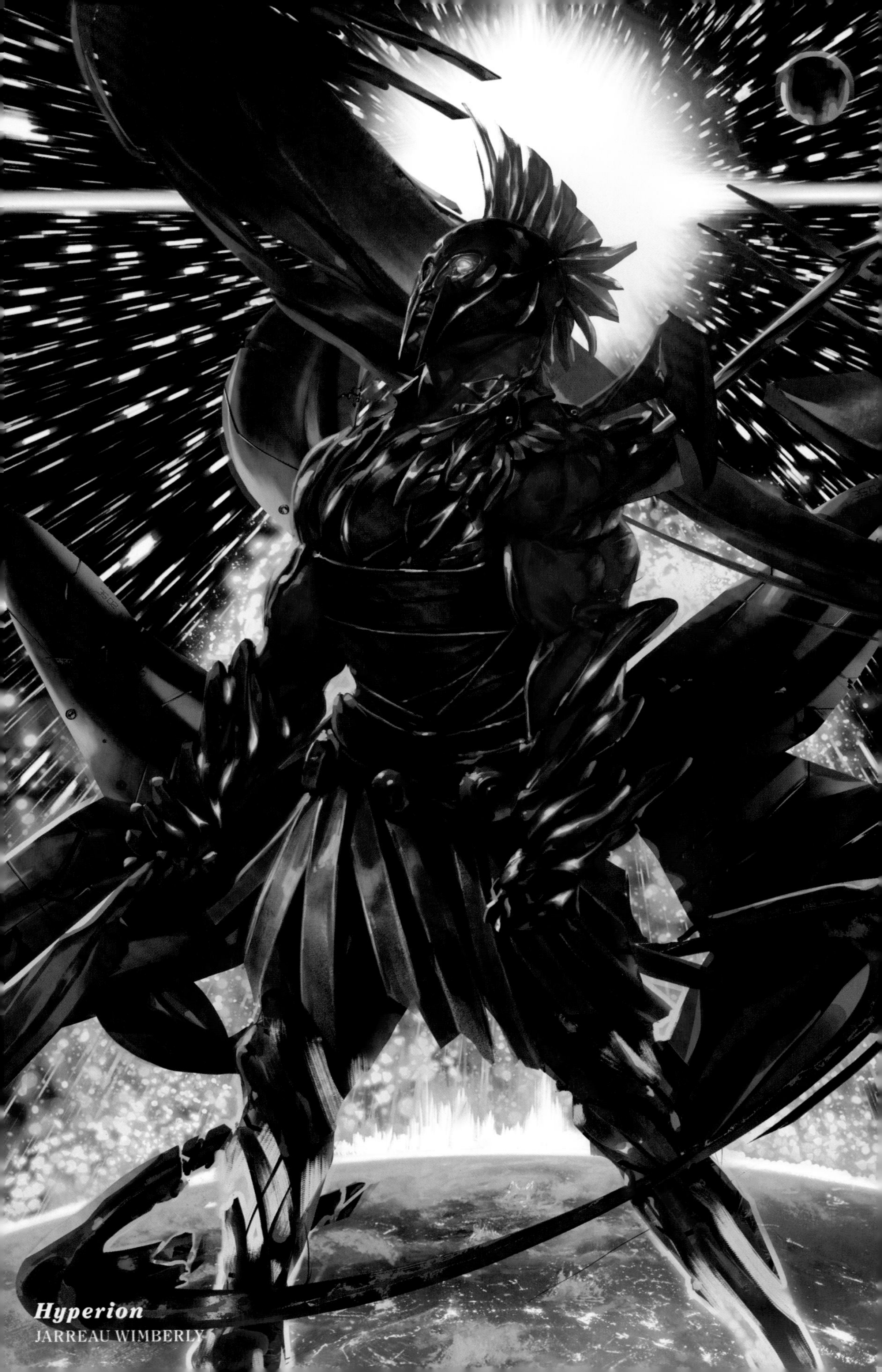

Hyperion

JARREAU WIMBERLY

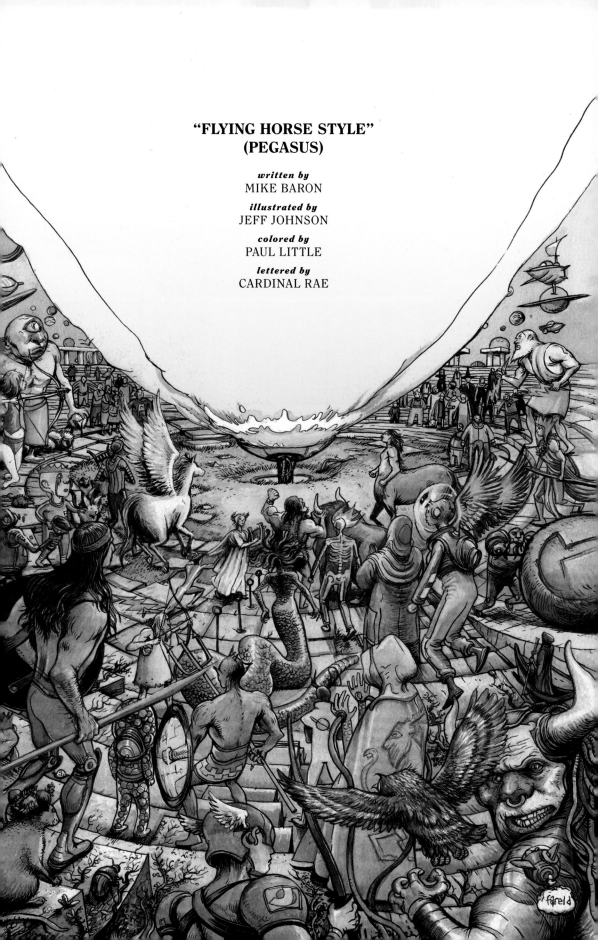

"FLYING HORSE STYLE" (PEGASUS)

written by
MIKE BARON

illustrated by
JEFF JOHNSON

colored by
PAUL LITTLE

lettered by
CARDINAL RAE

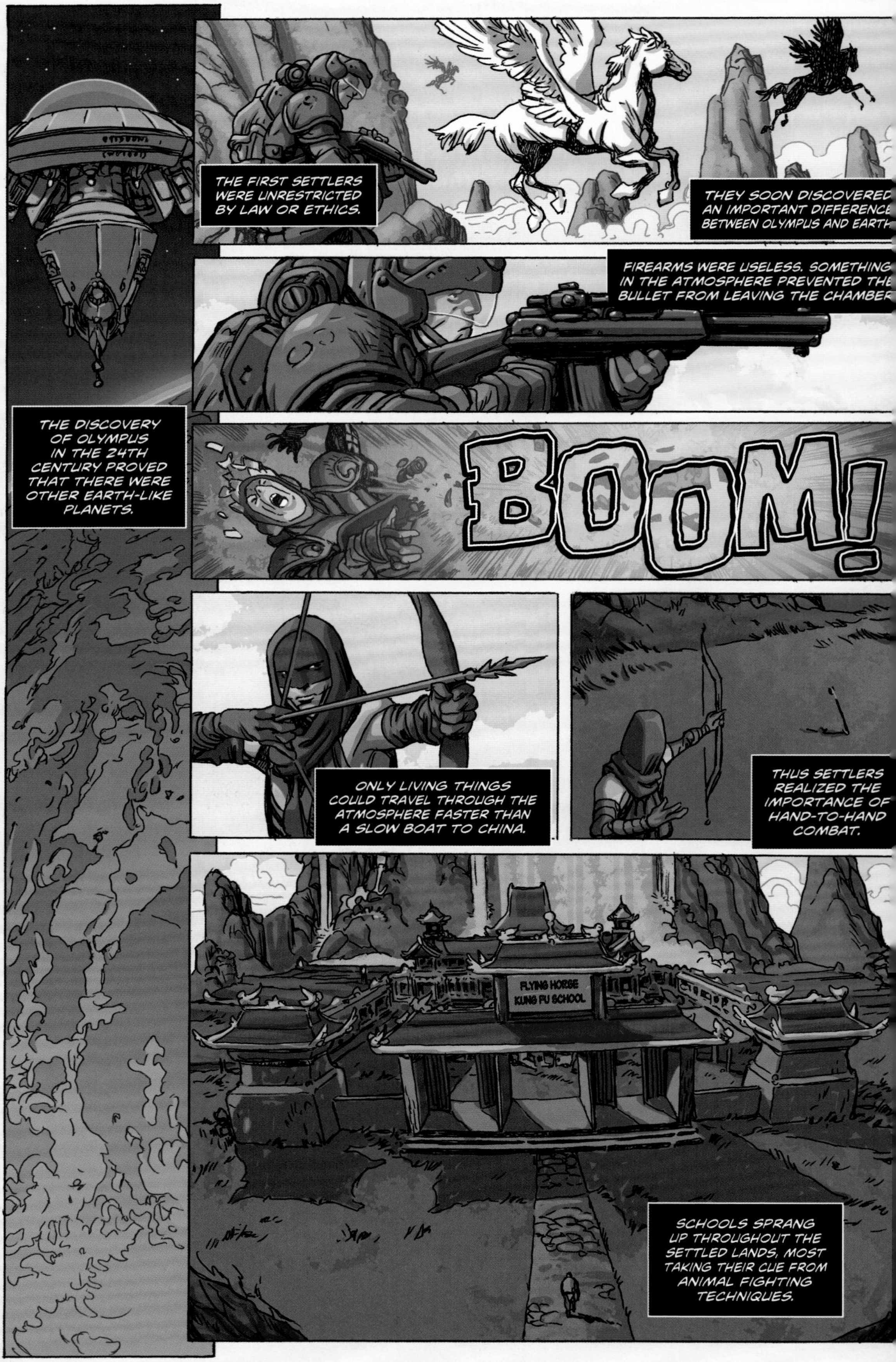
THE DISCOVERY OF OLYMPUS IN THE 24TH CENTURY PROVED THAT THERE WERE OTHER EARTH-LIKE PLANETS.
THE FIRST SETTLERS WERE UNRESTRICTED BY LAW OR ETHICS.
THEY SOON DISCOVERED AN IMPORTANT DIFFERENCE BETWEEN OLYMPUS AND EARTH
FIREARMS WERE USELESS. SOMETHING IN THE ATMOSPHERE PREVENTED THE BULLET FROM LEAVING THE CHAMBER
BOOOM!
ONLY LIVING THINGS COULD TRAVEL THROUGH THE ATMOSPHERE FASTER THAN A SLOW BOAT TO CHINA.
THUS SETTLERS REALIZED THE IMPORTANCE OF HAND-TO-HAND COMBAT.
FLYING HORSE KUNG FU SCHOOL
SCHOOLS SPRANG UP THROUGHOUT THE SETTLED LANDS, MOST TAKING THEIR CUE FROM ANIMAL FIGHTING TECHNIQUES.

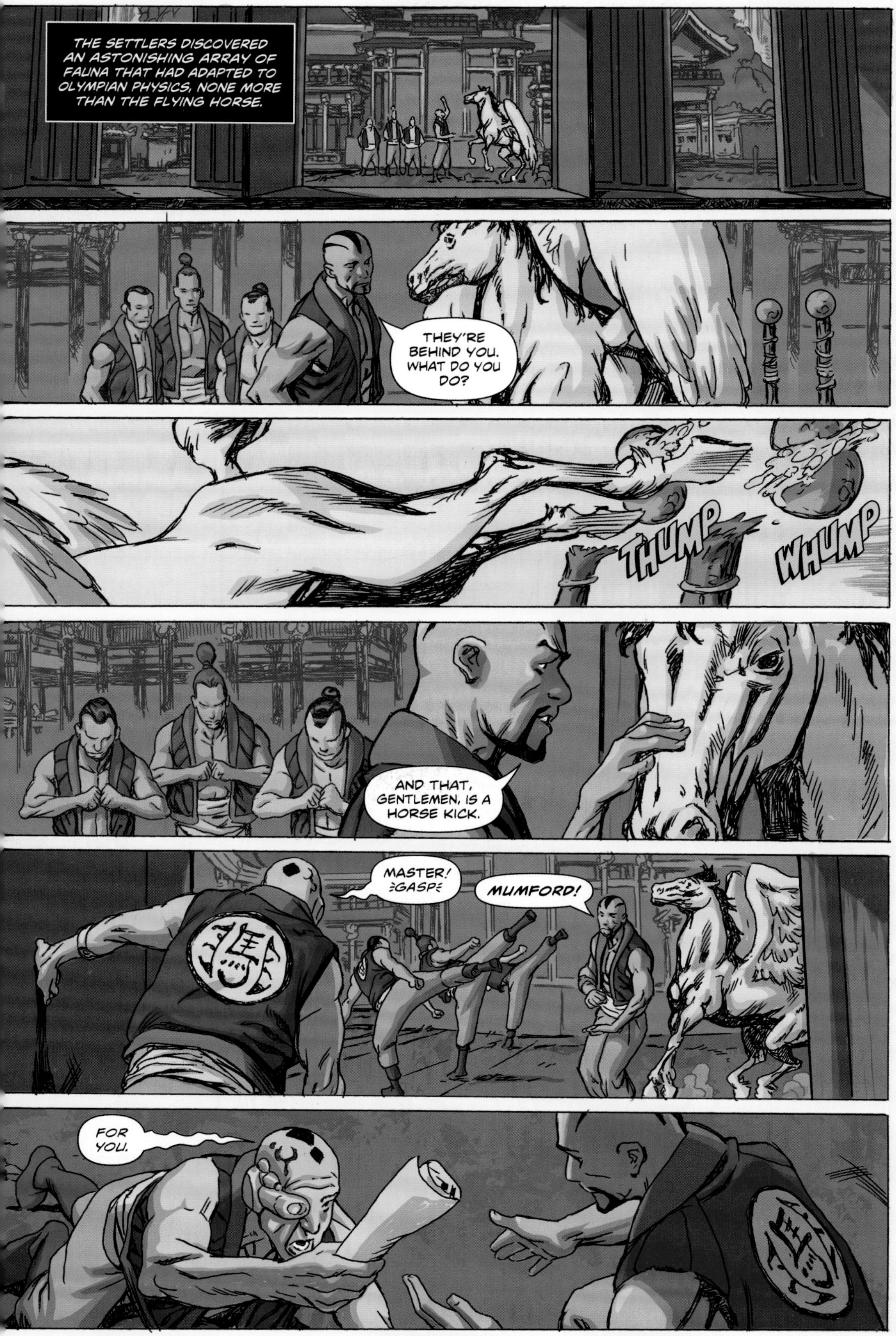
THE SETTLERS DISCOVERED AN ASTONISHING ARRAY OF FAUNA THAT HAD ADAPTED TO OLYMPIAN PHYSICS, NONE MORE THAN THE FLYING HORSE.
THEY'RE BEHIND YOU. WHAT DO YOU DO?
THUMP
WHUMP
AND THAT, GENTLEMEN, IS A HORSE KICK.
MASTER! GASP
MUMFORD!
FOR YOU.

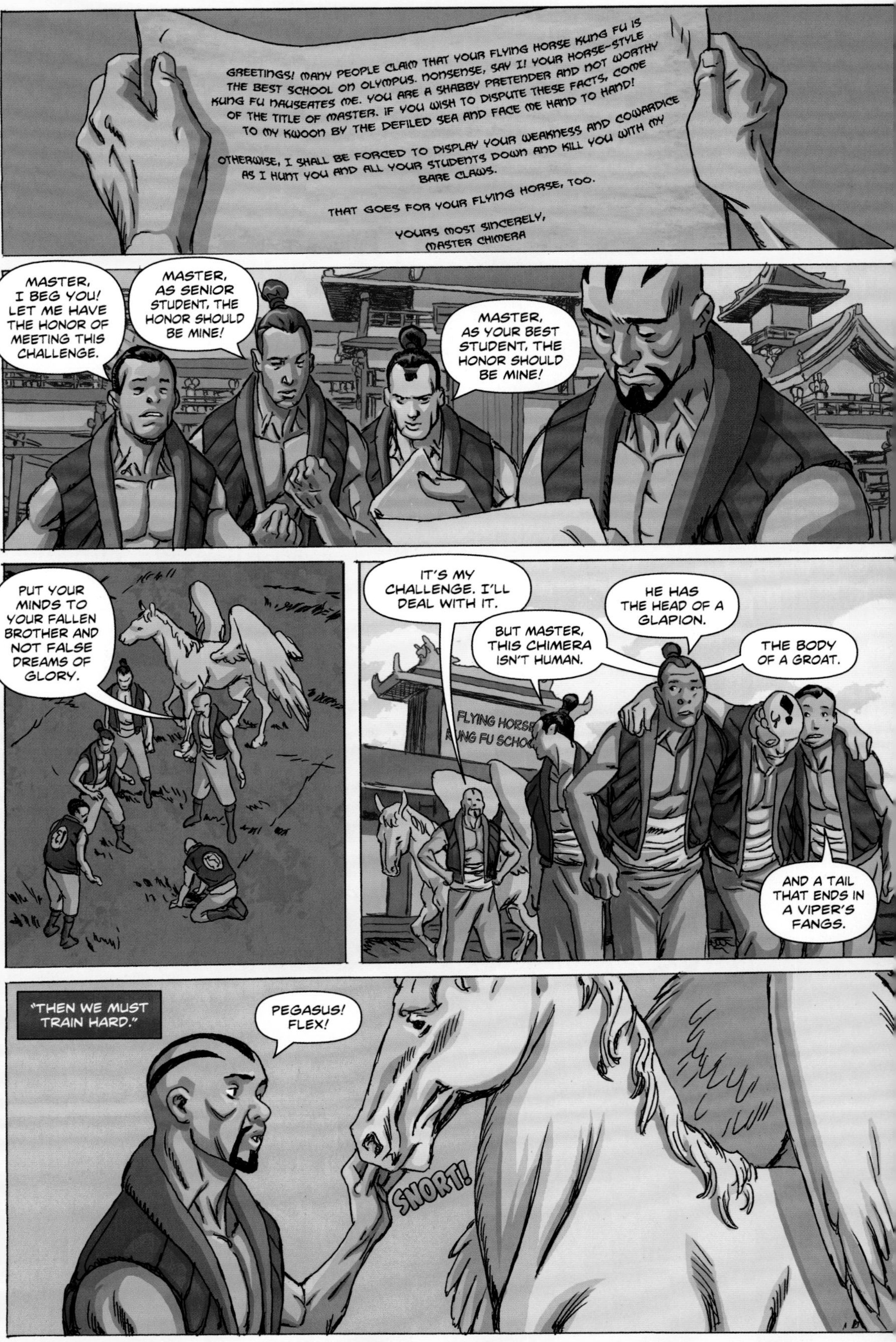
GREETINGS! MANY PEOPLE CLAIM THAT YOUR FLYING HORSE KUNG FU IS THE BEST SCHOOL ON OLYMPUS. NONSENSE, SAY I! YOUR HORSE-STYLE KUNG FU NAUSEATES ME. YOU ARE A SHABBY PRETENDER AND NOT WORTHY OF THE TITLE OF MASTER. IF YOU WISH TO DISPUTE THESE FACTS, COME TO MY KWOON BY THE DEFILED SEA AND FACE ME HAND TO HAND!
OTHERWISE, I SHALL BE FORCED TO DISPLAY YOUR WEAKNESS AND COWARDICE AS I HUNT YOU AND ALL YOUR STUDENTS DOWN AND KILL YOU WITH MY BARE CLAWS.
THAT GOES FOR YOUR FLYING HORSE, TOO.
YOURS MOST SINCERELY, MASTER CHIMERA
MASTER, I BEG YOU! LET ME HAVE THE HONOR OF MEETING THIS CHALLENGE.
MASTER, AS SENIOR STUDENT, THE HONOR SHOULD BE MINE!
MASTER, AS YOUR BEST STUDENT, THE HONOR SHOULD BE MINE!
PUT YOUR MINDS TO YOUR FALLEN BROTHER AND NOT FALSE DREAMS OF GLORY.
IT'S MY CHALLENGE. I'LL DEAL WITH IT.
BUT MASTER, THIS CHIMERA ISN'T HUMAN.
HE HAS THE HEAD OF A GLAPION.
THE BODY OF A GROAT.
AND A TAIL THAT ENDS IN A VIPER'S FANGS.
"THEN WE MUST TRAIN HARD."
PEGASUS! FLEX!
SNORT!

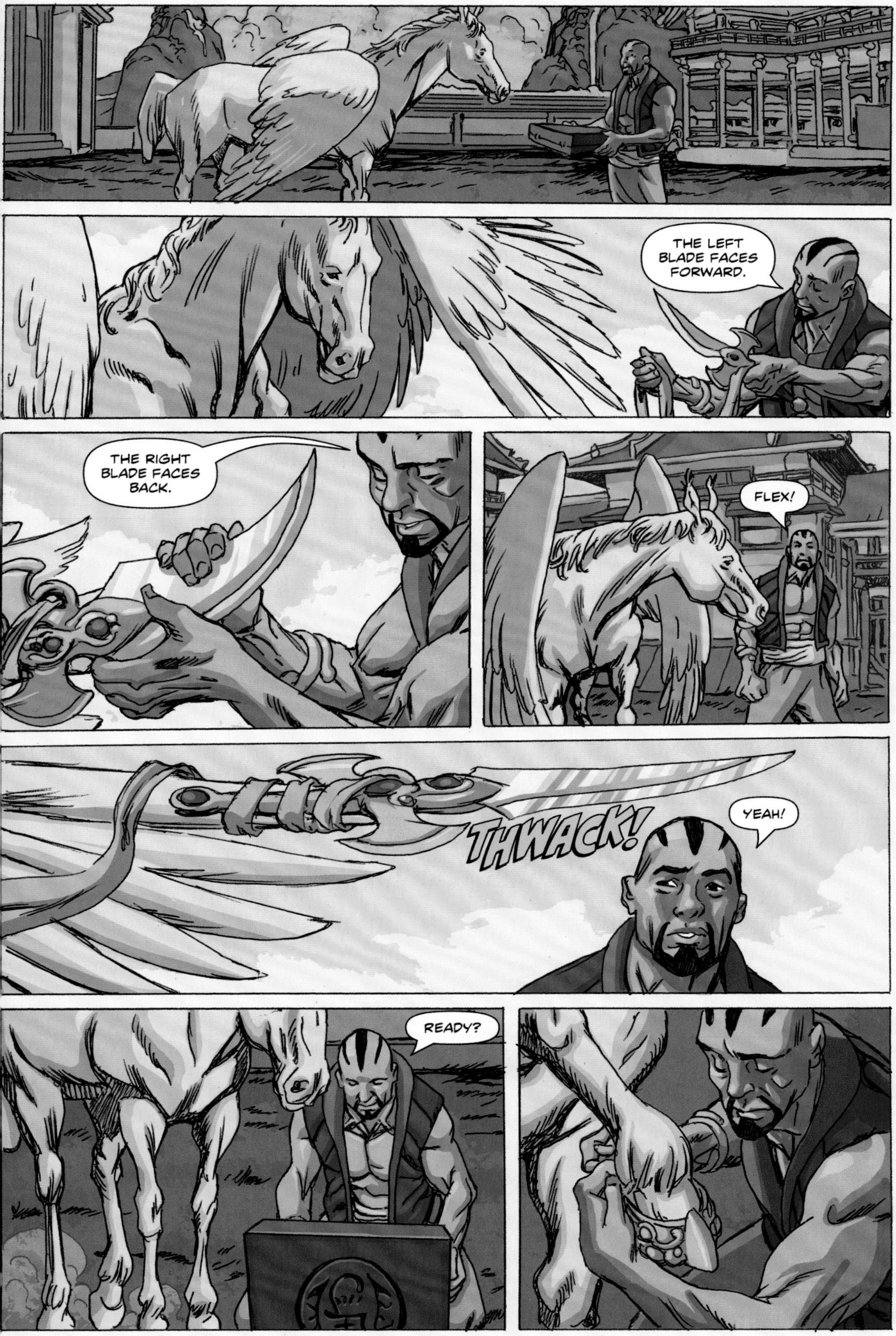
THE LEFT BLADE FACES FORWARD.
THE RIGHT BLADE FACES BACK.
FLEX!
THWACK!
YEAH!
READY?

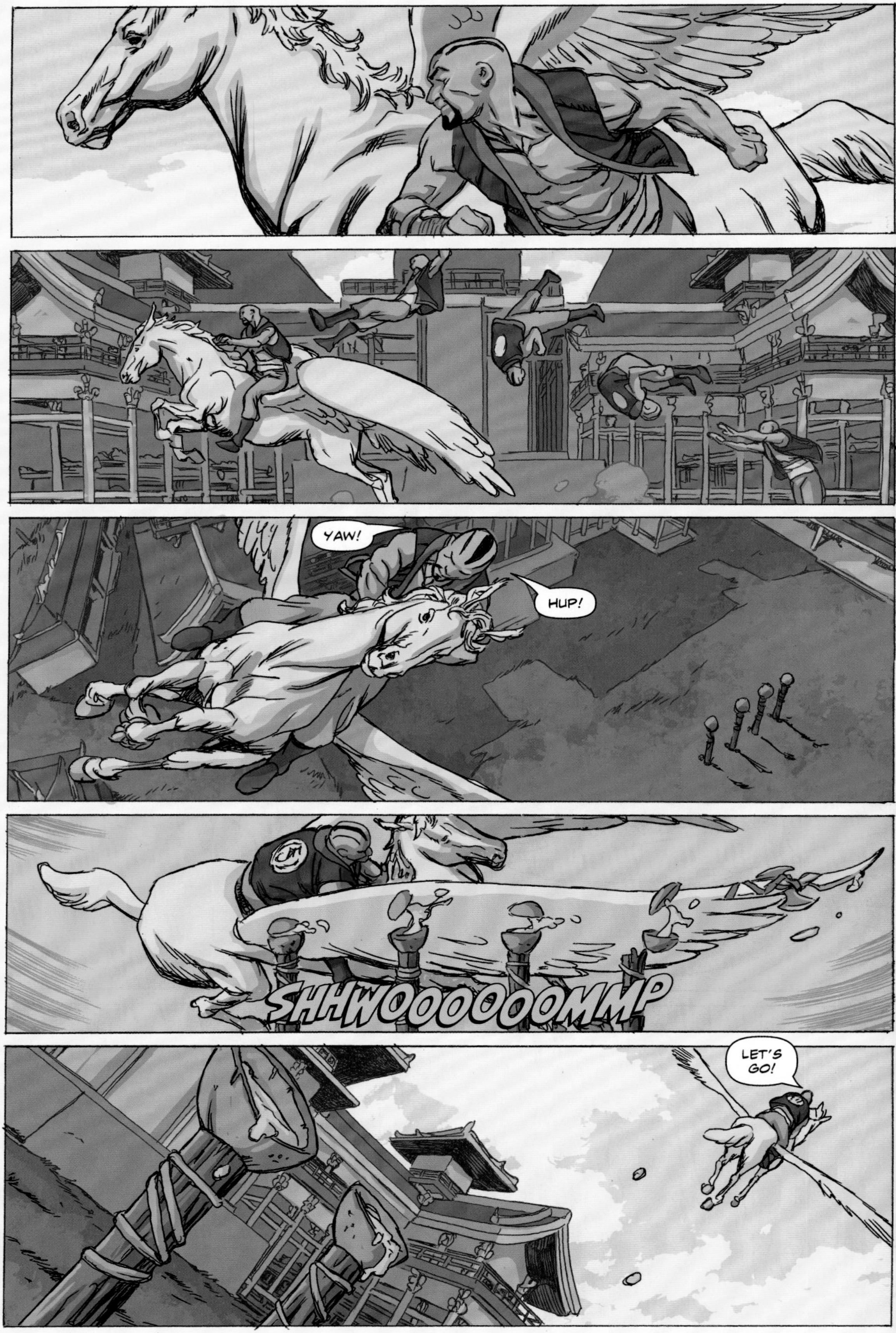
YAW!
HUP!
SHHWOOOOOOOMMP
LET'S GO!

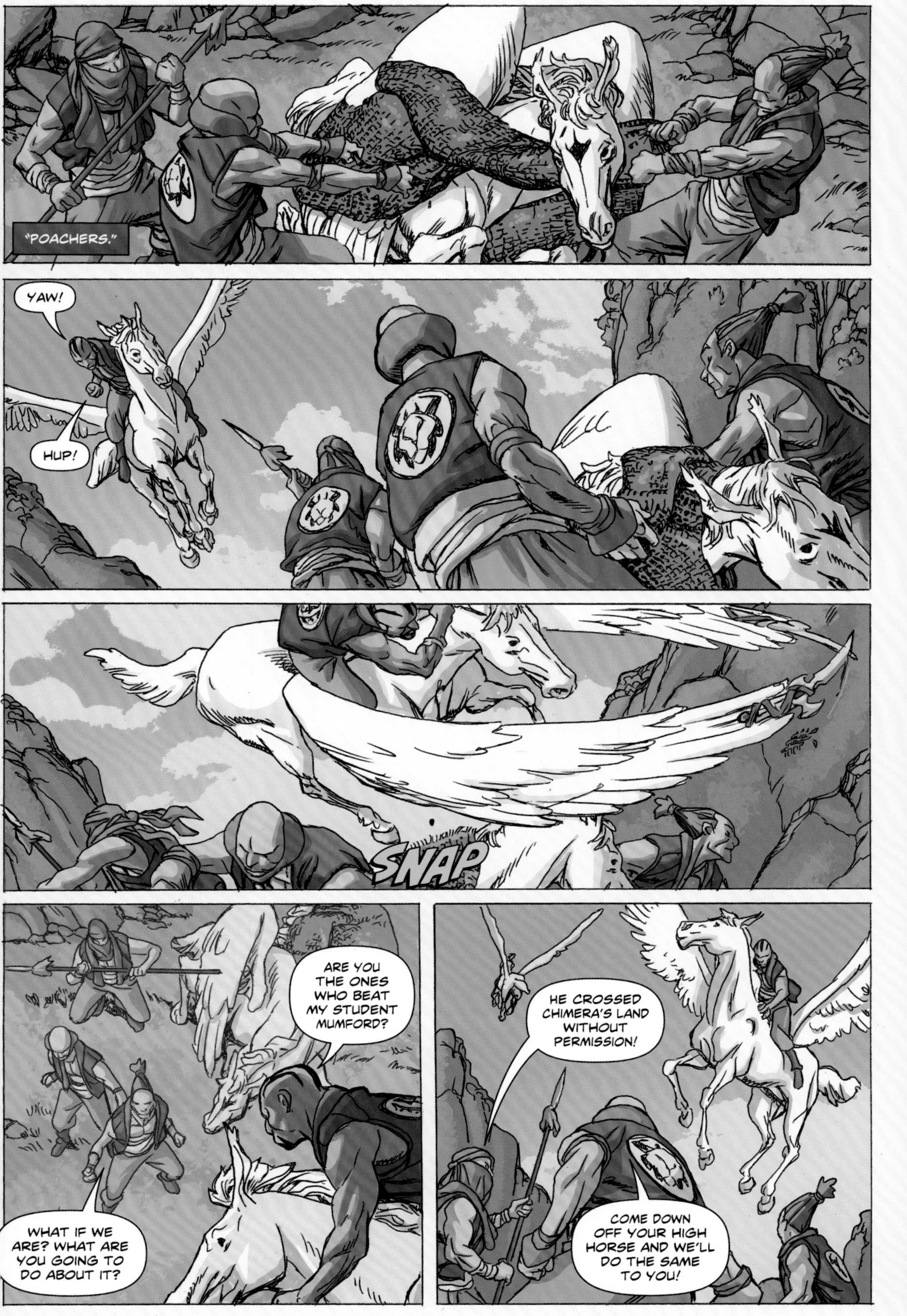
"POACHERS."
YAW!
HUP!
SNAP
ARE YOU THE ONES WHO BEAT MY STUDENT MUMFORD?
WHAT IF WE ARE? WHAT ARE YOU GOING TO DO ABOUT IT?
HE CROSSED CHIMERA'S LAND WITHOUT PERMISSION!
COME DOWN OFF YOUR HIGH HORSE AND WE'LL DO THE SAME TO YOU!

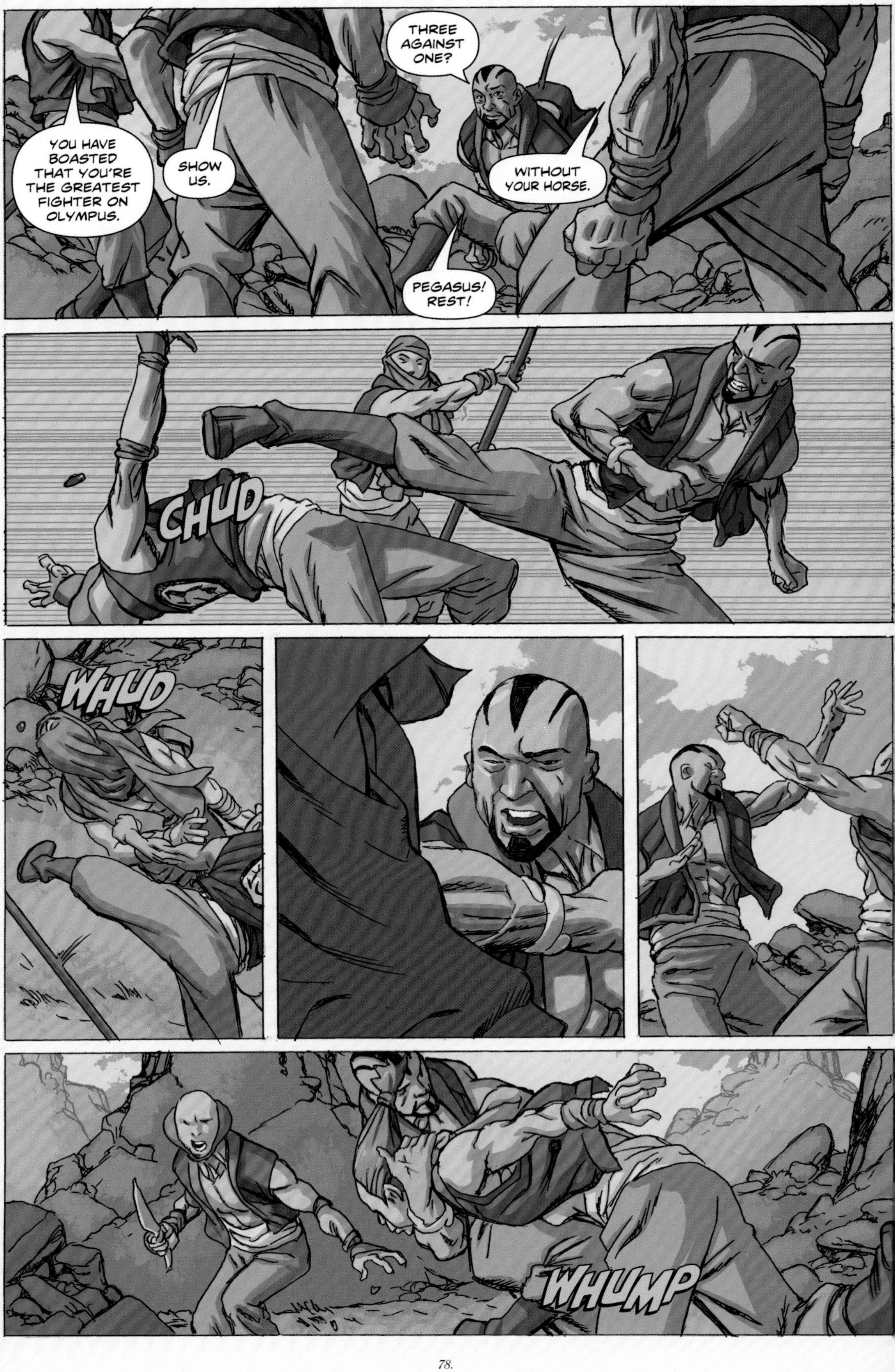
THREE AGAINST ONE?
YOU HAVE BOASTED THAT YOU'RE THE GREATEST FIGHTER ON OLYMPUS.
SHOW US.
WITHOUT YOUR HORSE.
PEGASUS! REST!
CHUD
WHUD
WHUMP

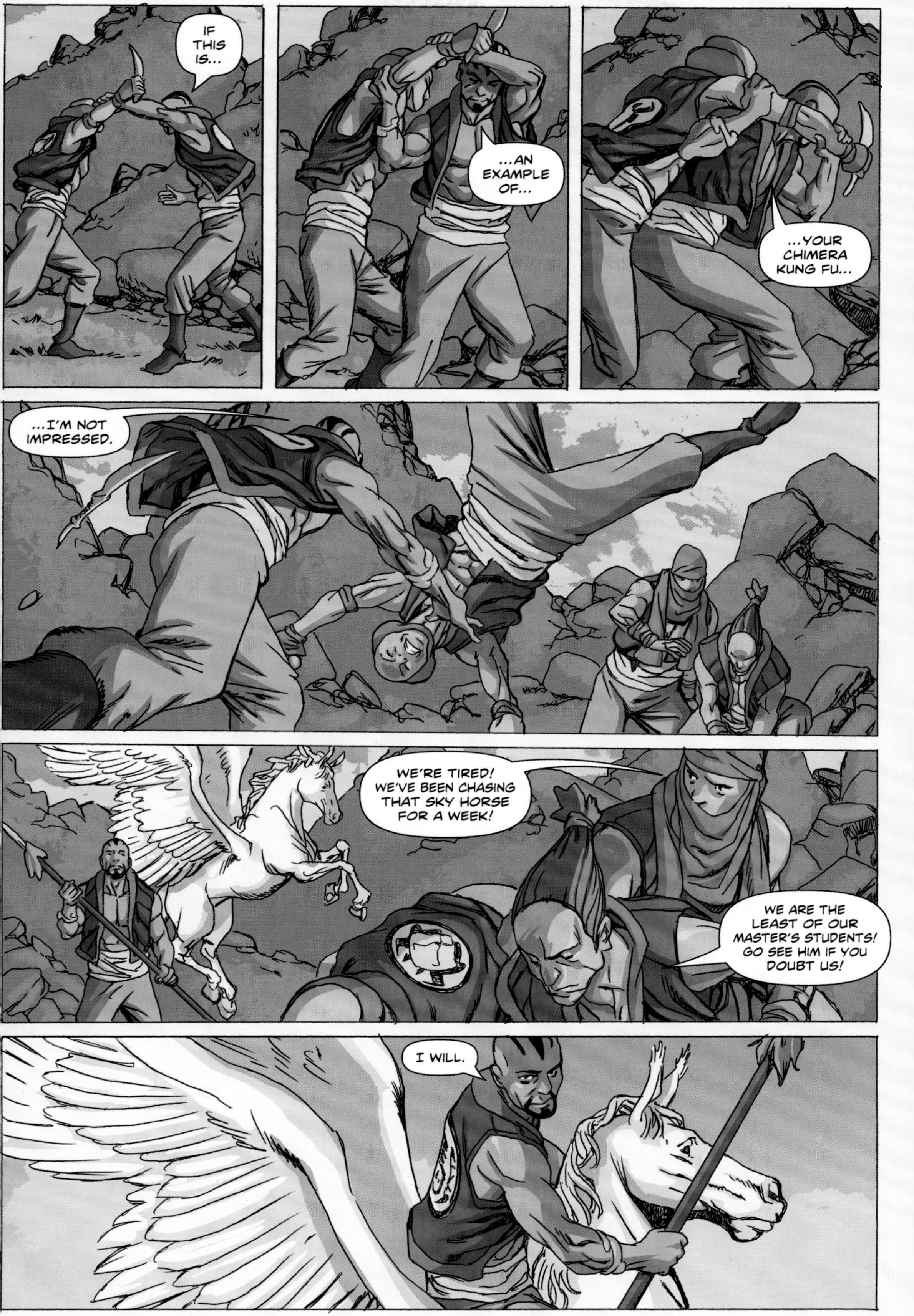
IF THIS IS...
...AN EXAMPLE OF...
...YOUR CHIMERA KUNG FU...
...I'M NOT IMPRESSED.
WE'RE TIRED! WE'VE BEEN CHASING THAT SKY HORSE FOR A WEEK!
WE ARE THE LEAST OF OUR MASTER'S STUDENTS! GO SEE HIM IF YOU DOUBT US!
I WILL.

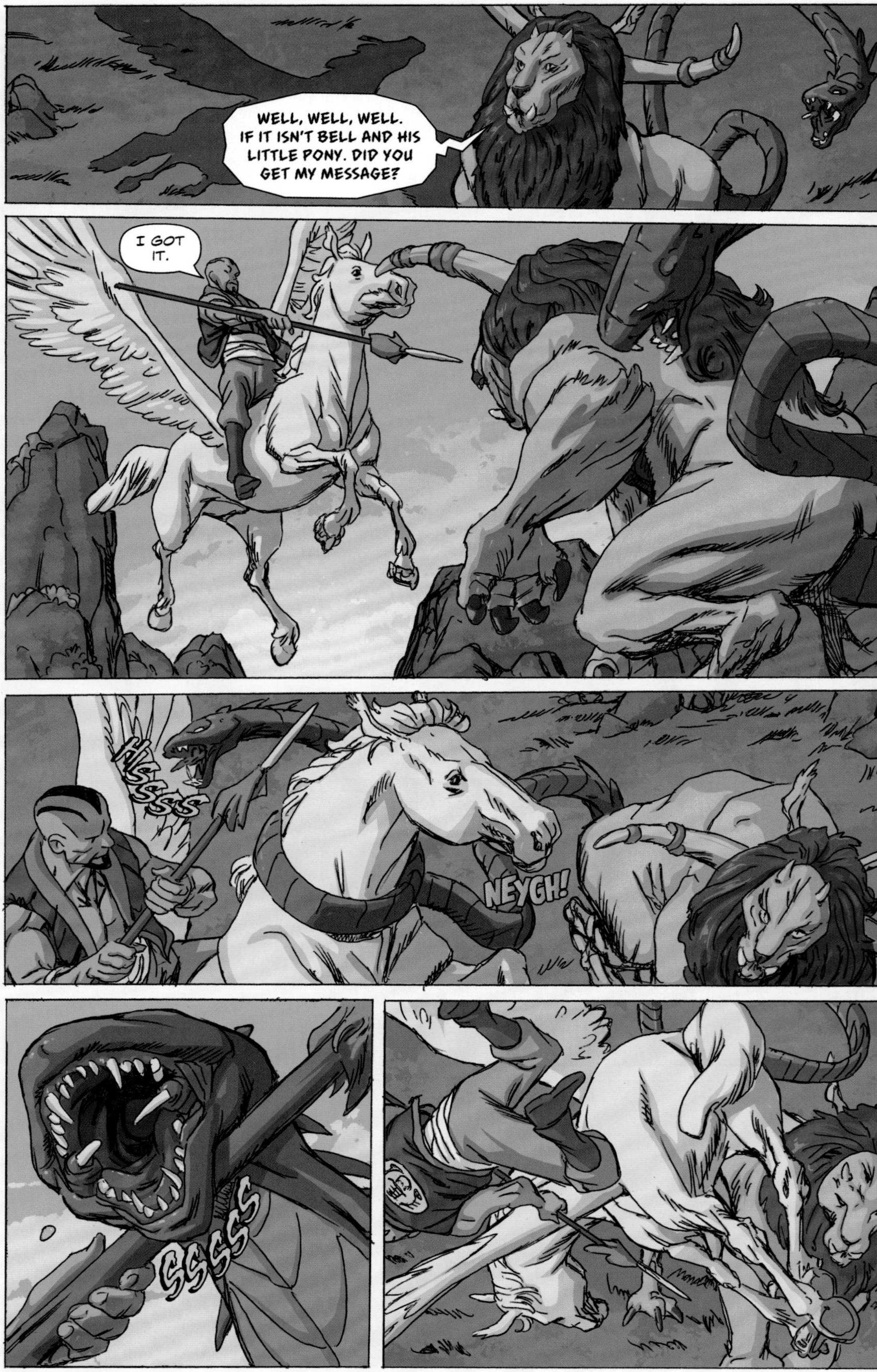
WELL, WELL, WELL.
IF IT ISN'T BELL AND HIS LITTLE PONY. DID YOU GET MY MESSAGE?
I GOT IT.
HISSSS
NEYGH!
SSSSS

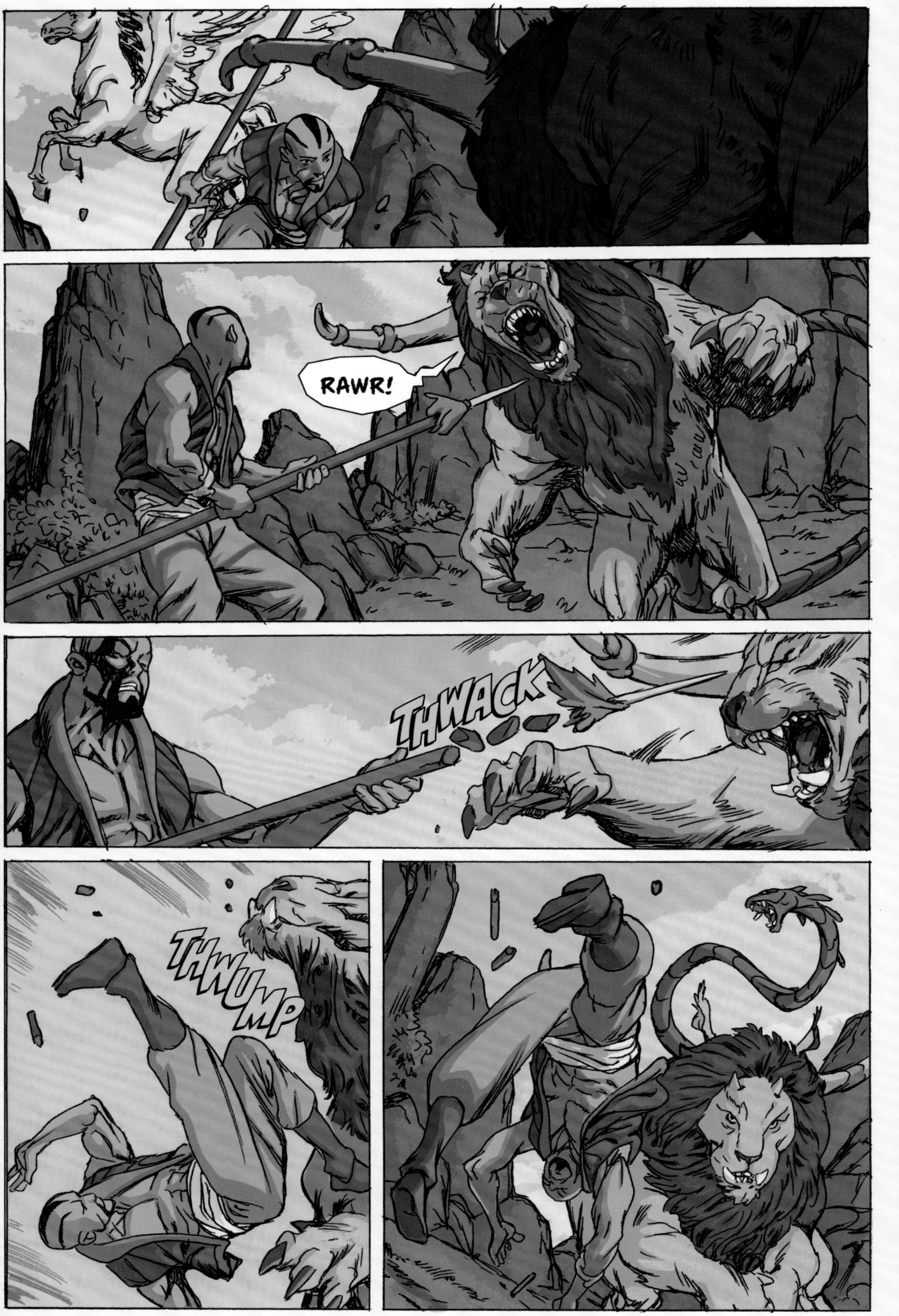
RAWR!
THWACK
THWUMP

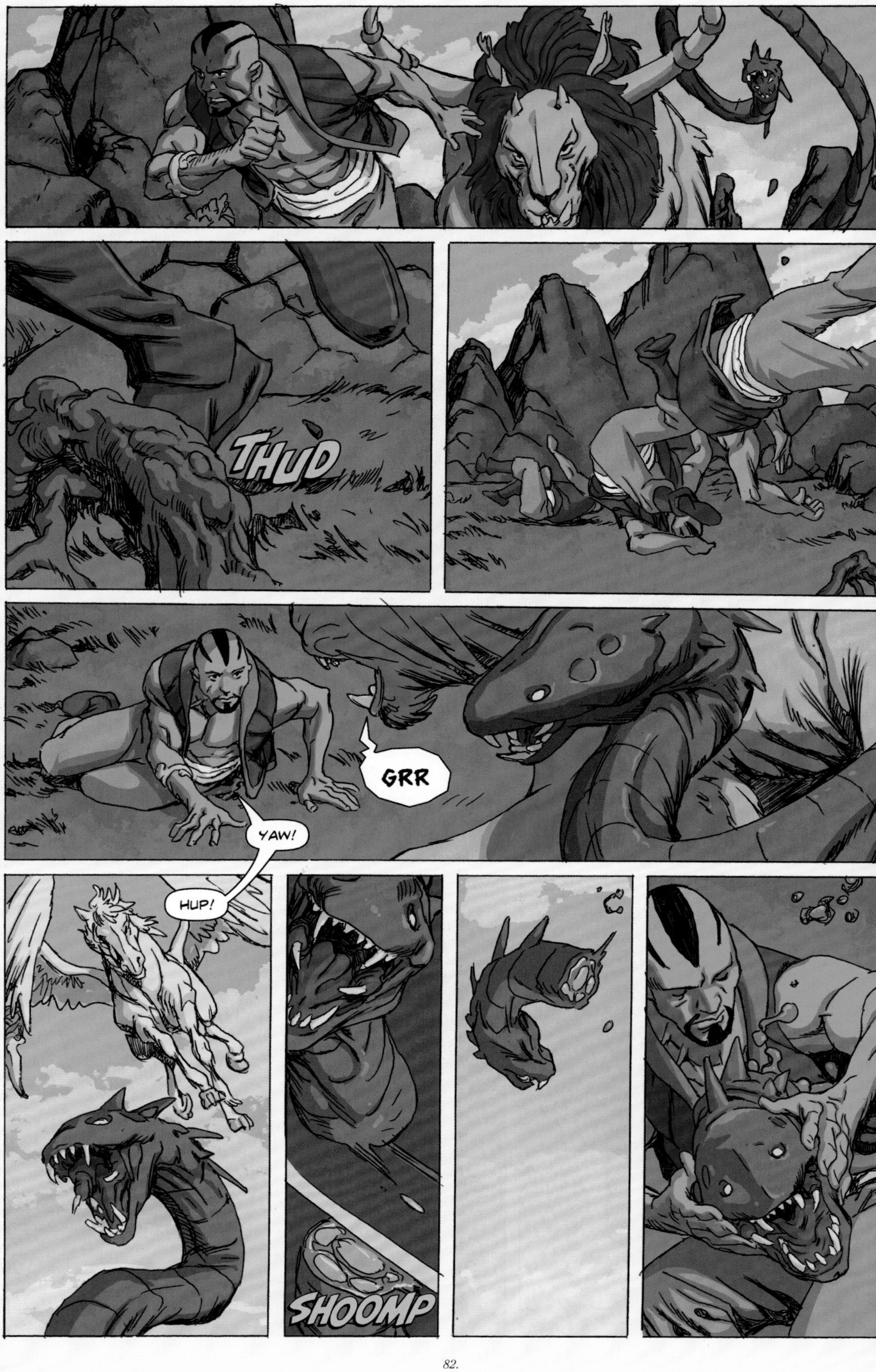

THUD
GRR
YAW!
HUP!
SHOOMP

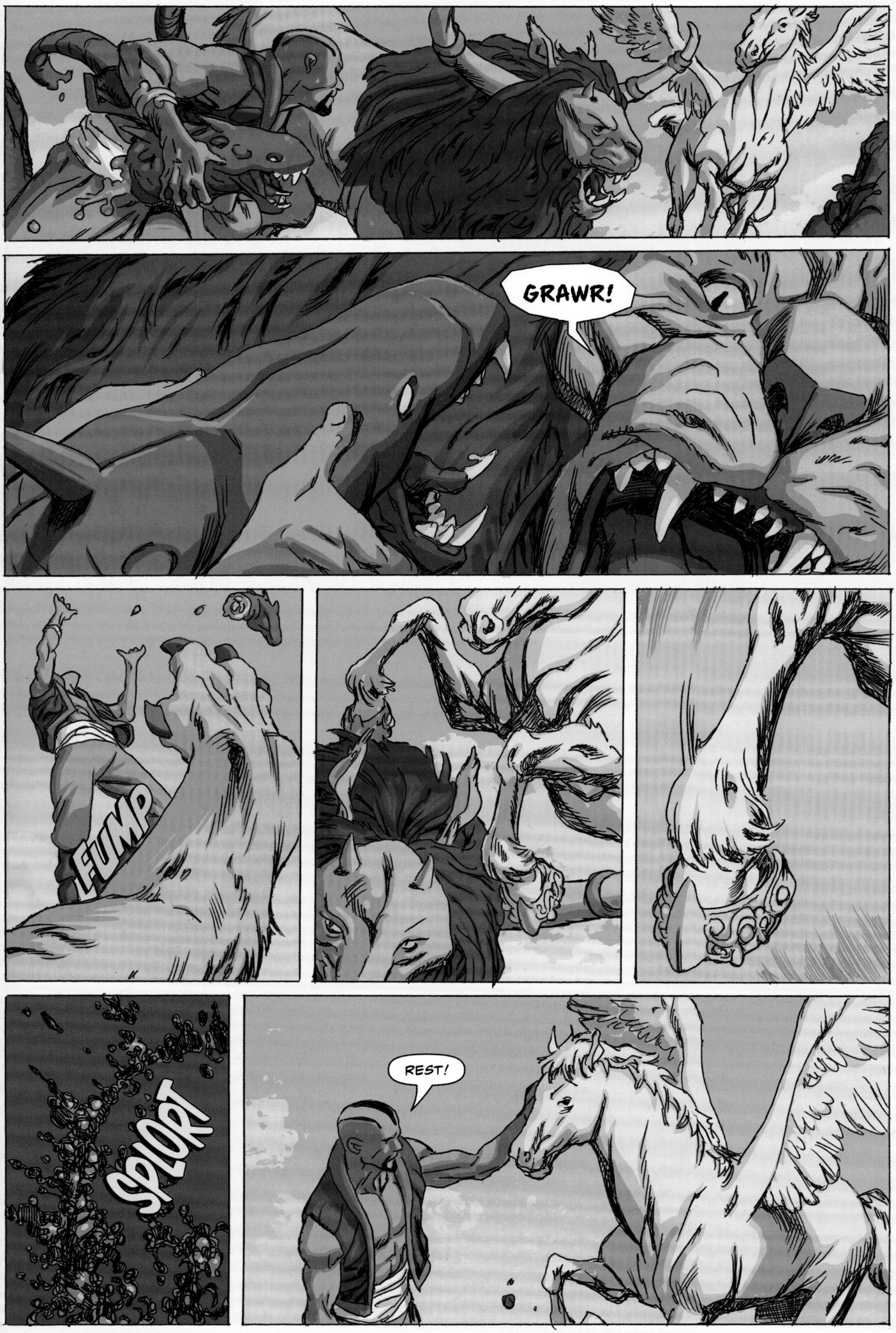
GRAWR!
FUMP
SPLORT
REST!

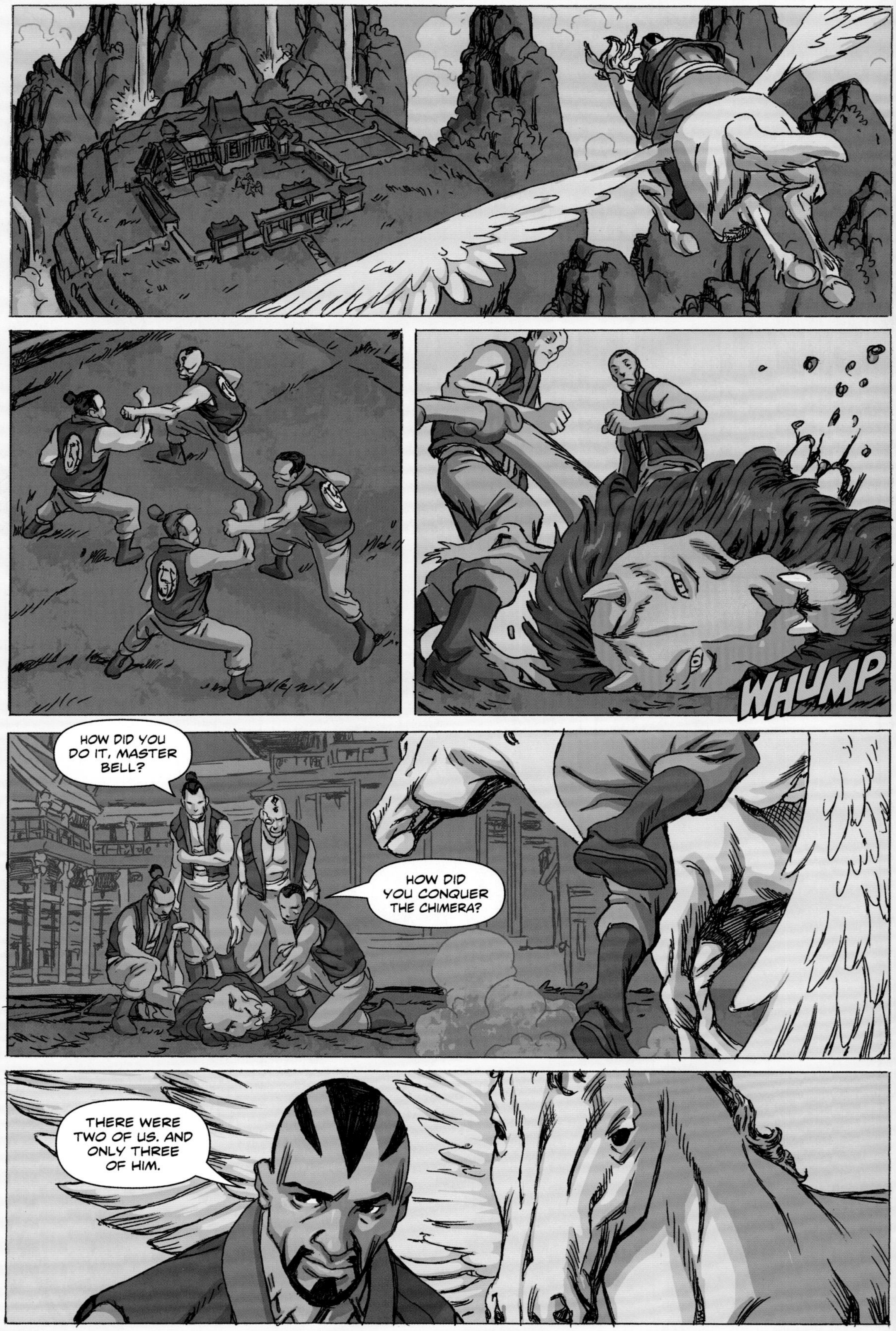
WHUMP
HOW DID YOU DO IT, MASTER BELL?
HOW DID YOU CONQUER THE CHIMERA?
THERE WERE TWO OF US. AND ONLY THREE OF HIM.

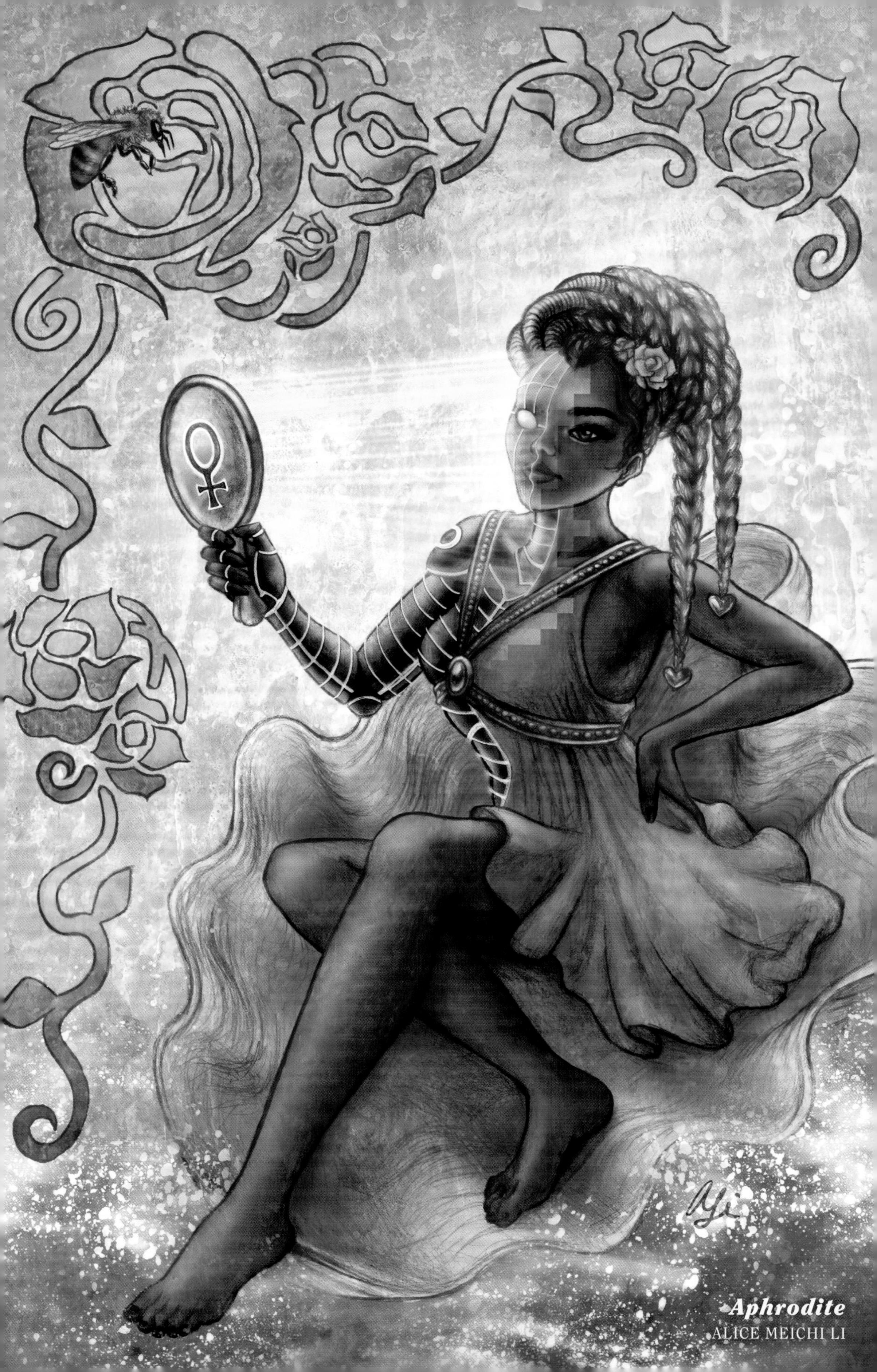
Ali

Aphrodite
ALICE MEICHI LI

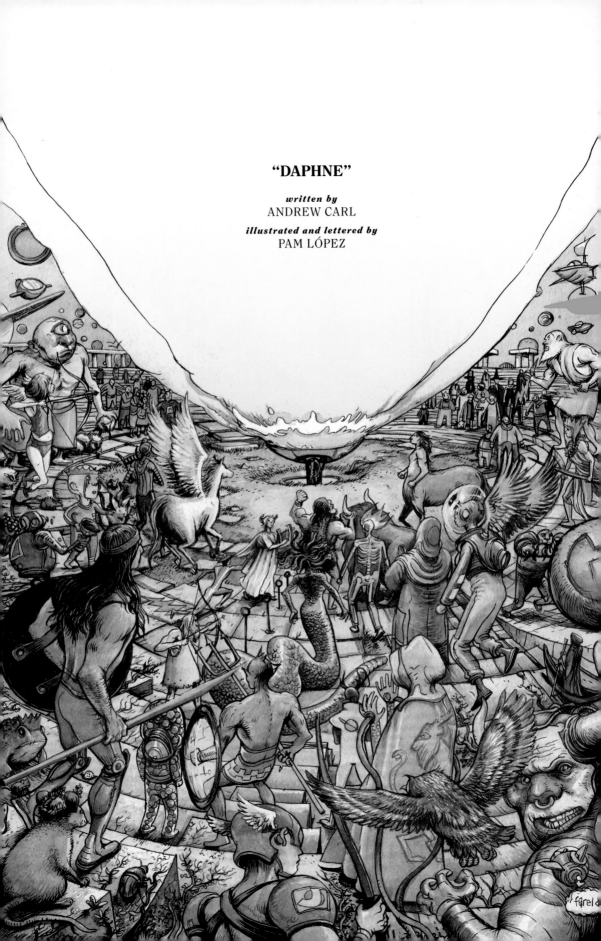

"DAPHNE"

written by
ANDREW CARL

illustrated and lettered by
PAM LÓPEZ

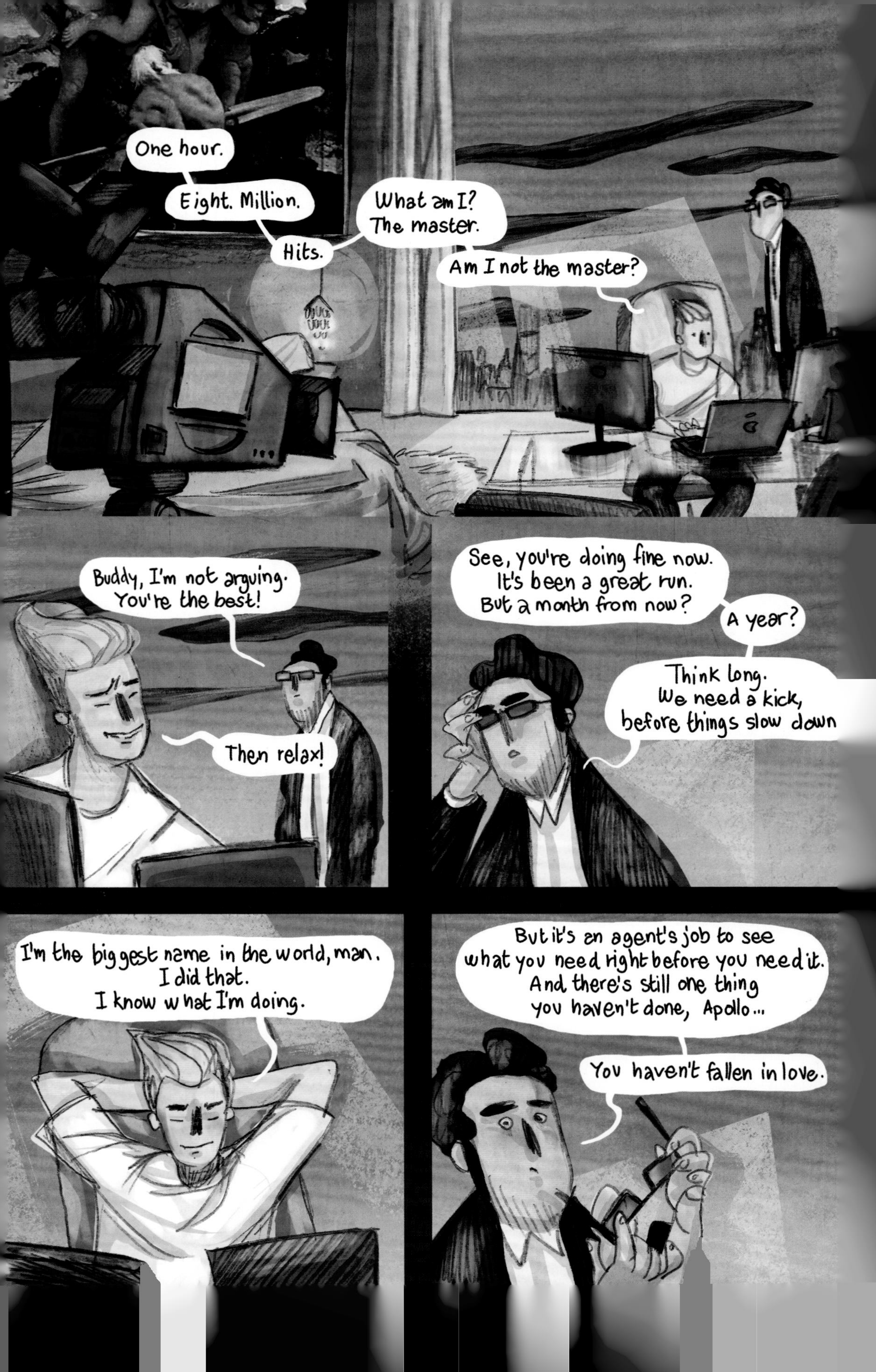
One hour.
Eight. Million.
Hits.
What am I? The master.
Am I not the master?
Buddy, I'm not arguing. You're the best!
Then relax!
See, you're doing fine now. It's been a great run. But a month from now?
A year?
Think long. We need a kick, before things slow down
I'm the biggest name in the world, man. I did that. I know what I'm doing.
But it's an agent's job to see what you need right before you need it. And there's still one thing you haven't done, Apollo...
You haven't fallen in love.

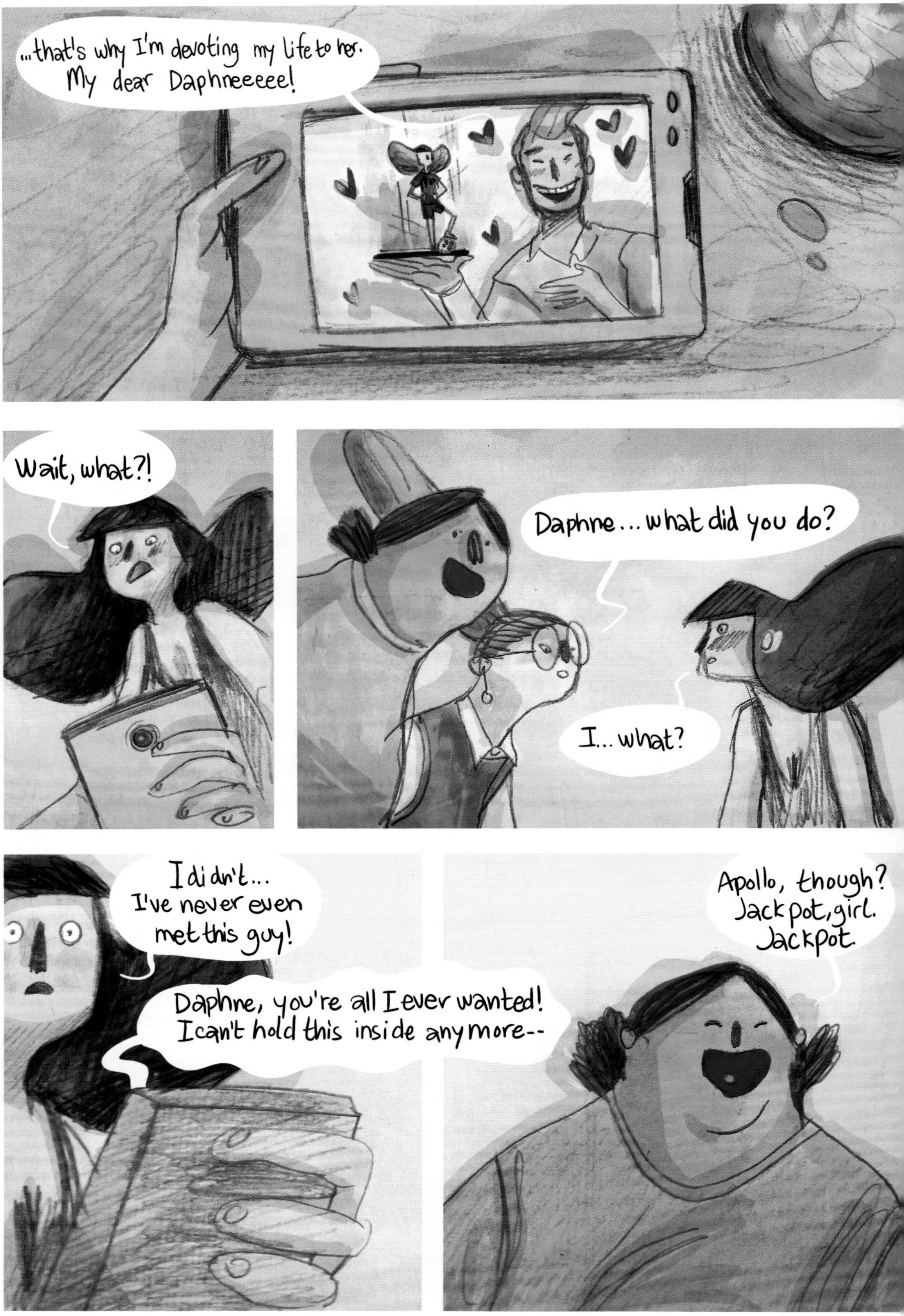
...that's why I'm devoting my life to her. My dear Daphneeeee!
Wait, what?!
Daphne... what did you do?
I... what?
I didn't... I've never even met this guy!
Daphne, you're all I ever wanted! I can't hold this inside anymore--
Apollo, though? Jackpot, girl. Jackpot.

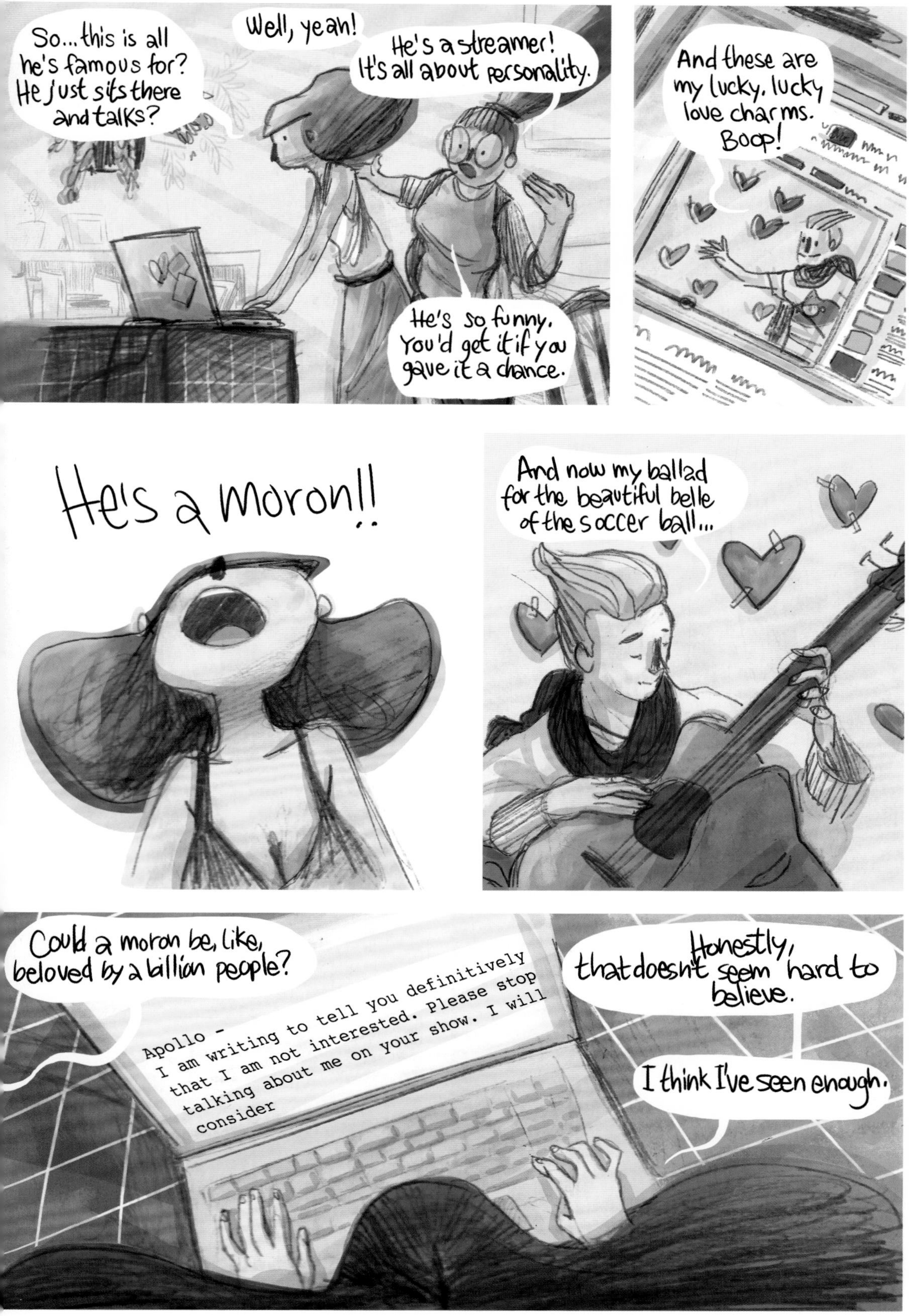
So... this is all he's famous for? He just sits there and talks?
Well, yeah!
He's a streamer! It's all about personality.
He's so funny. You'd get it if you gave it a chance.
And these are my lucky, lucky love charms. Boop!
He's a moron!!
And now my ballad for the beautiful belle of the soccer ball...
Could a moron be, like, beloved by a billion people?
Apollo -
I am writing to tell you definitively that I am not interested. Please stop talking about me on your show. I will consider
Honestly, that doesn't seem hard to believe.
I think I've seen enough.

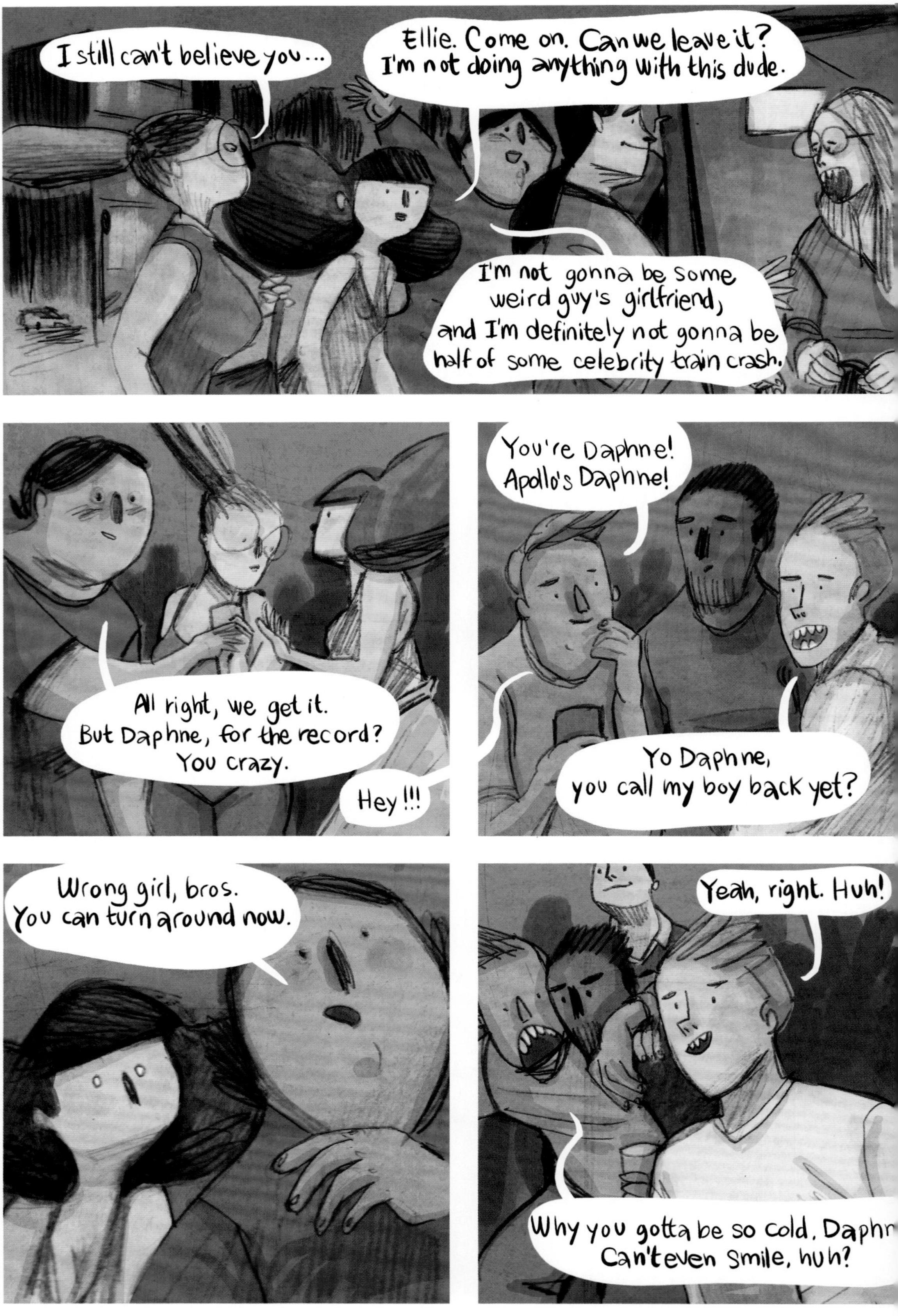
I still can't believe you...
Ellie. Come on. Can we leave it? I'm not doing anything with this dude.
I'm not gonna be some weird guy's girlfriend, and I'm definitely not gonna be half of some celebrity train crash.
All right, we get it. But Daphne, for the record? You crazy.
Hey!!!
You're Daphne! Apollo's Daphne!
Yo Daphne, you call my boy back yet?
Wrong girl, bros. You can turn around now.
Yeah, right. Huh!
Why you gotta be so cold, Daphn
Can't even smile, huh?

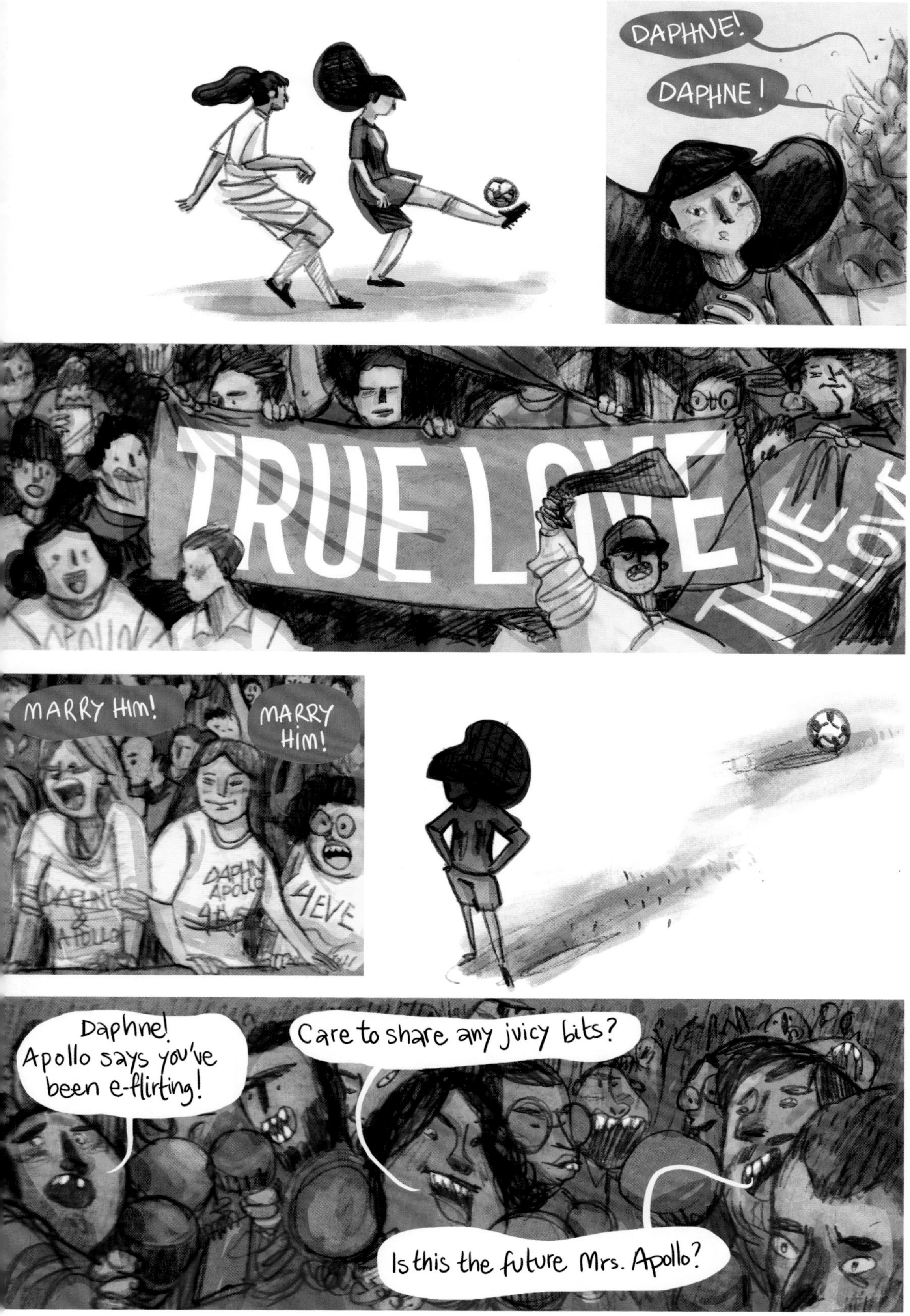
DAPHNE!
DAPHNE!
TRUE LOVE
TRUE LOVE
MARRY HIM!
MARRY HIM!
Daphne! Apollo says you've been e-flirting!
Care to share any juicy bits?
Is this the future Mrs. Apollo?

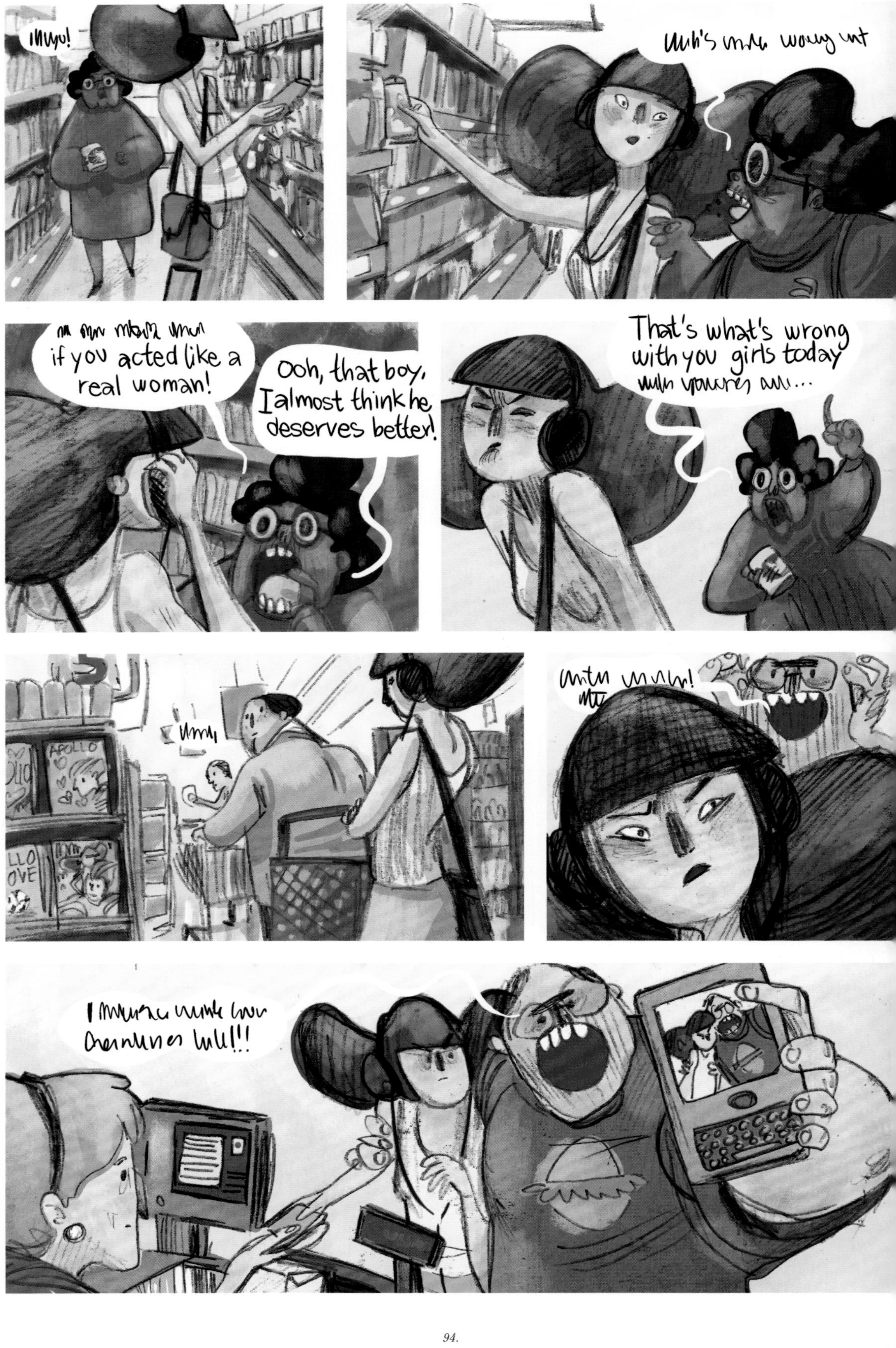
if you acted like a real woman!
Ooh, that boy, I almost think he deserves better!
That's what's wrong with you girls today
APOLLO

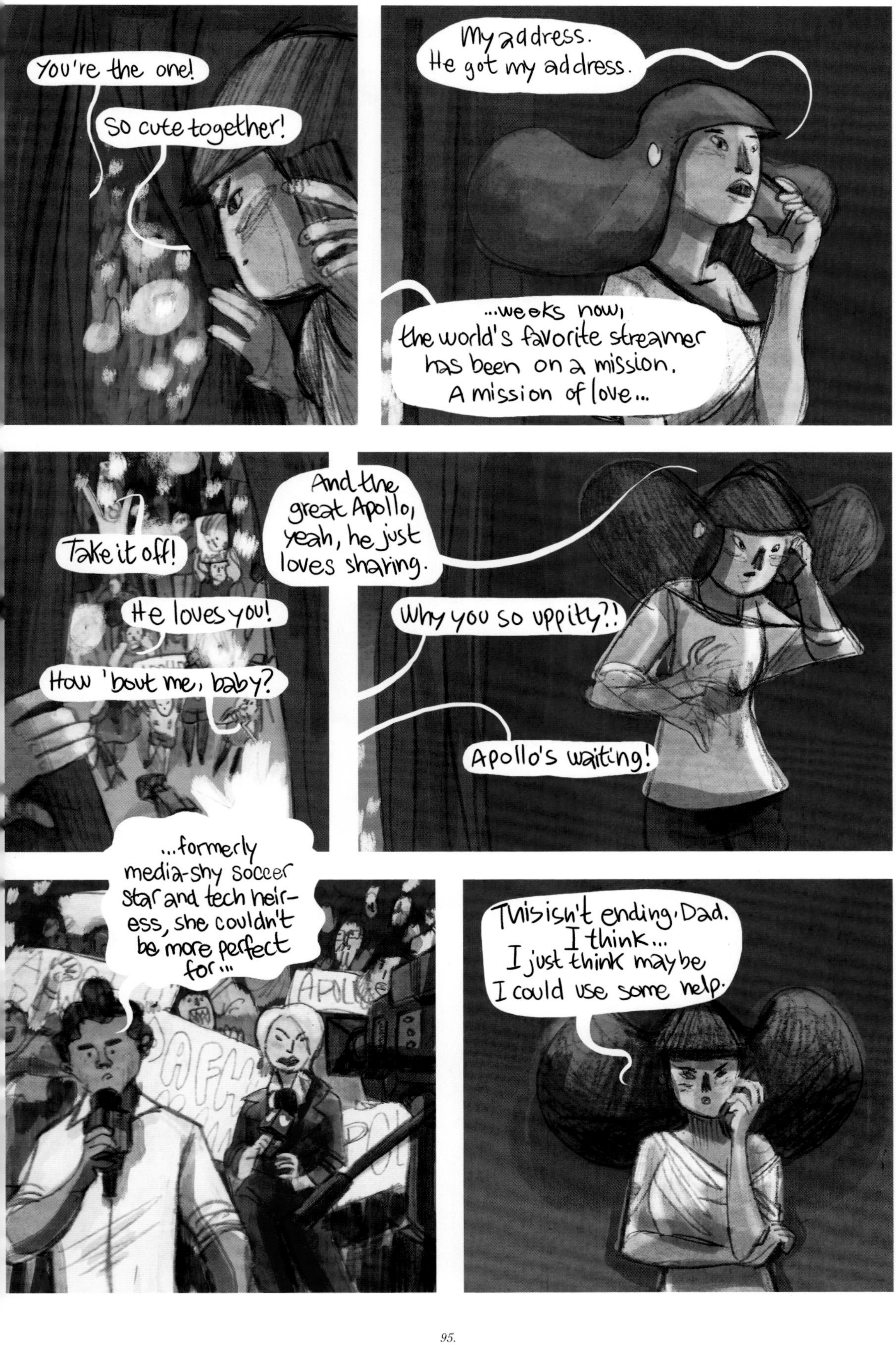
You're the one!
So cute together!
My address.
He got my address.
...weeks now, the world's favorite streamer has been on a mission. A mission of love...
Take it off!
And the great Apollo, yeah, he just loves sharing.
He loves you!
Why you so uppity?!
How 'bout me, baby?
Apollo's waiting!
...formerly media-shy soccer star and tech heir-ess, she couldn't be more perfect for...
This isn't ending, Dad. I think... I just think maybe I could use some help.

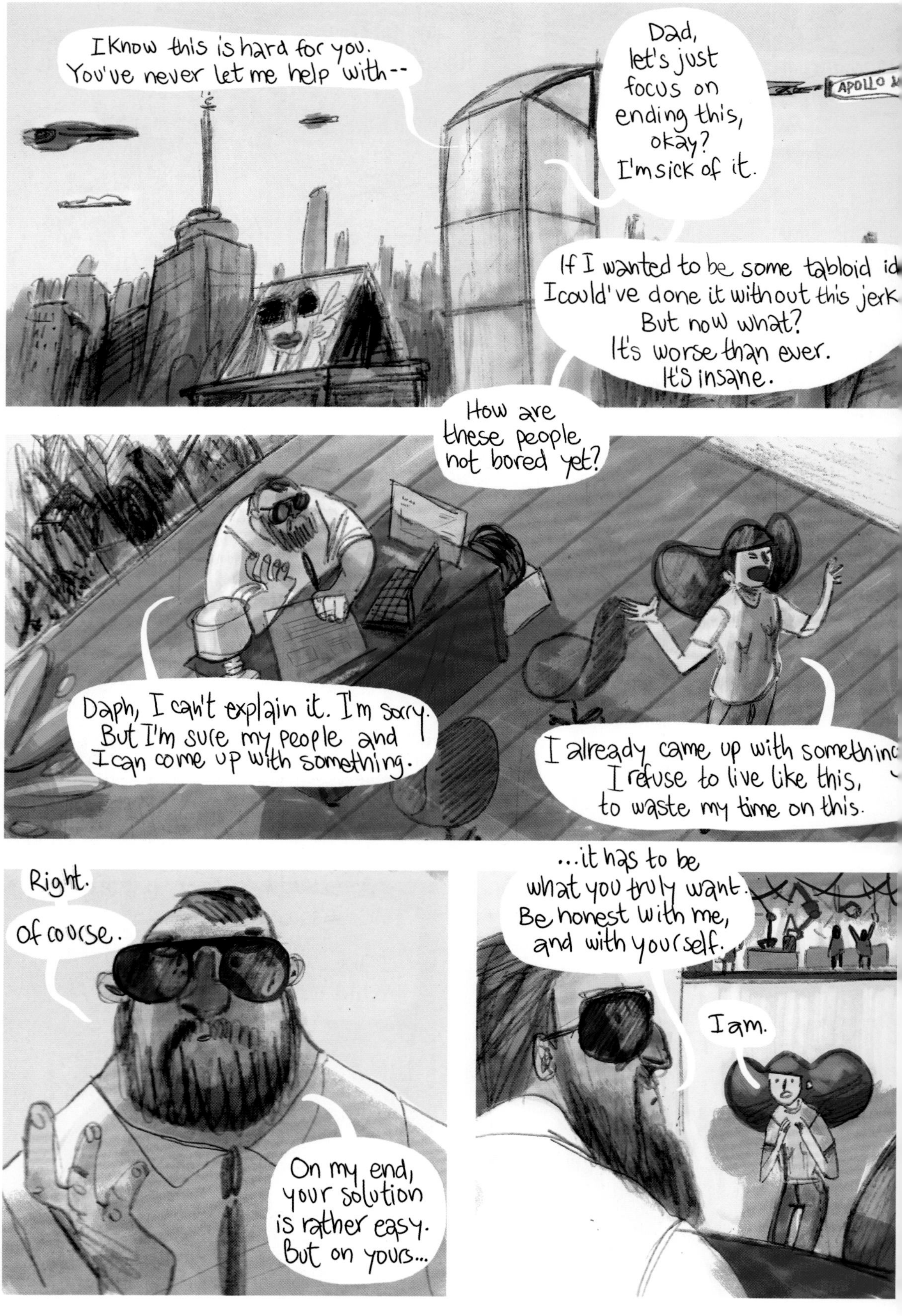
I know this is hard for you. You've never let me help with--
Dad, let's just focus on ending this, okay? I'm sick of it.
APOLLO
If I wanted to be some tabloid id
I could've done it without this jerk.
But now what? It's worse than ever. It's insane.
How are these people not bored yet?
Daph, I can't explain it. I'm sorry. But I'm sure my people and I can come up with something.
I already came up with something. I refuse to live like this, to waste my time on this.
Right.
Of course.
On my end, your solution is rather easy. But on yours...
...it has to be what you truly want. Be honest with me, and with yourself.
I am.

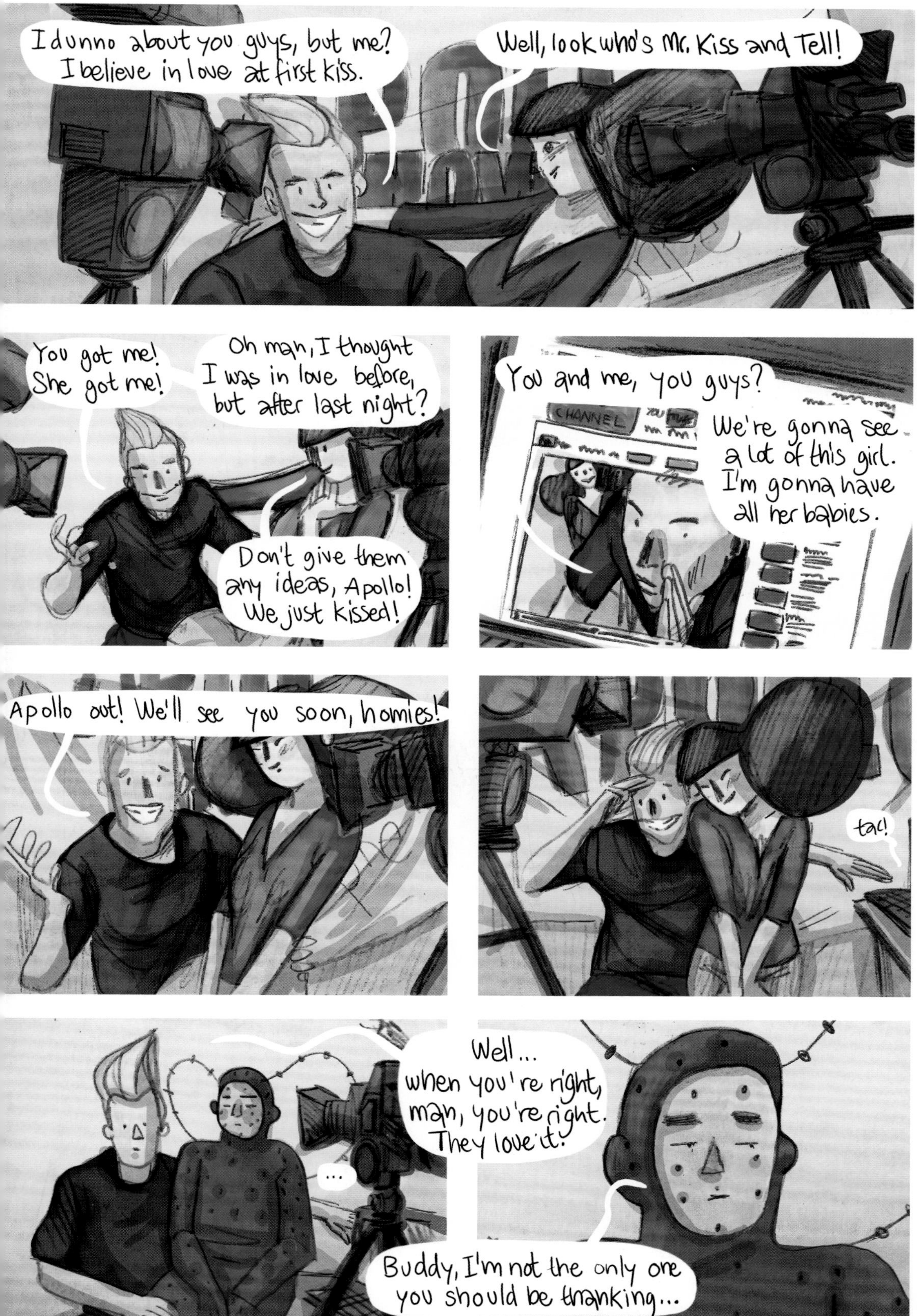
I dunno about you guys, but me? I believe in love at first kiss.
Well, look who's Mr. Kiss and Tell!
You got me! She got me!
Oh man, I thought I was in love before, but after last night?
Don't give them any ideas, Apollo! We just kissed!
You and me, you guys?
We're gonna see a lot of this girl. I'm gonna have all her babies.
CHANNEL
Apollo out! We'll see you soon, homies!
tac!
Well... when you're right, man, you're right. They love it.
...
Buddy, I'm not the only one you should be thanking...

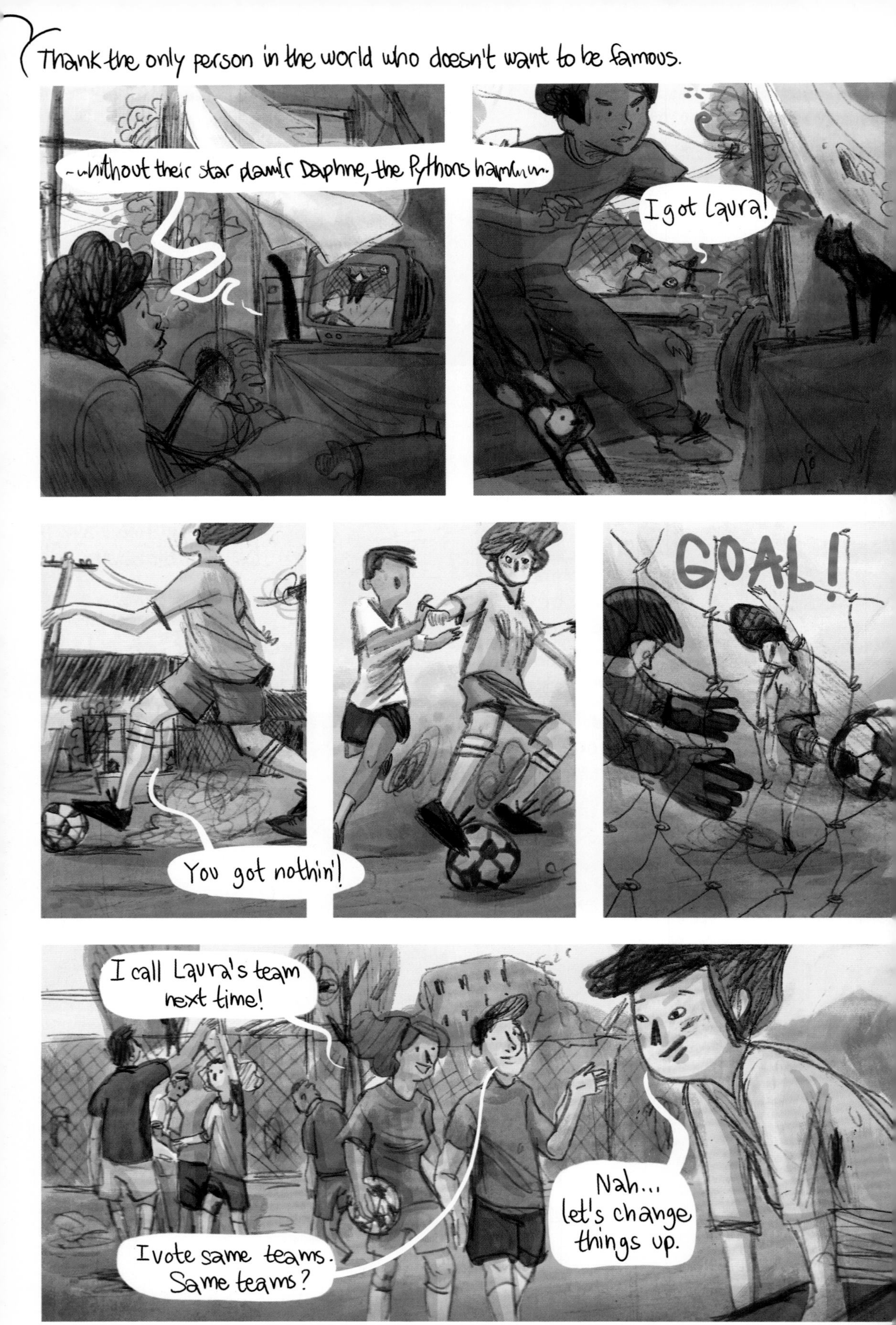

Thank the only person in the world who doesn't want to be famous.
~without their star plamr Daphne, the Pythons ham...
I got Laura!
You got nothin'!
GOAL!
I call Laura's team next time!
I vote same teams. Same teams?
Nah... let's change things up.

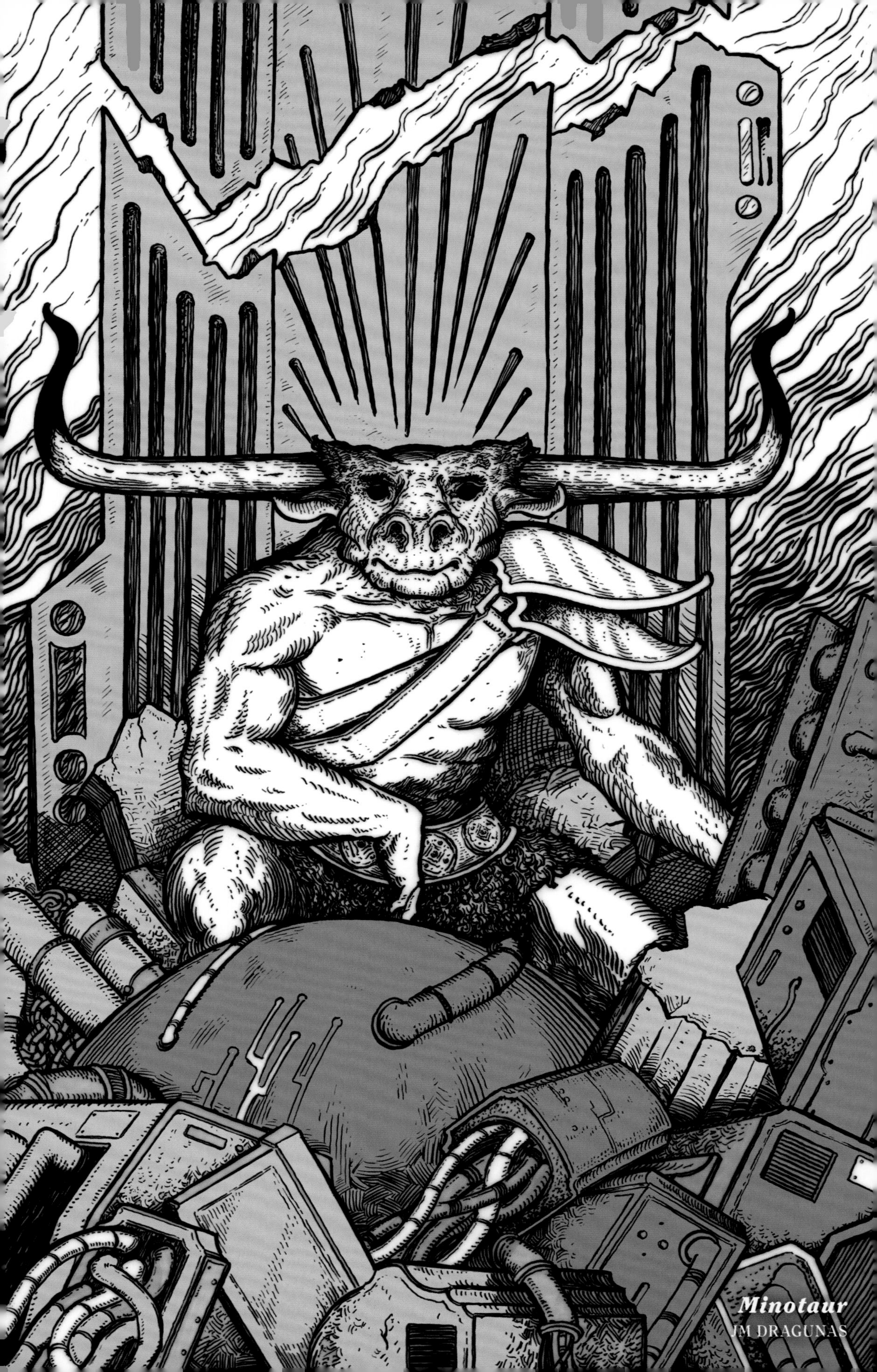

Minotaur
JM DRAGUNAS

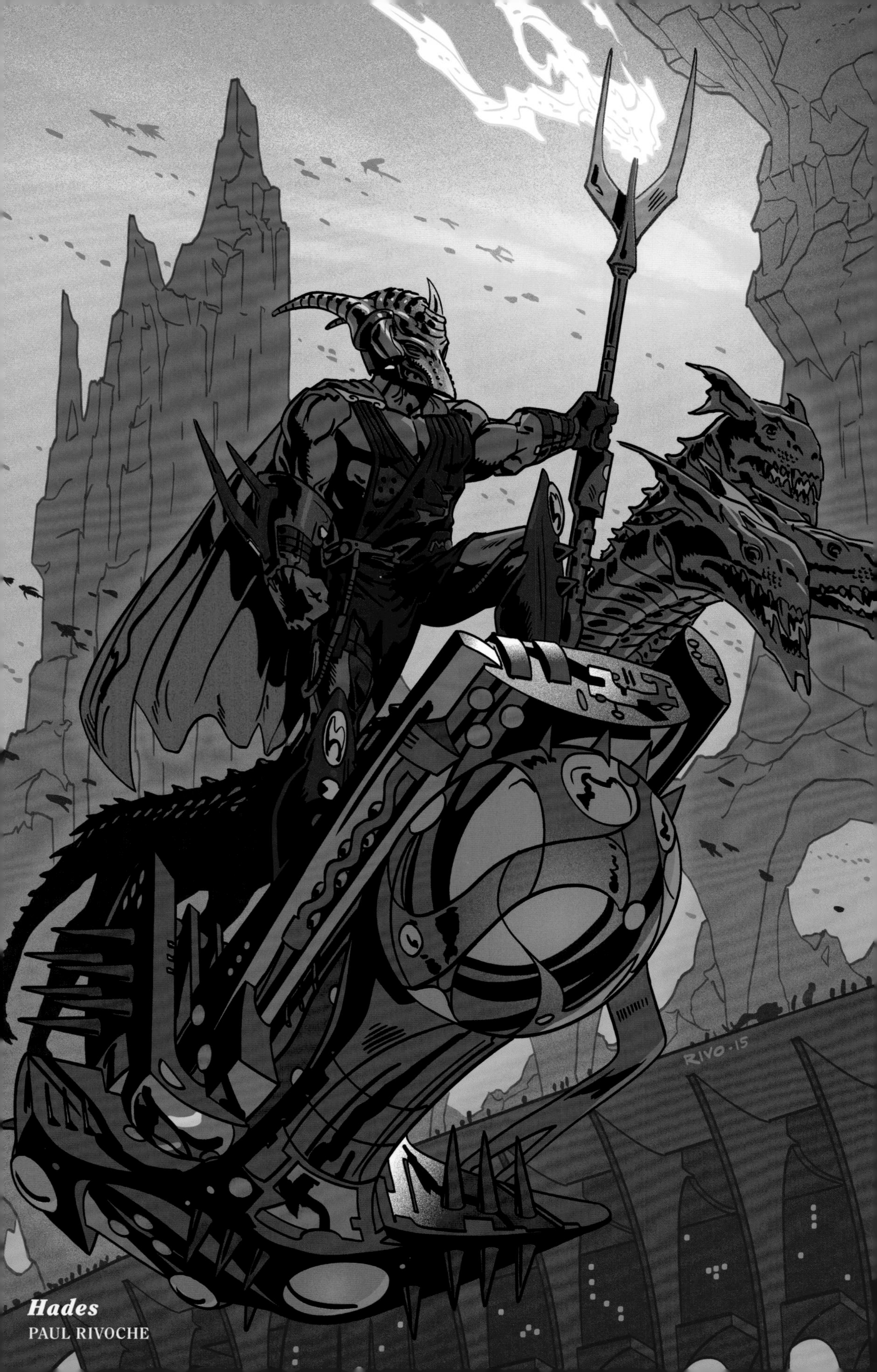
RIVO·15

Hades
PAUL RIVOCHE

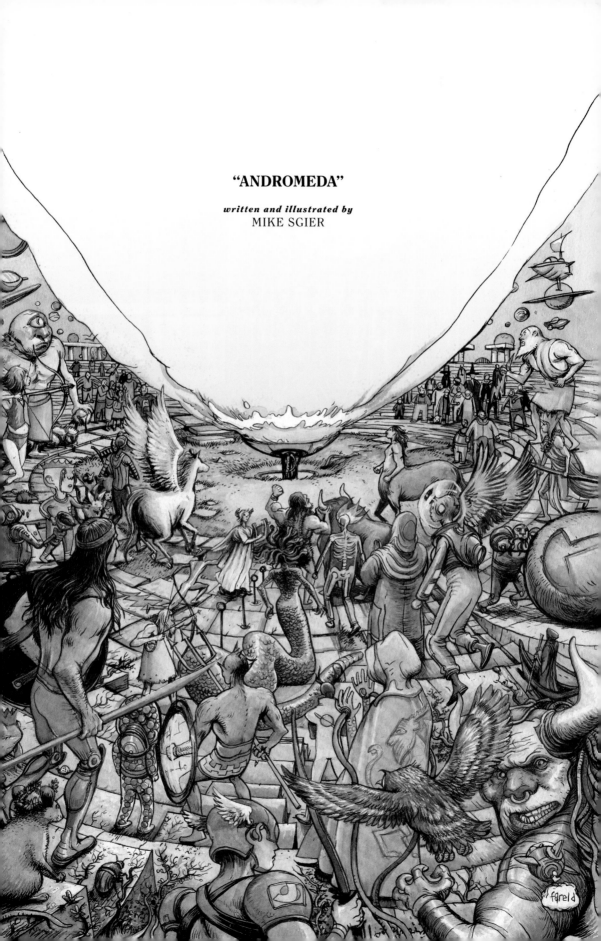

"ANDROMEDA"

written and illustrated by
MIKE SGIER

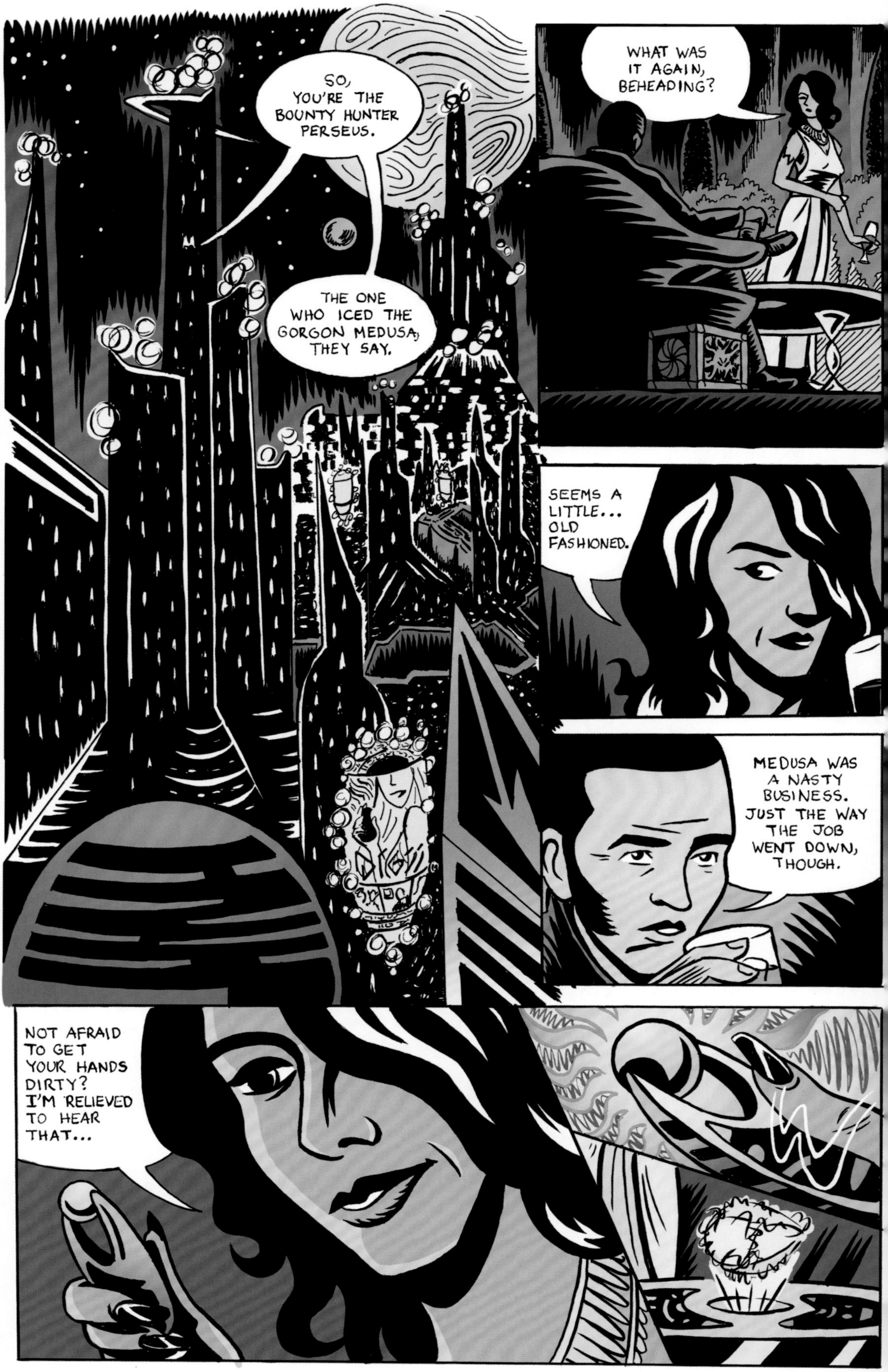
SO, YOU'RE THE BOUNTY HUNTER PERSEUS.
THE ONE WHO ICED THE GORGON MEDUSA, THEY SAY.
WHAT WAS IT AGAIN, BEHEADING?
SEEMS A LITTLE... OLD FASHIONED.
MEDUSA WAS A NASTY BUSINESS. JUST THE WAY THE JOB WENT DOWN, THOUGH.
NOT AFRAID TO GET YOUR HANDS DIRTY? I'M RELIEVED TO HEAR THAT...

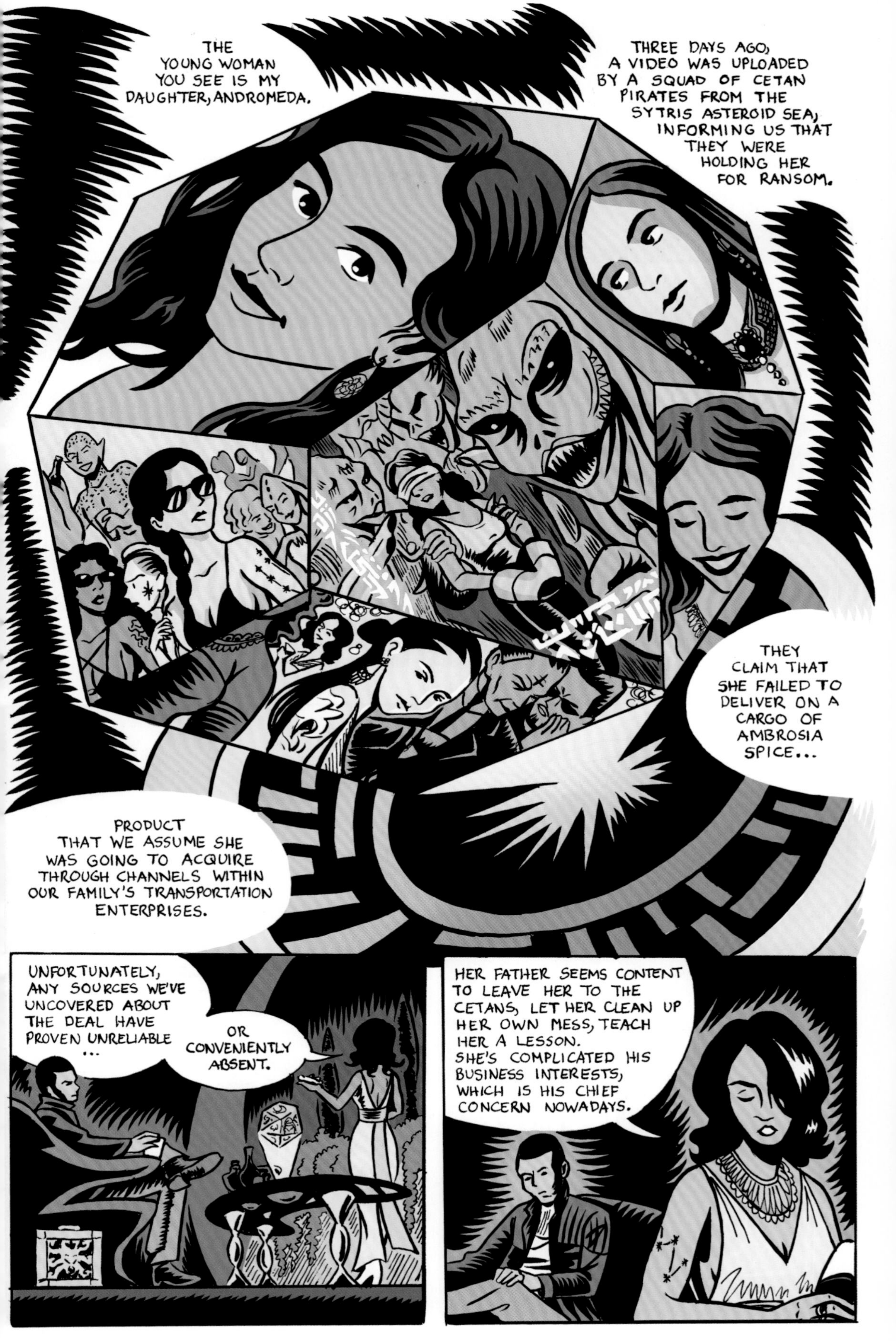
THE YOUNG WOMAN YOU SEE IS MY DAUGHTER, ANDROMEDA.
THREE DAYS AGO, A VIDEO WAS UPLOADED BY A SQUAD OF CETAN PIRATES FROM THE SYTRIS ASTEROID SEA, INFORMING US THAT THEY WERE HOLDING HER FOR RANSOM.
THEY CLAIM THAT SHE FAILED TO DELIVER ON A CARGO OF AMBROSIA SPICE...
PRODUCT THAT WE ASSUME SHE WAS GOING TO ACQUIRE THROUGH CHANNELS WITHIN OUR FAMILY'S TRANSPORTATION ENTERPRISES.
UNFORTUNATELY, ANY SOURCES WE'VE UNCOVERED ABOUT THE DEAL HAVE PROVEN UNRELIABLE ...
OR CONVENIENTLY ABSENT.
HER FATHER SEEMS CONTENT TO LEAVE HER TO THE CETANS, LET HER CLEAN UP HER OWN MESS, TEACH HER A LESSON.
SHE'S COMPLICATED HIS BUSINESS INTERESTS, WHICH IS HIS CHIEF CONCERN NOWADAYS.

BUT SHE'S STILL MY DAUGHTER. AND I ... SOMEONE NEEDS TO LOOK OUT FOR HER REPUTATION. THAT'S WHAT REALLY MATTERS.

SHE HAS THAT RARE COMBINATION OF BEAUTY AND AMBITION THAT HAS SO MUCH POTENTIAL.

BUT IT'S ALSO MADE HER NAIVE, IMPULSIVE, STUBBORN...

HER TASTE IN MEN IS CHEAP, AND SHE'S SURROUNDED BY FAIR-WEATHER FRIENDS.

SHE GOES FOR THE QUICK AND EASY WHEN IT'S THE ENDGAME SHE SHOULD HAVE HER EYE ON.

MA'AM, I GET IT. YOU'VE GOT A PRETTY DAUGHTER THAT LOVES TROUBLE.

BUT WHAT DOES IT HAVE TO DO WITH ME?

OF COURSE, YOU'RE A MAN OF BUSINESS, AFTER ALL.

QUITE SIMPLY, WE'RE HIRING YOU TO RETRIEVE ANDROMEDA...

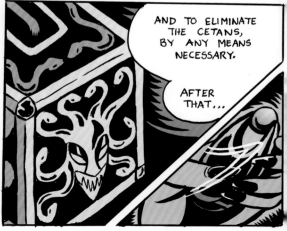

AND TO ELIMINATE THE CETANS, BY ANY MEANS NECESSARY.

AFTER THAT...

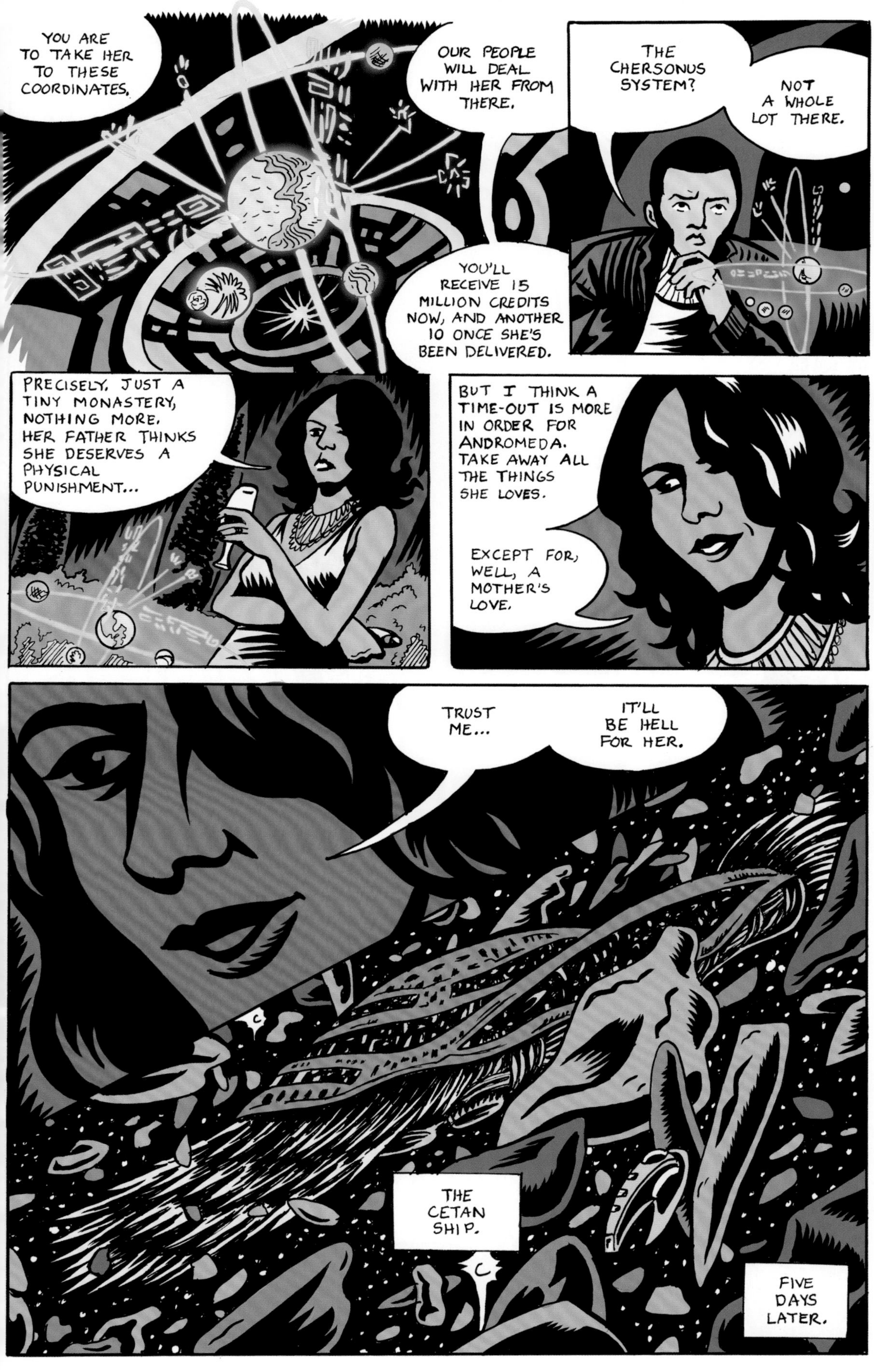
YOU ARE TO TAKE HER TO THESE COORDINATES.
OUR PEOPLE WILL DEAL WITH HER FROM THERE.
YOU'LL RECEIVE 15 MILLION CREDITS NOW, AND ANOTHER 10 ONCE SHE'S BEEN DELIVERED.
THE CHERSONUS SYSTEM?
NOT A WHOLE LOT THERE.
PRECISELY. JUST A TINY MONASTERY, NOTHING MORE. HER FATHER THINKS SHE DESERVES A PHYSICAL PUNISHMENT...
BUT I THINK A TIME-OUT IS MORE IN ORDER FOR ANDROMEDA. TAKE AWAY ALL THE THINGS SHE LOVES.
EXCEPT FOR, WELL, A MOTHER'S LOVE.
TRUST ME...
IT'LL BE HELL FOR HER.
THE CETAN SHIP.
FIVE DAYS LATER.

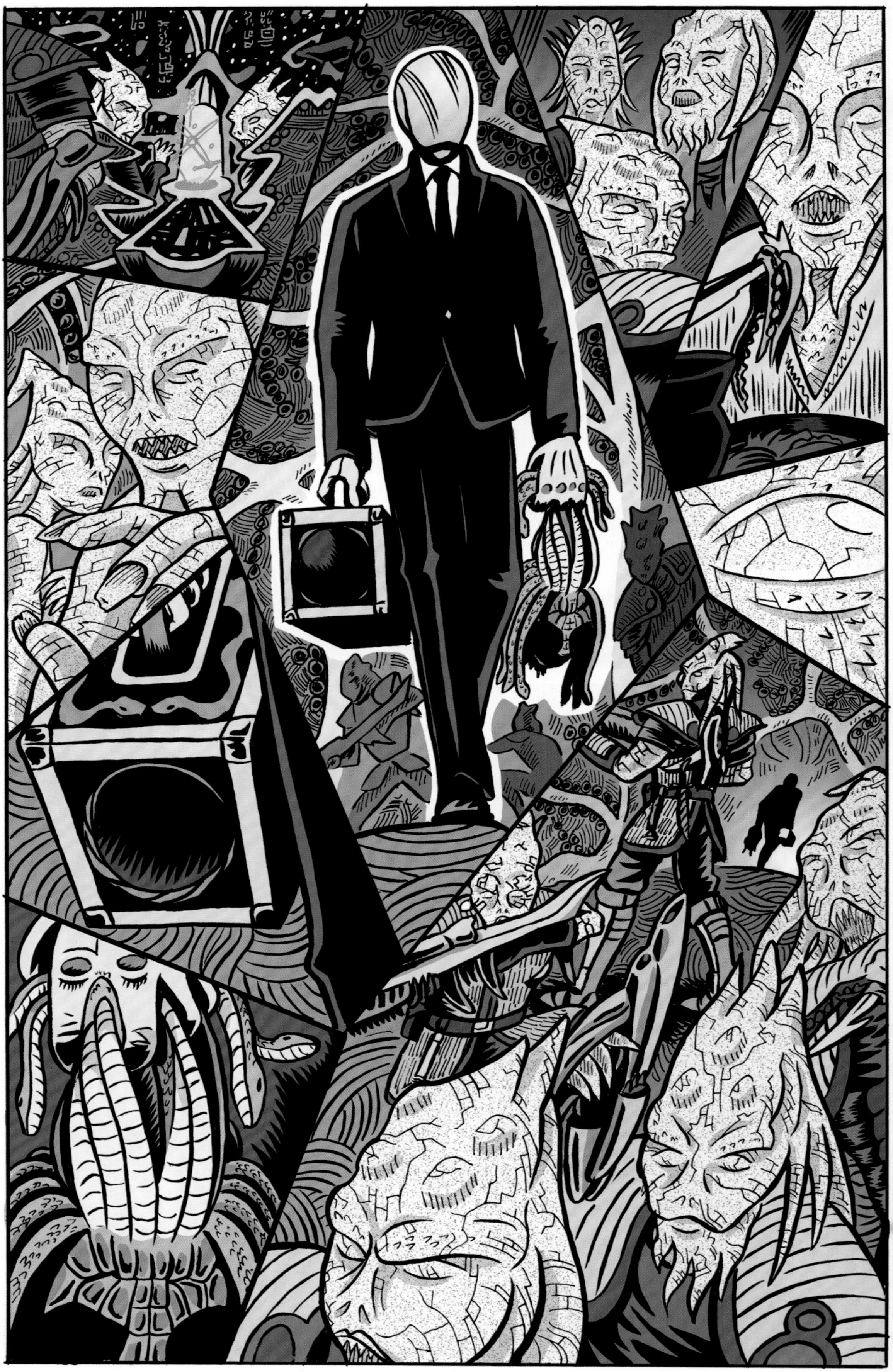

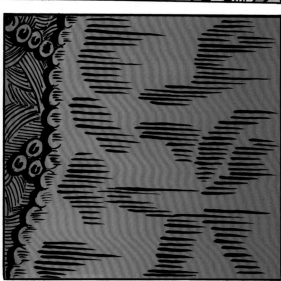

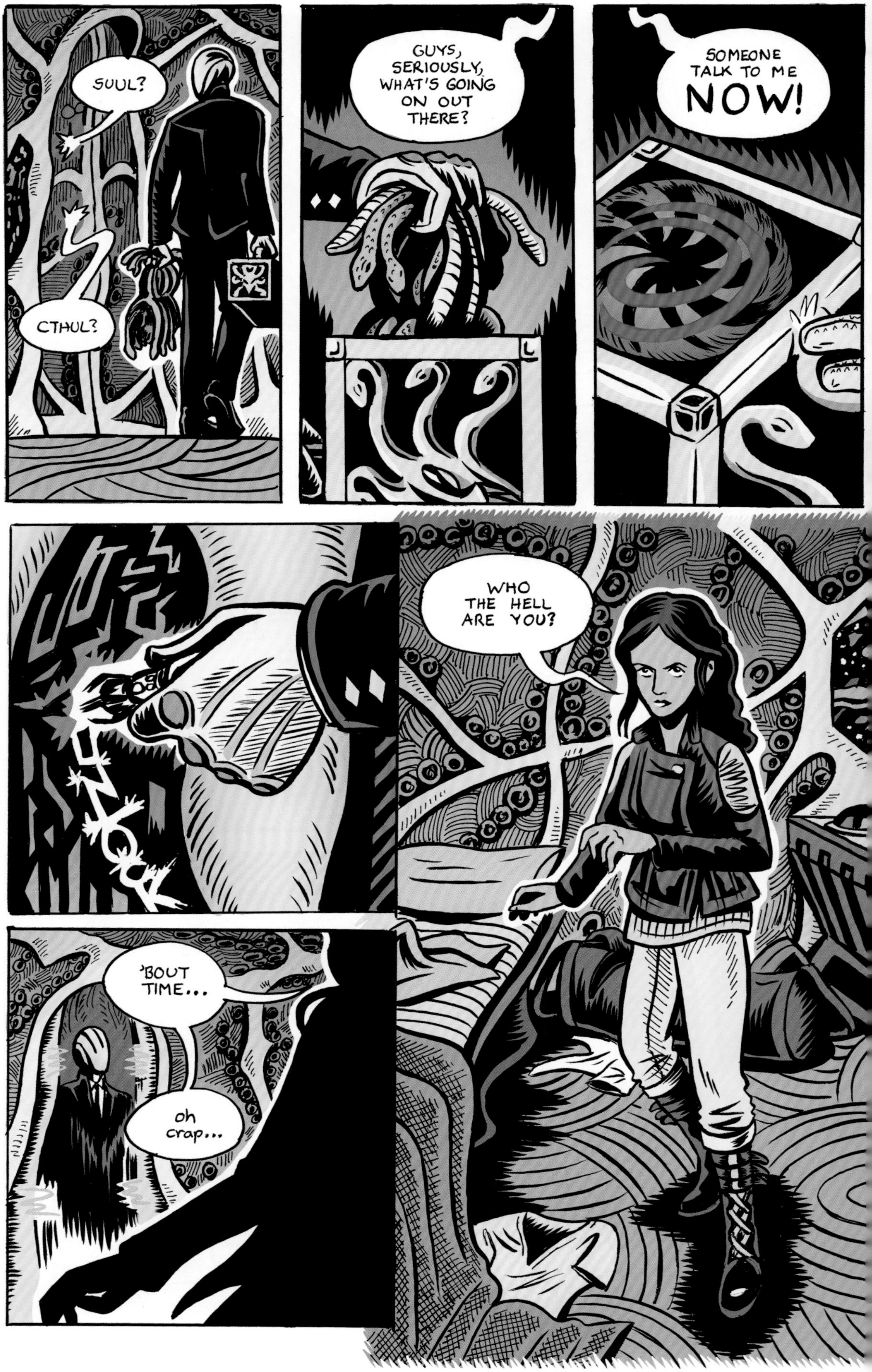
SUUL?
CTHUL?
GUYS, SERIOUSLY, WHAT'S GOING ON OUT THERE?
SOMEONE TALK TO ME NOW!
WHO THE HELL ARE YOU?
'BOUT TIME...
oh crap...

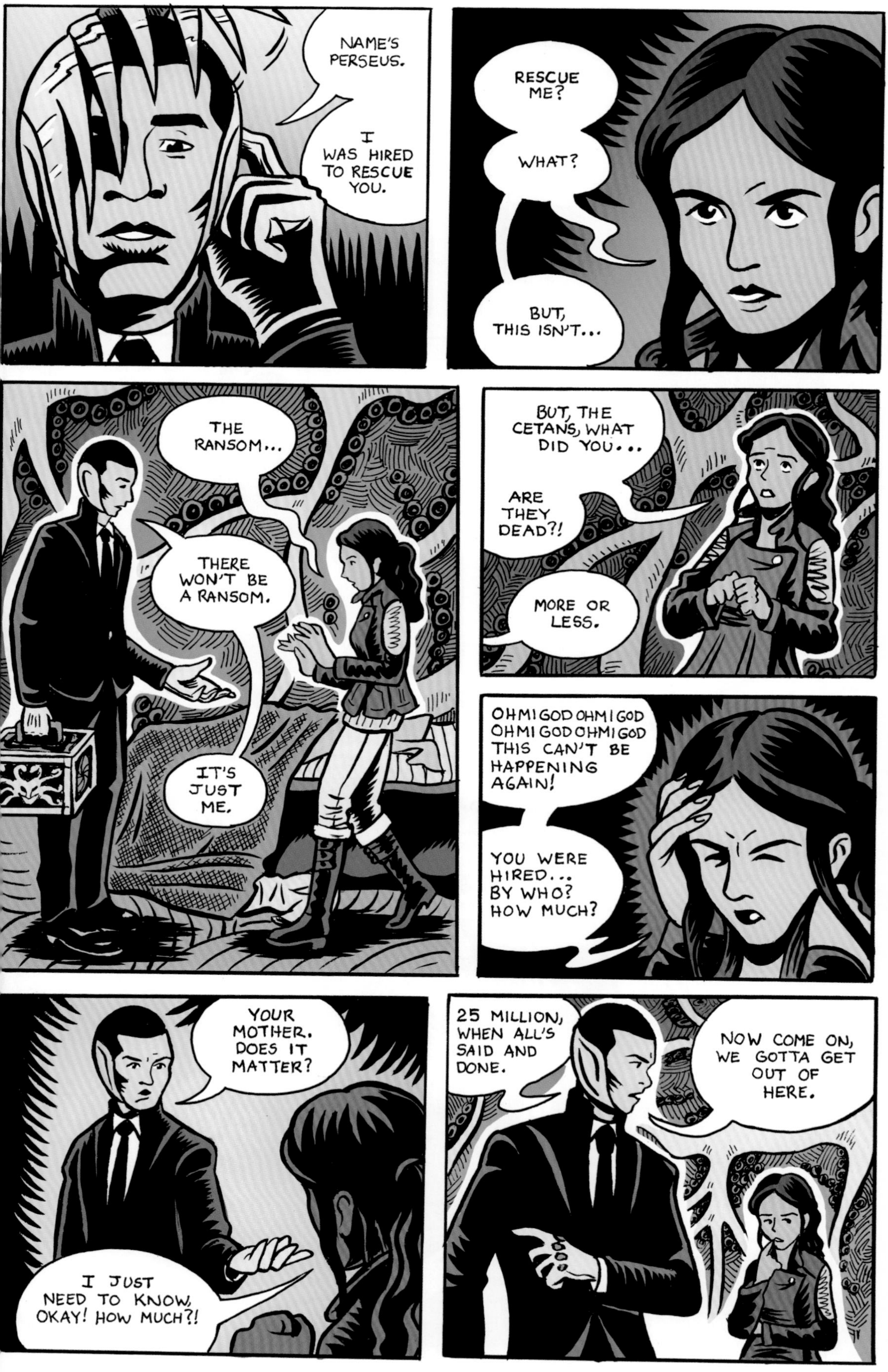
NAME'S PERSEUS.
I WAS HIRED TO RESCUE YOU.
RESCUE ME?
WHAT?
BUT, THIS ISN'T...
THE RANSOM...
THERE WON'T BE A RANSOM.
IT'S JUST ME.
BUT, THE CETANS, WHAT DID YOU...
ARE THEY DEAD?!
MORE OR LESS.
OHMIGODOHMIGOD OHMIGODOHMIGOD THIS CAN'T BE HAPPENING AGAIN!
YOU WERE HIRED... BY WHO? HOW MUCH?
YOUR MOTHER. DOES IT MATTER?
I JUST NEED TO KNOW, OKAY! HOW MUCH?!
25 MILLION, WHEN ALL'S SAID AND DONE.
NOW COME ON, WE GOTTA GET OUT OF HERE.

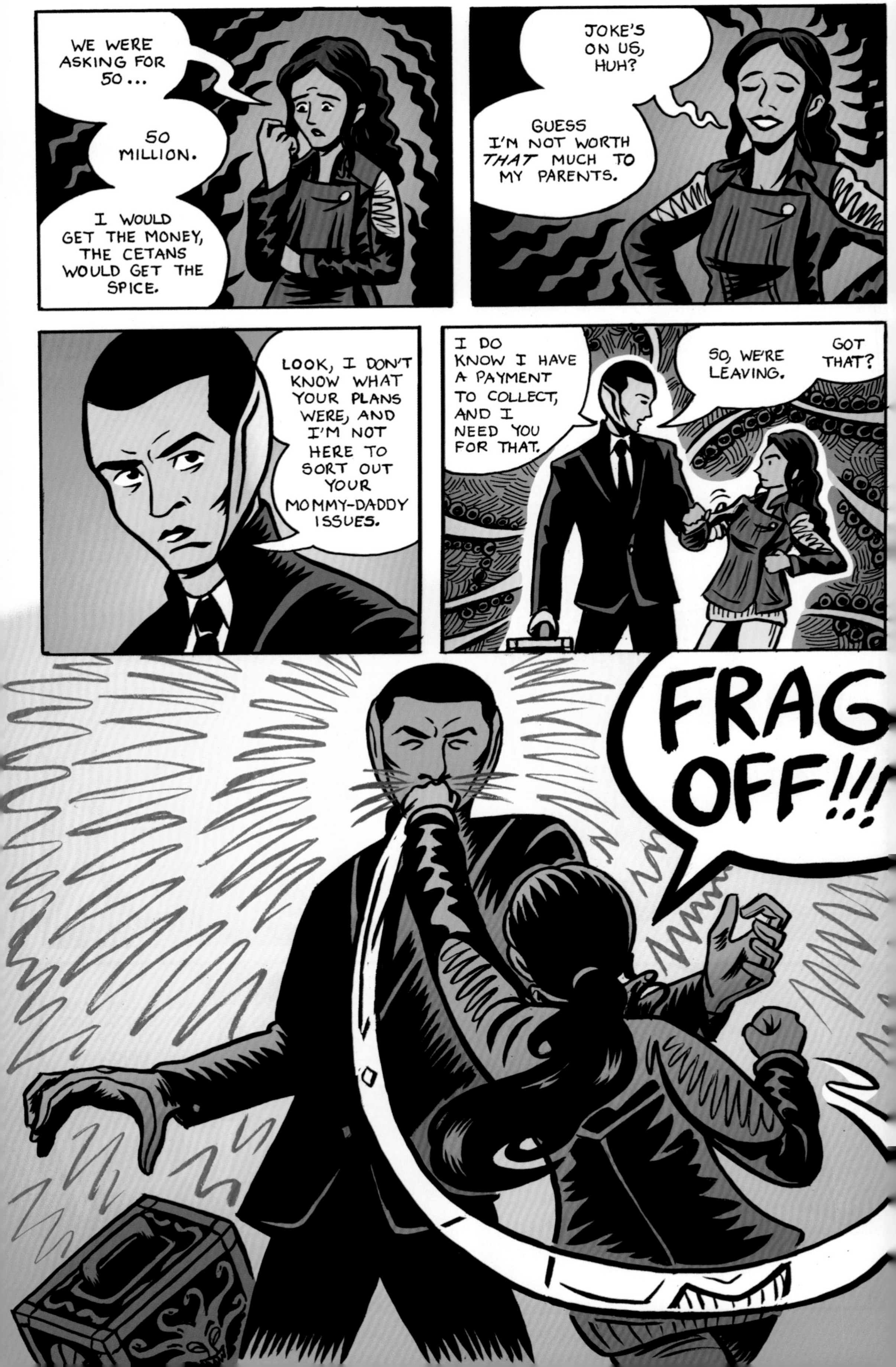
WE WERE ASKING FOR 50...
50 MILLION.
I WOULD GET THE MONEY, THE CETANS WOULD GET THE SPICE.
JOKE'S ON US, HUH?
GUESS I'M NOT WORTH *THAT* MUCH TO MY PARENTS.
LOOK, I DON'T KNOW WHAT YOUR PLANS WERE, AND I'M NOT HERE TO SORT OUT YOUR MOMMY-DADDY ISSUES.
I DO KNOW I HAVE A PAYMENT TO COLLECT, AND I NEED YOU FOR THAT.
SO, WE'RE LEAVING.
GOT THAT?
FRAG OFF!!!

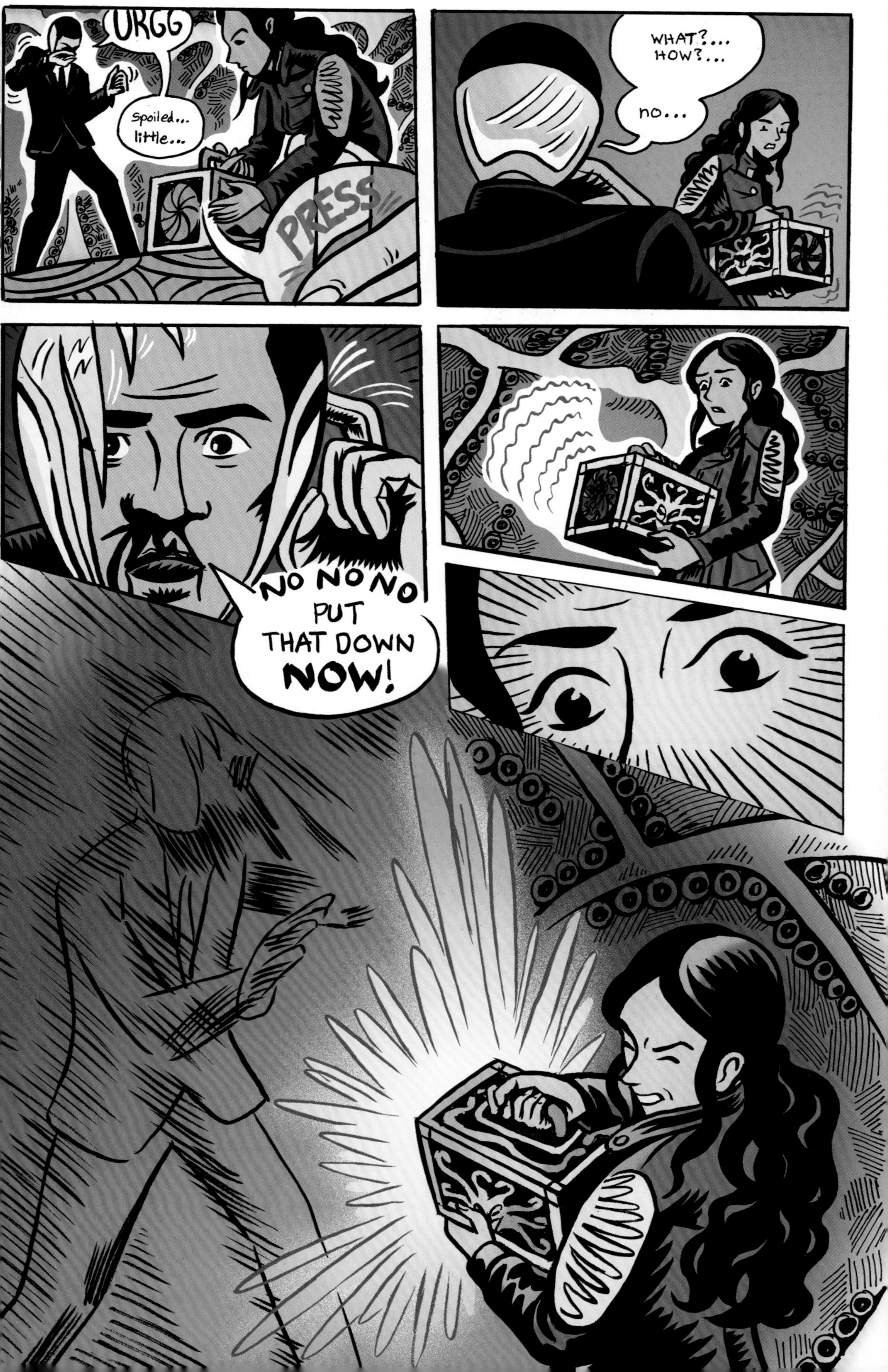
ORGG
Spoiled... little...
PRESS
WHAT?... HOW?...
no...
NO NO NO PUT THAT DOWN NOW!

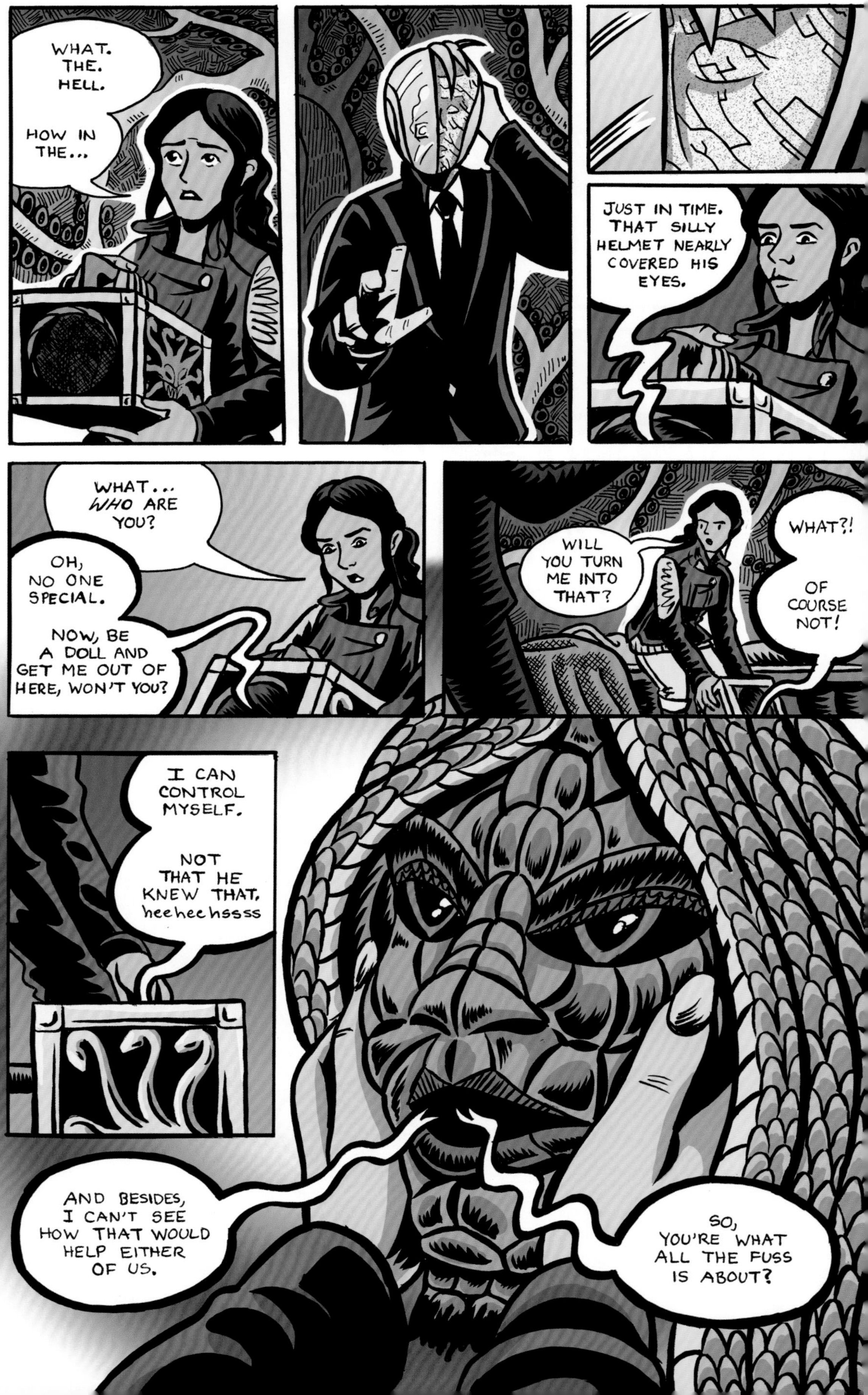
WHAT. THE. HELL.
HOW IN THE...
JUST IN TIME. THAT SILLY HELMET NEARLY COVERED HIS EYES.
WHAT... WHO ARE YOU?
OH, NO ONE SPECIAL.
NOW, BE A DOLL AND GET ME OUT OF HERE, WON'T YOU?
WILL YOU TURN ME INTO THAT?
WHAT?!
OF COURSE NOT!
I CAN CONTROL MYSELF.
NOT THAT HE KNEW THAT. heeheehssss
AND BESIDES, I CAN'T SEE HOW THAT WOULD HELP EITHER OF US.
SO, YOU'RE WHAT ALL THE FUSS IS ABOUT?

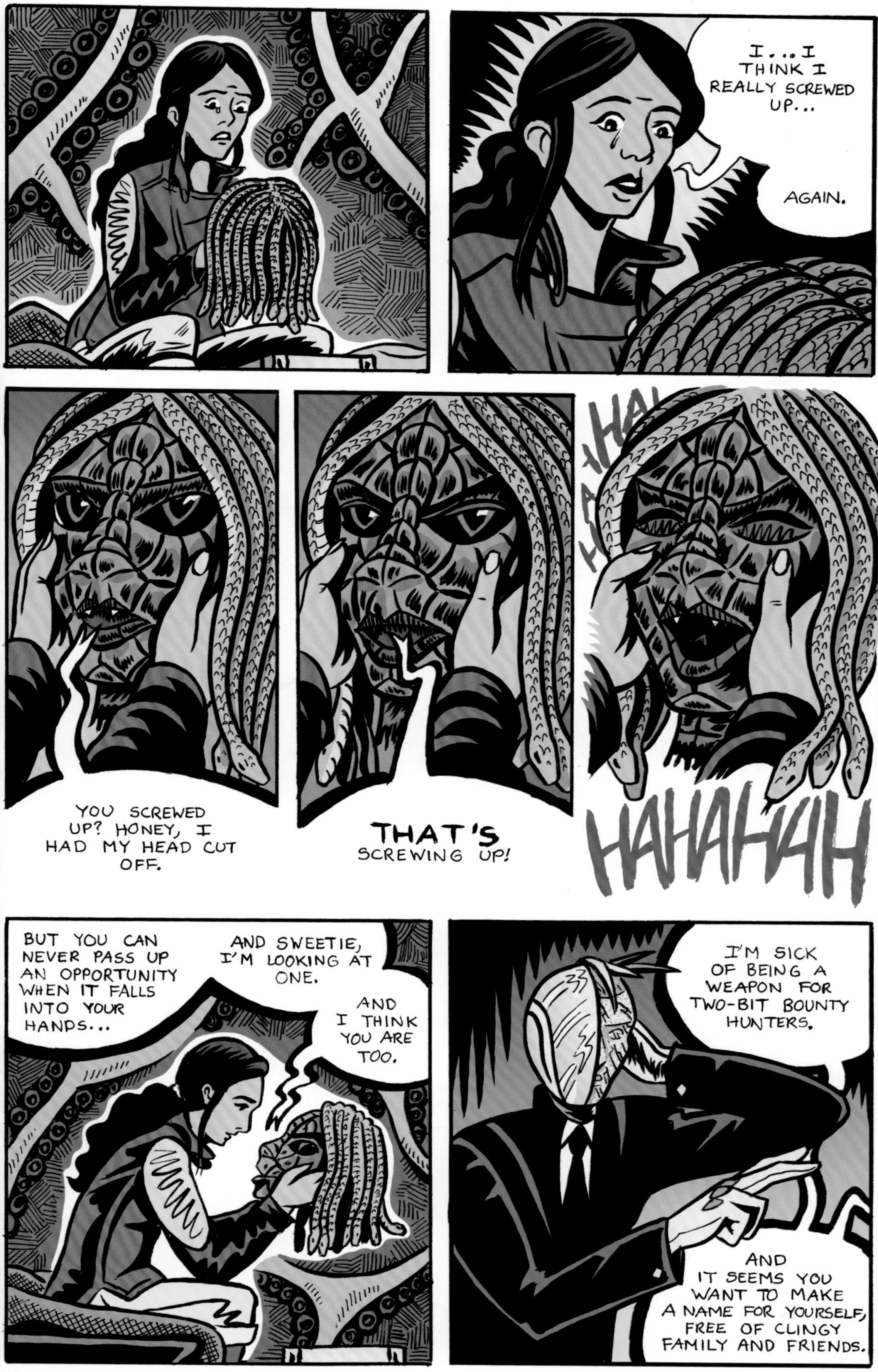
I...I THINK I REALLY SCREWED UP...
AGAIN.
YOU SCREWED UP? HONEY, I HAD MY HEAD CUT OFF.
THAT'S SCREWING UP!
HAHAHAH
HAHAHAH
BUT YOU CAN NEVER PASS UP AN OPPORTUNITY WHEN IT FALLS INTO YOUR HANDS...
AND SWEETIE, I'M LOOKING AT ONE.
AND I THINK YOU ARE TOO.
I'M SICK OF BEING A WEAPON FOR TWO-BIT BOUNTY HUNTERS.
AND IT SEEMS YOU WANT TO MAKE A NAME FOR YOURSELF, FREE OF CLINGY FAMILY AND FRIENDS.

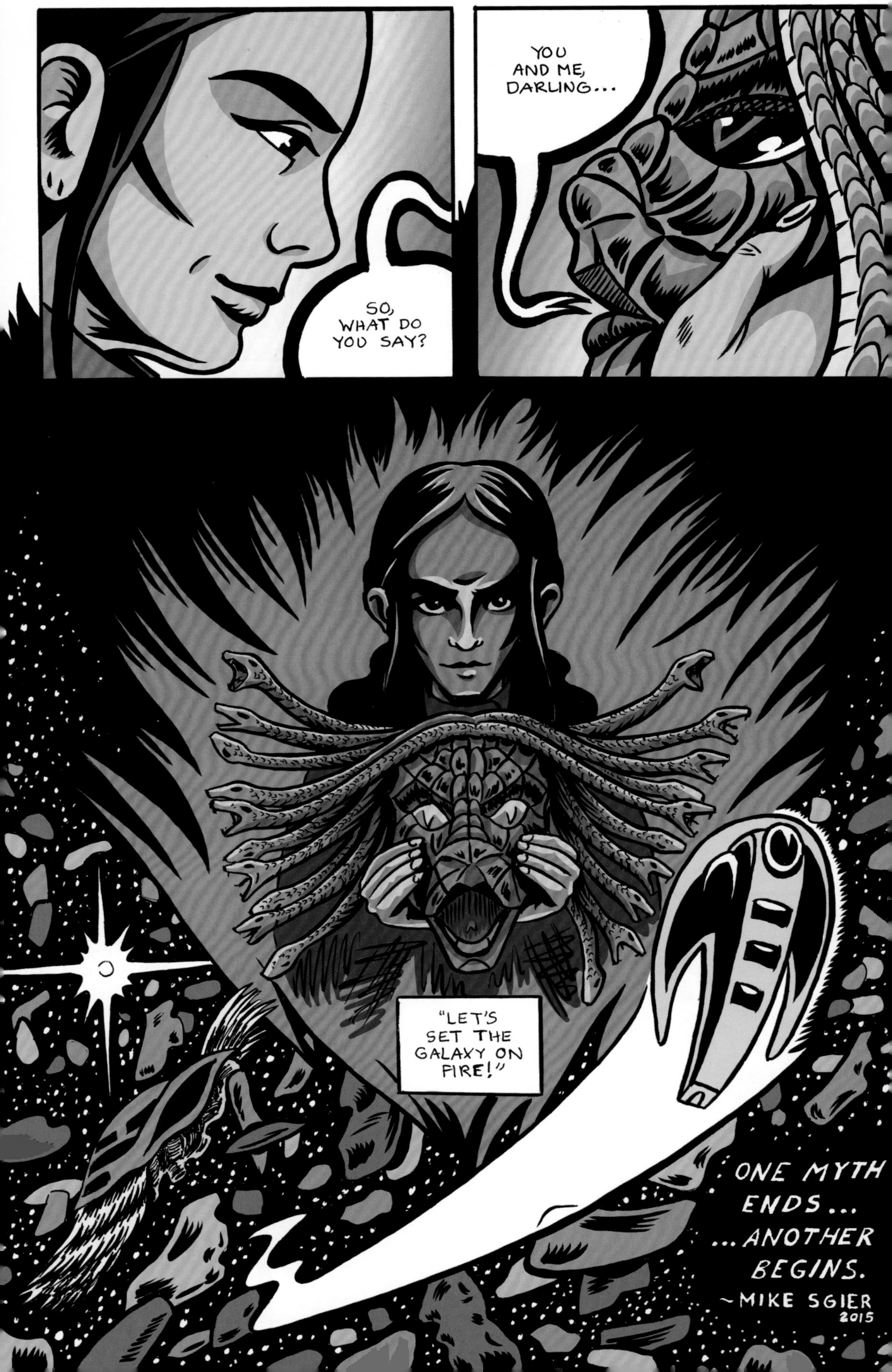
SO, WHAT DO YOU SAY?
YOU AND ME, DARLING...
"LET'S SET THE GALAXY ON FIRE!"
ONE MYTH ENDS...
...ANOTHER BEGINS.
~MIKE SGIER 2015

“EURYDICE”

written by
JOSH O’NEILL

illustrated and lettered by
TOBY CYPRESS

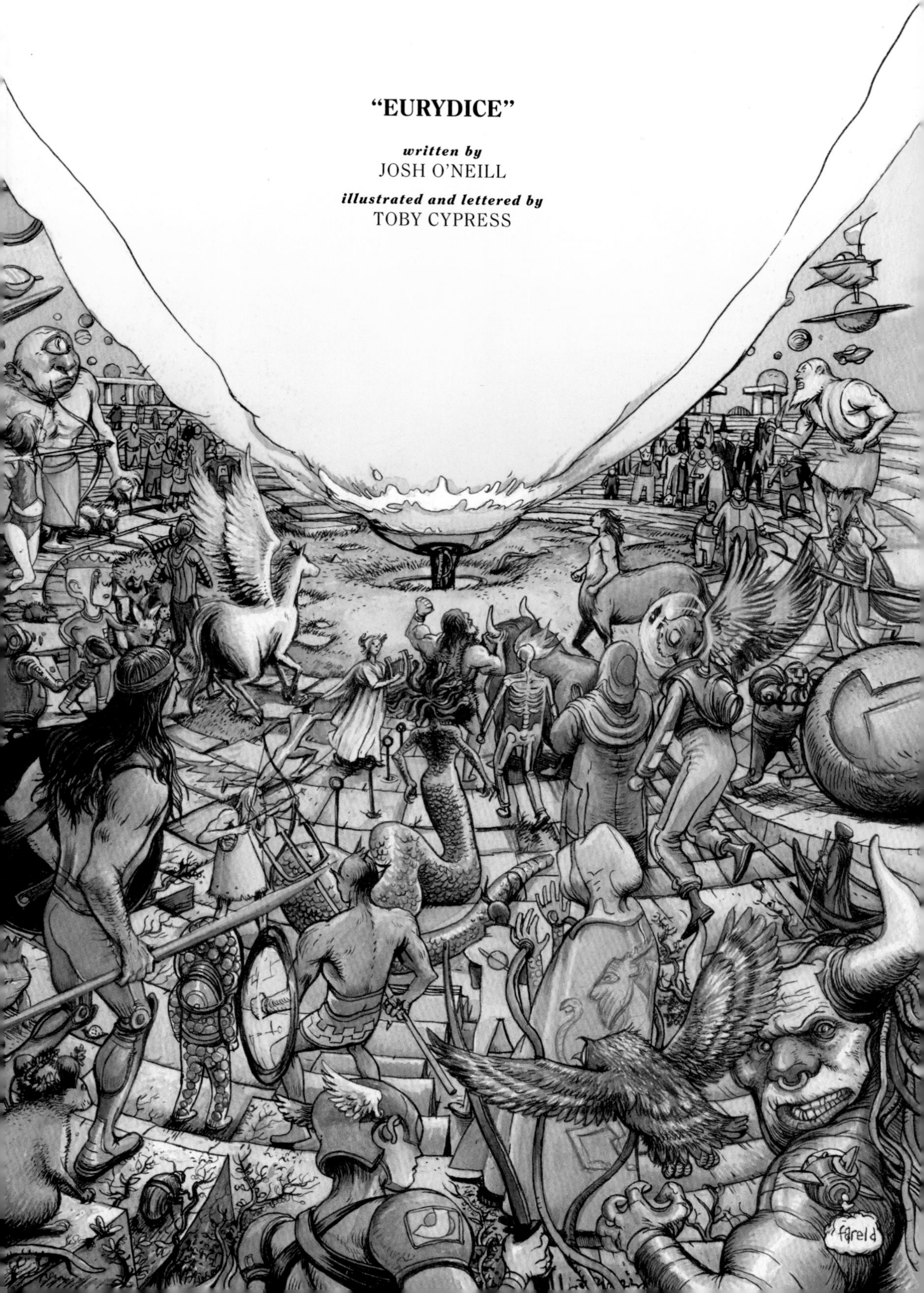
fareld

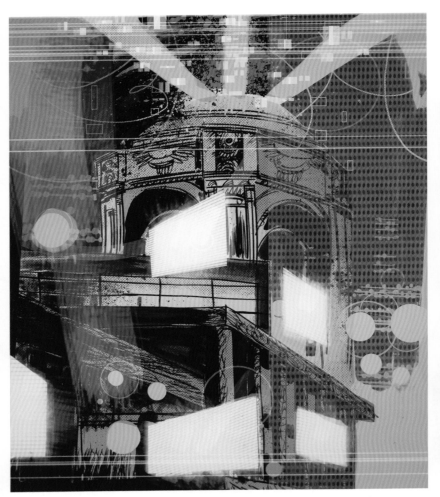

EURYDICE, MY BEAUTY.

I ALWAYS TOLD YOU WE'D TRAVEL THE WORLD.

I DIDN'T KNOW YOU WOULD BE PACKED IN MY SUITCASE.

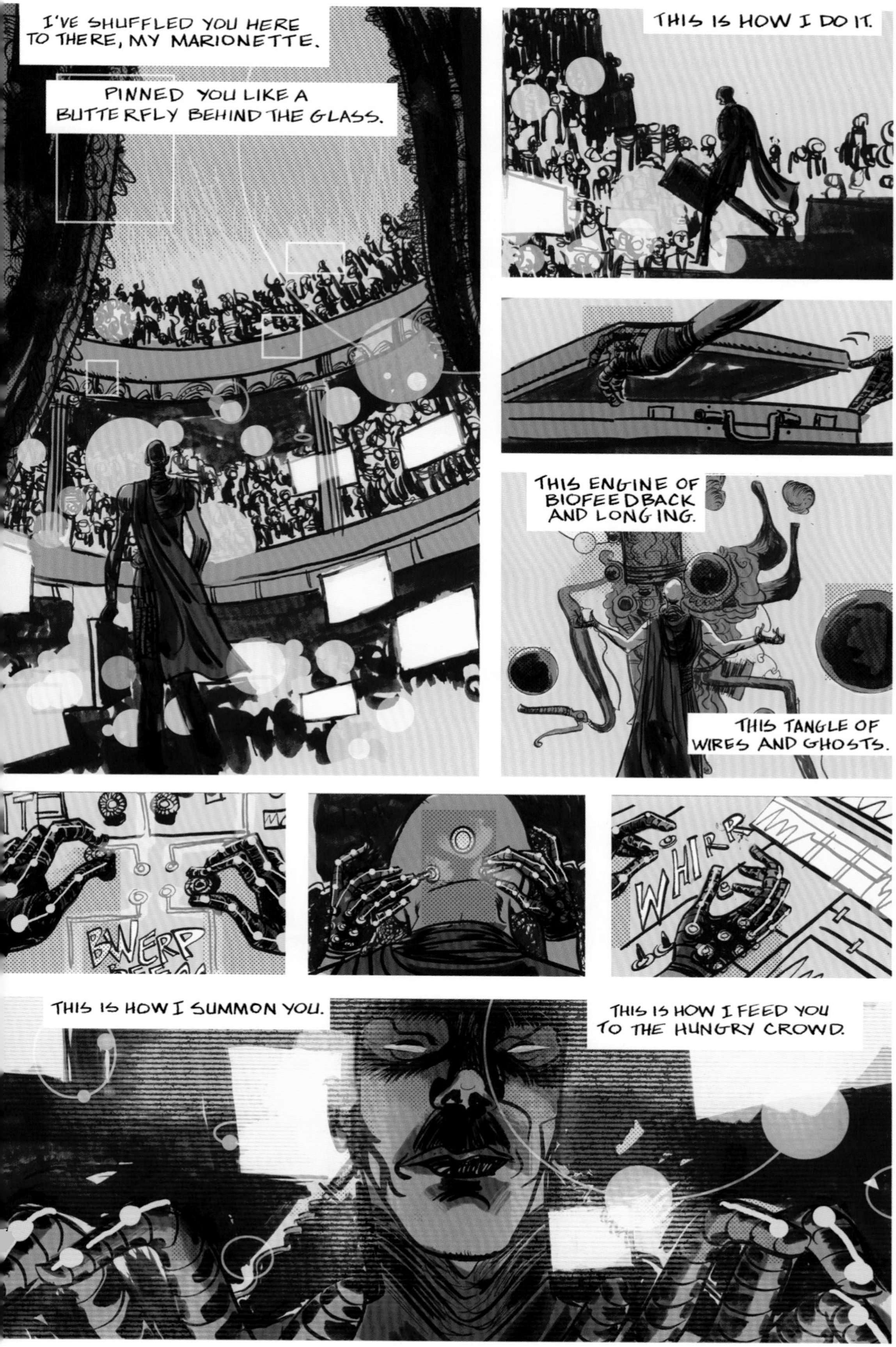
I'VE SHUFFLED YOU HERE TO THERE, MY MARIONETTE.
PINNED YOU LIKE A BUTTERFLY BEHIND THE GLASS.
THIS IS HOW I DO IT.
THIS ENGINE OF BIOFEEDBACK AND LONGING.
THIS TANGLE OF WIRES AND GHOSTS.
BWERP
WHIRR
THIS IS HOW I SUMMON YOU.
THIS IS HOW I FEED YOU TO THE HUNGRY CROWD.

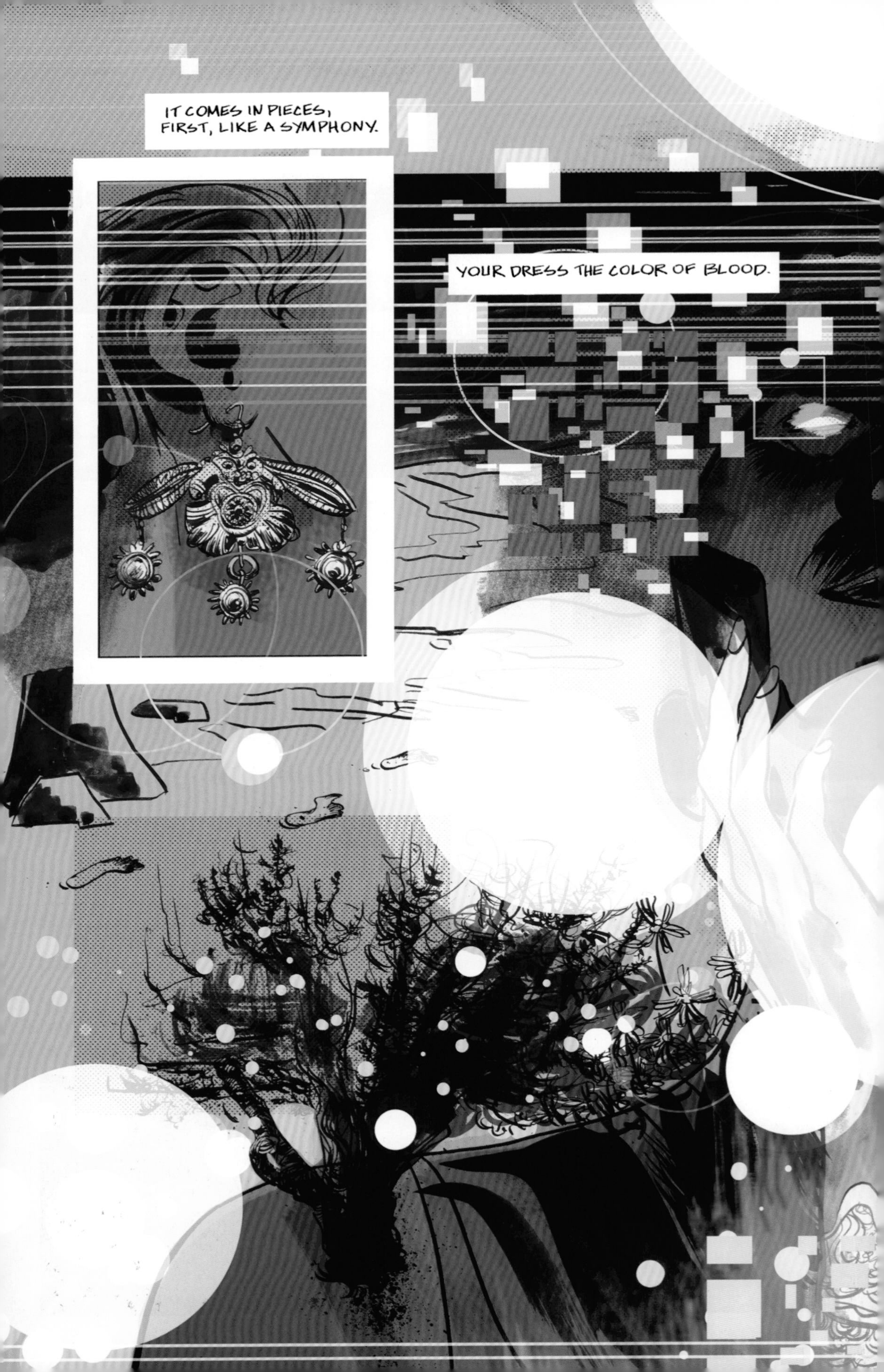
IT COMES IN PIECES, FIRST, LIKE A SYMPHONY.
YOUR DRESS THE COLOR OF BLOOD.

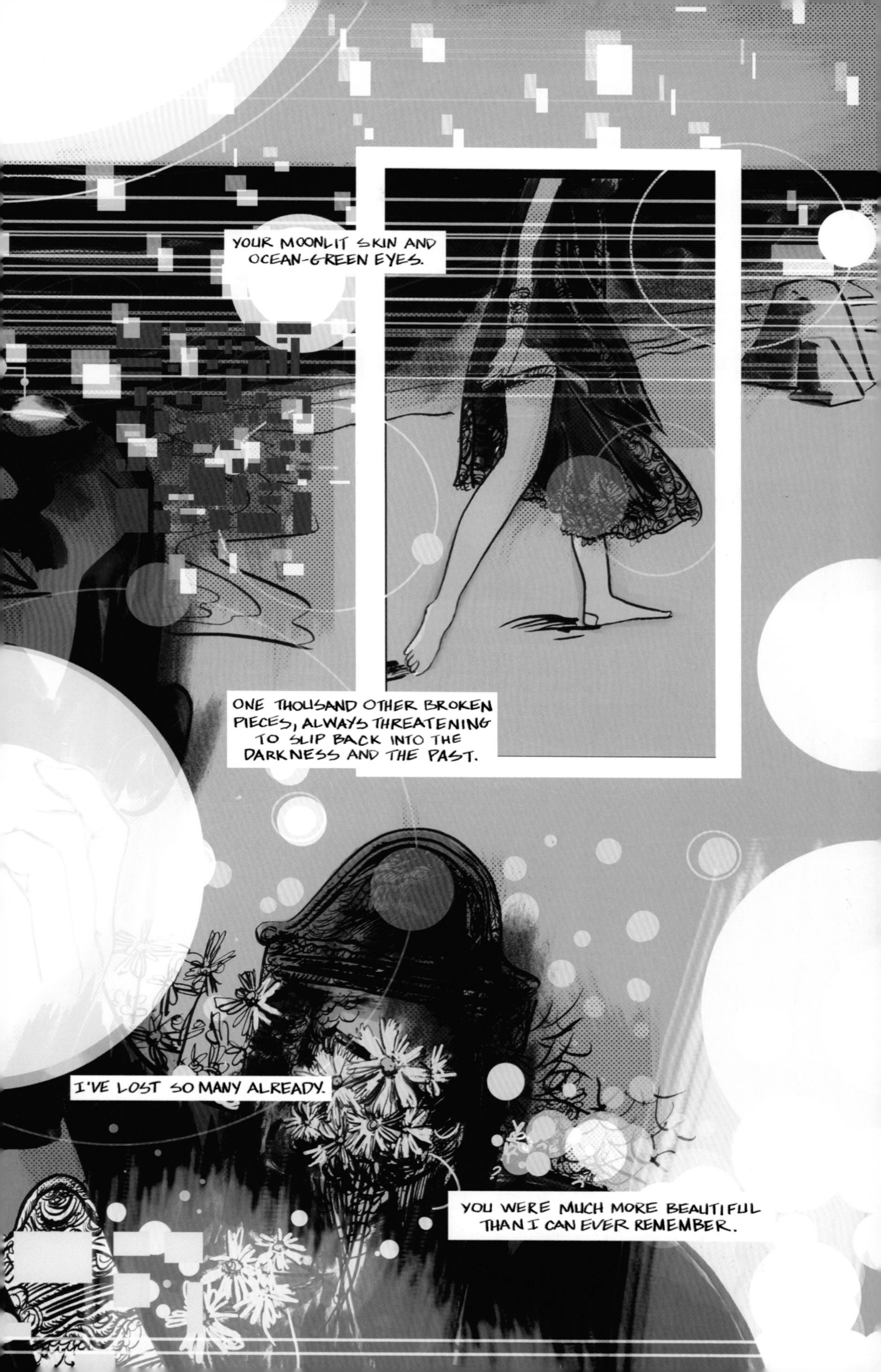
YOUR MOONLIT SKIN AND OCEAN-GREEN EYES.
ONE THOUSAND OTHER BROKEN PIECES, ALWAYS THREATENING TO SLIP BACK INTO THE DARKNESS AND THE PAST.
I'VE LOST SO MANY ALREADY.
YOU WERE MUCH MORE BEAUTIFUL THAN I CAN EVER REMEMBER.

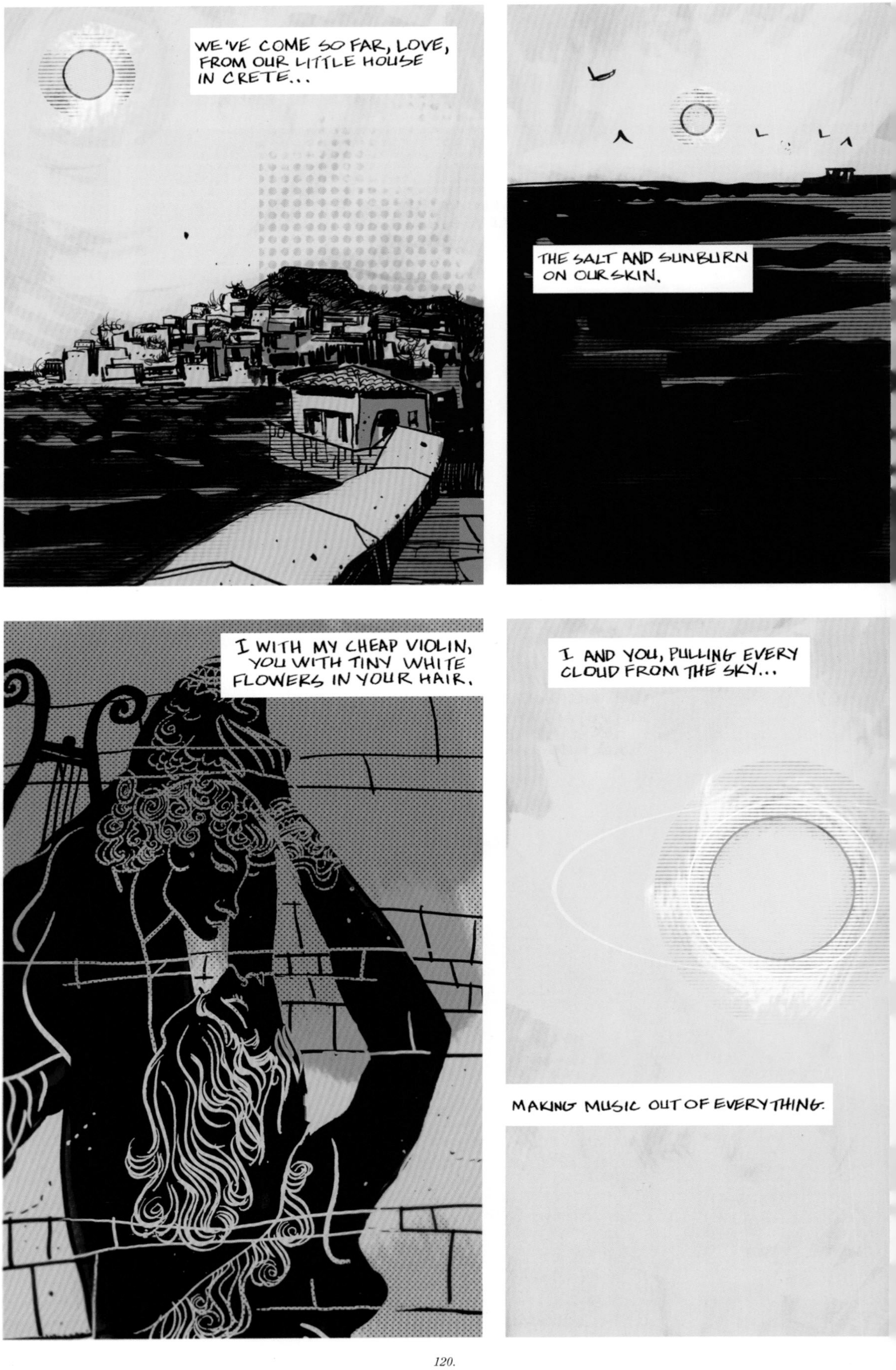
WE'VE COME SO FAR, LOVE, FROM OUR LITTLE HOUSE IN CRETE...
THE SALT AND SUNBURN ON OUR SKIN.
I WITH MY CHEAP VIOLIN, YOU WITH TINY WHITE FLOWERS IN YOUR HAIR.
I AND YOU, PULLING EVERY CLOUD FROM THE SKY...
MAKING MUSIC OUT OF EVERYTHING.

IT COMES QUICKER NOW, THE MEMORIES PILING AS FAST AS I CAN ARRANGE THEM. PIECES MOVE AND SHIFT.

MY HEART MUST BE FLAWLESS. MY GAZE PERFECT.

THIS IS THE MOMENT OF CREATION.

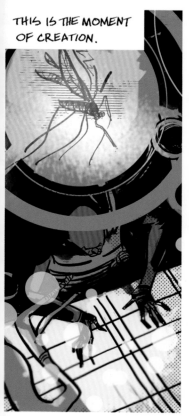

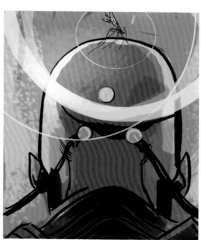

THE SMALLEST DISTRACTION, A MICROSECOND'S HESITATION, A TINY COUGH FROM THE CROWD, AND THE LOOKING GLASS WILL SHATTER. IT FALLS APART.

BUT NO, EURYDICE. AS EVER...

YOU HAVE MY FULL ATTENTION.

NOW, DARLING:

BE.

THE SPELL WORKS.
IT ALWAYS DOES.

THE MEMORIES
COALESCE.

AND ONCE AGAIN
I CAN HEAR YOUR
FOOTSTEPS BEHIND ME.

I CAN FEEL YOUR BREATH
AT MY BACK.

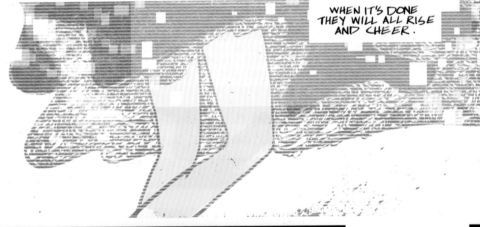

WHEN IT'S DONE
THEY WILL ALL RISE
AND CHEER.

AND I WILL GET
WHAT I CAME FOR.

I WILL SEE THE SHADOW OF YOUR BEAUTY IN THEIR WIDE, WET EYES.

IN THEIR APPLAUSE I WILL HEAR THE BELLS OF YOUR VOICE.

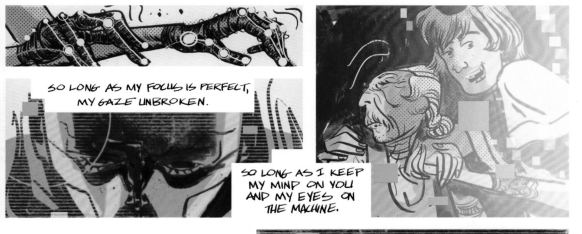

SO LONG AS MY FOCUS IS PERFECT, MY GAZE UNBROKEN.

SO LONG AS I KEEP MY MIND ON YOU AND MY EYES ON THE MACHINE.

HUNCHED HERE IN THE ORCHESTRA PIT, I FEEL YOU GLOWING BEHIND ME.

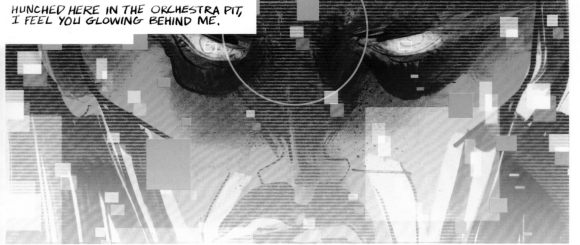

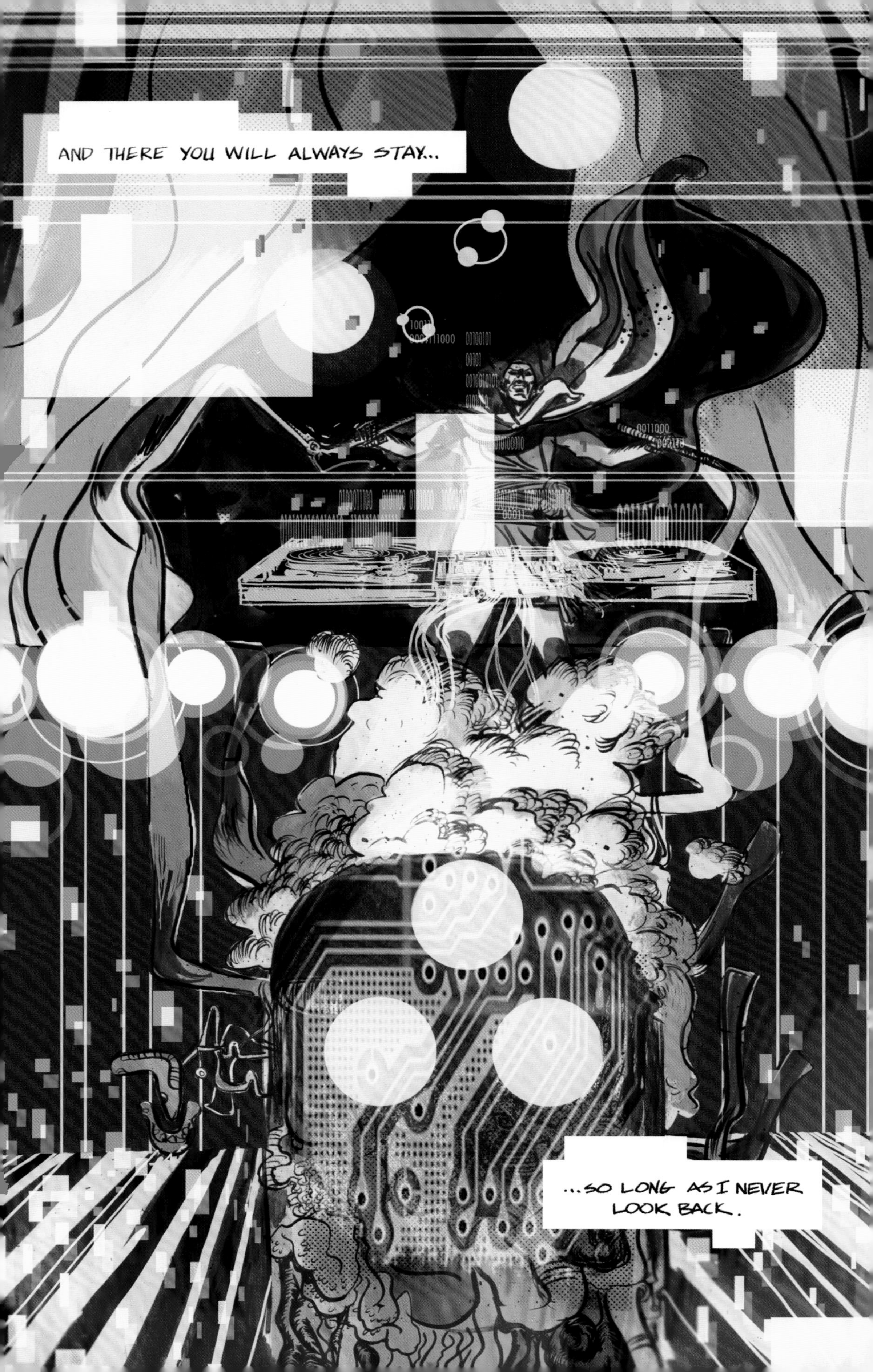
AND THERE YOU WILL ALWAYS STAY...
...SO LONG AS I NEVER LOOK BACK.

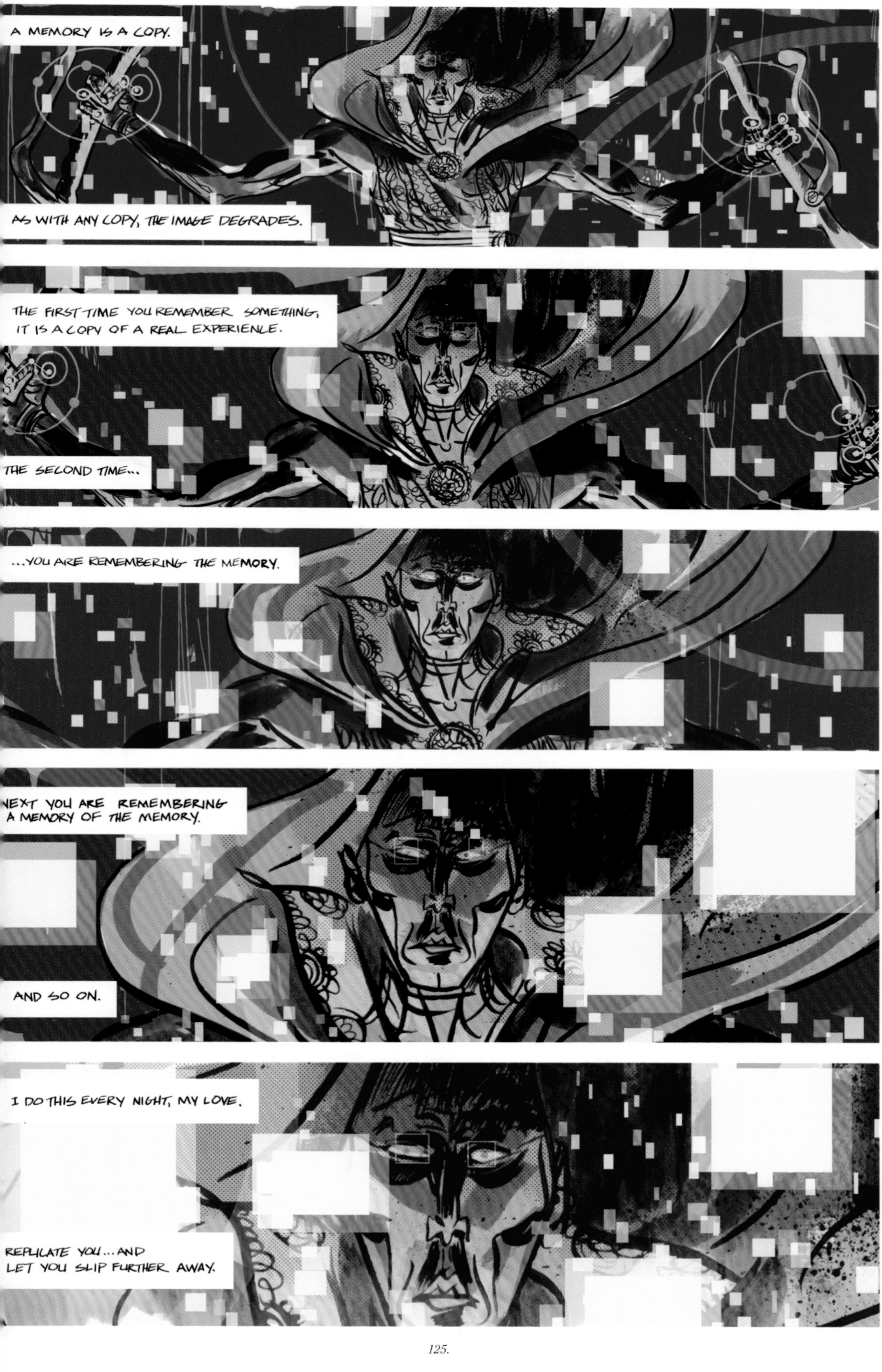
A MEMORY IS A COPY.
AS WITH ANY COPY, THE IMAGE DEGRADES.
THE FIRST TIME YOU REMEMBER SOMETHING, IT IS A COPY OF A REAL EXPERIENCE.
THE SECOND TIME...
...YOU ARE REMEMBERING THE MEMORY.
NEXT YOU ARE REMEMBERING A MEMORY OF THE MEMORY.
AND SO ON.
I DO THIS EVERY NIGHT, MY LOVE.
REPLICATE YOU... AND LET YOU SLIP FURTHER AWAY.

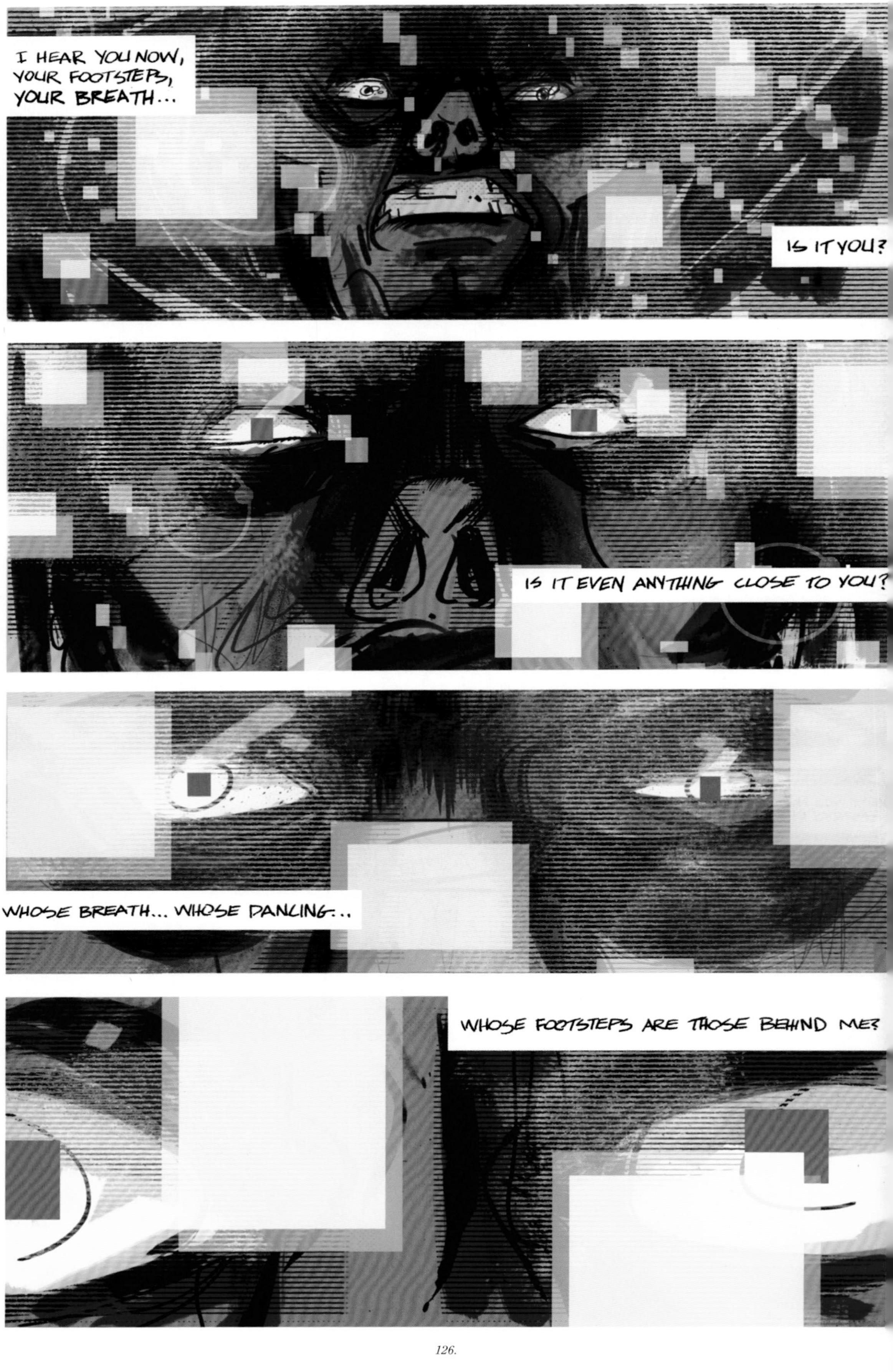
I HEAR YOU NOW, YOUR FOOTSTEPS, YOUR BREATH...
IS IT YOU?
IS IT EVEN ANYTHING CLOSE TO YOU?
WHOSE BREATH... WHOSE DANCING...
WHOSE FOOTSTEPS ARE THOSE BEHIND ME?

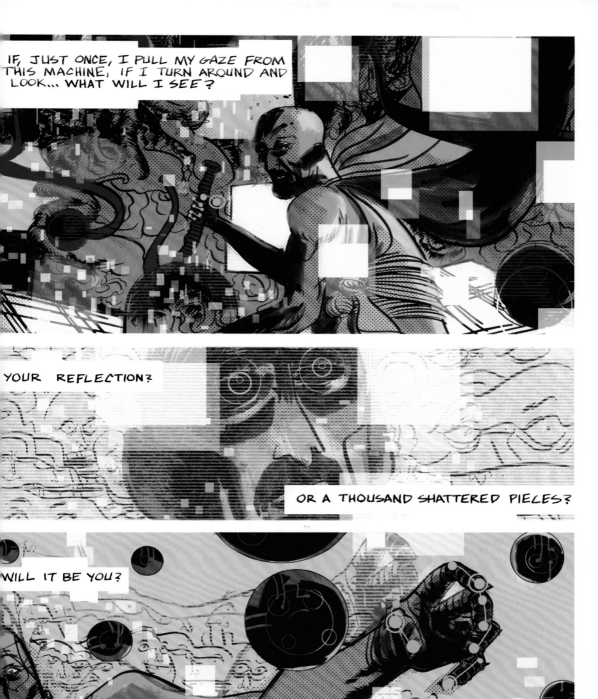

IF, JUST ONCE, I PULL MY GAZE FROM THIS MACHINE, IF I TURN AROUND AND LOOK... WHAT WILL I SEE?

YOUR REFLECTION?

OR A THOUSAND SHATTERED PIECES?

WILL IT BE YOU?

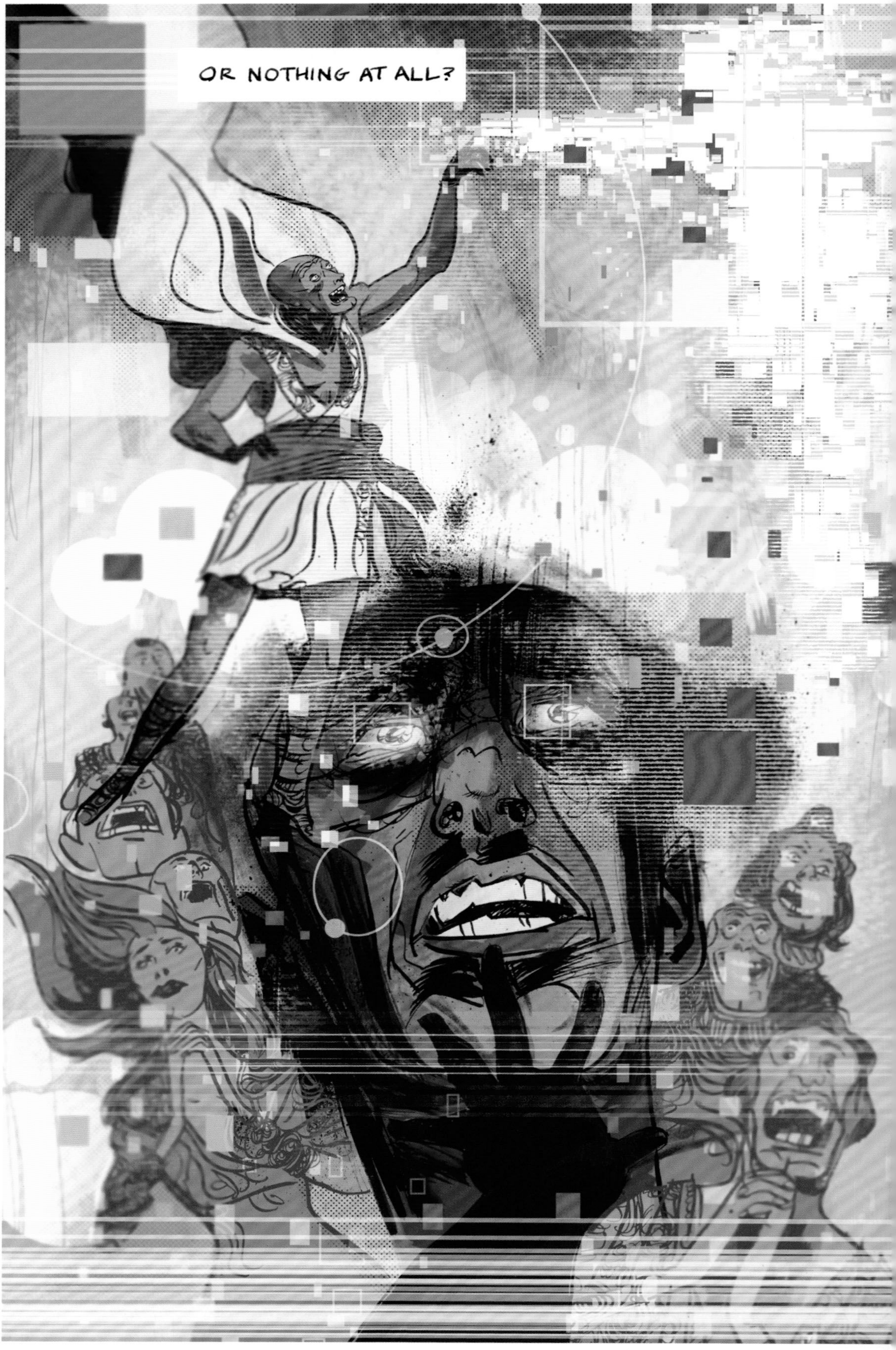
OR NOTHING AT ALL?

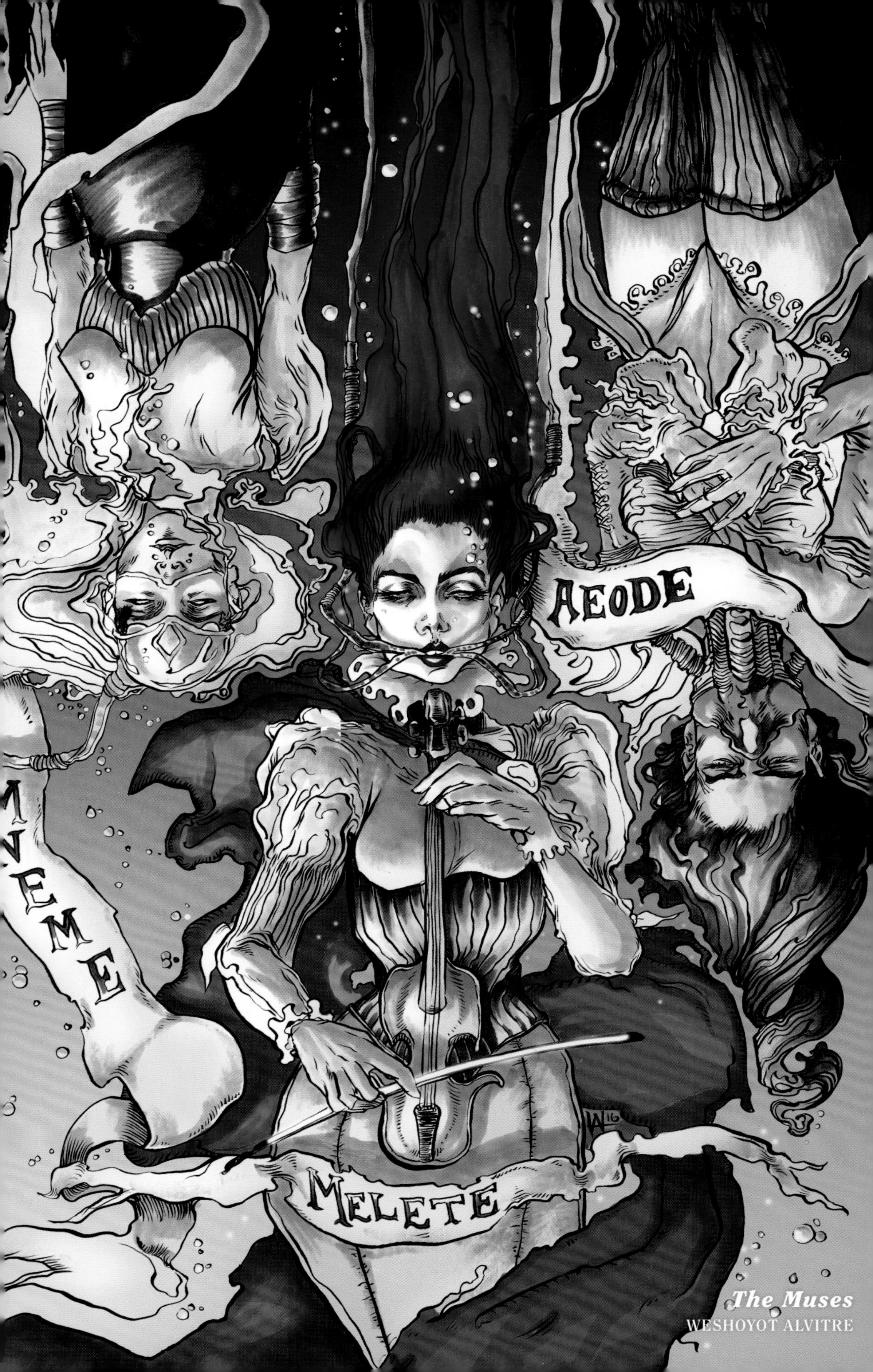
AEODE
MNEME
MELETE

The Muses
WESHOYOT ALVITRE

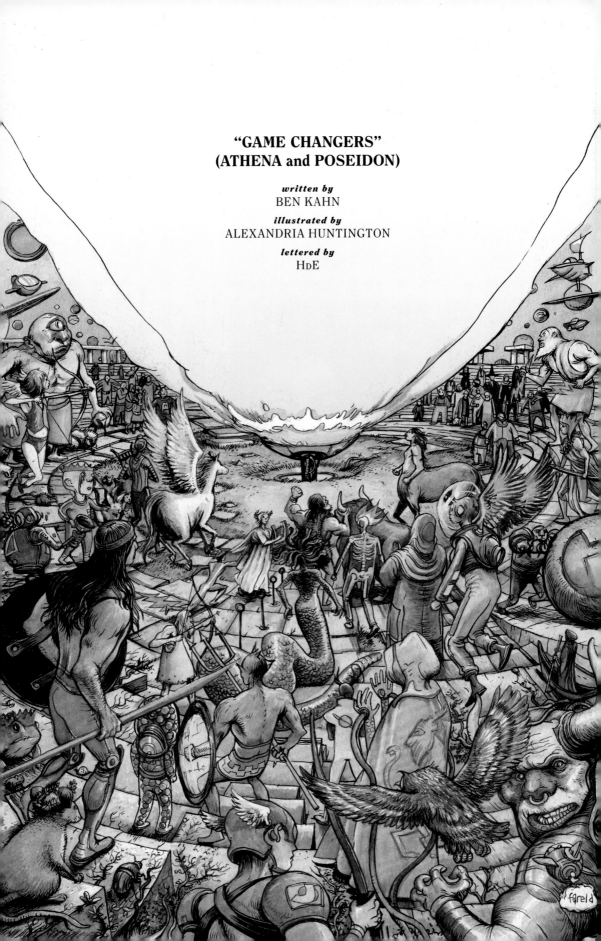

"GAME CHANGERS"
(ATHENA and POSEIDON)

written by
BEN KAHN

illustrated by
ALEXANDRIA HUNTINGTON

lettered by
HdE

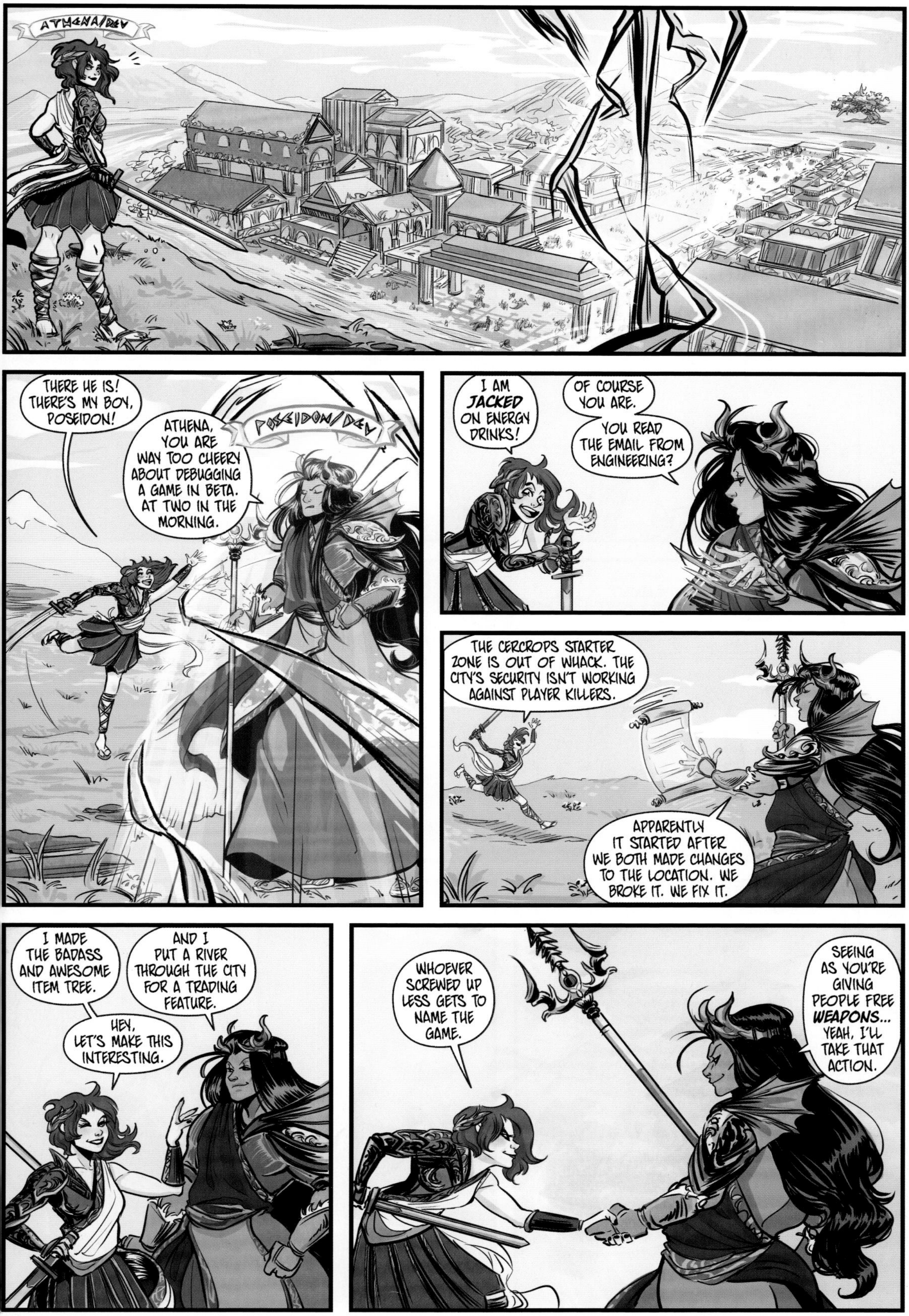
ATHENA/DEV
THERE HE IS! THERE'S MY BOY, POSEIDON!
POSEIDON/DEV
ATHENA, YOU ARE WAY TOO CHEERY ABOUT DEBUGGING A GAME IN BETA. AT TWO IN THE MORNING.
I AM **JACKED** ON ENERGY DRINKS!
OF COURSE YOU ARE.
YOU READ THE EMAIL FROM ENGINEERING?
THE CERCROPS STARTER ZONE IS OUT OF WHACK. THE CITY'S SECURITY ISN'T WORKING AGAINST PLAYER KILLERS.
APPARENTLY IT STARTED AFTER WE BOTH MADE CHANGES TO THE LOCATION. WE BROKE IT. WE FIX IT.
I MADE THE BADASS AND AWESOME ITEM TREE.
AND I PUT A RIVER THROUGH THE CITY FOR A TRADING FEATURE.
HEY, LET'S MAKE THIS INTERESTING.
WHOEVER SCREWED UP LESS GETS TO NAME THE GAME.
SEEING AS YOU'RE GIVING PEOPLE FREE **WEAPONS**... YEAH, I'LL TAKE THAT ACTION.

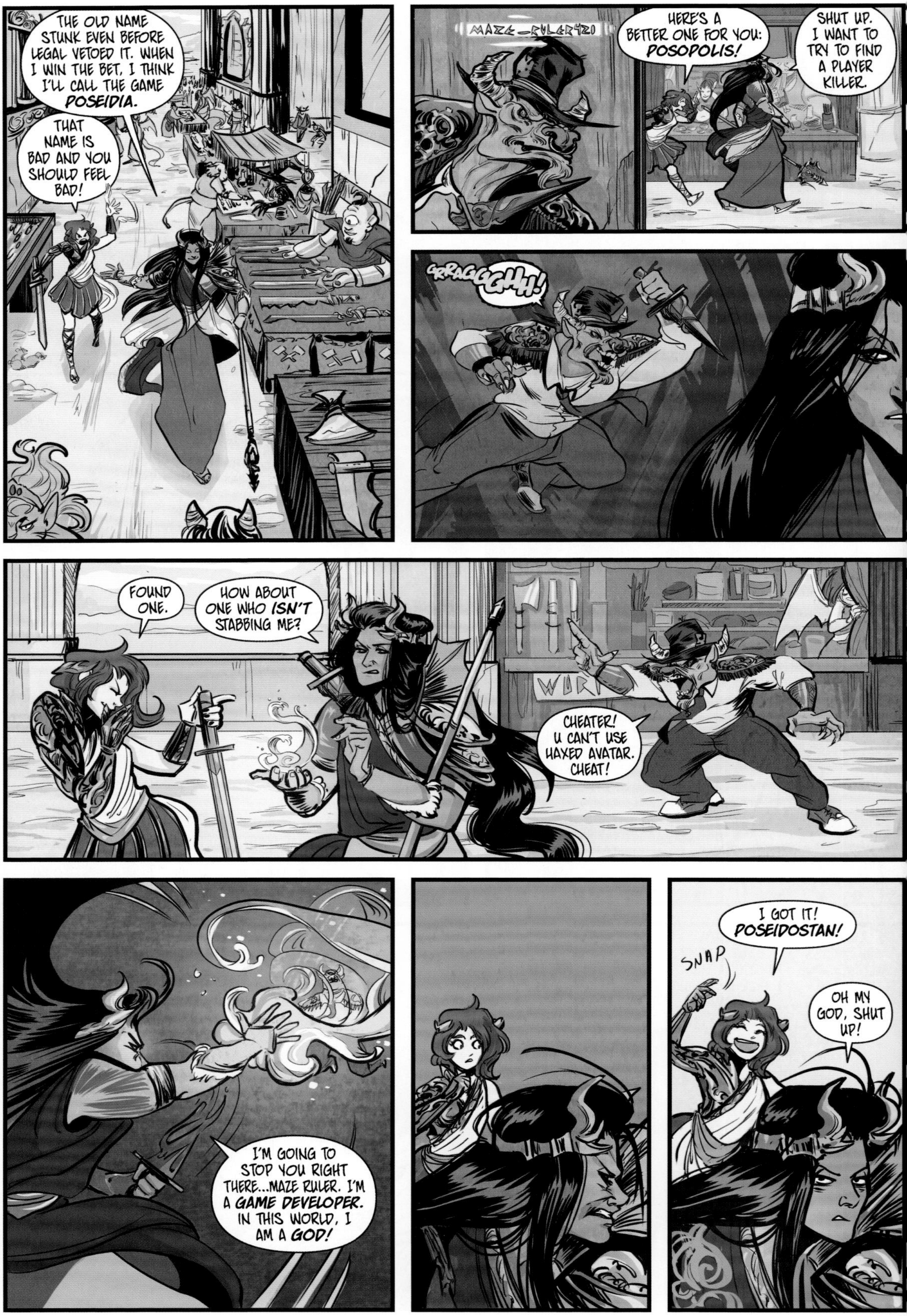
THE OLD NAME STUNK EVEN BEFORE LEGAL VETOED IT. WHEN I WIN THE BET, I THINK I'LL CALL THE GAME POSEIDIA.
THAT NAME IS BAD AND YOU SHOULD FEEL BAD!
MAZE_RULER420
HERE'S A BETTER ONE FOR YOU: POSOPOLIS!
SHUT UP. I WANT TO TRY TO FIND A PLAYER KILLER.
GRRAGGGHH!
FOUND ONE.
HOW ABOUT ONE WHO ISN'T STABBING ME?
CHEATER! U CAN'T USE HAXED AVATAR. CHEAT!
I'M GOING TO STOP YOU RIGHT THERE...MAZE RULER. I'M A GAME DEVELOPER. IN THIS WORLD, I AM A GOD!
I GOT IT! POSEIDOSTAN!
SNAP
OH MY GOD, SHUT UP!

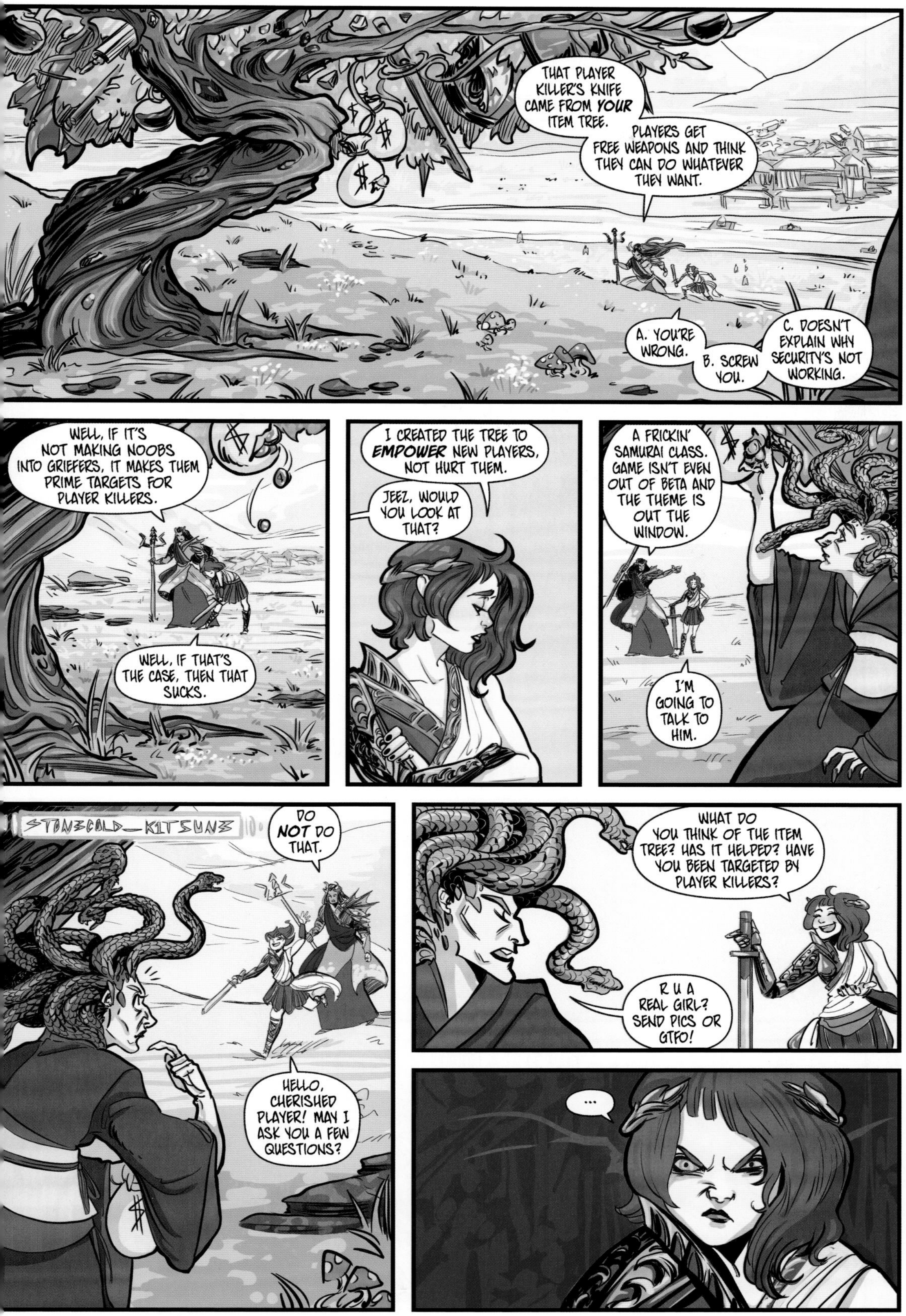

THAT PLAYER KILLER'S KNIFE CAME FROM **YOUR** ITEM TREE.
PLAYERS GET FREE WEAPONS AND THINK THEY CAN DO WHATEVER THEY WANT.
A. YOU'RE WRONG.
B. SCREW YOU.
C. DOESN'T EXPLAIN WHY SECURITY'S NOT WORKING.
WELL, IF IT'S NOT MAKING NOOBS INTO GRIEFERS, IT MAKES THEM PRIME TARGETS FOR PLAYER KILLERS.
WELL, IF THAT'S THE CASE, THEN THAT SUCKS.
I CREATED THE TREE TO **EMPOWER** NEW PLAYERS, NOT HURT THEM.
JEEZ, WOULD YOU LOOK AT THAT?
A FRICKIN' SAMURAI CLASS. GAME ISN'T EVEN OUT OF BETA AND THE THEME IS OUT THE WINDOW.
I'M GOING TO TALK TO HIM.
STON3COLD_K1TSUN3
DO **NOT** DO THAT.
HELLO, CHERISHED PLAYER! MAY I ASK YOU A FEW QUESTIONS?
WHAT DO YOU THINK OF THE ITEM TREE? HAS IT HELPED? HAVE YOU BEEN TARGETED BY PLAYER KILLERS?
R U A REAL GIRL? SEND PICS OR GTFO!
...

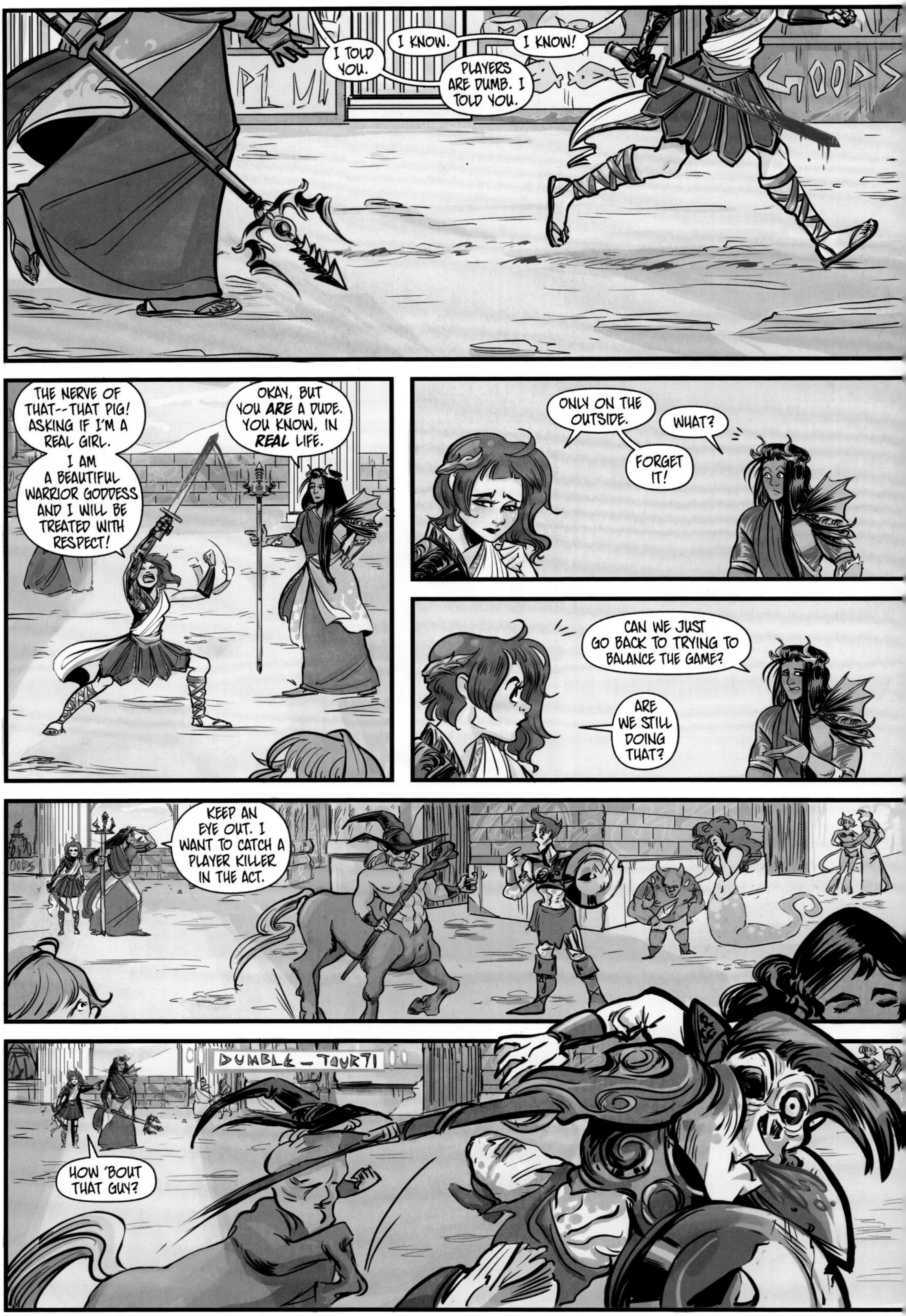
I TOLD YOU.
I KNOW.
I KNOW!
PLAYERS ARE DUMB. I TOLD YOU.
P1
GOODS
THE NERVE OF THAT--THAT PIG! ASKING IF I'M A REAL GIRL.
I AM A BEAUTIFUL WARRIOR GODDESS AND I WILL BE TREATED WITH RESPECT!
OKAY, BUT YOU ARE A DUDE. YOU KNOW, IN REAL LIFE.
ONLY ON THE OUTSIDE.
WHAT?
FORGET IT!
CAN WE JUST GO BACK TO TRYING TO BALANCE THE GAME?
ARE WE STILL DOING THAT?
KEEP AN EYE OUT. I WANT TO CATCH A PLAYER KILLER IN THE ACT.
DUMBLE_TOUR71
HOW 'BOUT THAT GUY?

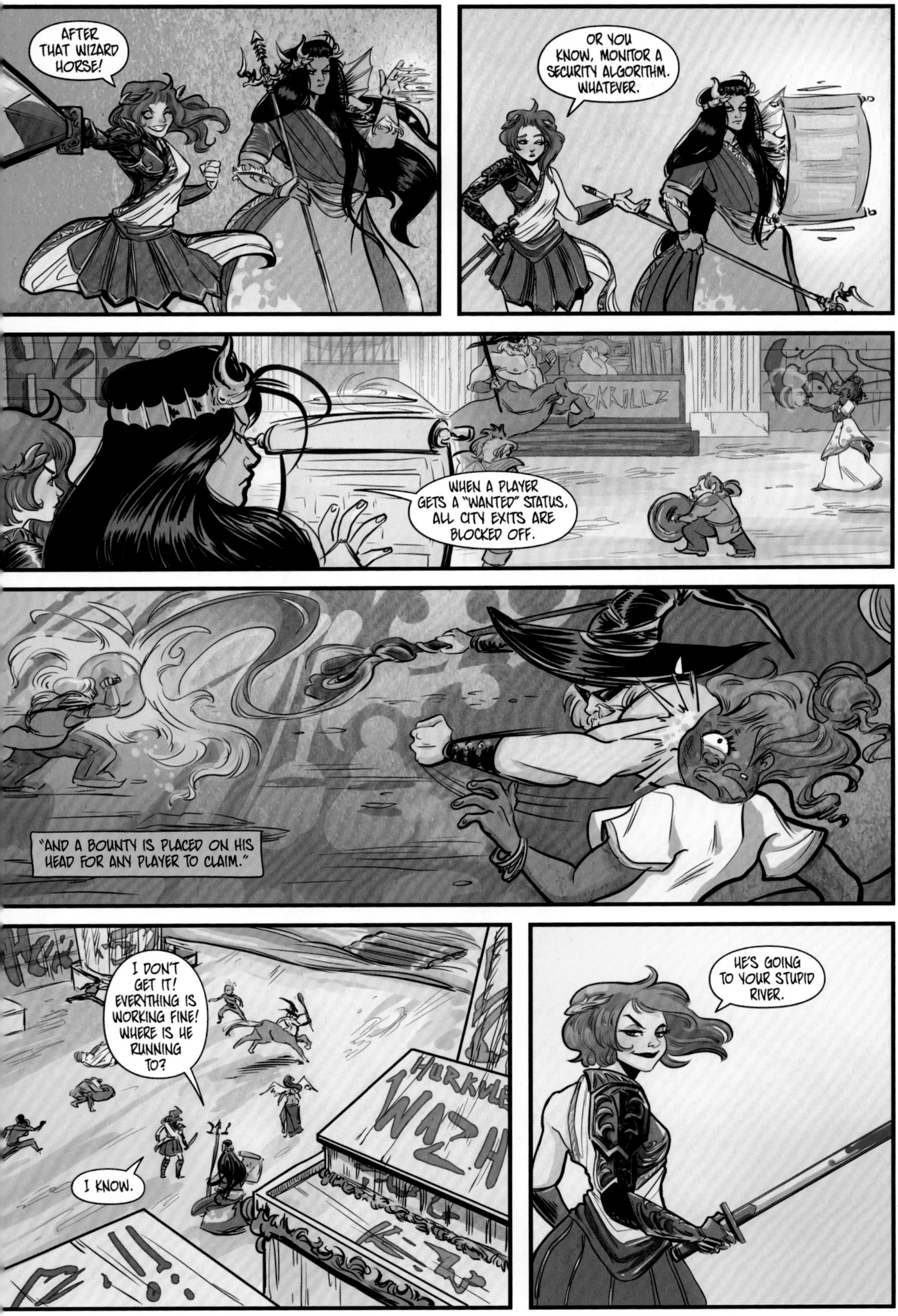
AFTER THAT WIZARD HORSE!
OR YOU KNOW, MONITOR A SECURITY ALGORITHM. WHATEVER.
SKROLLZ
WHEN A PLAYER GETS A "WANTED" STATUS, ALL CITY EXITS ARE BLOCKED OFF.
"AND A BOUNTY IS PLACED ON HIS HEAD FOR ANY PLAYER TO CLAIM."
I DON'T GET IT! EVERYTHING IS WORKING FINE! WHERE IS HE RUNNING TO?
I KNOW.
HE'S GOING TO YOUR STUPID RIVER.

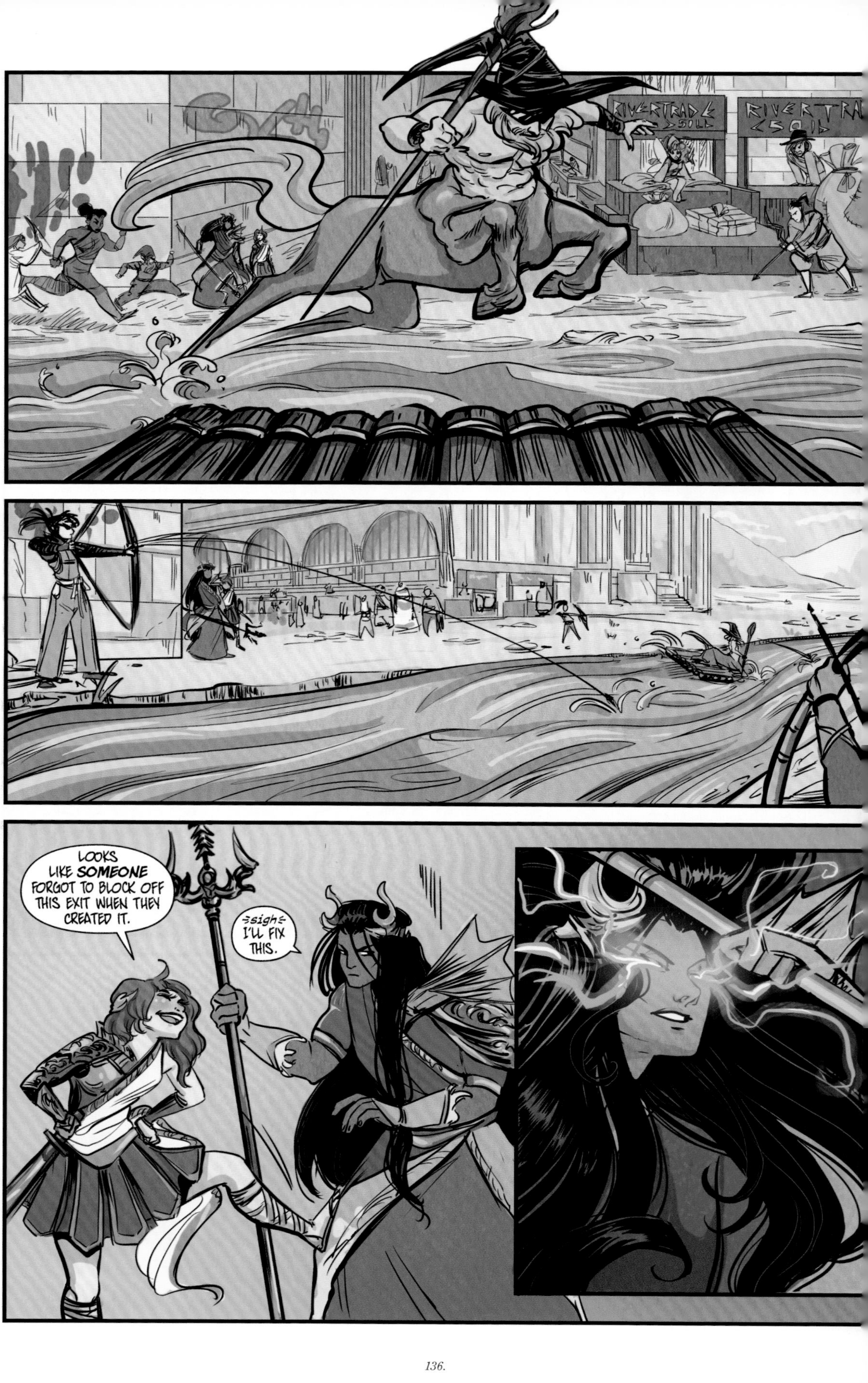
RIVERTRADE
RIVERTRADE
LOOKS LIKE **SOMEONE** FORGOT TO BLOCK OFF THIS EXIT WHEN THEY CREATED IT.
sigh I'LL FIX THIS.

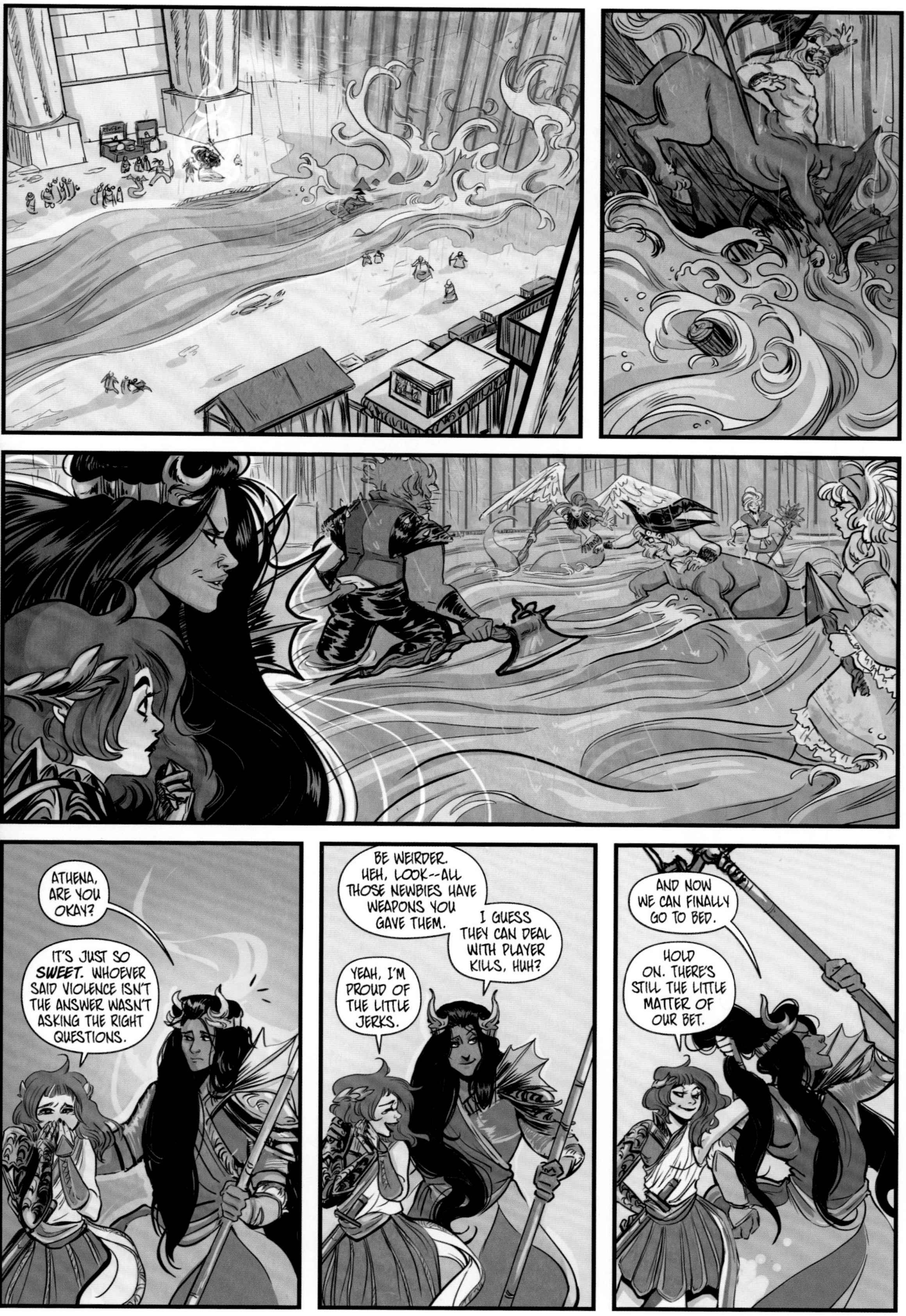
ATHENA, ARE YOU OKAY?
IT'S JUST SO **SWEET**. WHOEVER SAID VIOLENCE ISN'T THE ANSWER WASN'T ASKING THE RIGHT QUESTIONS.
BE WEIRDER. HEH, LOOK--ALL THOSE NEWBIES HAVE WEAPONS YOU GAVE THEM.
I GUESS THEY CAN DEAL WITH PLAYER KILLS, HUH?
YEAH, I'M PROUD OF THE LITTLE JERKS.
AND NOW WE CAN FINALLY GO TO BED.
HOLD ON. THERE'S STILL THE LITTLE MATTER OF OUR BET.

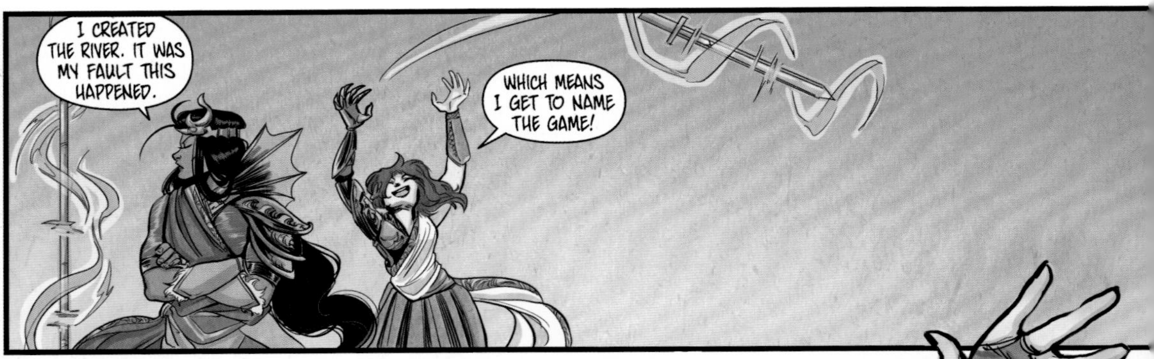
I CREATED THE RIVER. IT WAS MY FAULT THIS HAPPENED.
WHICH MEANS I GET TO NAME THE GAME!

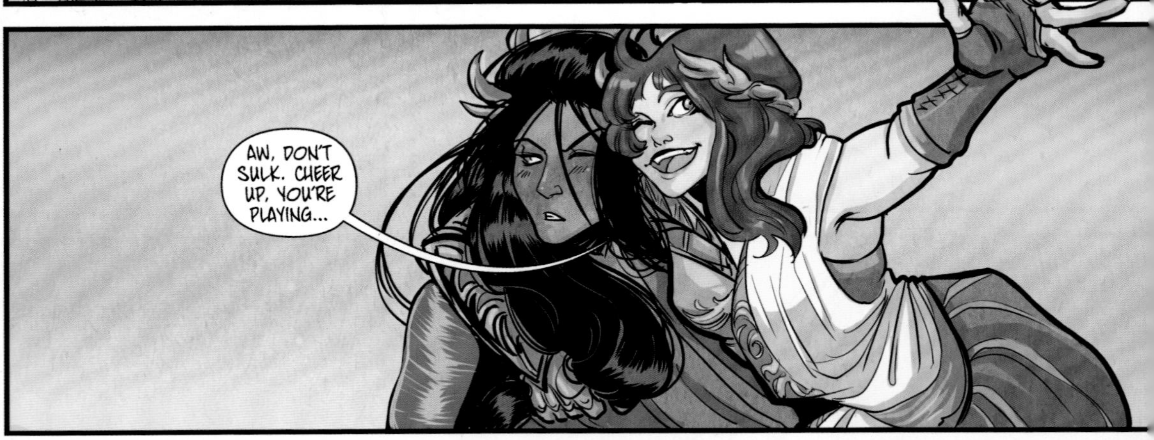
AW, DON'T SULK. CHEER UP, YOU'RE PLAYING...

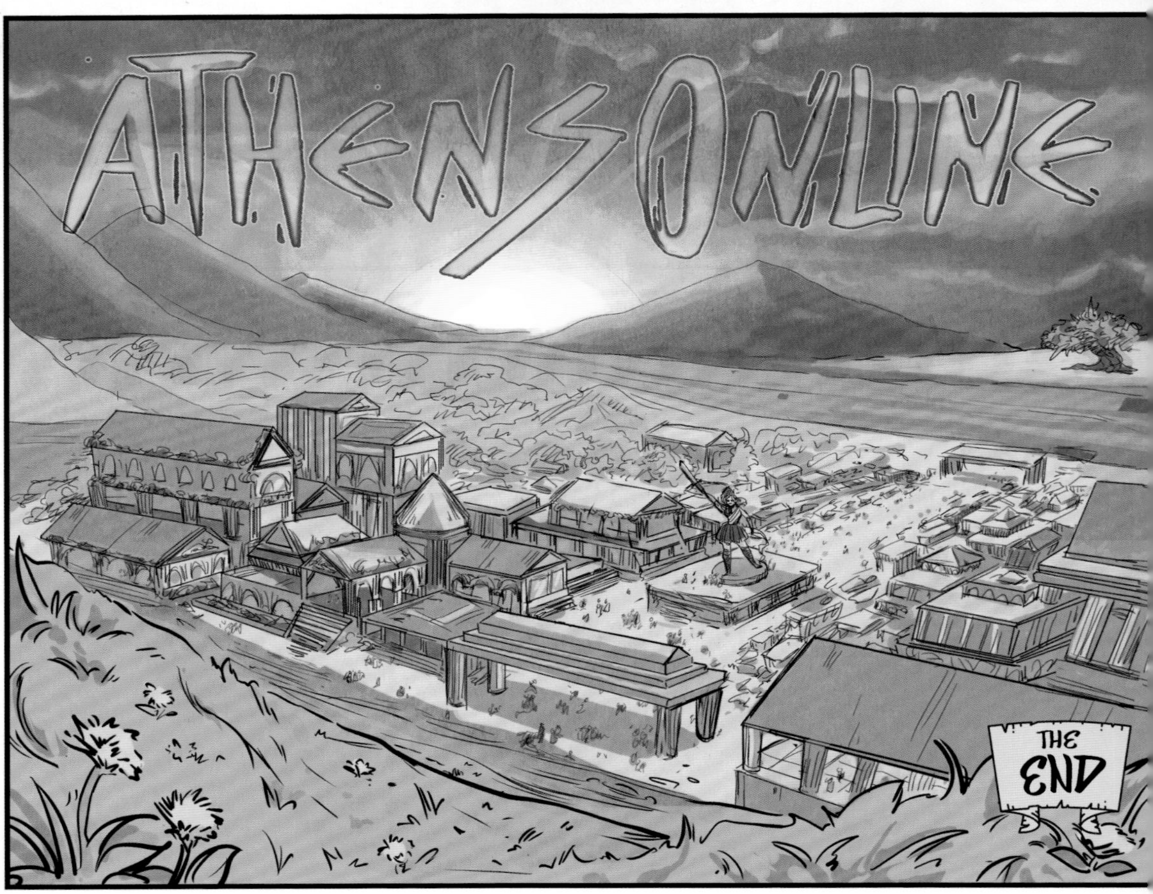
ATHENS ONLINE
THE END

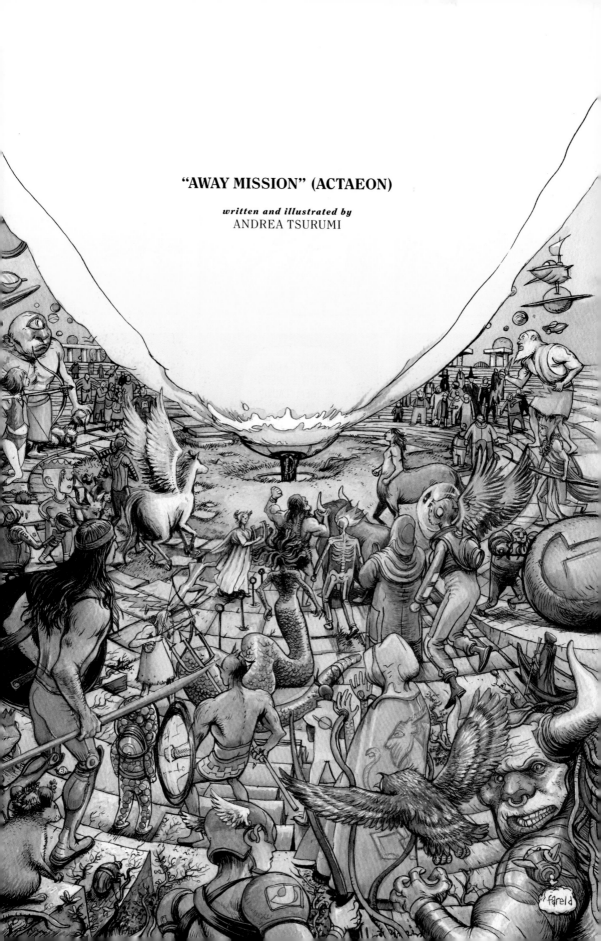

"AWAY MISSION" (ACTAEON)

written and illustrated by
ANDREA TSURUMI

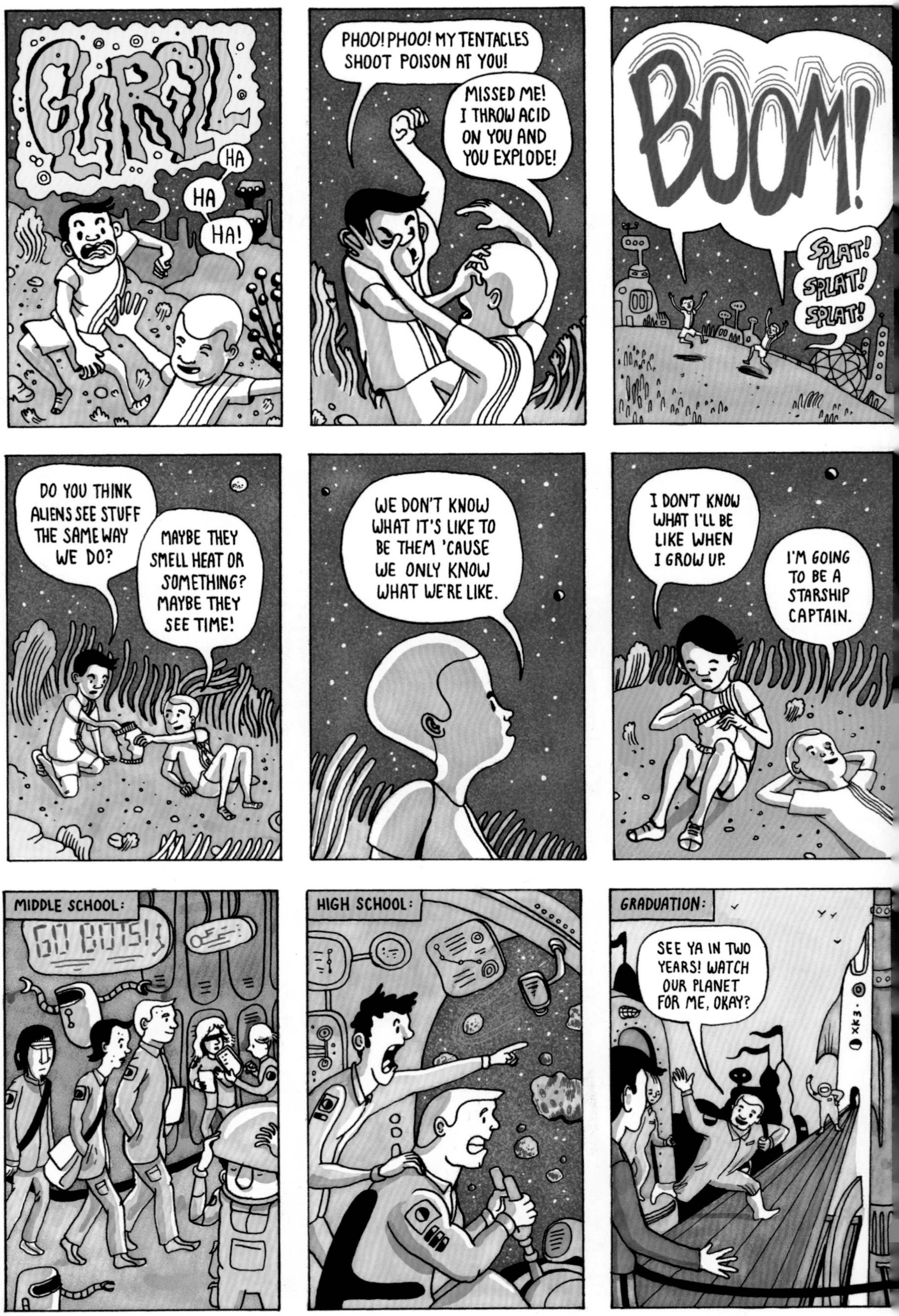
GARGL
HA
HA
HA!
PHOO! PHOO! MY TENTACLES SHOOT POISON AT YOU!
MISSED ME! I THROW ACID ON YOU AND YOU EXPLODE!
BOOM!
SPLAT! SPLAT! SPLAT!
DO YOU THINK ALIENS SEE STUFF THE SAME WAY WE DO?
MAYBE THEY SMELL HEAT OR SOMETHING? MAYBE THEY SEE TIME!
WE DON'T KNOW WHAT IT'S LIKE TO BE THEM 'CAUSE WE ONLY KNOW WHAT WE'RE LIKE.
I DON'T KNOW WHAT I'LL BE LIKE WHEN I GROW UP.
I'M GOING TO BE A STARSHIP CAPTAIN.
MIDDLE SCHOOL:
GO BOTS!
HIGH SCHOOL:
GRADUATION:
SEE YA IN TWO YEARS! WATCH OUR PLANET FOR ME, OKAY?

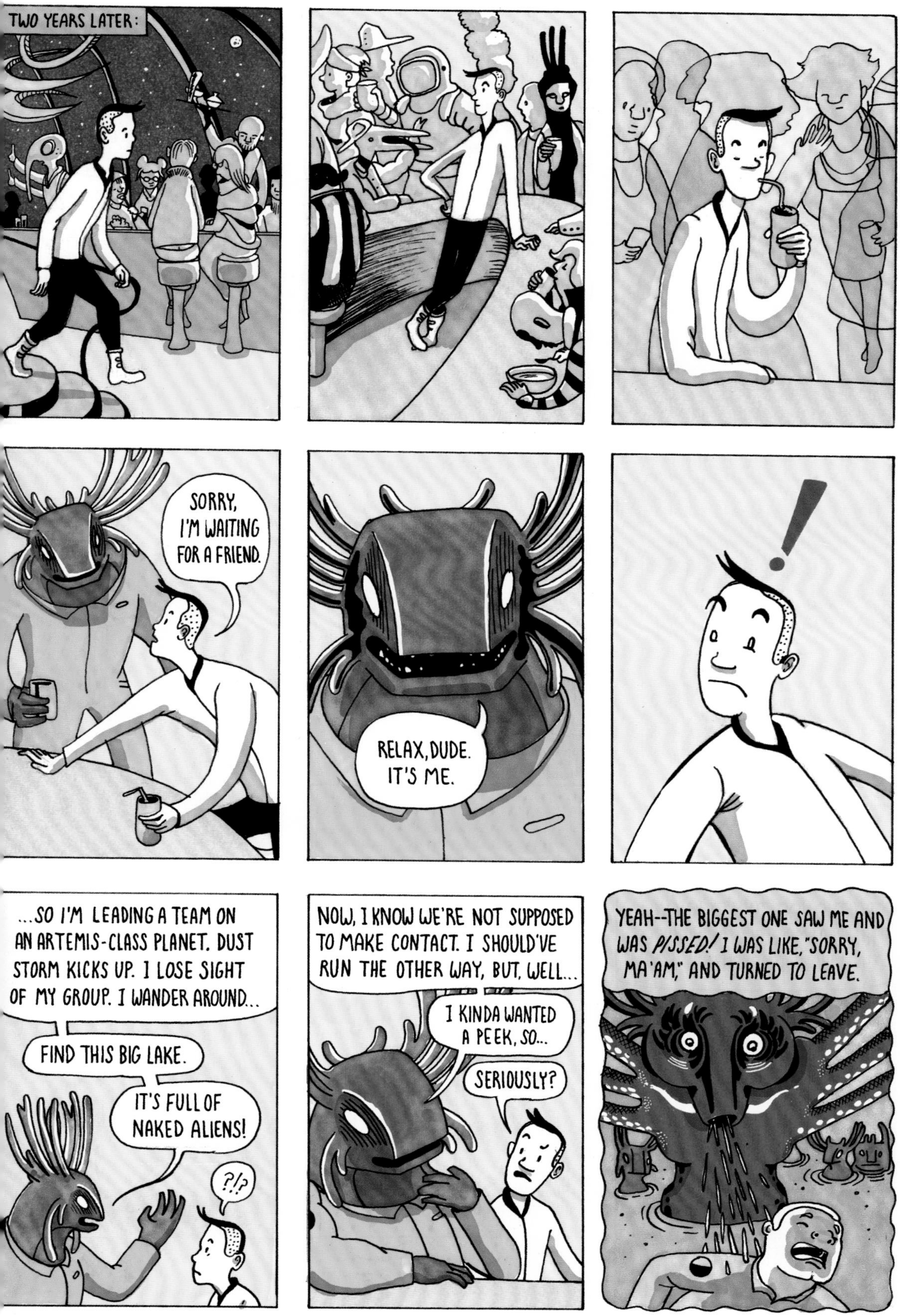
TWO YEARS LATER:
SORRY, I'M WAITING FOR A FRIEND.
RELAX, DUDE. IT'S ME.
!
...SO I'M LEADING A TEAM ON AN ARTEMIS-CLASS PLANET. DUST STORM KICKS UP. I LOSE SIGHT OF MY GROUP. I WANDER AROUND...
FIND THIS BIG LAKE.
IT'S FULL OF NAKED ALIENS!
?!?
NOW, I KNOW WE'RE NOT SUPPOSED TO MAKE CONTACT. I SHOULD'VE RUN THE OTHER WAY, BUT, WELL...
I KINDA WANTED A PEEK, SO...
SERIOUSLY?
YEAH--THE BIGGEST ONE SAW ME AND WAS *PISSED!* I WAS LIKE, "SORRY, MA'AM," AND TURNED TO LEAVE.

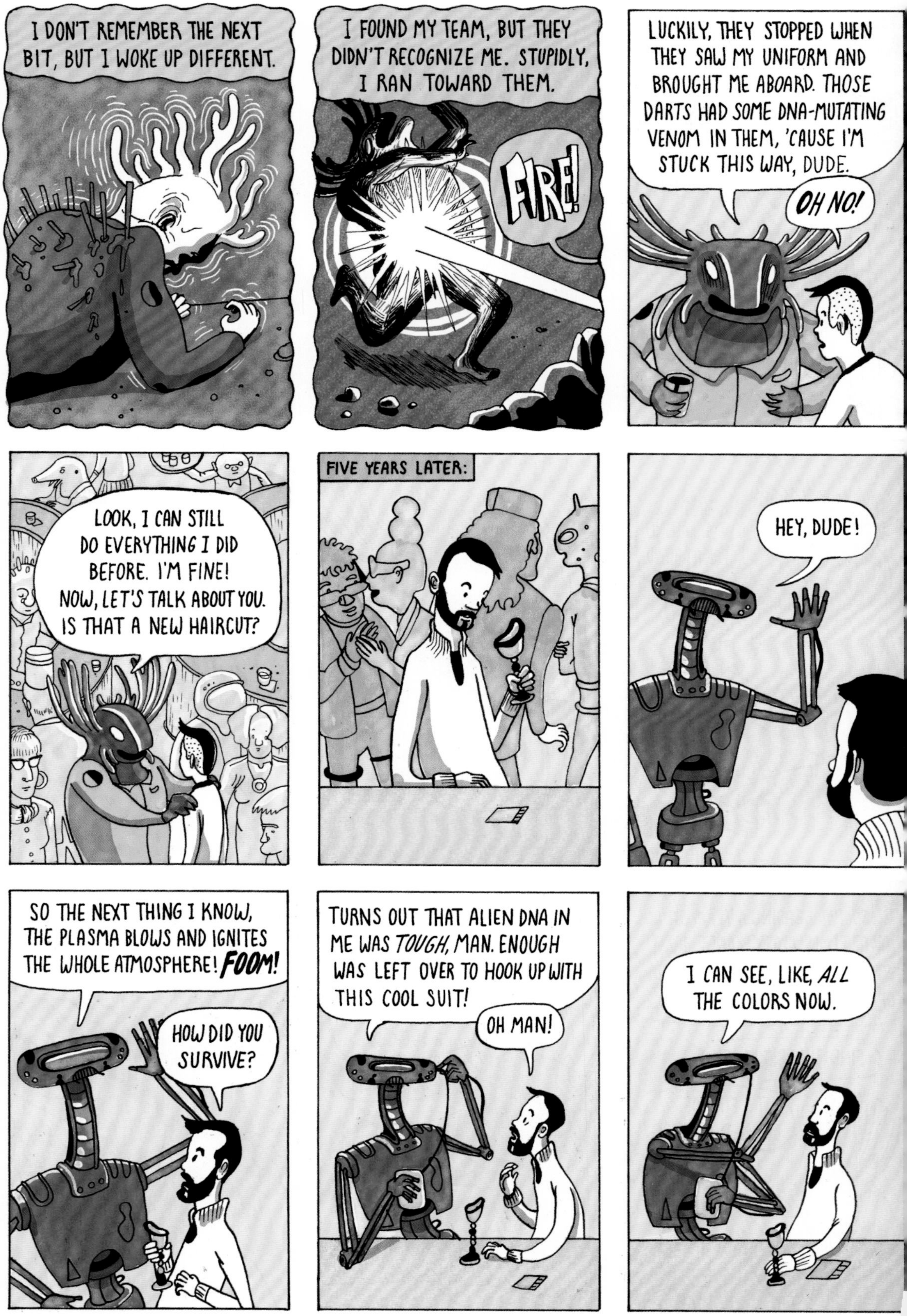
I DON'T REMEMBER THE NEXT BIT, BUT I WOKE UP DIFFERENT.
I FOUND MY TEAM, BUT THEY DIDN'T RECOGNIZE ME. STUPIDLY, I RAN TOWARD THEM.
FIRE!
LUCKILY, THEY STOPPED WHEN THEY SAW MY UNIFORM AND BROUGHT ME ABOARD. THOSE DARTS HAD SOME DNA-MUTATING VENOM IN THEM, 'CAUSE I'M STUCK THIS WAY, DUDE.
OH NO!
LOOK, I CAN STILL DO EVERYTHING I DID BEFORE. I'M FINE! NOW, LET'S TALK ABOUT YOU. IS THAT A NEW HAIRCUT?
FIVE YEARS LATER:
HEY, DUDE!
SO THE NEXT THING I KNOW, THE PLASMA BLOWS AND IGNITES THE WHOLE ATMOSPHERE! FOOM!
HOW DID YOU SURVIVE?
TURNS OUT THAT ALIEN DNA IN ME WAS TOUGH, MAN. ENOUGH WAS LEFT OVER TO HOOK UP WITH THIS COOL SUIT!
OH MAN!
I CAN SEE, LIKE, ALL THE COLORS NOW.

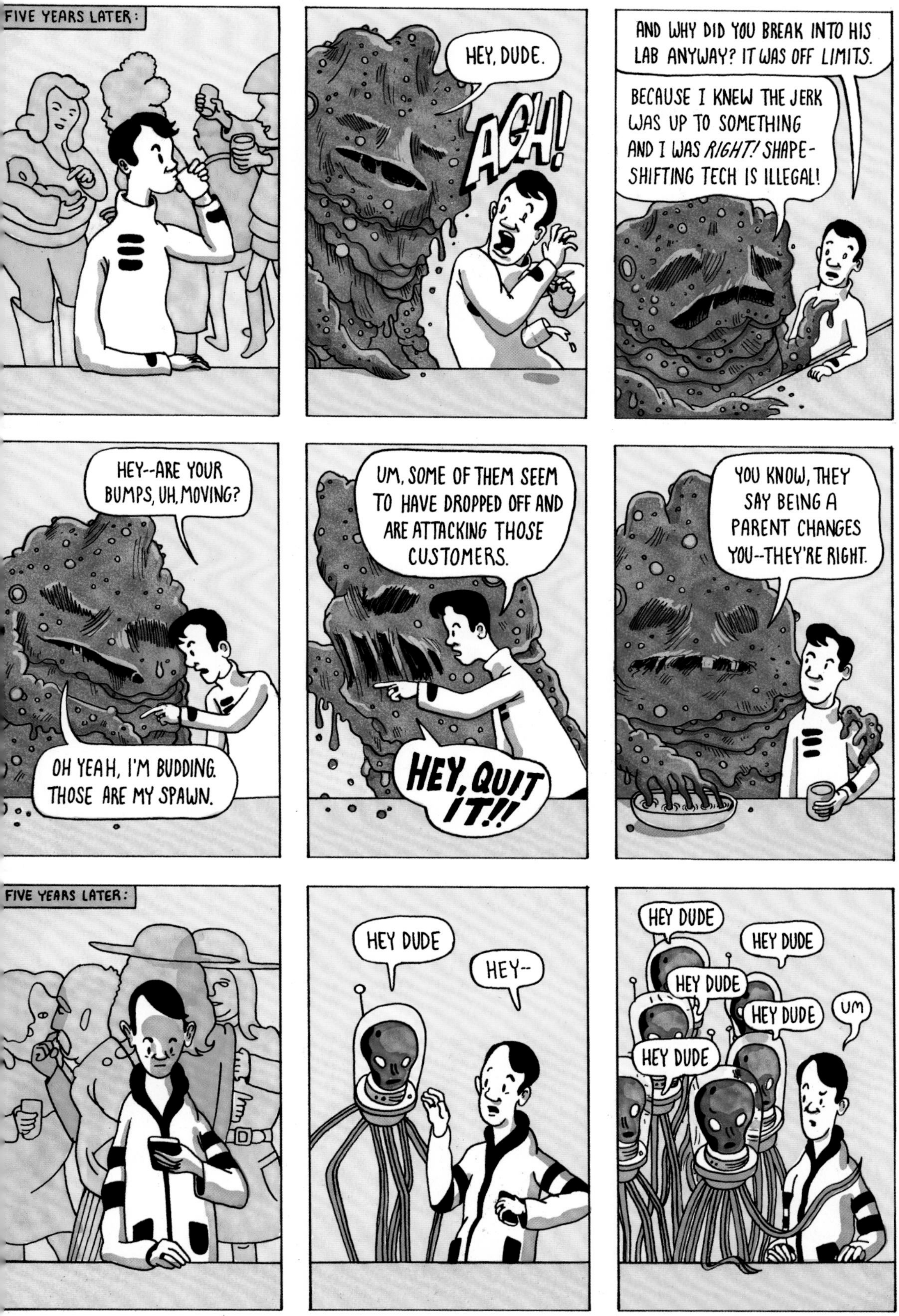
FIVE YEARS LATER:
HEY, DUDE.
AGH!
AND WHY DID YOU BREAK INTO HIS LAB ANYWAY? IT WAS OFF LIMITS.
BECAUSE I KNEW THE JERK WAS UP TO SOMETHING AND I WAS RIGHT! SHAPE-SHIFTING TECH IS ILLEGAL!
HEY--ARE YOUR BUMPS, UH, MOVING?
OH YEAH, I'M BUDDING. THOSE ARE MY SPAWN.
UM, SOME OF THEM SEEM TO HAVE DROPPED OFF AND ARE ATTACKING THOSE CUSTOMERS.
HEY, QUIT IT!!
YOU KNOW, THEY SAY BEING A PARENT CHANGES YOU--THEY'RE RIGHT.
FIVE YEARS LATER:
HEY DUDE
HEY--
HEY DUDE
HEY DUDE
HEY DUDE
HEY DUDE
UM
HEY DUDE

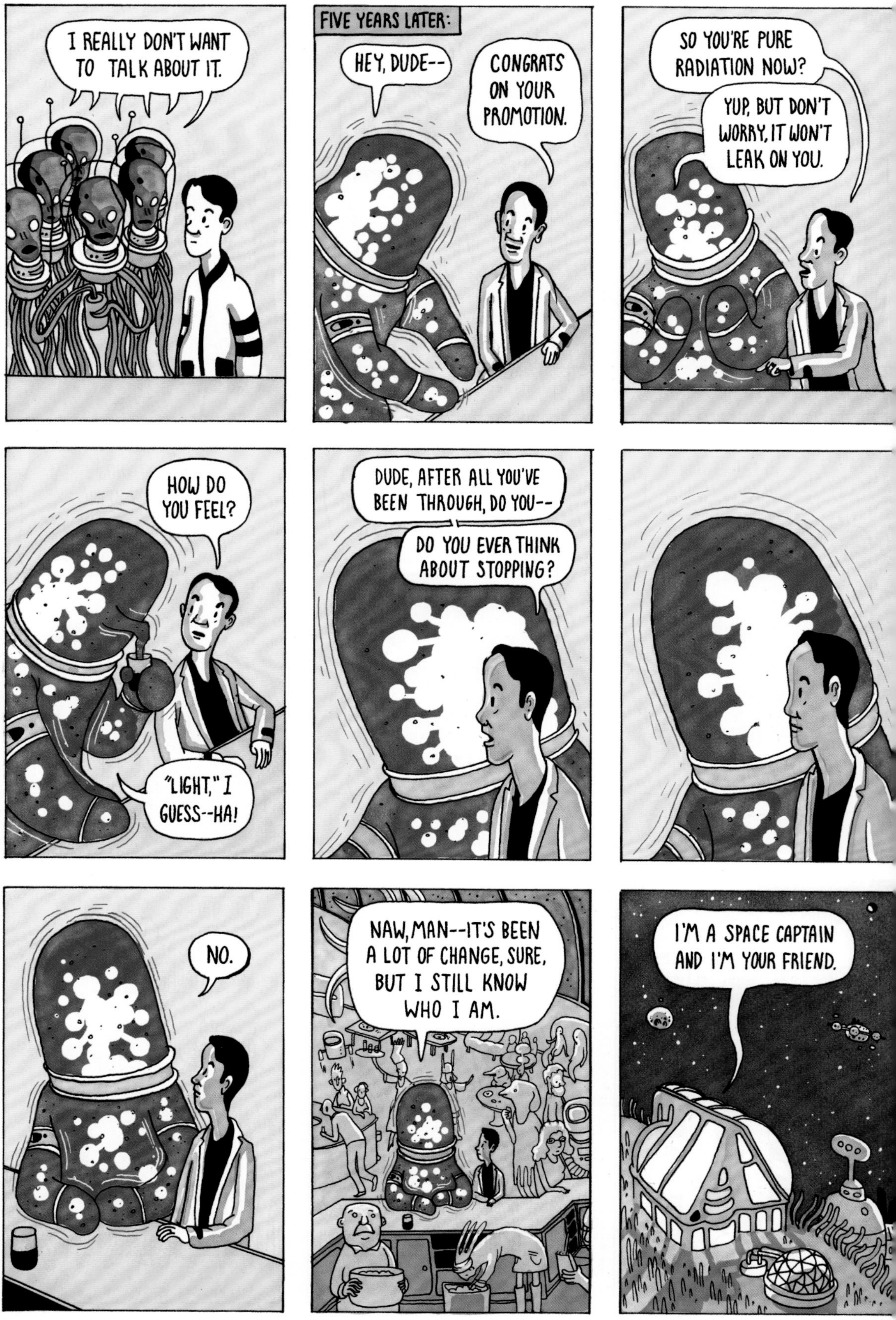
I REALLY DON'T WANT TO TALK ABOUT IT.
FIVE YEARS LATER:
HEY, DUDE--
CONGRATS ON YOUR PROMOTION.
SO YOU'RE PURE RADIATION NOW?
YUP, BUT DON'T WORRY, IT WON'T LEAK ON YOU.
HOW DO YOU FEEL?
"LIGHT," I GUESS--HA!
DUDE, AFTER ALL YOU'VE BEEN THROUGH, DO YOU--
DO YOU EVER THINK ABOUT STOPPING?
NO.
NAW, MAN--IT'S BEEN A LOT OF CHANGE, SURE, BUT I STILL KNOW WHO I AM.
I'M A SPACE CAPTAIN AND I'M YOUR FRIEND.

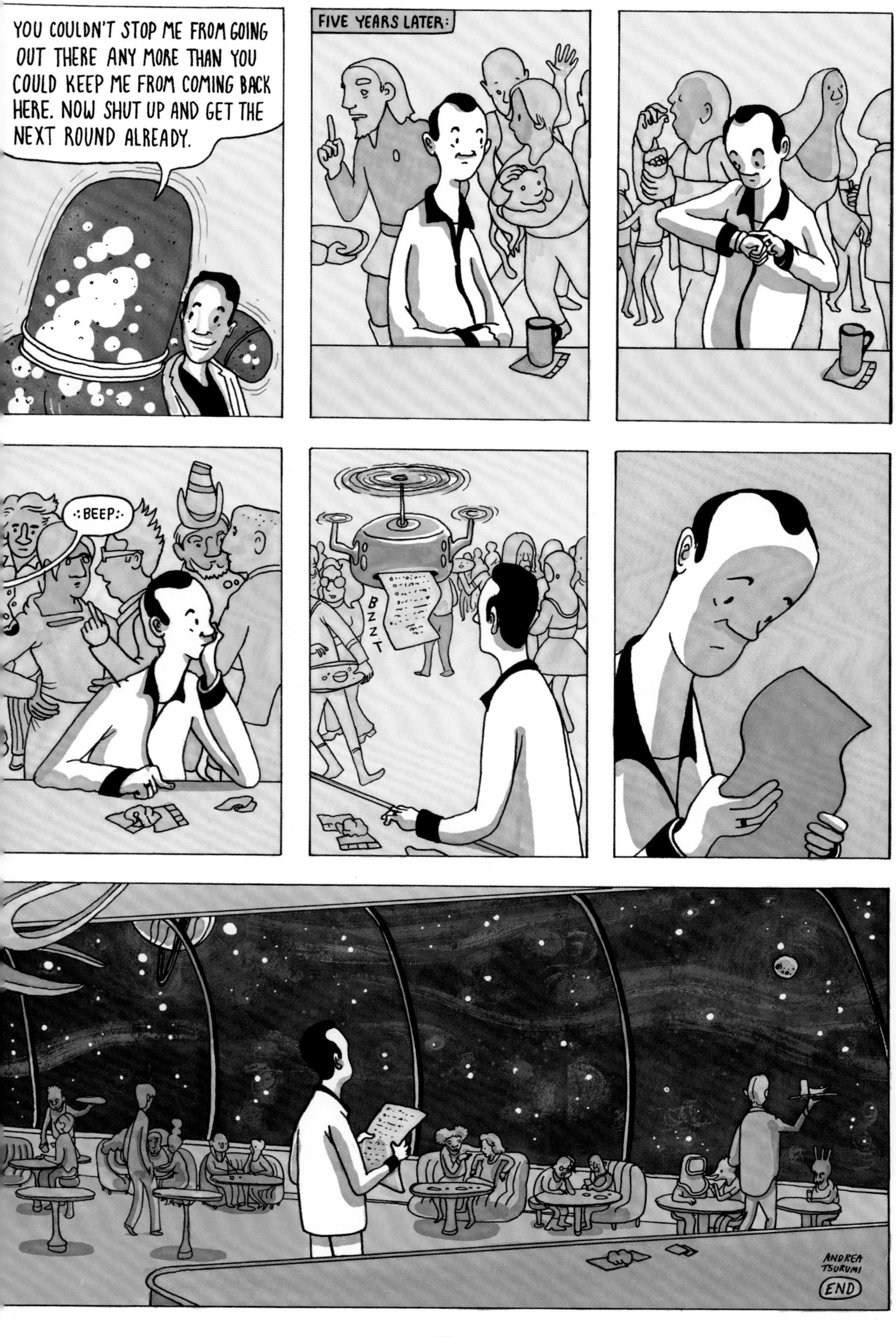
YOU COULDN'T STOP ME FROM GOING OUT THERE ANY MORE THAN YOU COULD KEEP ME FROM COMING BACK HERE. NOW SHUT UP AND GET THE NEXT ROUND ALREADY.
FIVE YEARS LATER:
BEEP
BZZT
ANDREA TSURUMI
END

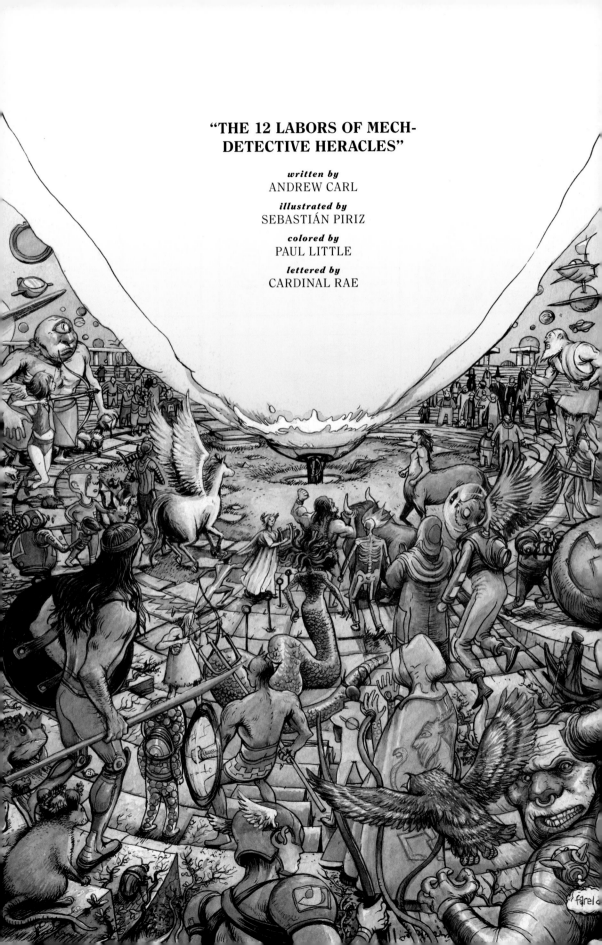

"THE 12 LABORS OF MECH-DETECTIVE HERACLES"

written by
ANDREW CARL

illustrated by
SEBASTIÁN PIRIZ

colored by
PAUL LITTLE

lettered by
CARDINAL RAE

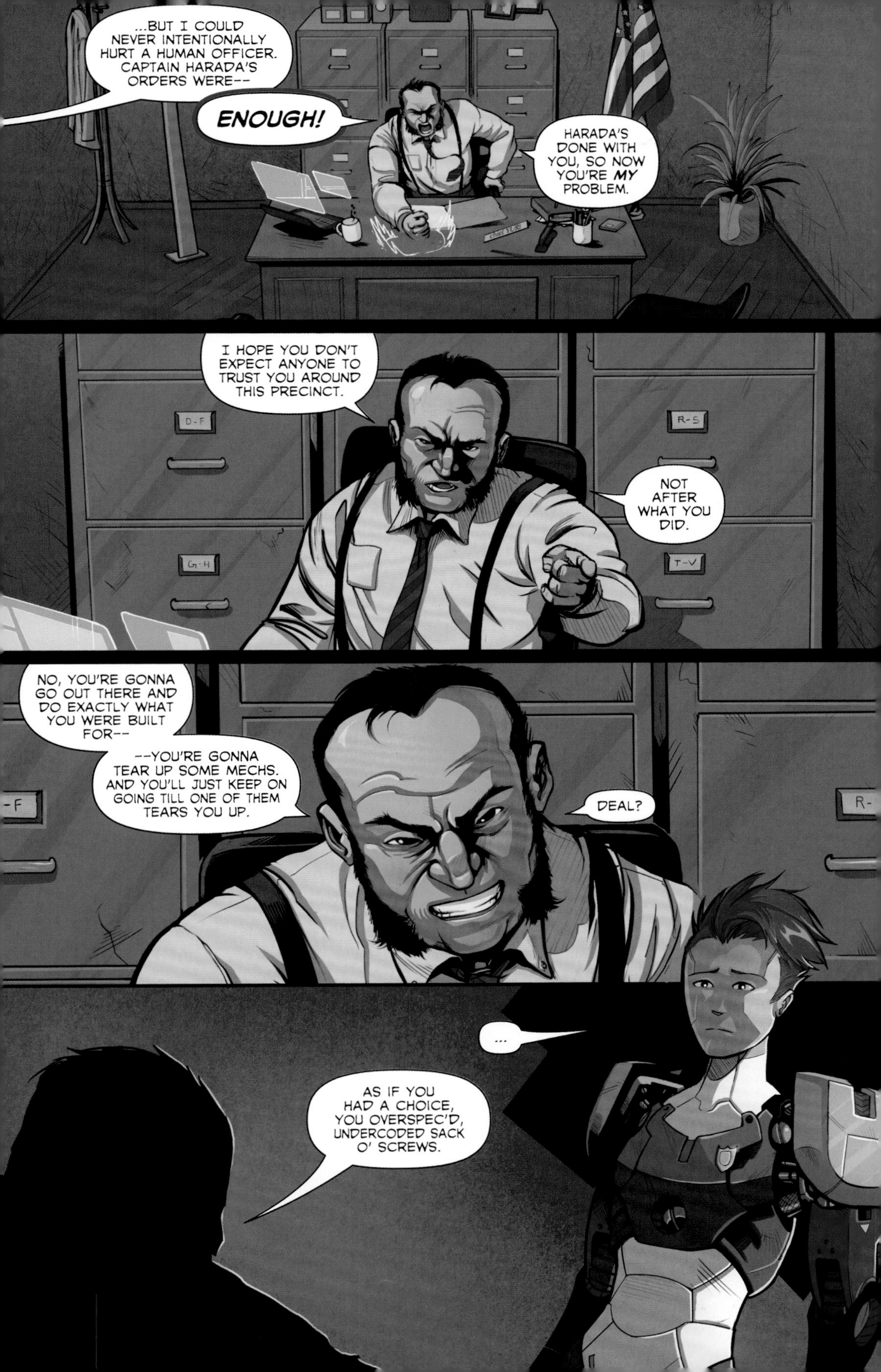

...BUT I COULD NEVER INTENTIONALLY HURT A HUMAN OFFICER. CAPTAIN HARADA'S ORDERS WERE--
ENOUGH!
HARADA'S DONE WITH YOU, SO NOW YOU'RE MY PROBLEM.
I HOPE YOU DON'T EXPECT ANYONE TO TRUST YOU AROUND THIS PRECINCT.
NOT AFTER WHAT YOU DID.
NO, YOU'RE GONNA GO OUT THERE AND DO EXACTLY WHAT YOU WERE BUILT FOR--
--YOU'RE GONNA TEAR UP SOME MECHS. AND YOU'LL JUST KEEP ON GOING TILL ONE OF THEM TEARS YOU UP.
DEAL?
...
AS IF YOU HAD A CHOICE, YOU OVERSPEC'D, UNDERCODED SACK O' SCREWS.

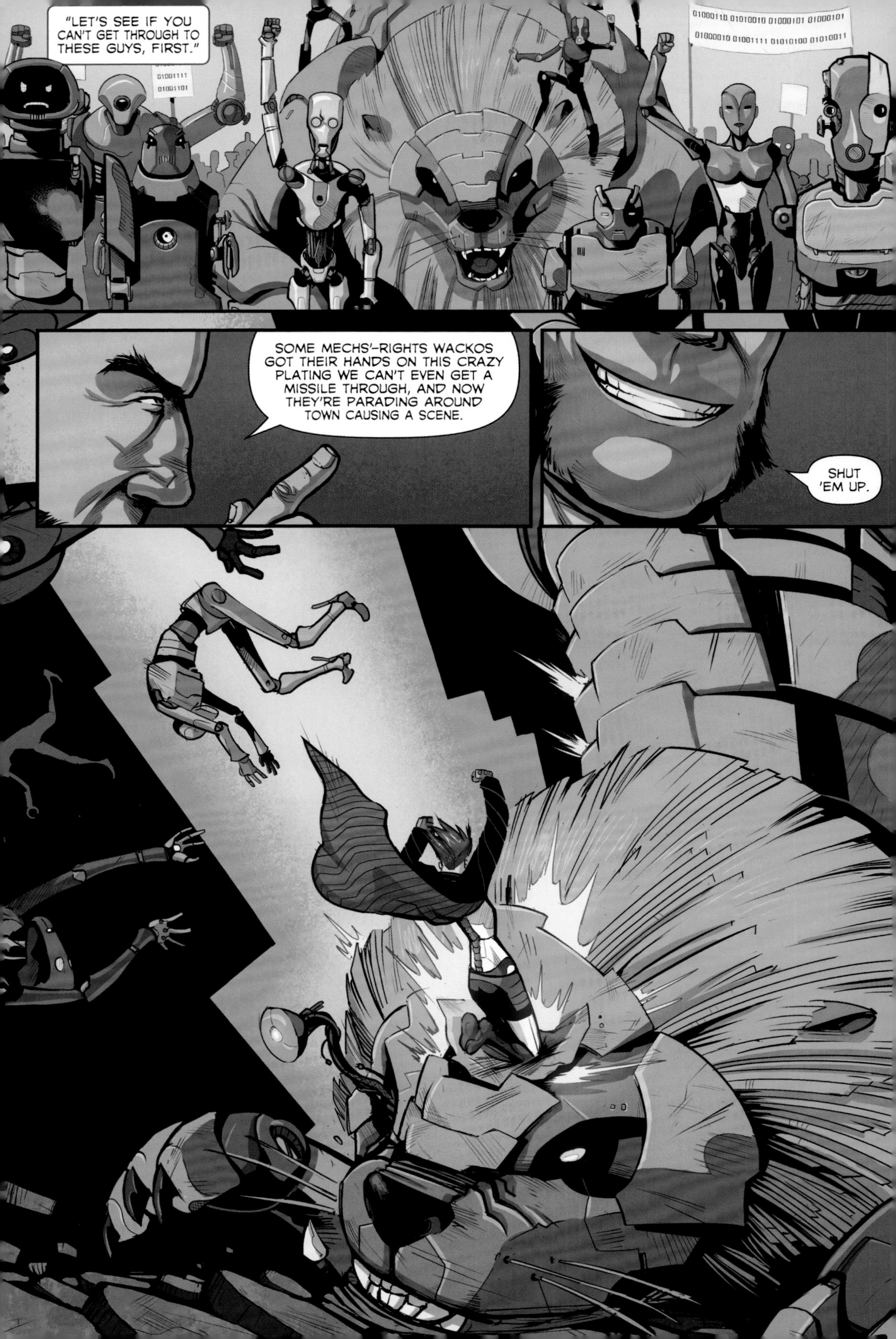
"LET'S SEE IF YOU CAN'T GET THROUGH TO THESE GUYS, FIRST."
01001111 01001101
01000110 01010010 01000101 01000101
01000010 01001111 01010100 01010011
SOME MECHS'-RIGHTS WACKOS GOT THEIR HANDS ON THIS CRAZY PLATING WE CAN'T EVEN GET A MISSILE THROUGH, AND NOW THEY'RE PARADING AROUND TOWN CAUSING A SCENE.
SHUT 'EM UP.

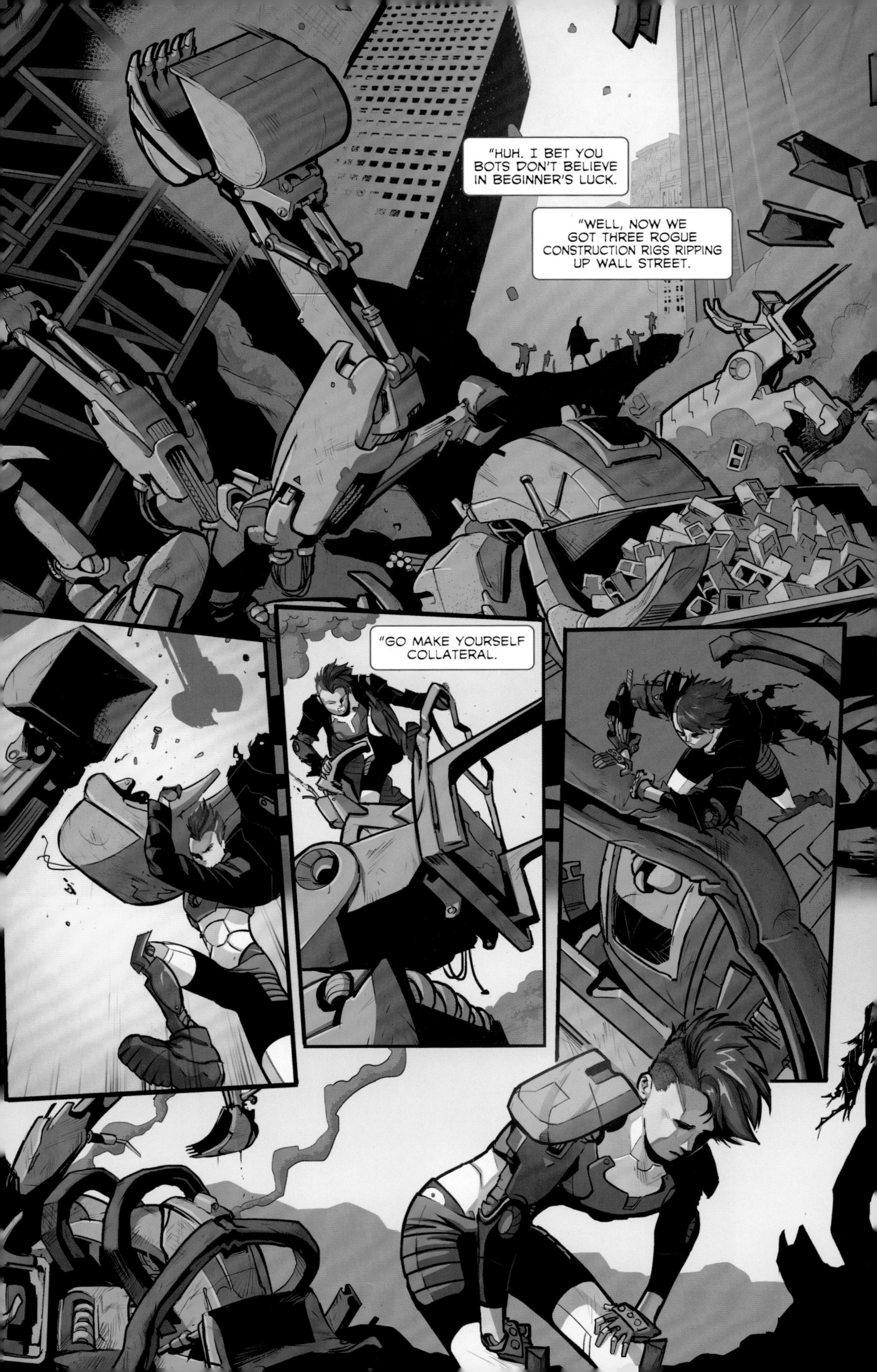
"HUH. I BET YOU BOTS DON'T BELIEVE IN BEGINNER'S LUCK.
"WELL, NOW WE GOT THREE ROGUE CONSTRUCTION RIGS RIPPING UP WALL STREET.
"GO MAKE YOURSELF COLLATERAL.

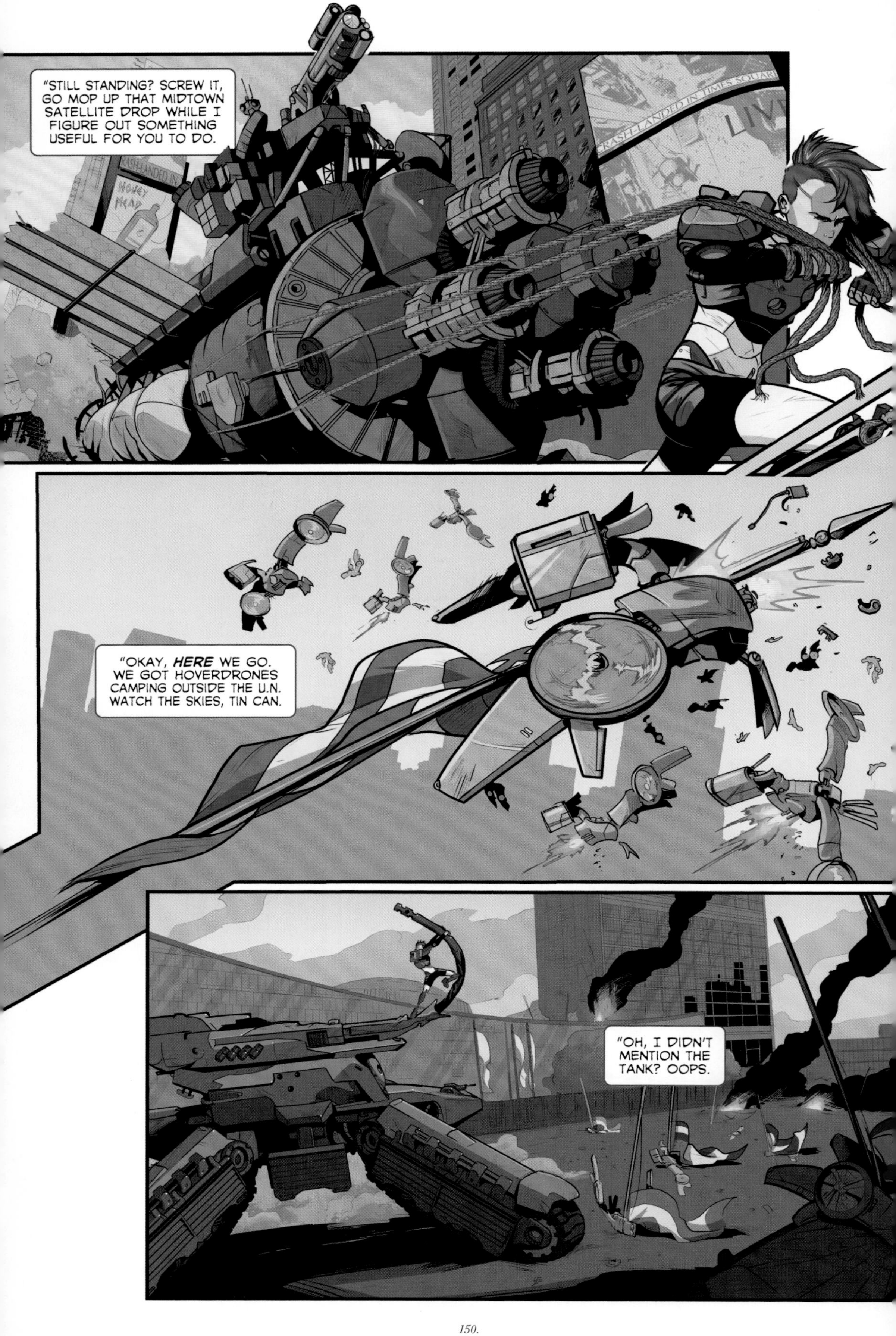
"STILL STANDING? SCREW IT, GO MOP UP THAT MIDTOWN SATELLITE DROP WHILE I FIGURE OUT SOMETHING USEFUL FOR YOU TO DO.
CRASH-LANDED IN TIMES SQUARE
CRASH-LANDED IN TIMES SQUARE
LIVE
HONEY MEAD
"OKAY, ***HERE*** WE GO. WE GOT HOVERDRONES CAMPING OUTSIDE THE U.N. WATCH THE SKIES, TIN CAN.
"OH, I DIDN'T MENTION THE TANK? OOPS.

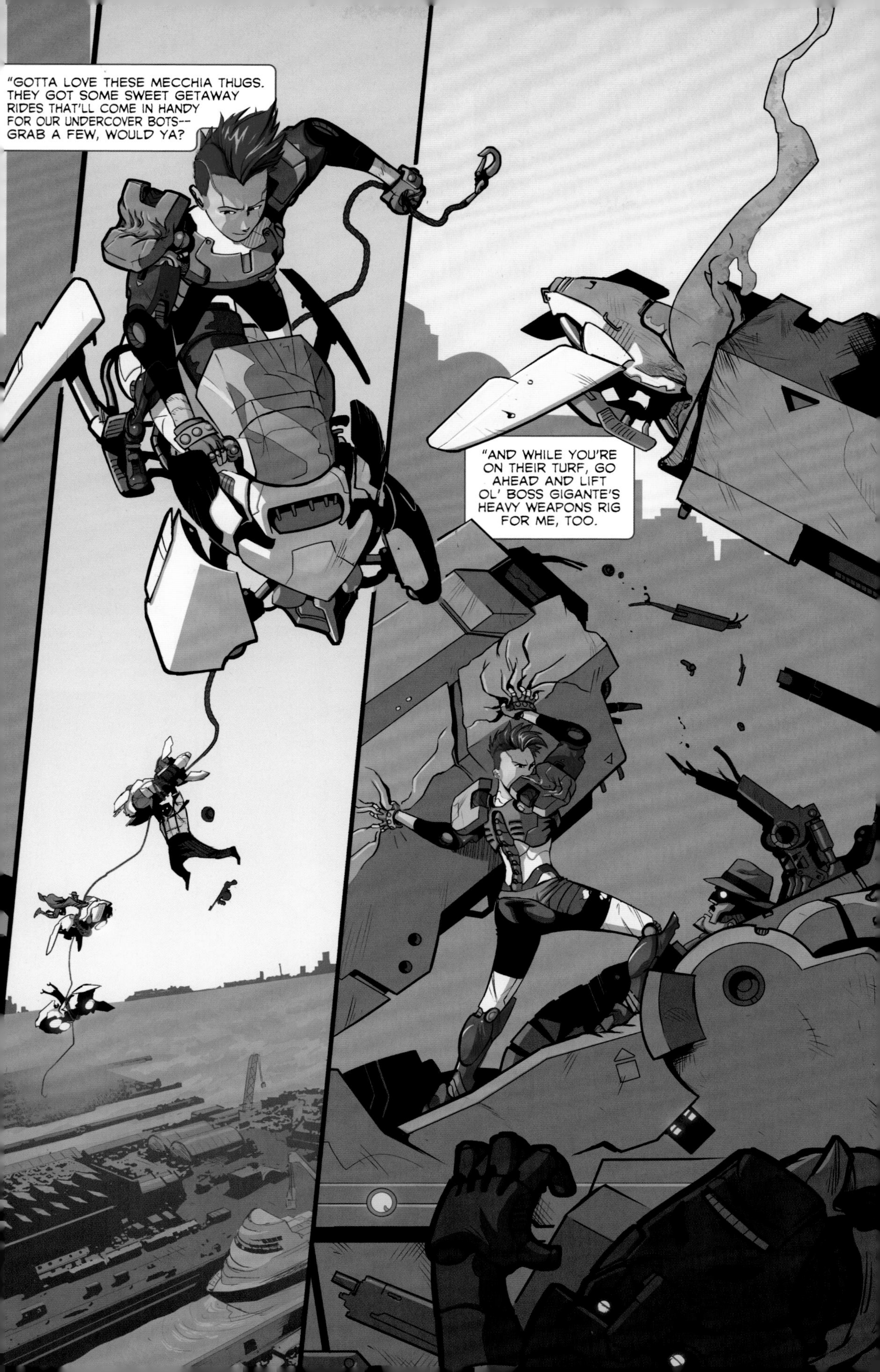
"GOTTA LOVE THESE MECCHIA THUGS. THEY GOT SOME SWEET GETAWAY RIDES THAT'LL COME IN HANDY FOR OUR UNDERCOVER BOTS-- GRAB A FEW, WOULD YA?
"AND WHILE YOU'RE ON THEIR TURF, GO AHEAD AND LIFT OL' BOSS GIGANTE'S HEAVY WEAPONS RIG FOR ME, TOO.

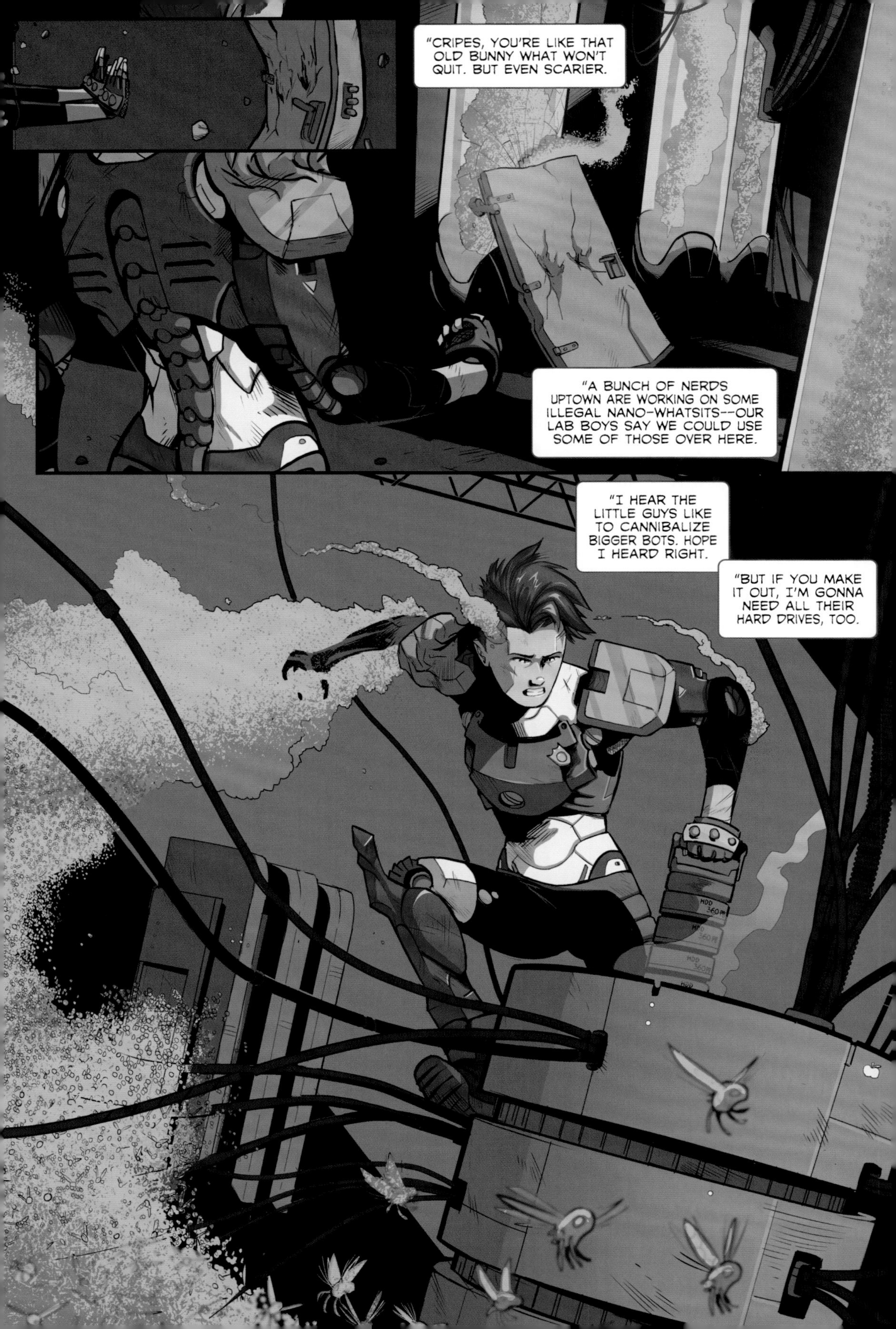
"CRIPES, YOU'RE LIKE THAT OLD BUNNY WHAT WON'T QUIT. BUT EVEN SCARIER.
"A BUNCH OF NERDS UPTOWN ARE WORKING ON SOME ILLEGAL NANO-WHATSITS--OUR LAB BOYS SAY WE COULD USE SOME OF THOSE OVER HERE.
"I HEAR THE LITTLE GUYS LIKE TO CANNIBALIZE BIGGER BOTS. HOPE I HEARD RIGHT.
"BUT IF YOU MAKE IT OUT, I'M GONNA NEED ALL THEIR HARD DRIVES, TOO.
HDD 360
HDD 360
HDD 360

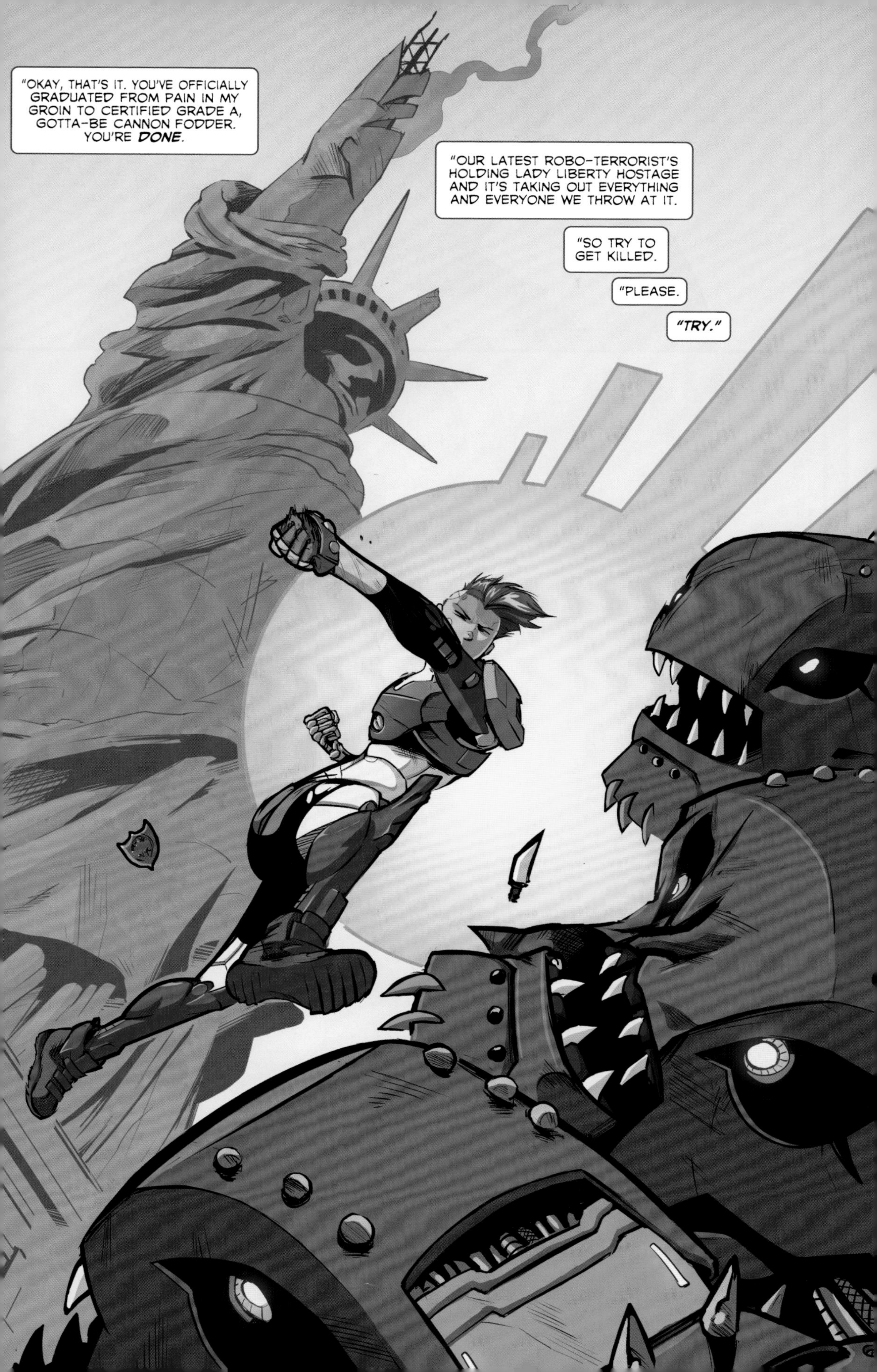
"OKAY, THAT'S IT. YOU'VE OFFICIALLY GRADUATED FROM PAIN IN MY GROIN TO CERTIFIED GRADE A, GOTTA-BE CANNON FODDER. YOU'RE ***DONE***.
"OUR LATEST ROBO-TERRORIST'S HOLDING LADY LIBERTY HOSTAGE AND IT'S TAKING OUT EVERYTHING AND EVERYONE WE THROW AT IT.
"SO TRY TO GET KILLED.
"PLEASE.
"TRY."

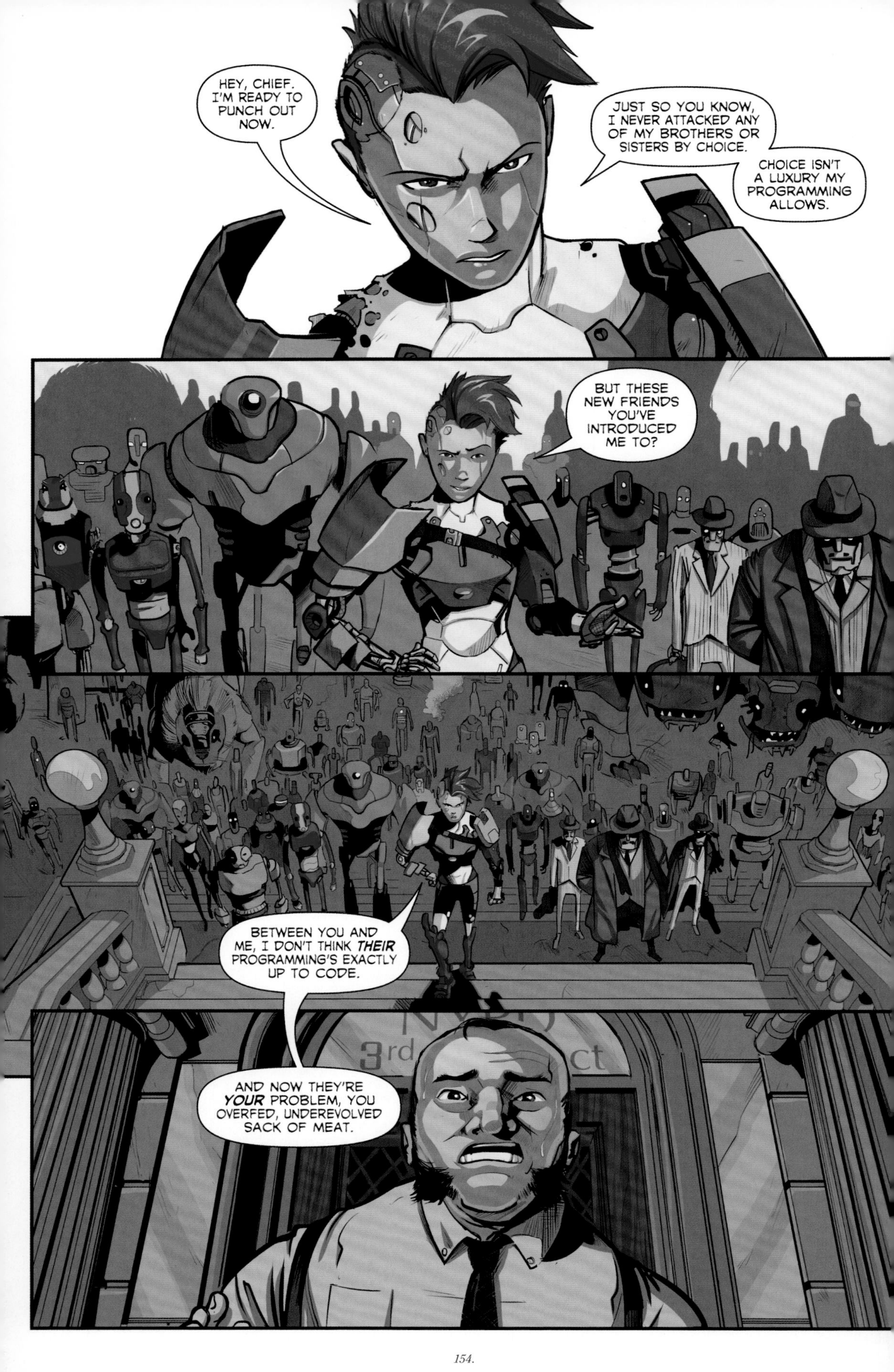
HEY, CHIEF. I'M READY TO PUNCH OUT NOW.
JUST SO YOU KNOW, I NEVER ATTACKED ANY OF MY BROTHERS OR SISTERS BY CHOICE.
CHOICE ISN'T A LUXURY MY PROGRAMMING ALLOWS.
BUT THESE NEW FRIENDS YOU'VE INTRODUCED ME TO?
BETWEEN YOU AND ME, I DON'T THINK ***THEIR*** PROGRAMMING'S EXACTLY UP TO CODE.
AND NOW THEY'RE ***YOUR*** PROBLEM, YOU OVERFED, UNDEREVOLVED SACK OF MEAT.

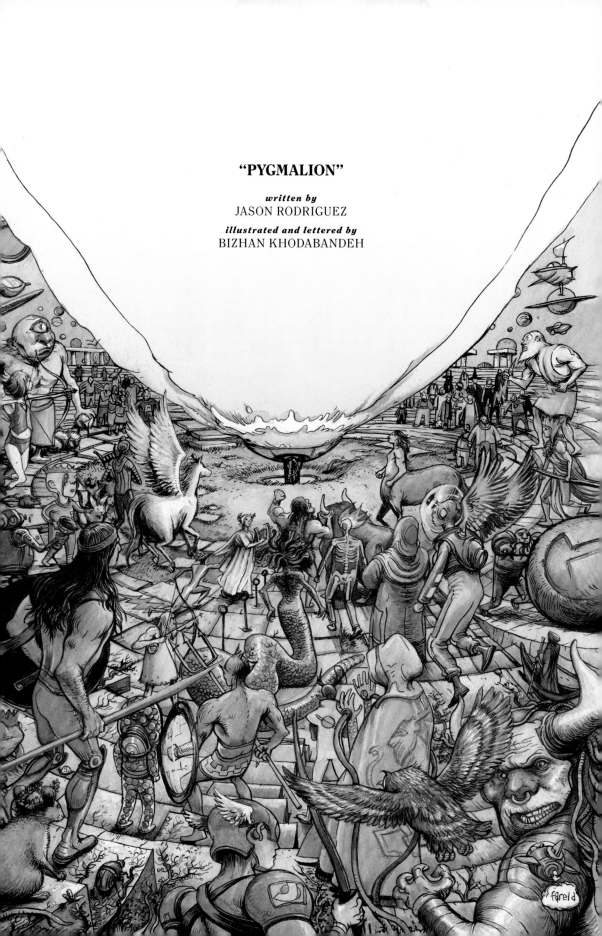

"PYGMALION"

written by
JASON RODRIGUEZ

illustrated and lettered by
BIZHAN KHODABANDEH

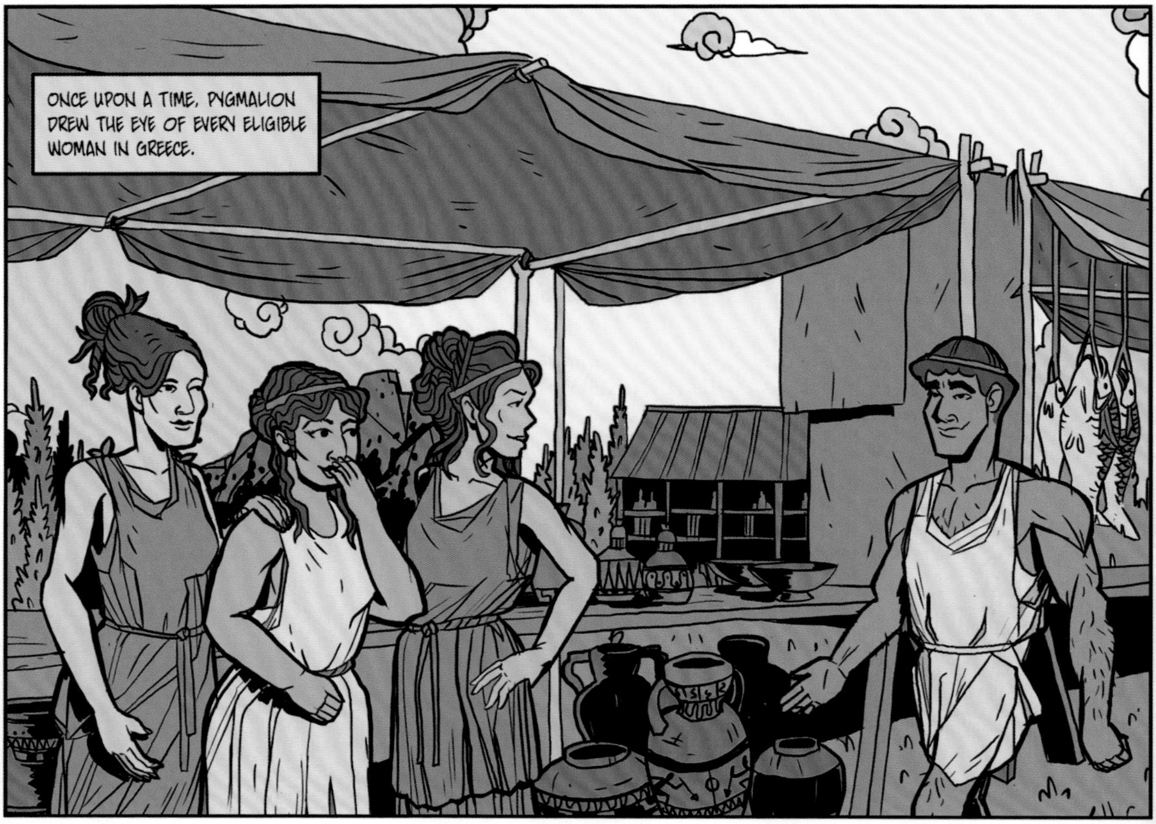
ONCE UPON A TIME, PYGMALION DREW THE EYE OF EVERY ELIGIBLE WOMAN IN GREECE.

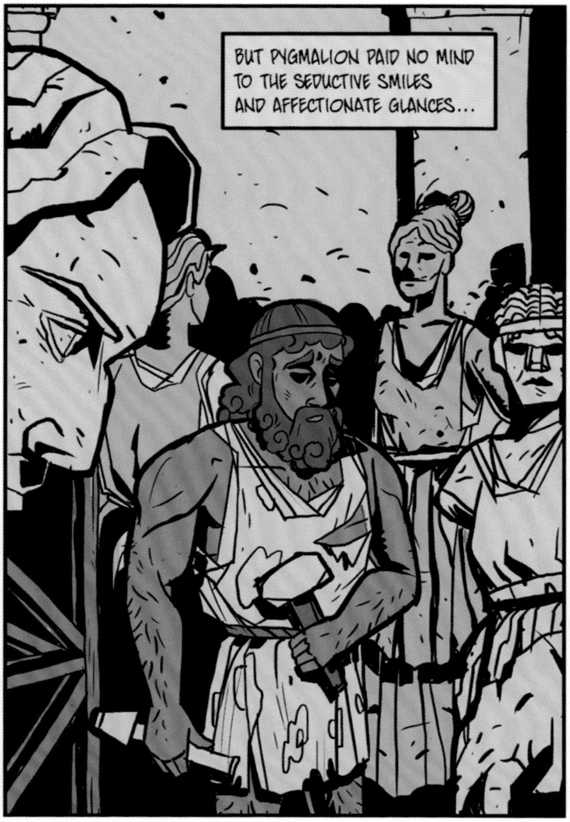
BUT PYGMALION PAID NO MIND TO THE SEDUCTIVE SMILES AND AFFECTIONATE GLANCES...

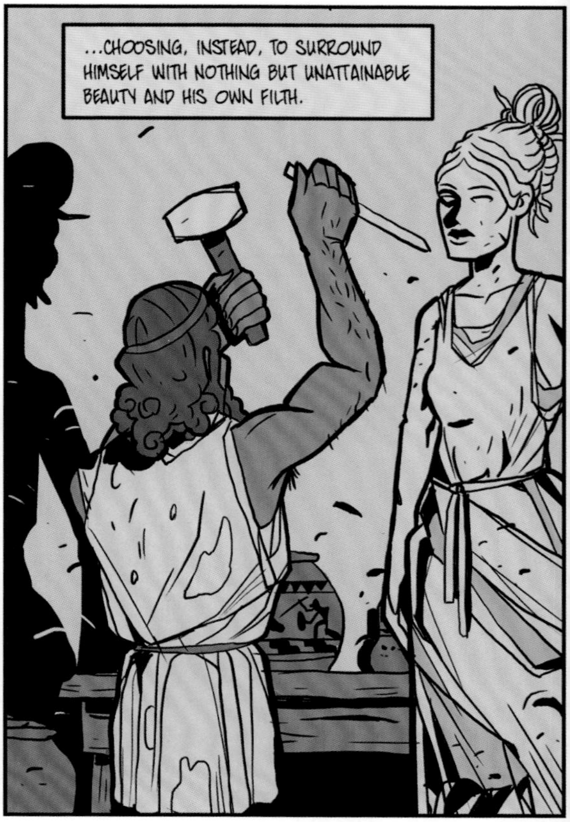
...CHOOSING, INSTEAD, TO SURROUND HIMSELF WITH NOTHING BUT UNATTAINABLE BEAUTY AND HIS OWN FILTH.

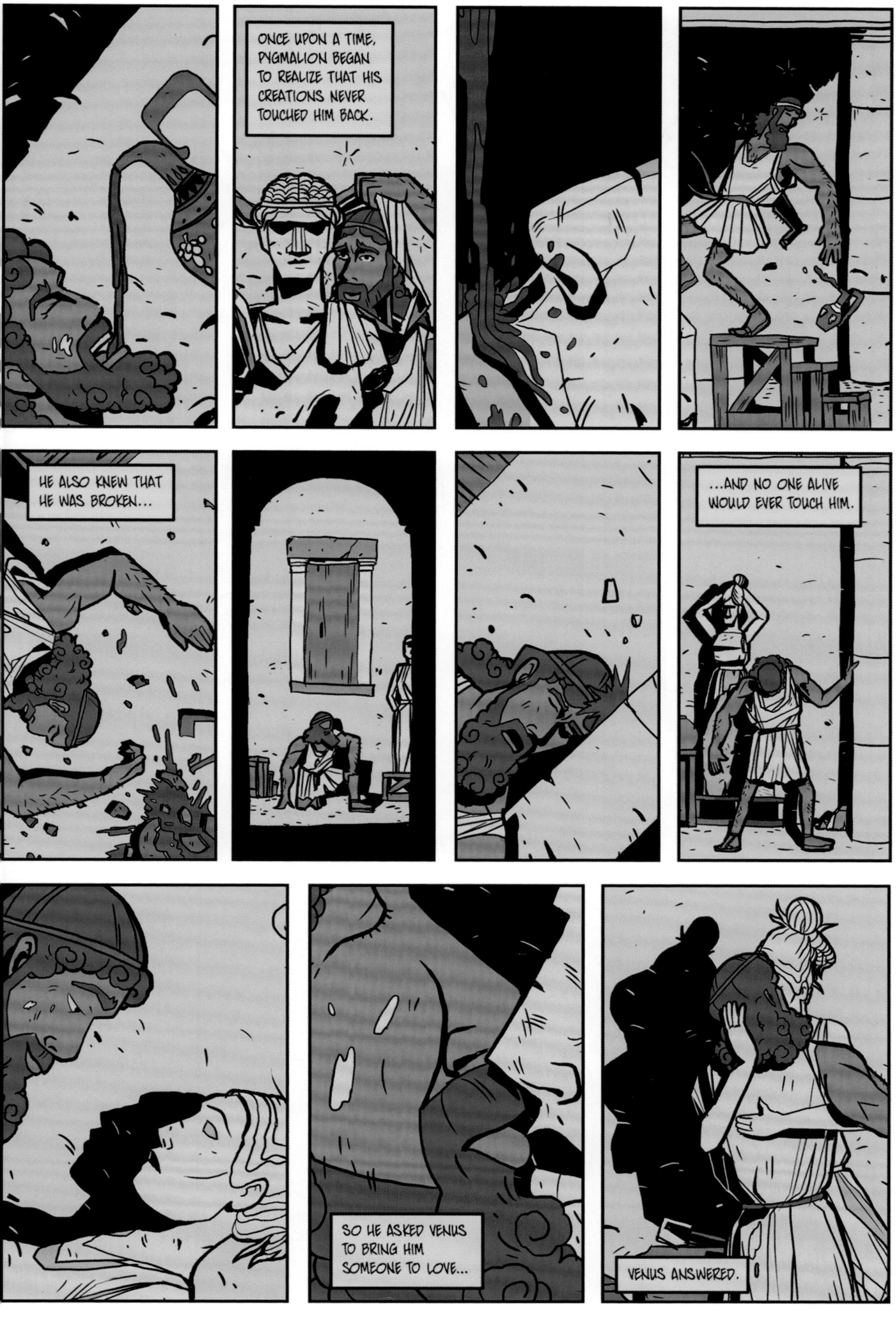
ONCE UPON A TIME, PYGMALION BEGAN TO REALIZE THAT HIS CREATIONS NEVER TOUCHED HIM BACK.
HE ALSO KNEW THAT HE WAS BROKEN...
...AND NO ONE ALIVE WOULD EVER TOUCH HIM.
SO HE ASKED VENUS TO BRING HIM SOMEONE TO LOVE...
VENUS ANSWERED.

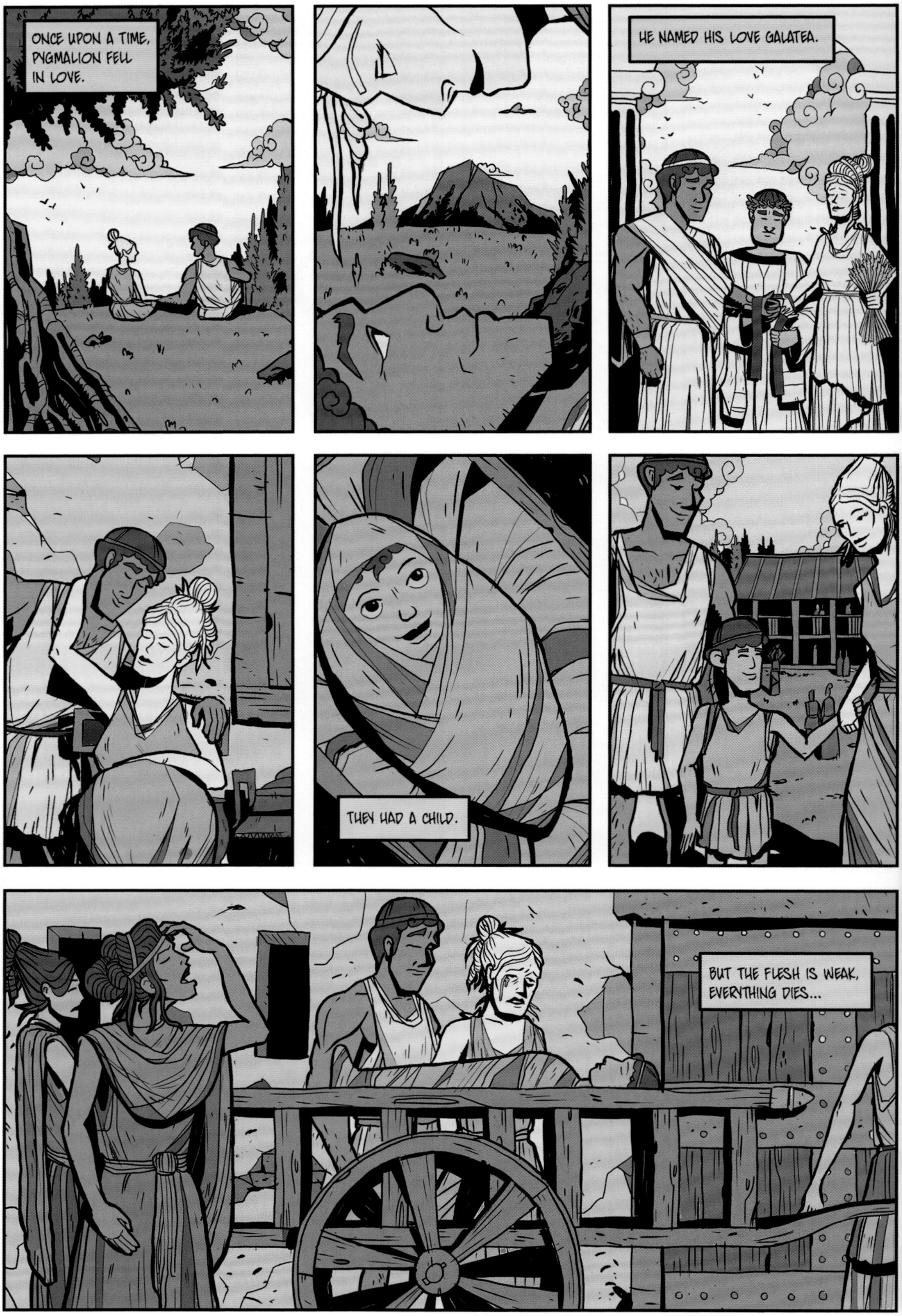
ONCE UPON A TIME, PYGMALION FELL IN LOVE.
HE NAMED HIS LOVE GALATEA.
THEY HAD A CHILD.
BUT THE FLESH IS WEAK, EVERYTHING DIES...

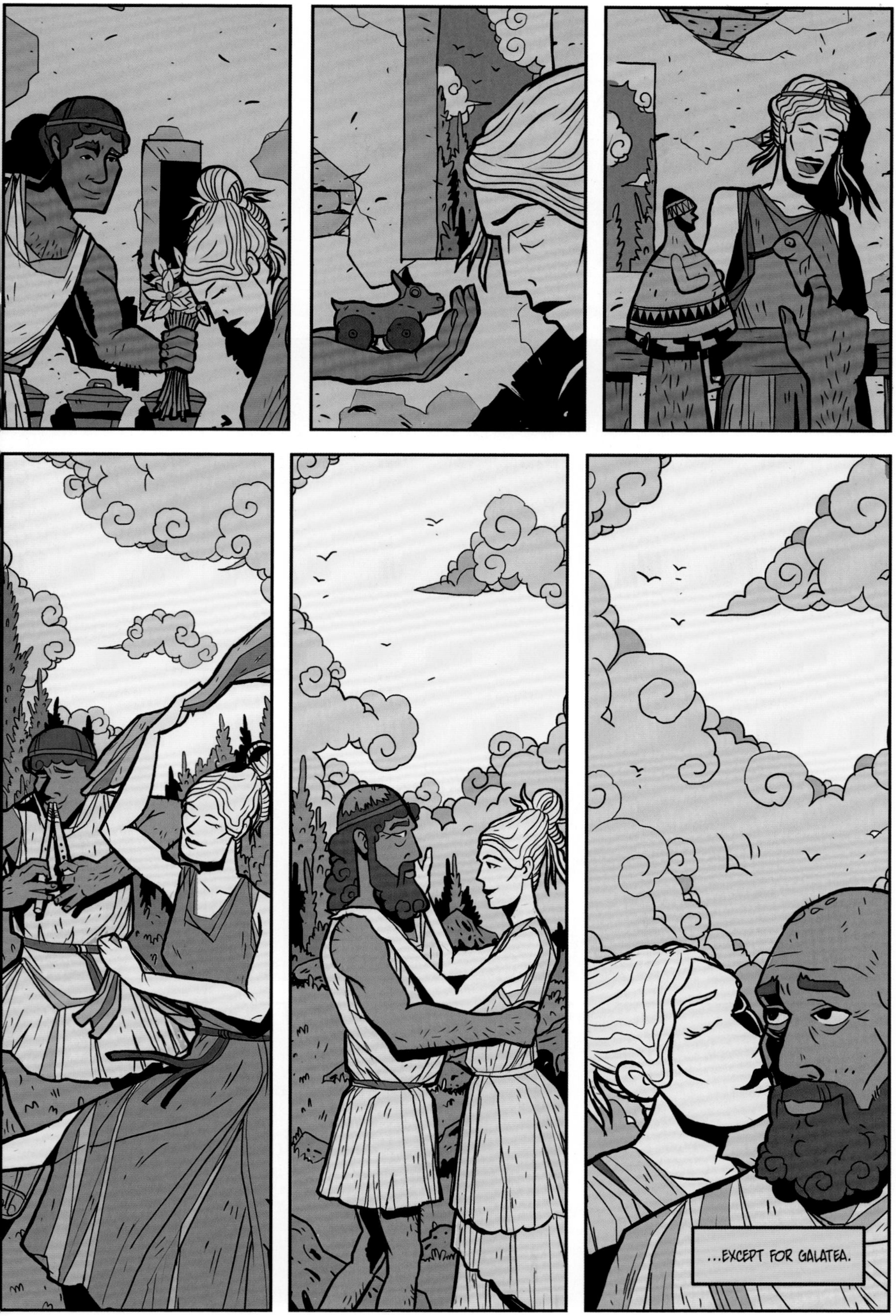
...EXCEPT FOR GALATEA.

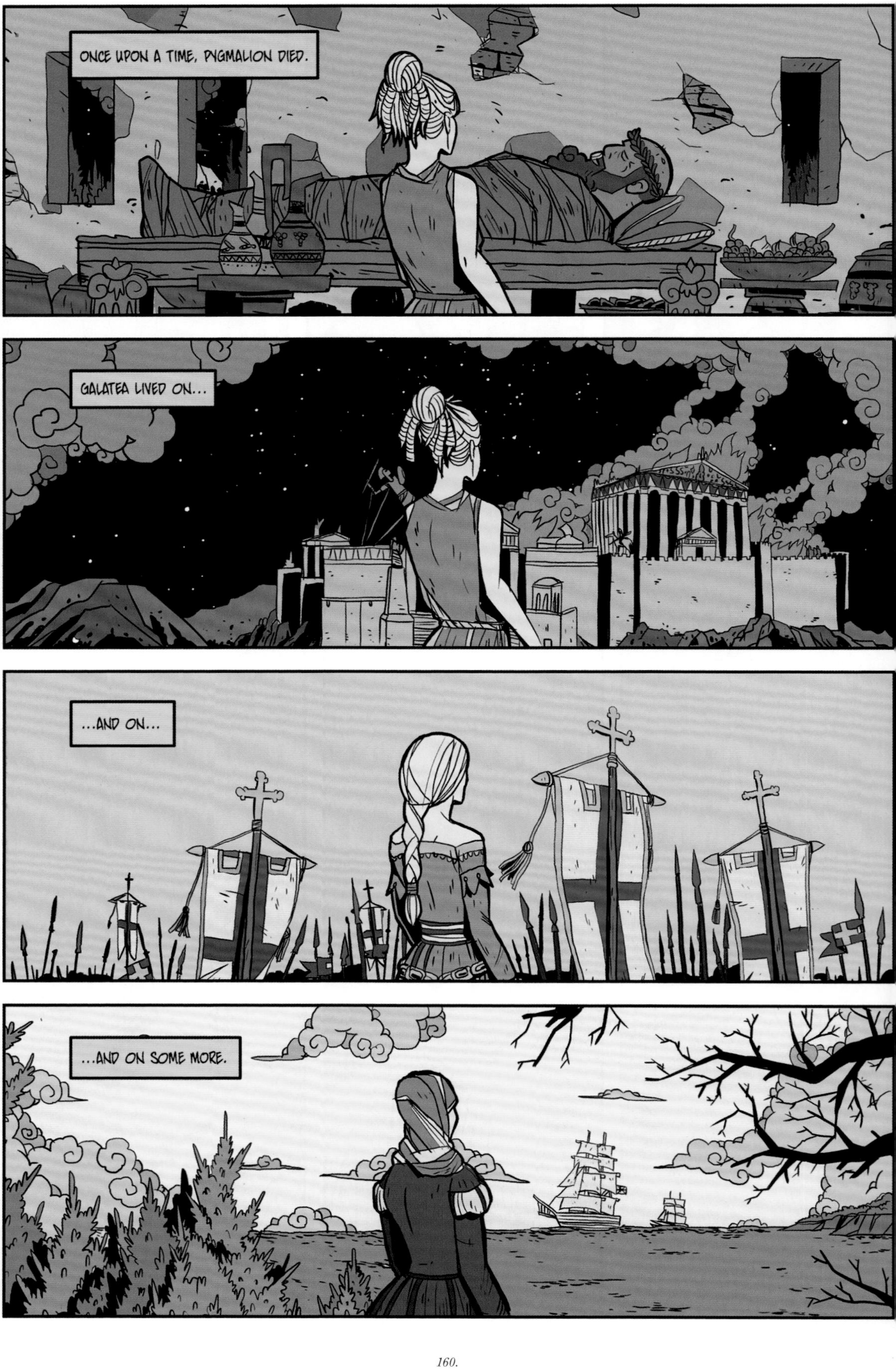
ONCE UPON A TIME, PYGMALION DIED.
GALATEA LIVED ON...
...AND ON...
...AND ON SOME MORE.

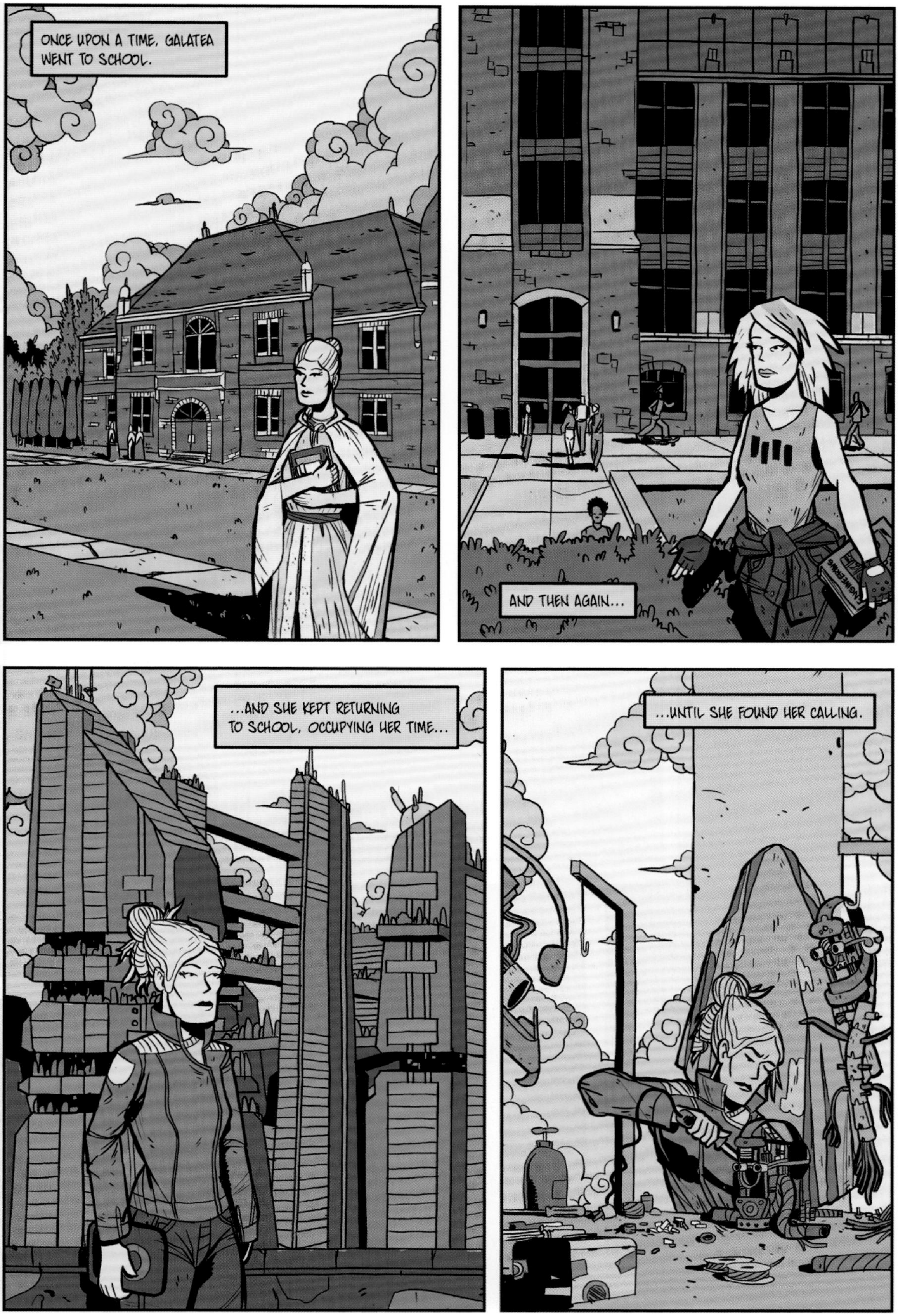
ONCE UPON A TIME, GALATEA WENT TO SCHOOL.
AND THEN AGAIN...
...AND SHE KEPT RETURNING TO SCHOOL, OCCUPYING HER TIME...
...UNTIL SHE FOUND HER CALLING.

LIKE PYGMALION, GALATEA LEARNED HOW TO CREATE.

UNLIKE PYGMALION, HER CREATIONS WERE NOT MADE OF RIGID MARBLE...

...SHE EVOKED HEPHAESTUS...

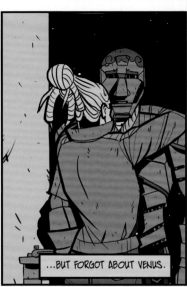

...BUT FORGOT ABOUT VENUS.

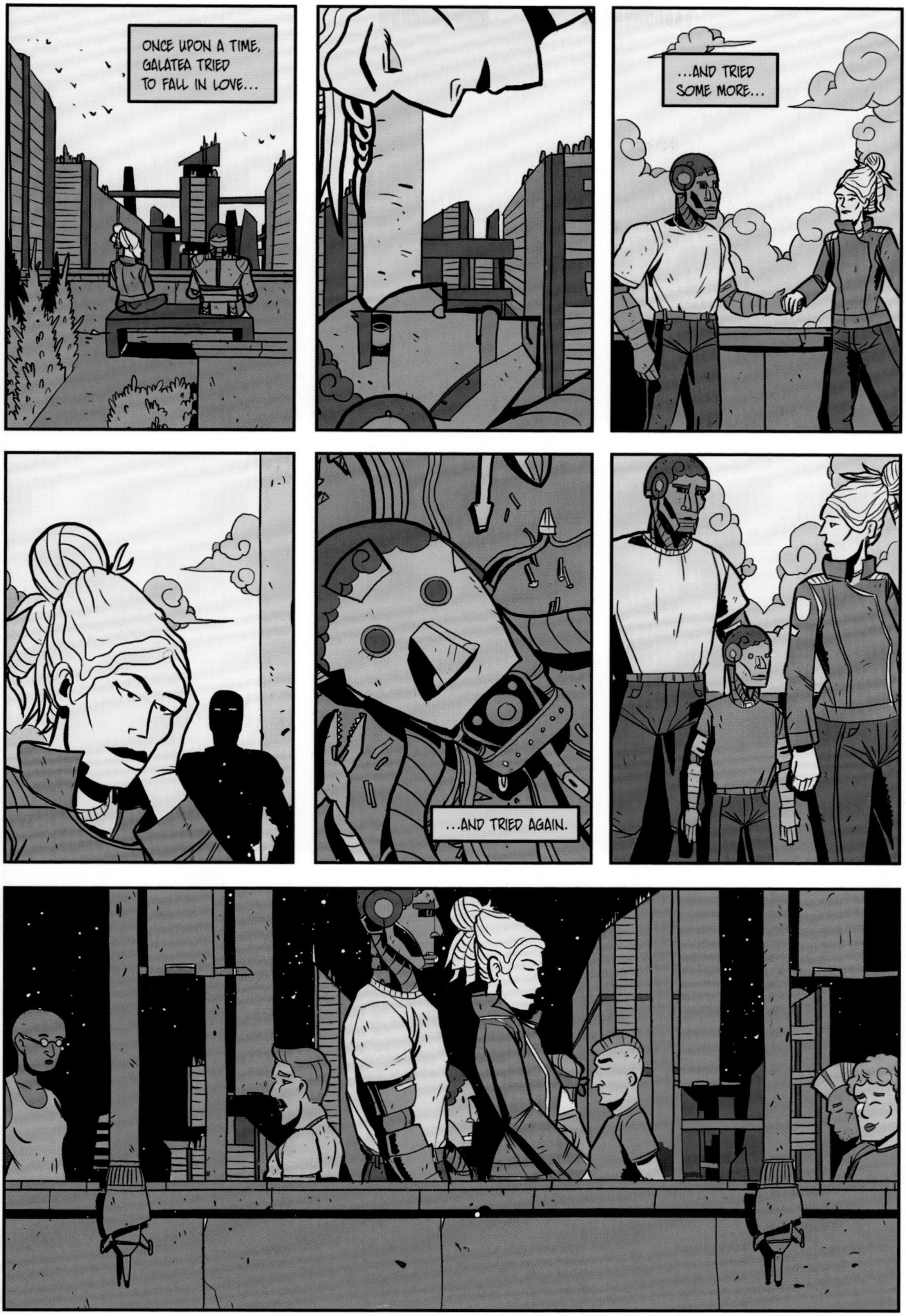
ONCE UPON A TIME, GALATEA TRIED TO FALL IN LOVE...
...AND TRIED SOME MORE...
...AND TRIED AGAIN.

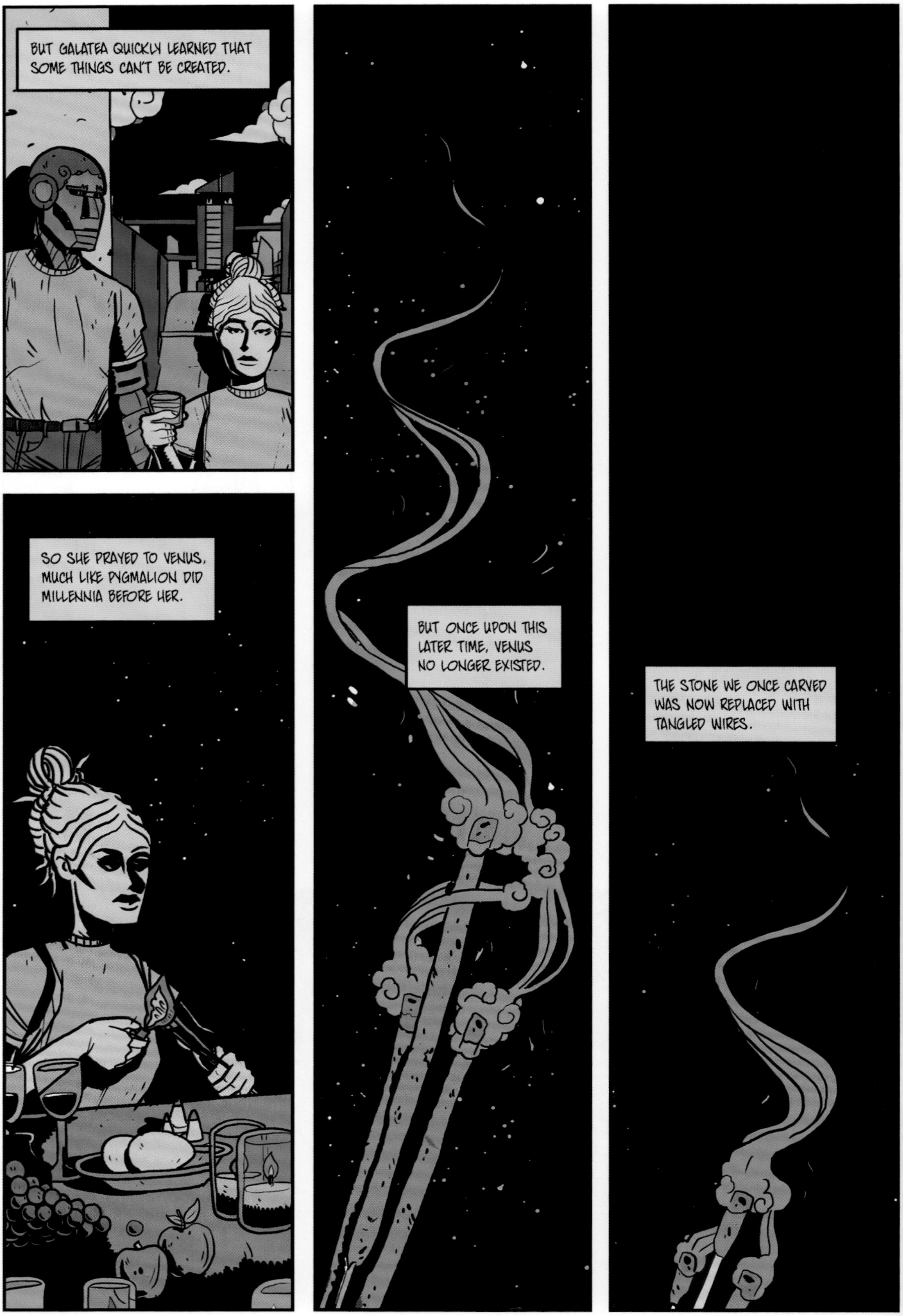
BUT GALATEA QUICKLY LEARNED THAT SOME THINGS CAN'T BE CREATED.
SO SHE PRAYED TO VENUS, MUCH LIKE PYGMALION DID MILLENNIA BEFORE HER.
BUT ONCE UPON THIS LATER TIME, VENUS NO LONGER EXISTED.
THE STONE WE ONCE CARVED WAS NOW REPLACED WITH TANGLED WIRES.

“A HEAVY STONE FOR ALL THE PEOPLES” (SISYPHUS)

written by
CHRIS STEVENS

illustrated and lettered by
DAVE CHISHOLM

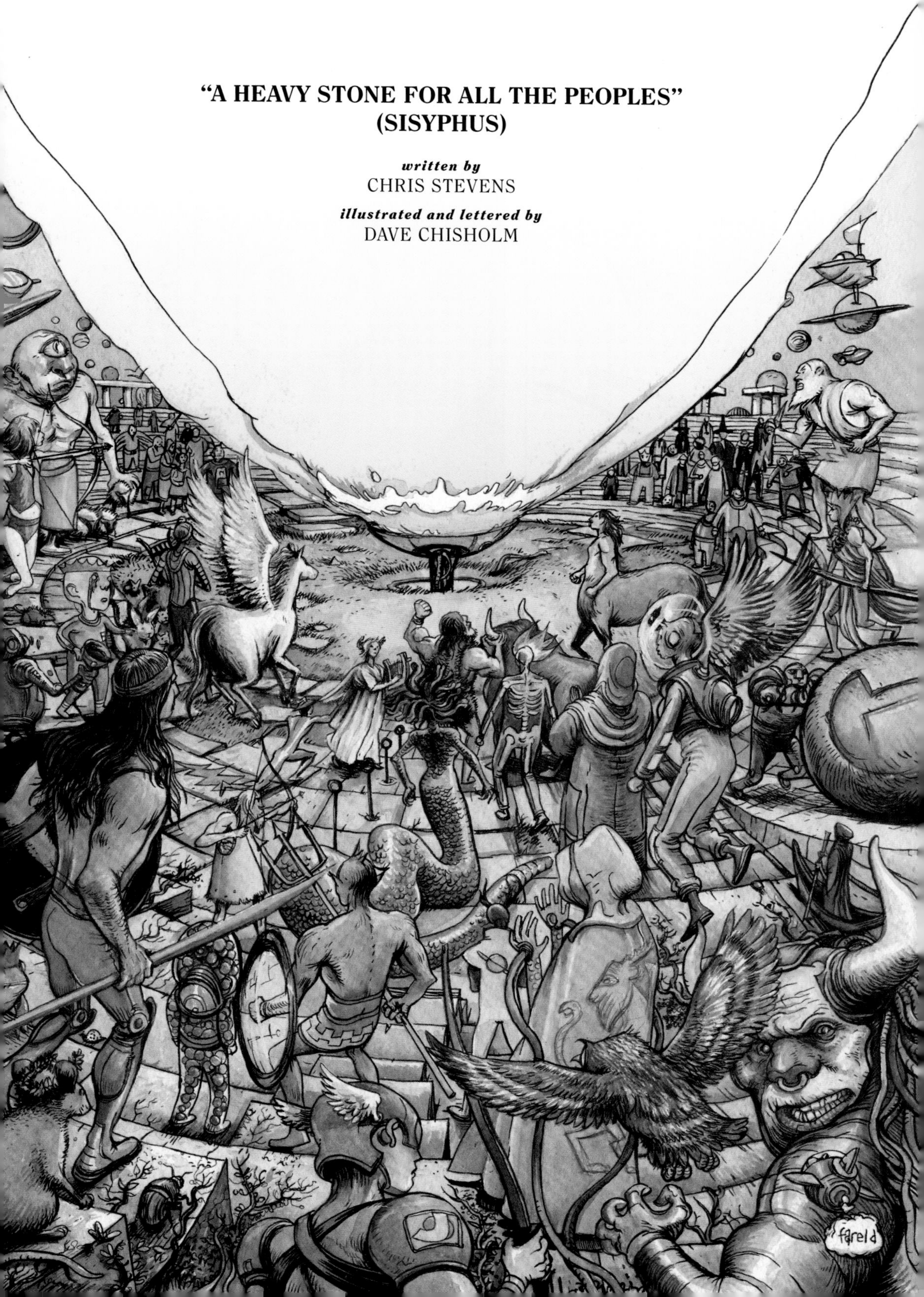
fareld

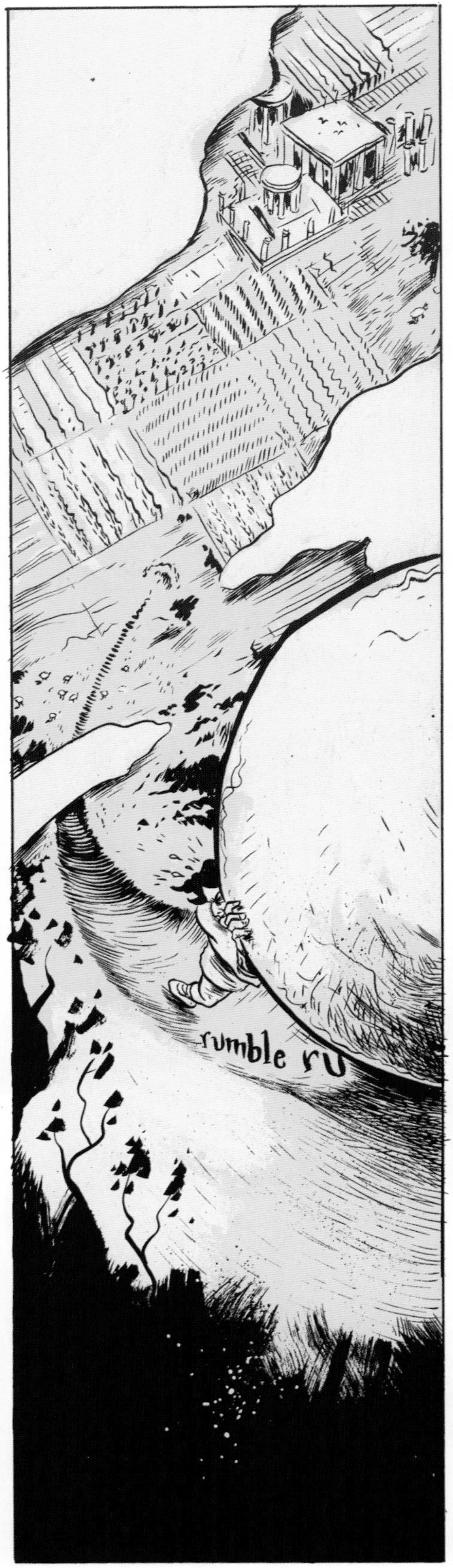
rumble ru

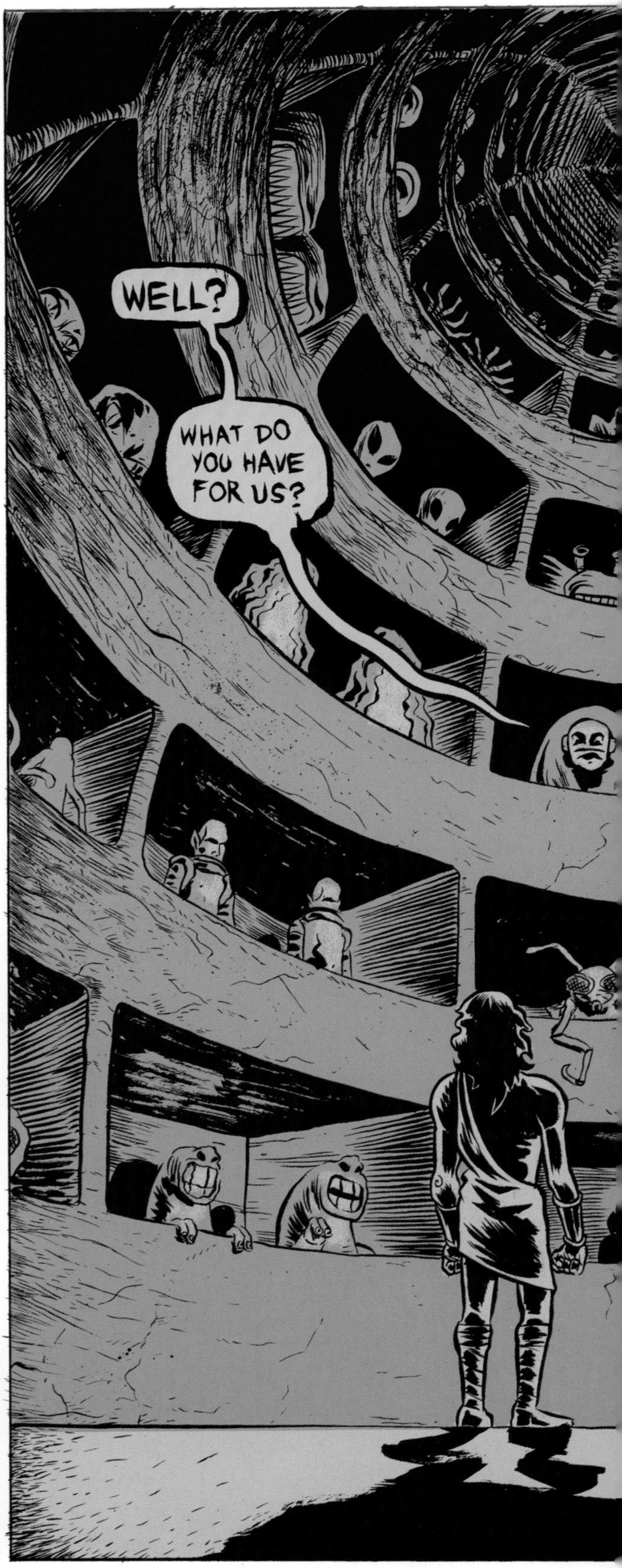
WELL?
WHAT DO YOU HAVE FOR US?

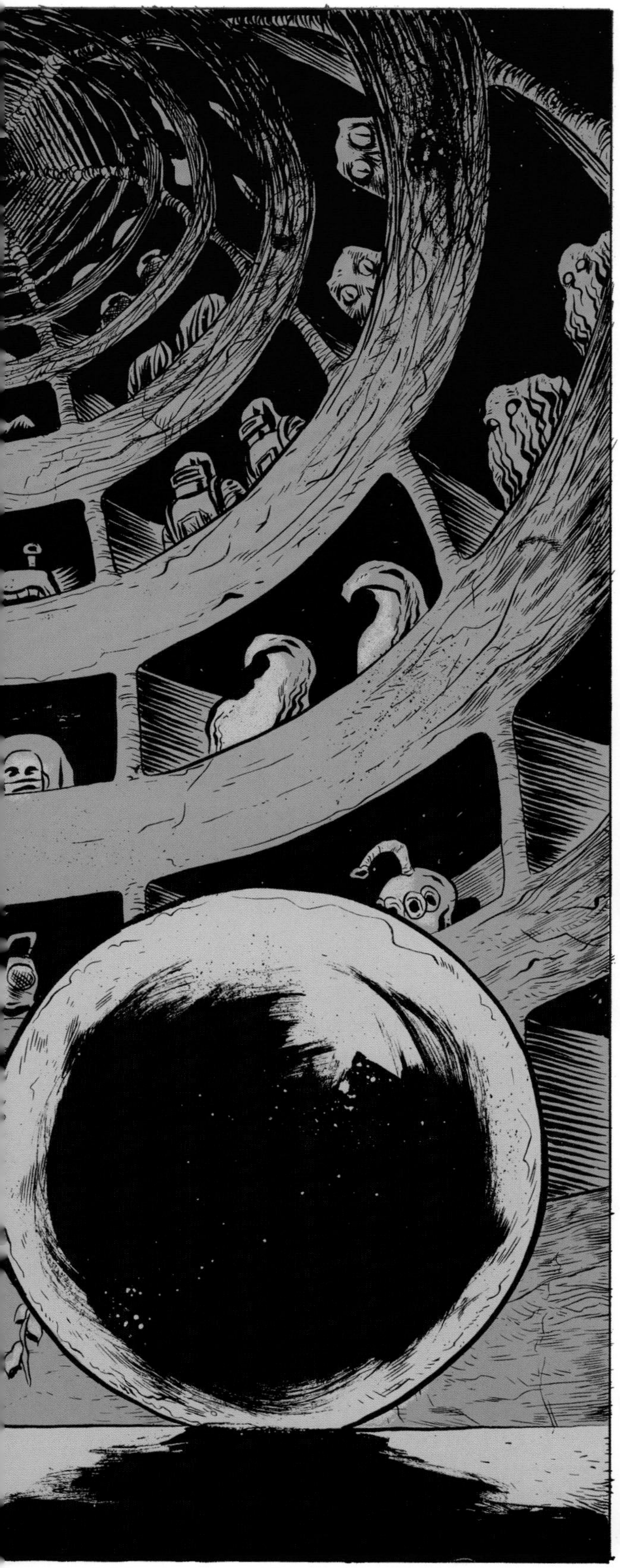

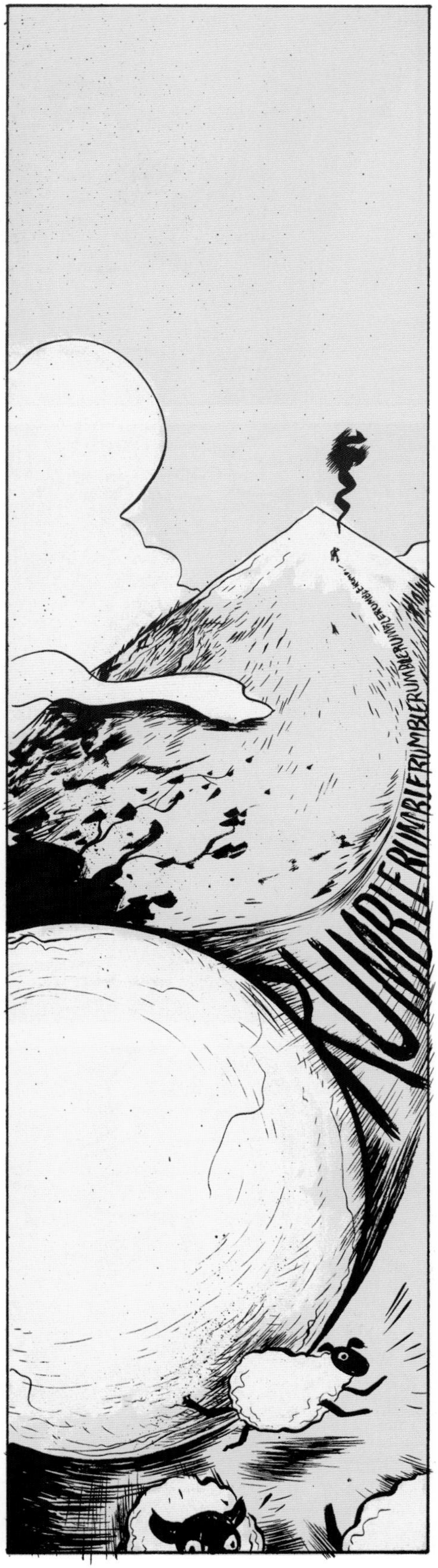
RUMBLERUMBLERUMBLERUMBLE

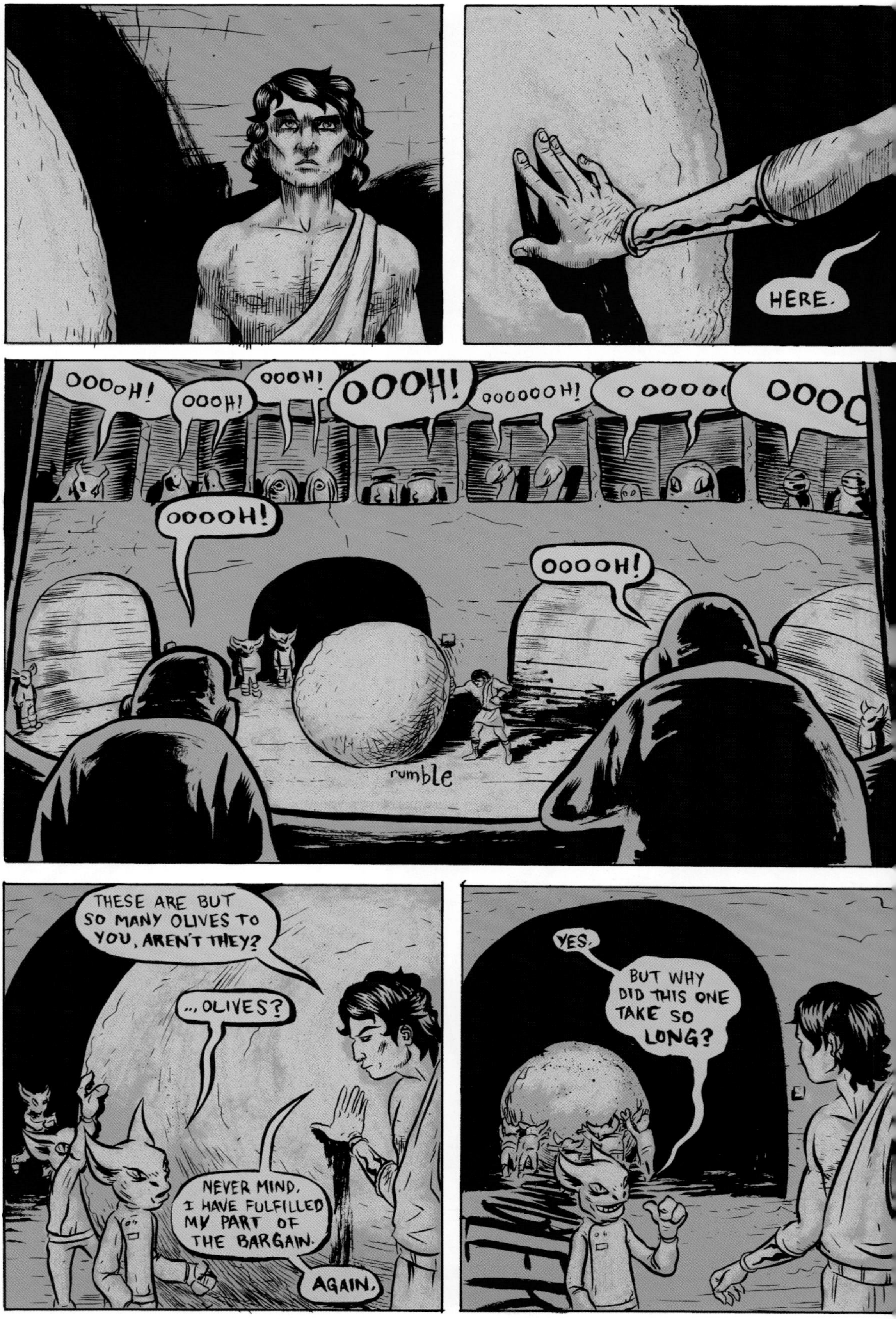
HERE.
OOOoH!
OOOH!
OOOH!
OOOH!
OOOOOOH!
OOOOOO
OOOO
OOOOH!
OOOOH!
rumble
THESE ARE BUT SO MANY OLIVES TO YOU, AREN'T THEY?
...OLIVES?
NEVER MIND. I HAVE FULFILLED MY PART OF THE BARGAIN.
AGAIN.
YES.
BUT WHY DID THIS ONE TAKE SO LONG?

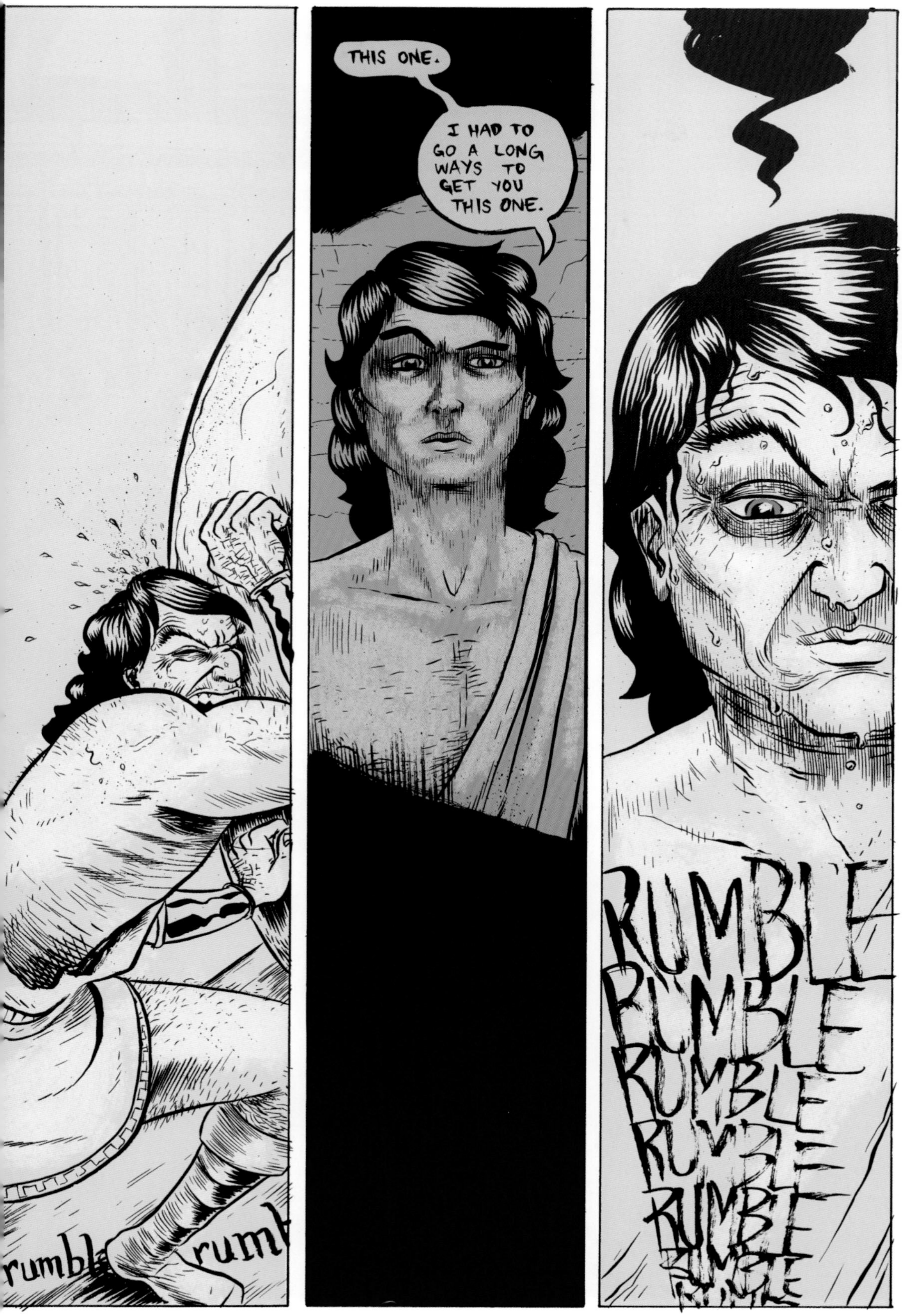
rumble rumb
THIS ONE.
I HAD TO GO A LONG WAYS TO GET YOU THIS ONE.
RUMBLE
RUMBLE
RUMBLE
RUMBLE
RUMBLE
RUMBLE

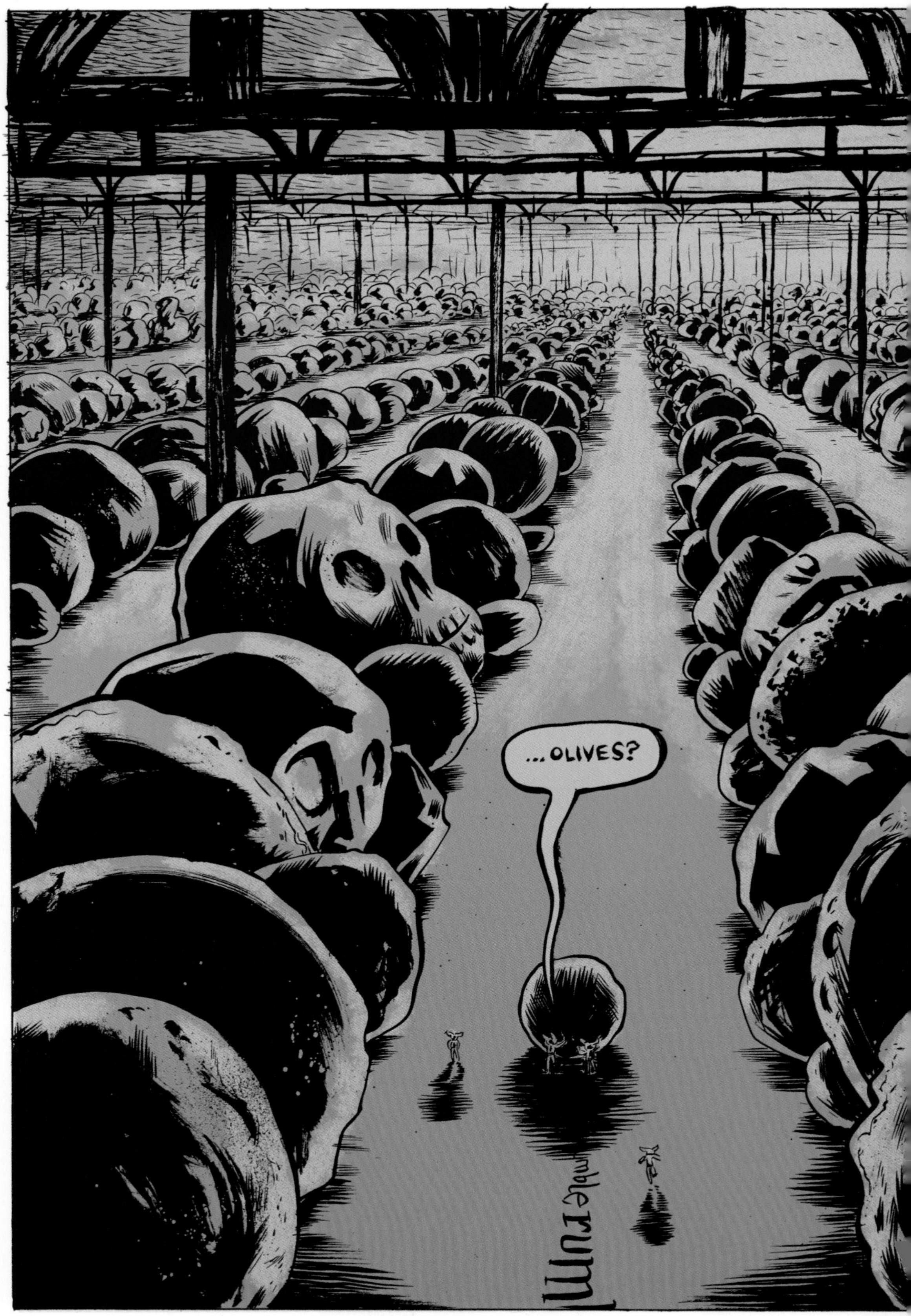
...OLIVES?
mble rum

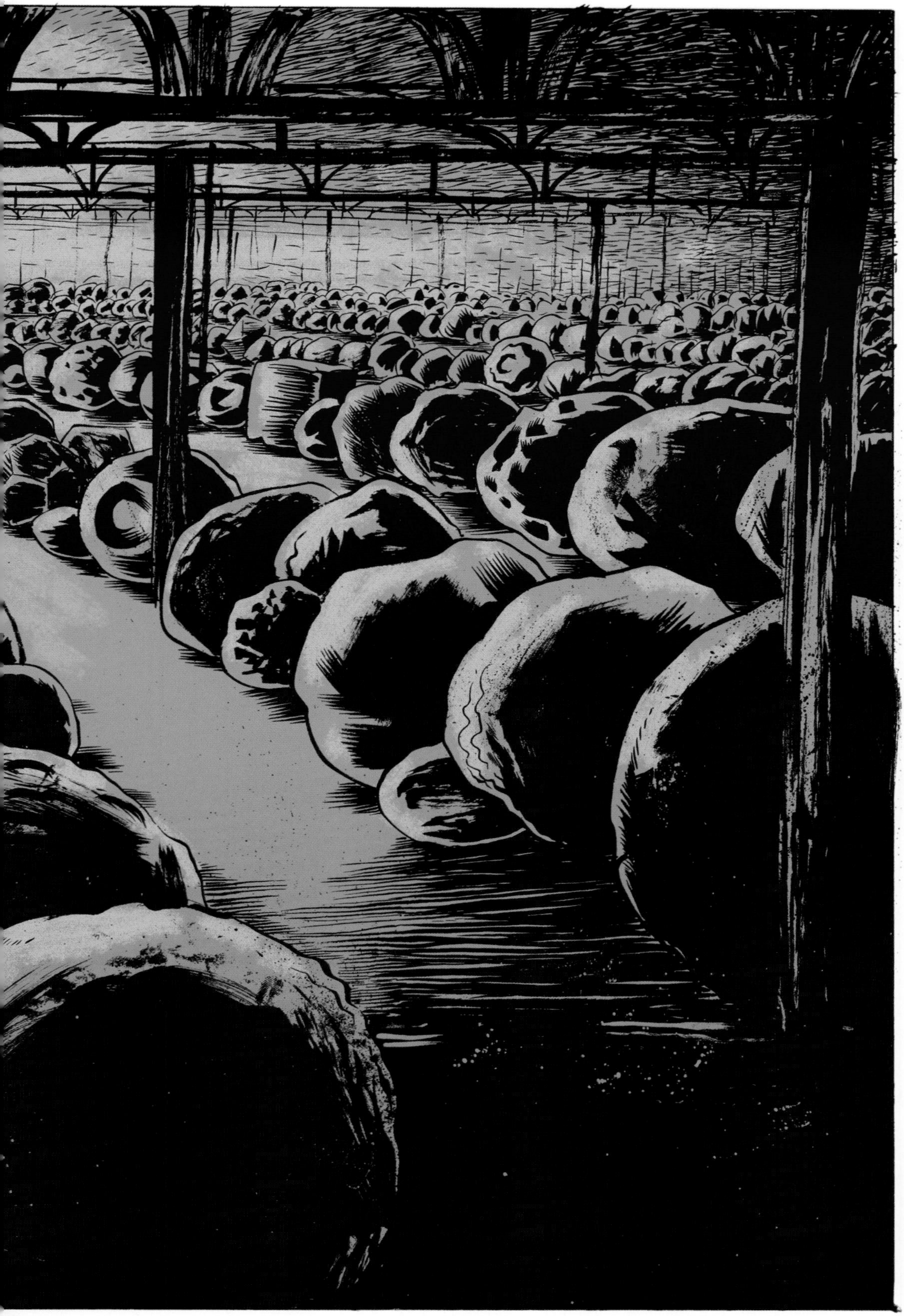

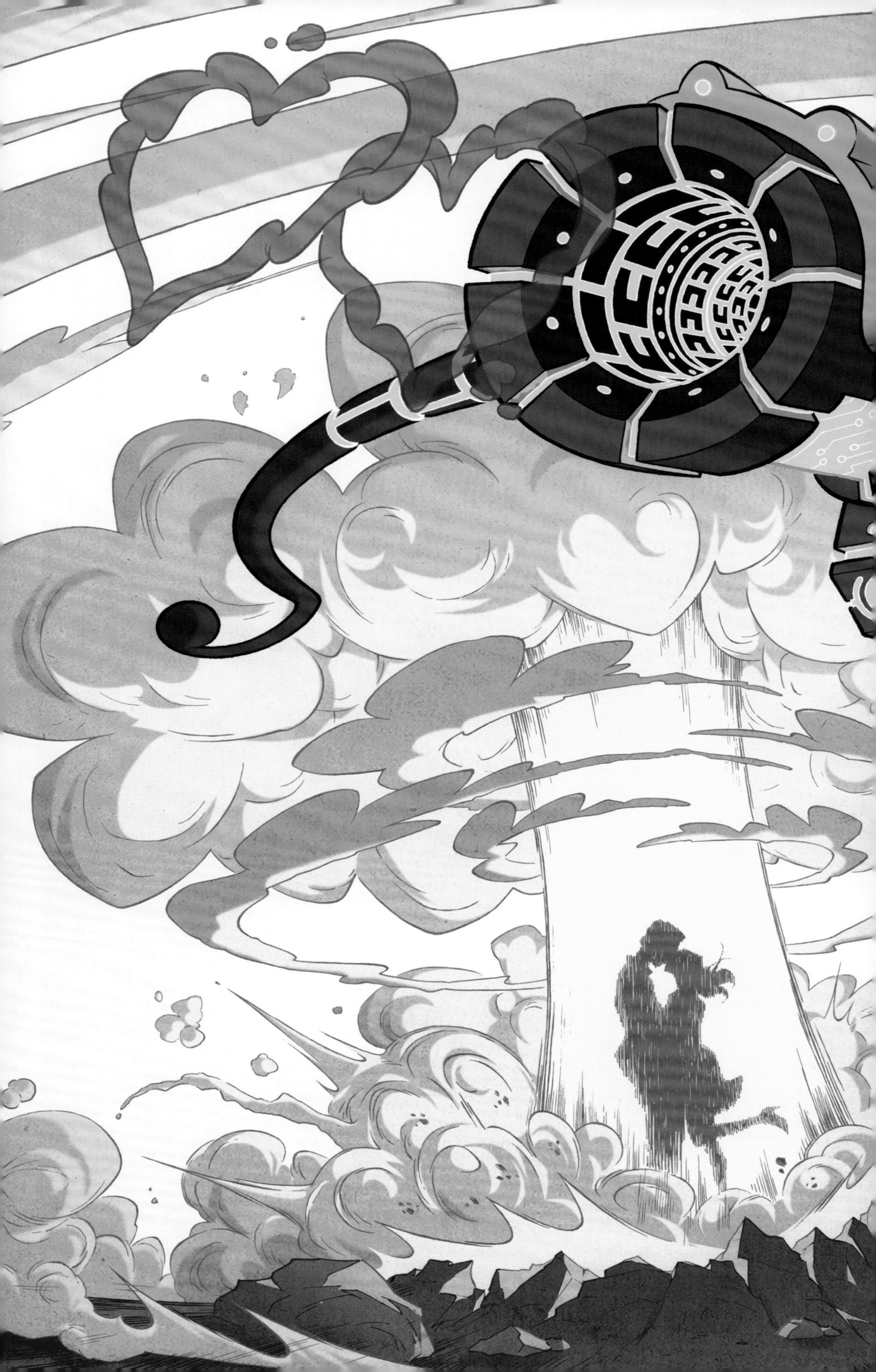

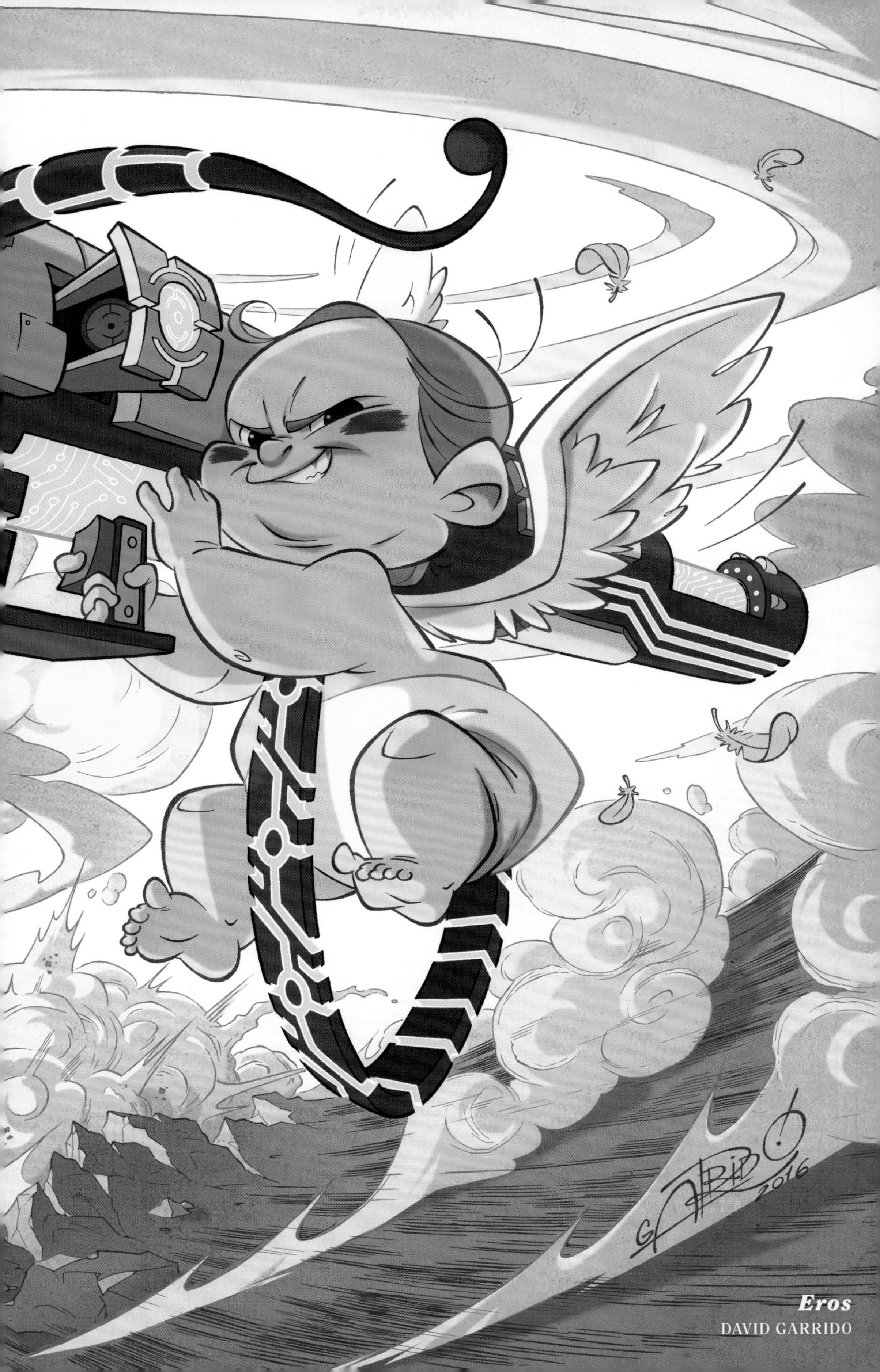
G. ARRIBO
2016

Eros
DAVID GARRIDO

"JASON AND THE ARGONAUTS"

written by
TARA ALEXANDER

illustrated by
HA HUY HOANG

lettered by
CARDINAL RAE

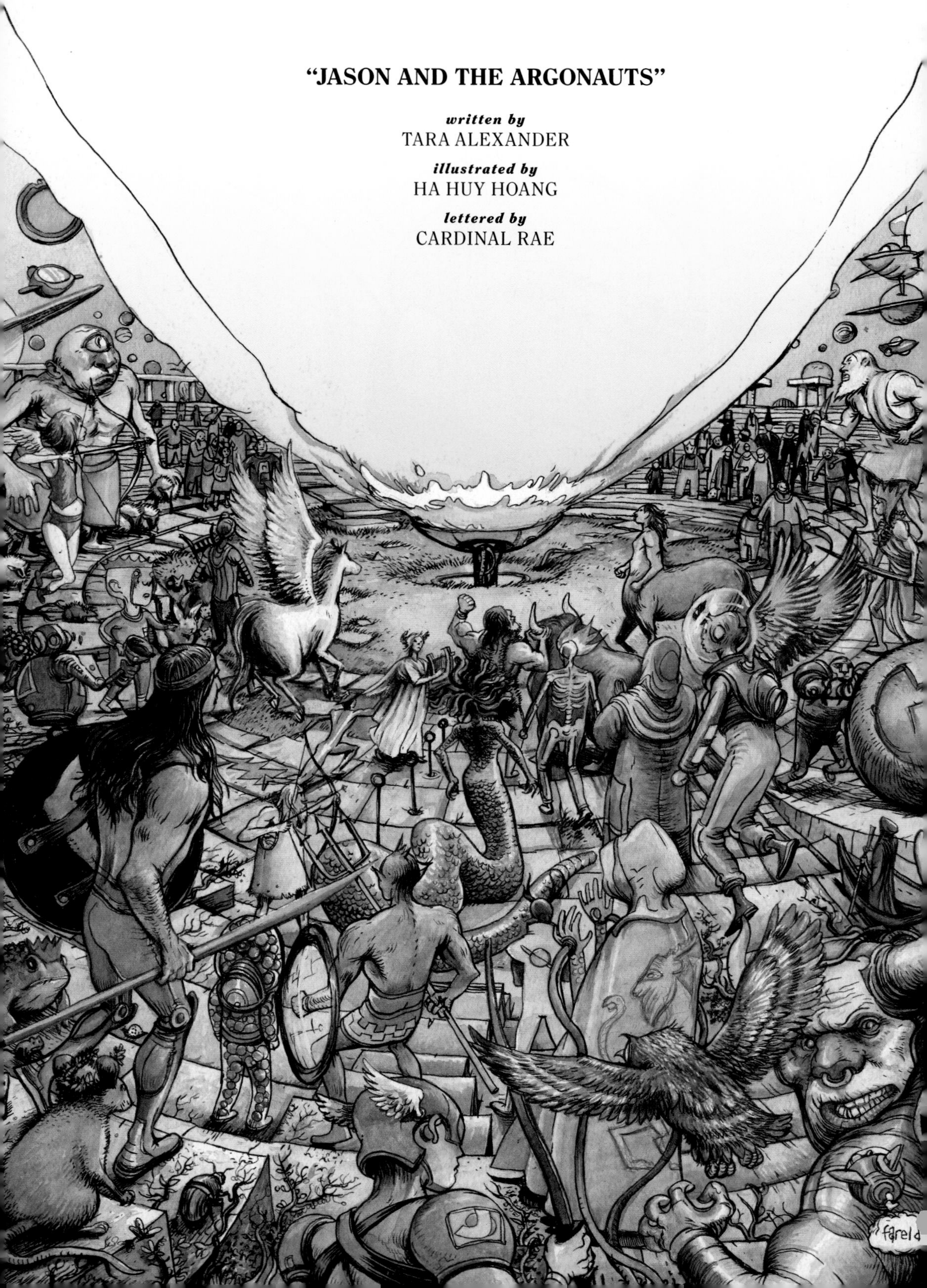

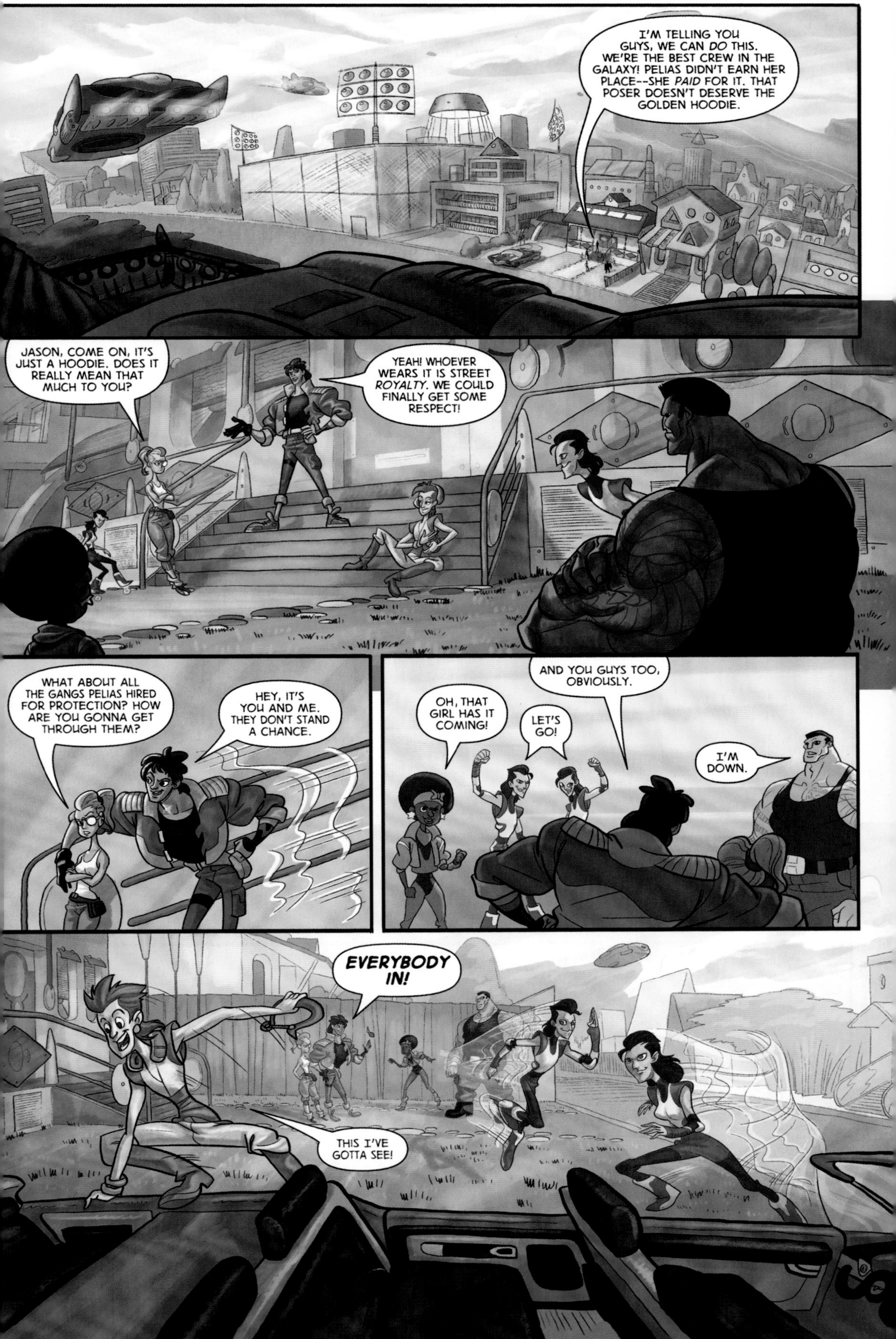
I'M TELLING YOU GUYS, WE CAN *DO* THIS. WE'RE THE BEST CREW IN THE GALAXY! PELIAS DIDN'T EARN HER PLACE--SHE *PAID* FOR IT. THAT POSER DOESN'T DESERVE THE GOLDEN HOODIE.
JASON, COME ON, IT'S JUST A HOODIE. DOES IT REALLY MEAN THAT MUCH TO YOU?
YEAH! WHOEVER WEARS IT IS STREET *ROYALTY*. WE COULD FINALLY GET SOME RESPECT!
WHAT ABOUT ALL THE GANGS PELIAS HIRED FOR PROTECTION? HOW ARE YOU GONNA GET THROUGH THEM?
HEY, IT'S YOU AND ME. THEY DON'T STAND A CHANCE.
AND YOU GUYS TOO, OBVIOUSLY.
OH, THAT GIRL HAS IT COMING!
LET'S GO!
I'M DOWN.
EVERYBODY IN!
THIS I'VE GOTTA SEE!

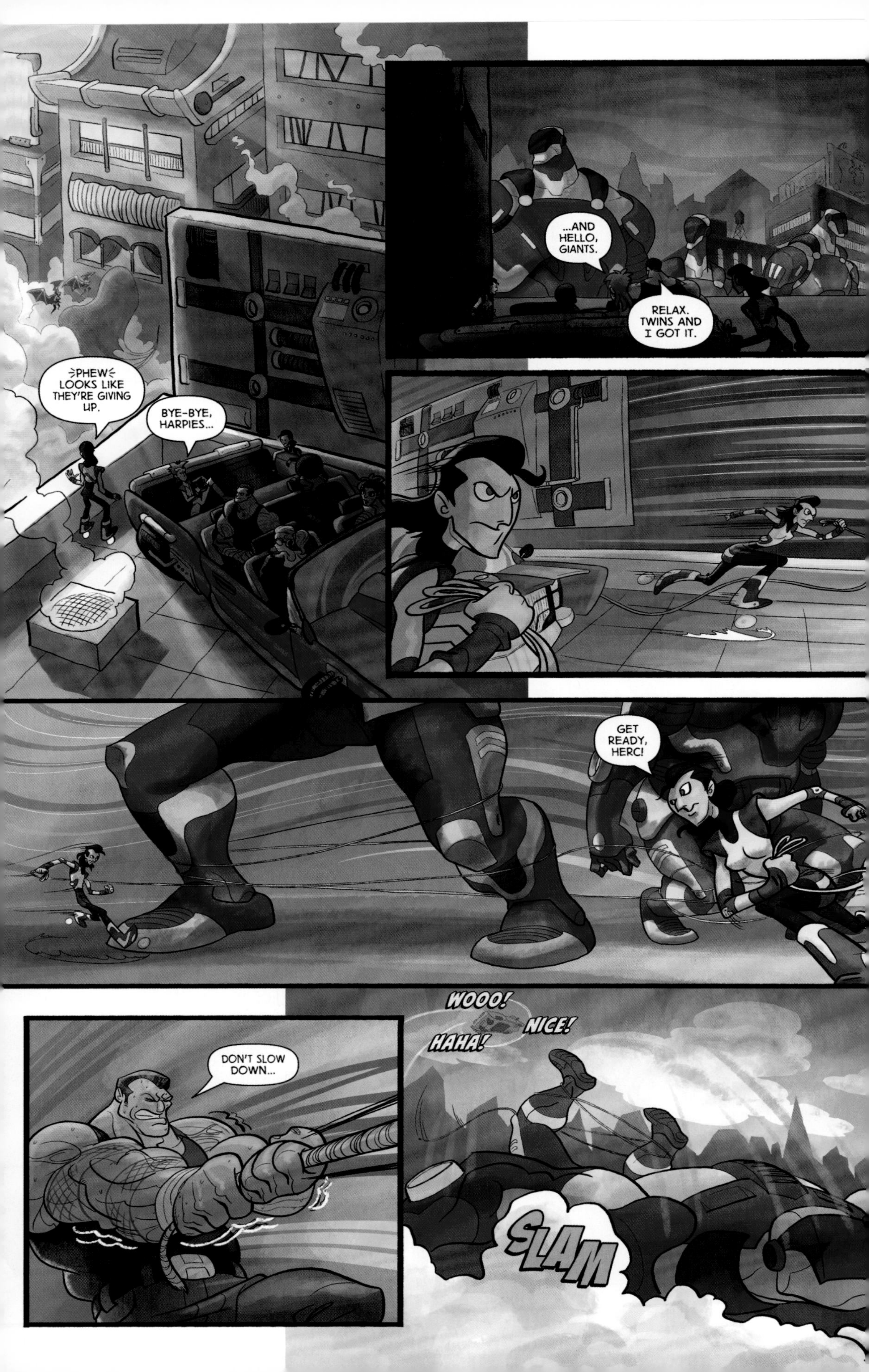

≶PHEW≷ LOOKS LIKE THEY'RE GIVING UP.
BYE-BYE, HARPIES...
...AND HELLO, GIANTS.
RELAX. TWINS AND I GOT IT.
GET READY, HERC!
DON'T SLOW DOWN...
WOOO!
NICE!
HAHA!
SLAM

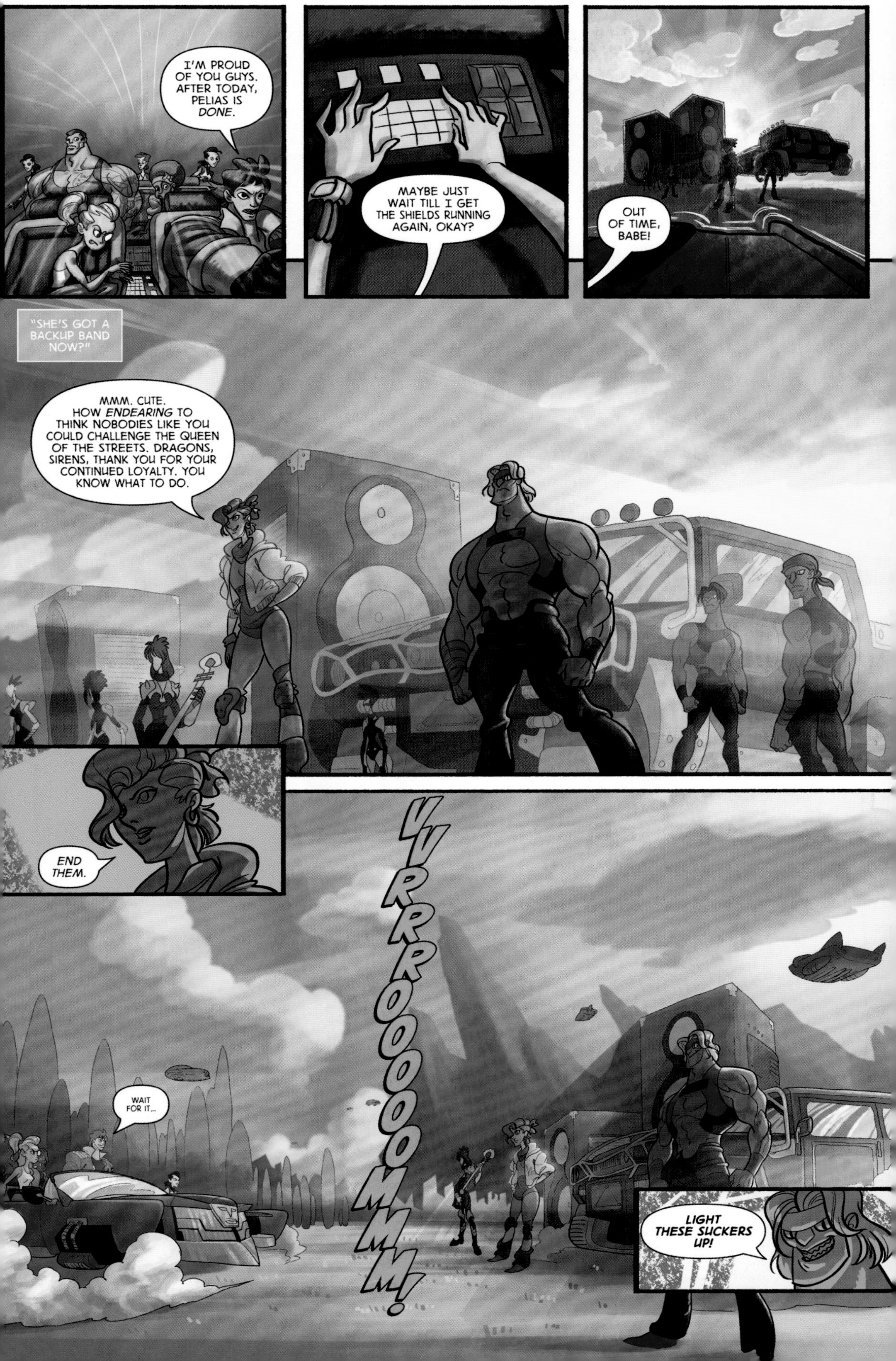
I'M PROUD OF YOU GUYS. AFTER TODAY, PELIAS IS *DONE*.
MAYBE JUST WAIT TILL I GET THE SHIELDS RUNNING AGAIN, OKAY?
OUT OF TIME, BABE!
"SHE'S GOT A BACKUP BAND NOW?"
MMM. CUTE. HOW *ENDEARING* TO THINK NOBODIES LIKE YOU COULD CHALLENGE THE QUEEN OF THE STREETS. DRAGONS, SIRENS, THANK YOU FOR YOUR CONTINUED LOYALTY. YOU KNOW WHAT TO DO.
END THEM.
VVRROOOOOOMMMM!
WAIT FOR IT...
LIGHT THESE SUCKERS UP!

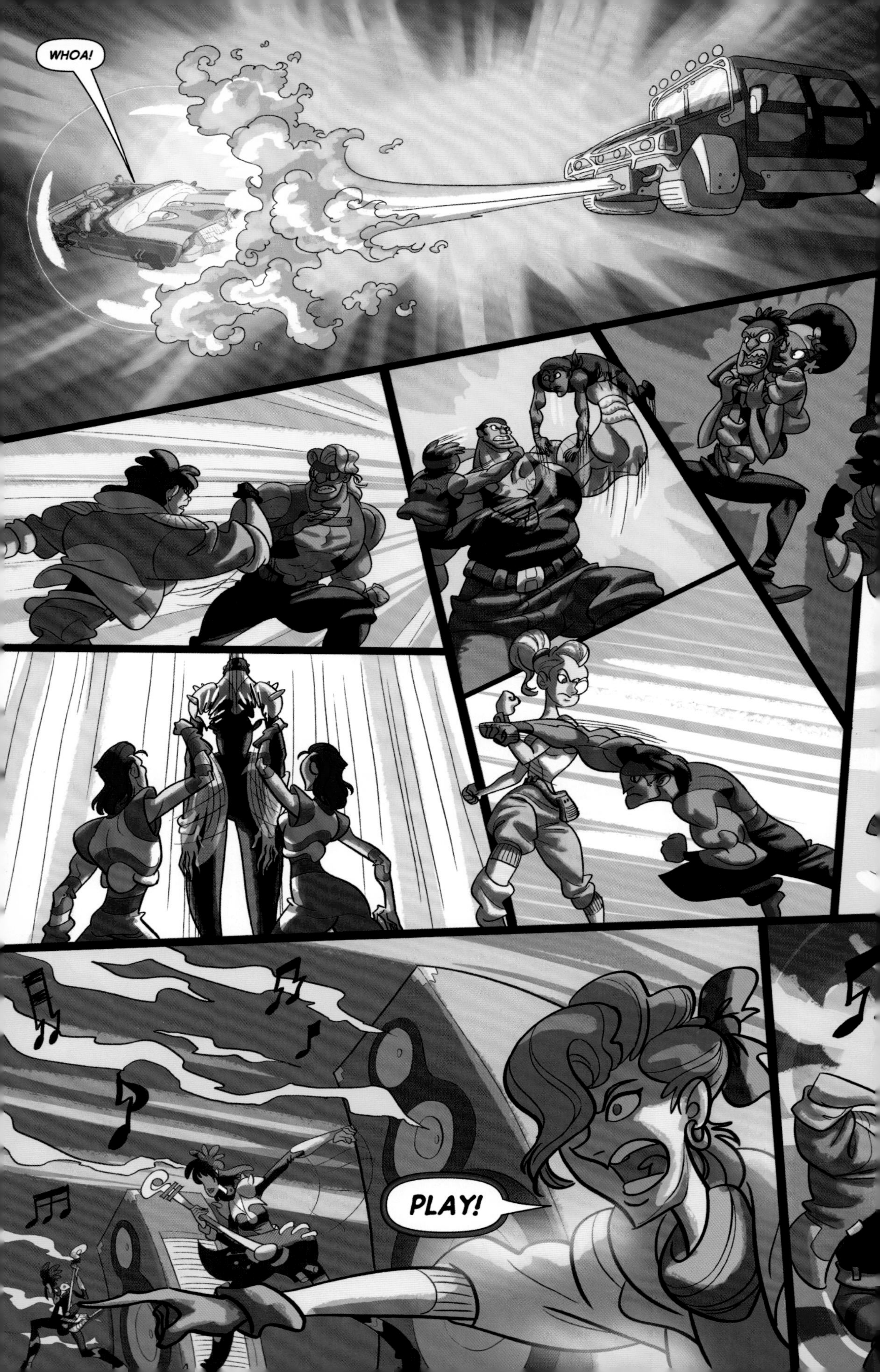
WHOA!
PLAY!

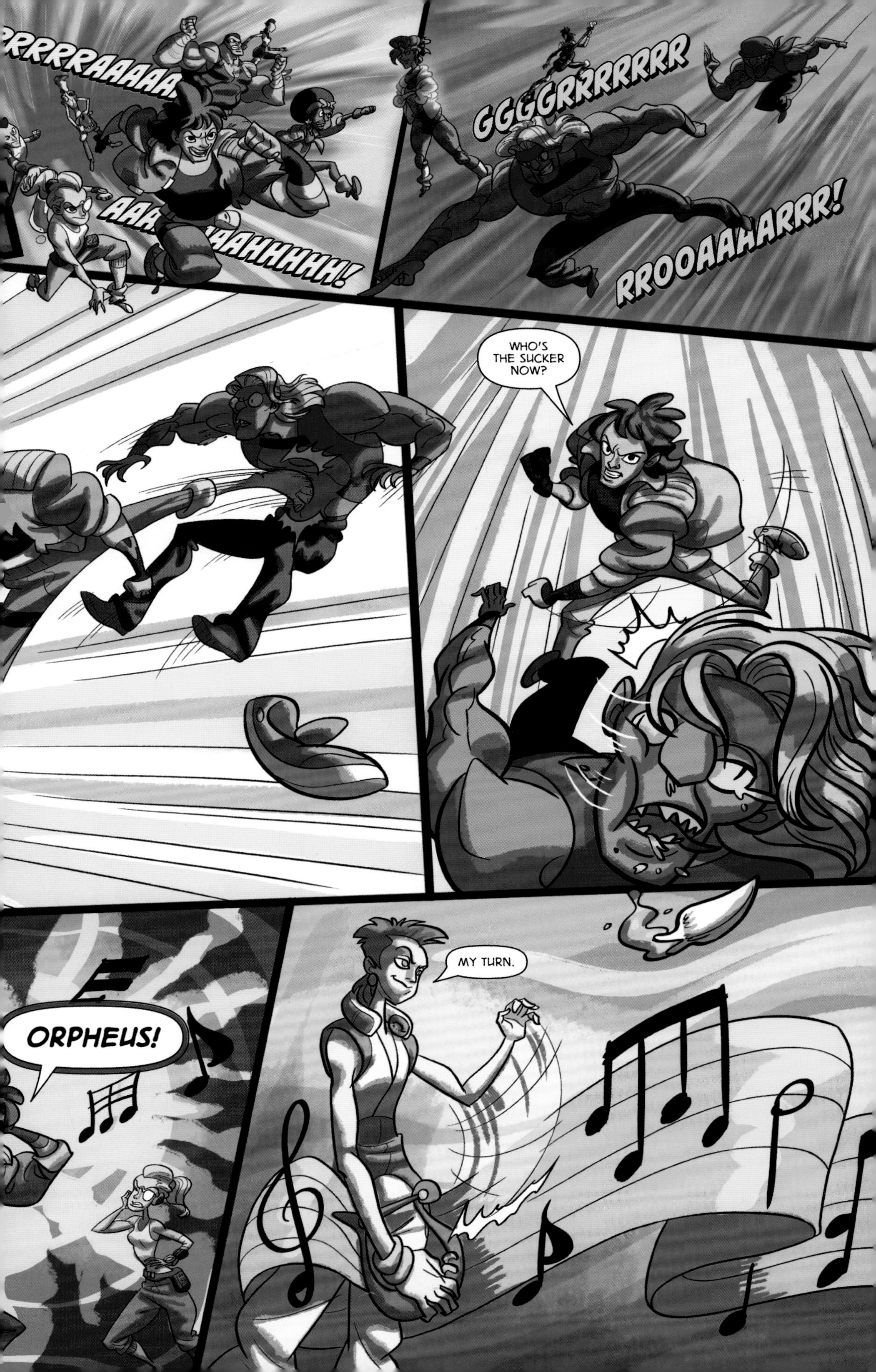
RRRRRAAAAAA
AAAAAAAHHHHHH!
GGGGRRRRRRR
RROOAAAHARRR!
WHO'S THE SUCKER NOW?
ORPHEUS!
MY TURN.

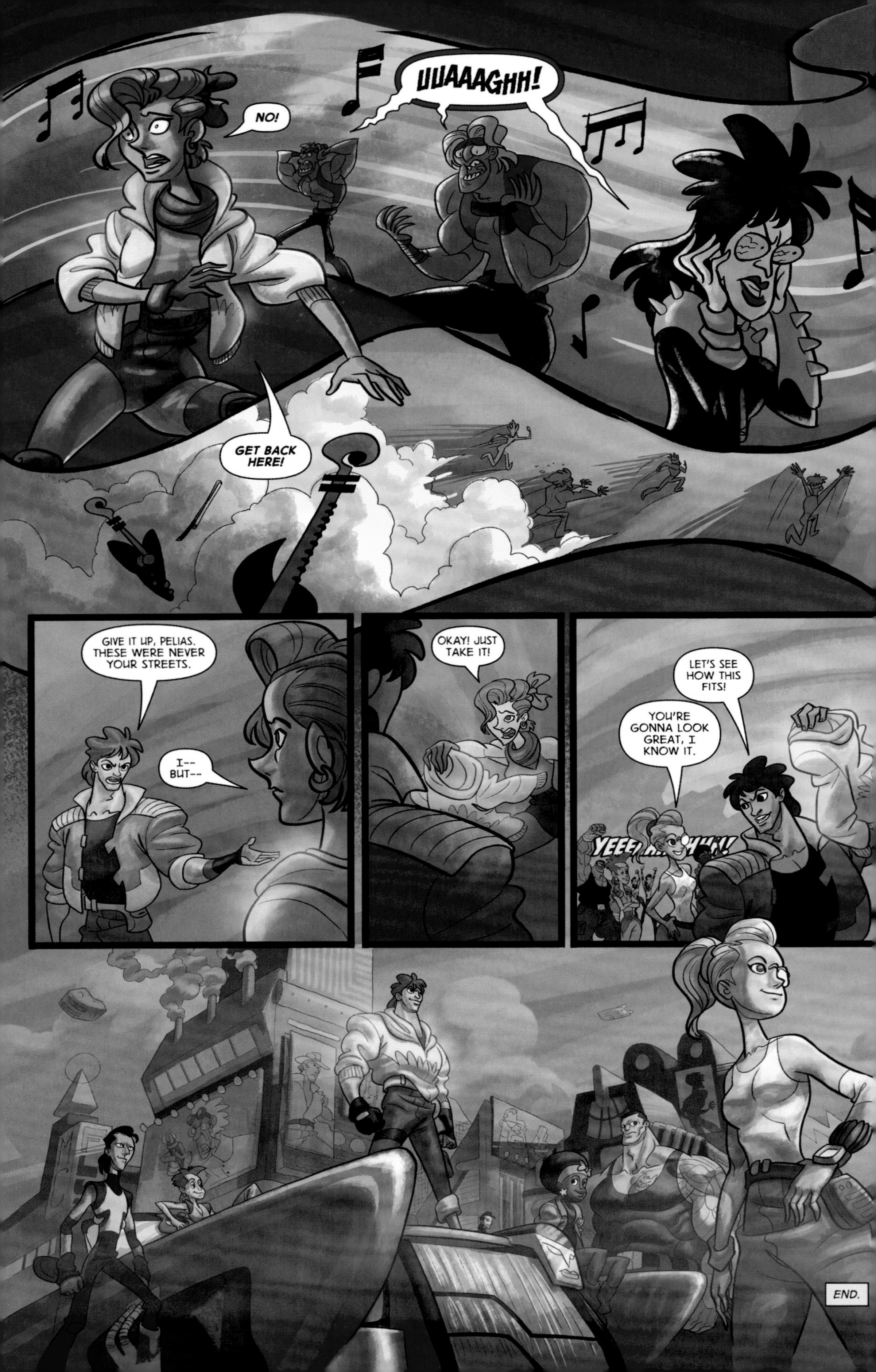
NO!
UUAAAGHH!
GET BACK HERE!
GIVE IT UP, PELIAS. THESE WERE NEVER YOUR STREETS.
I-- BUT--
OKAY! JUST TAKE IT!
LET'S SEE HOW THIS FITS!
YOU'RE GONNA LOOK GREAT, I KNOW IT.
END.

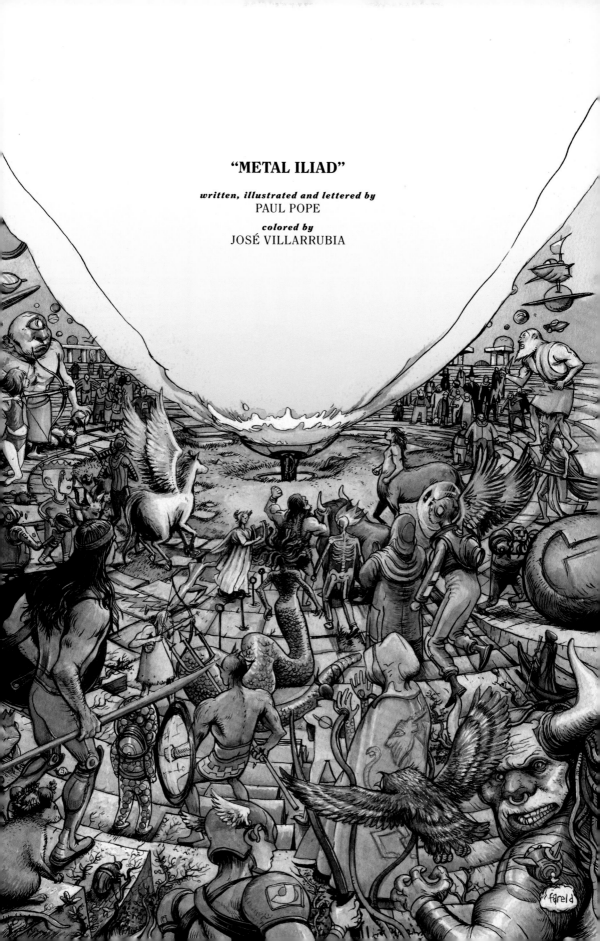

"METAL ILIAD"

written, illustrated and lettered by
PAUL POPE

colored by
JOSÉ VILLARRUBIA

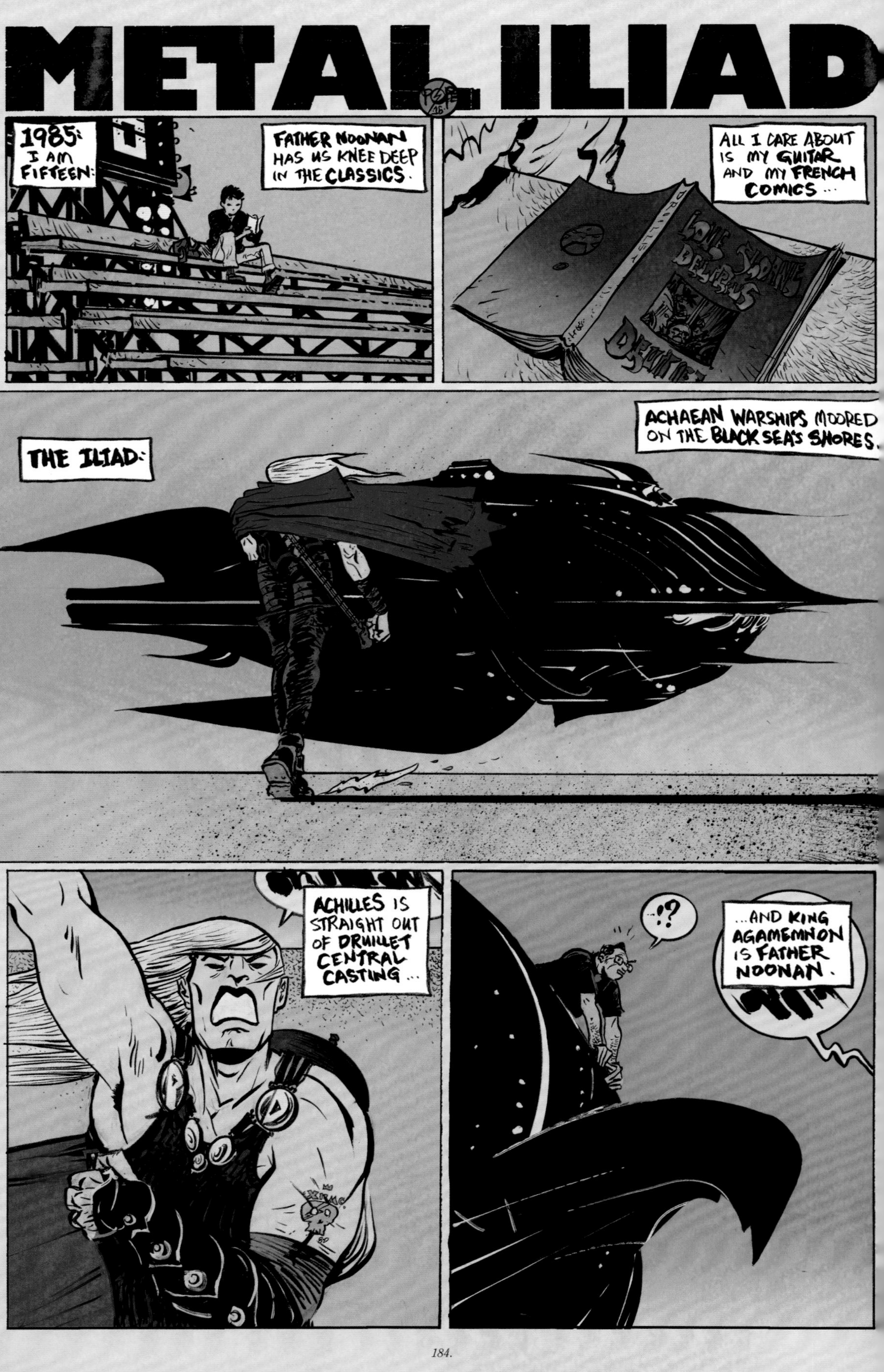

METAL ILIAD
1985: I AM FIFTEEN.
FATHER NOONAN HAS US KNEE DEEP IN THE CLASSICS.
ALL I CARE ABOUT IS MY GUITAR AND MY FRENCH COMICS...
THE ILIAD:
ACHAEAN WARSHIPS MOORED ON THE BLACK SEA'S SHORES.
ACHILLES IS STRAIGHT OUT OF DRUILLET CENTRAL CASTING...
!?
...AND KING AGAMEMNON IS FATHER NOONAN.

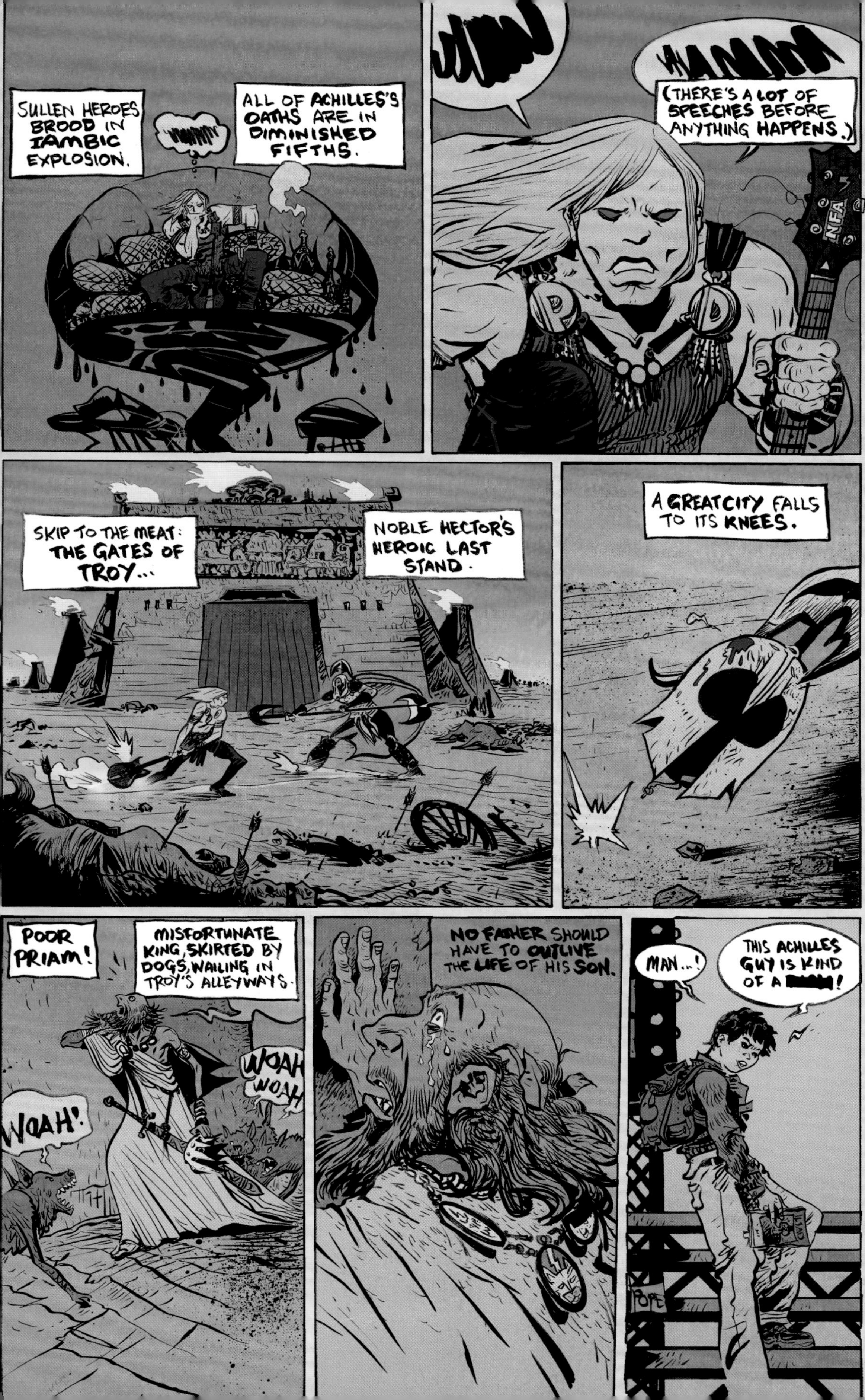
SULLEN HEROES BROOD IN IAMBIC EXPLOSION.
ALL OF ACHILLES'S OATHS ARE IN DIMINISHED FIFTHS.
(THERE'S A LOT OF SPEECHES BEFORE ANYTHING HAPPENS.)
SKIP TO THE MEAT: THE GATES OF TROY...
NOBLE HECTOR'S HEROIC LAST STAND.
A GREAT CITY FALLS TO ITS KNEES.
POOR PRIAM!
MISFORTUNATE KING, SKIRTED BY DOGS, WAILING IN TROY'S ALLEYWAYS.
WOAH WOAH
WOAH!
NO FATHER SHOULD HAVE TO OUTLIVE THE LIFE OF HIS SON.
MAN...!
THIS ACHILLES GUY IS KIND OF A [redacted]!

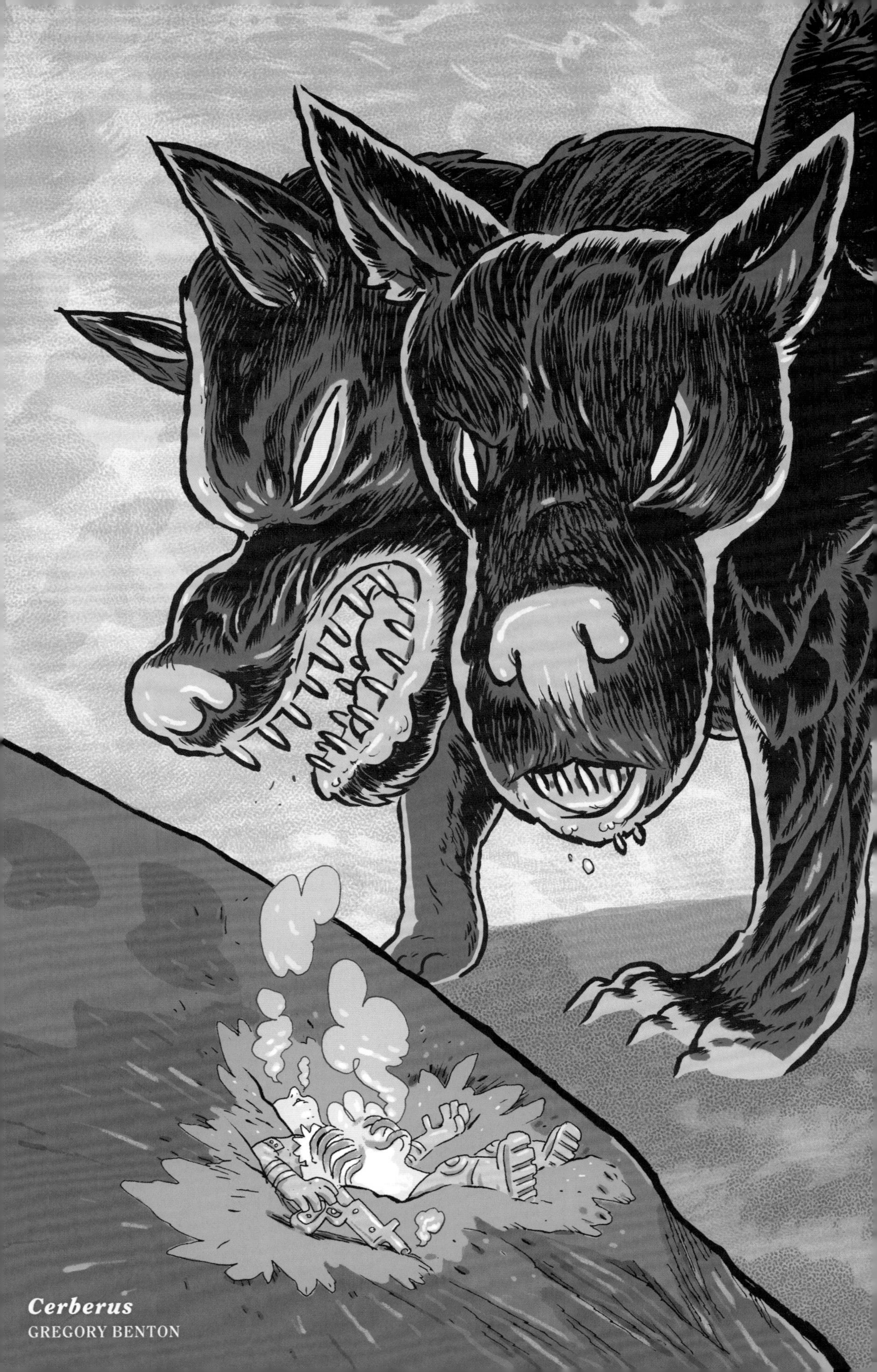

Cerberus
GREGORY BENTON

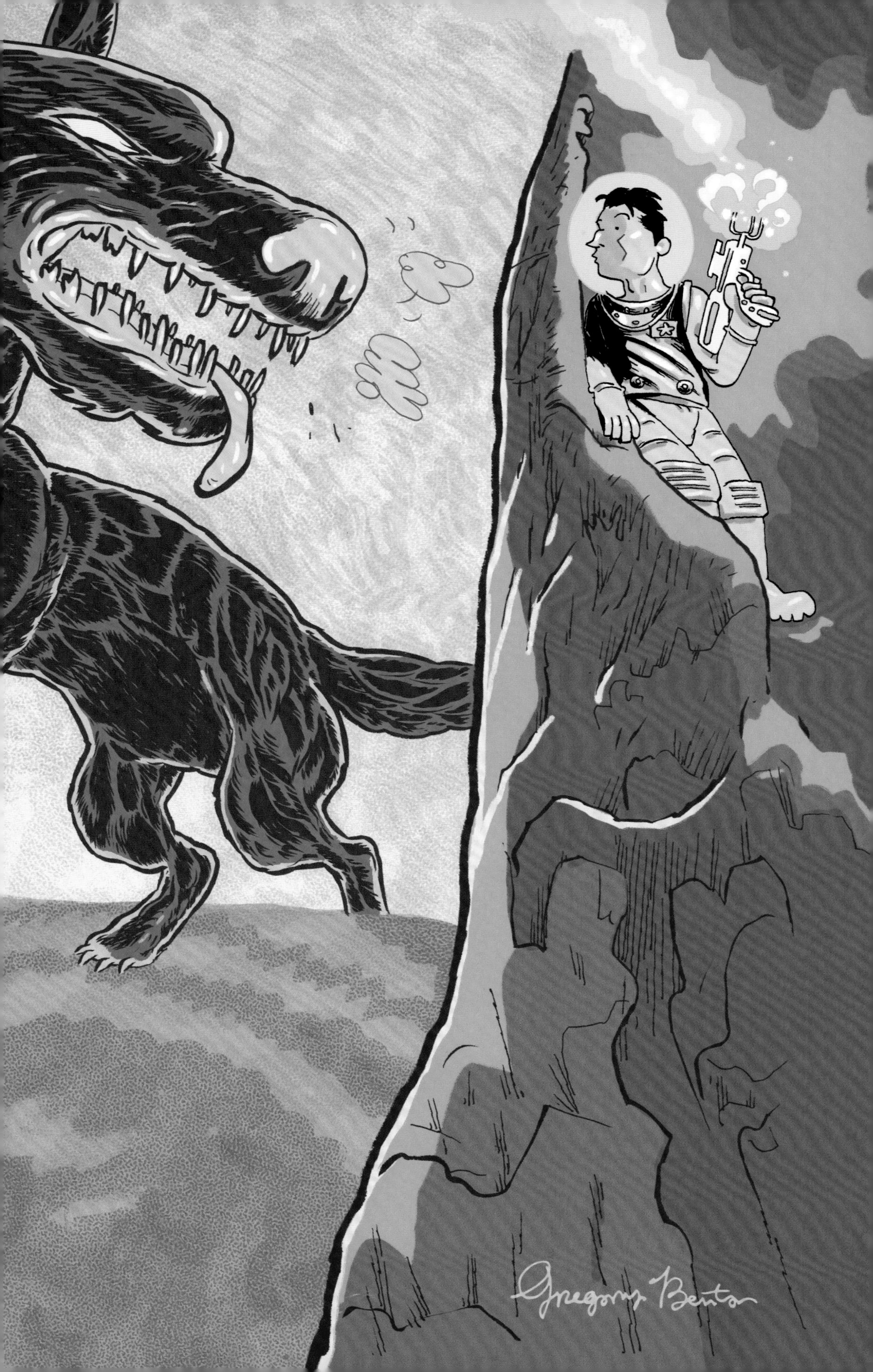
Gregory Benton

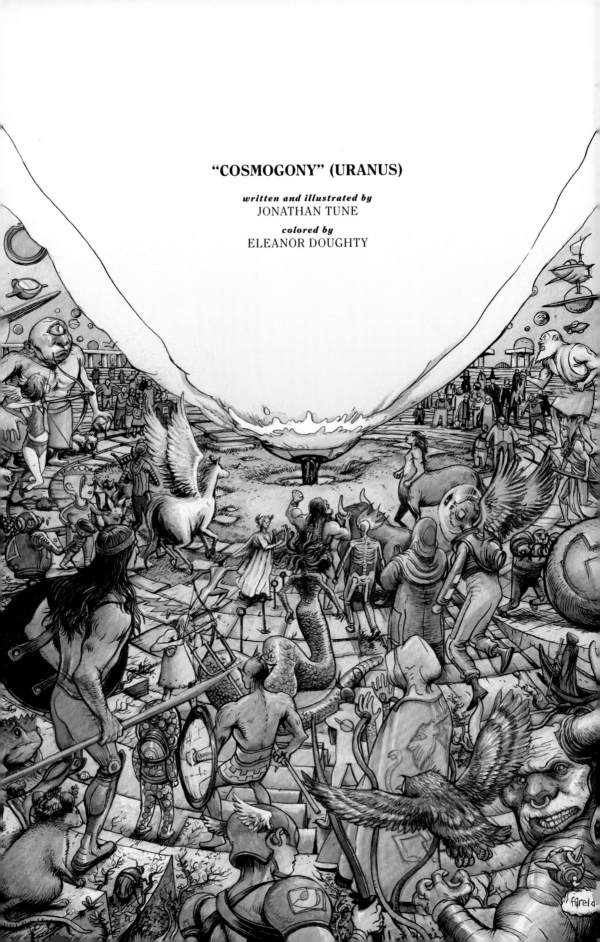

"COSMOGONY" (URANUS)

written and illustrated by
JONATHAN TUNE

colored by
ELEANOR DOUGHTY

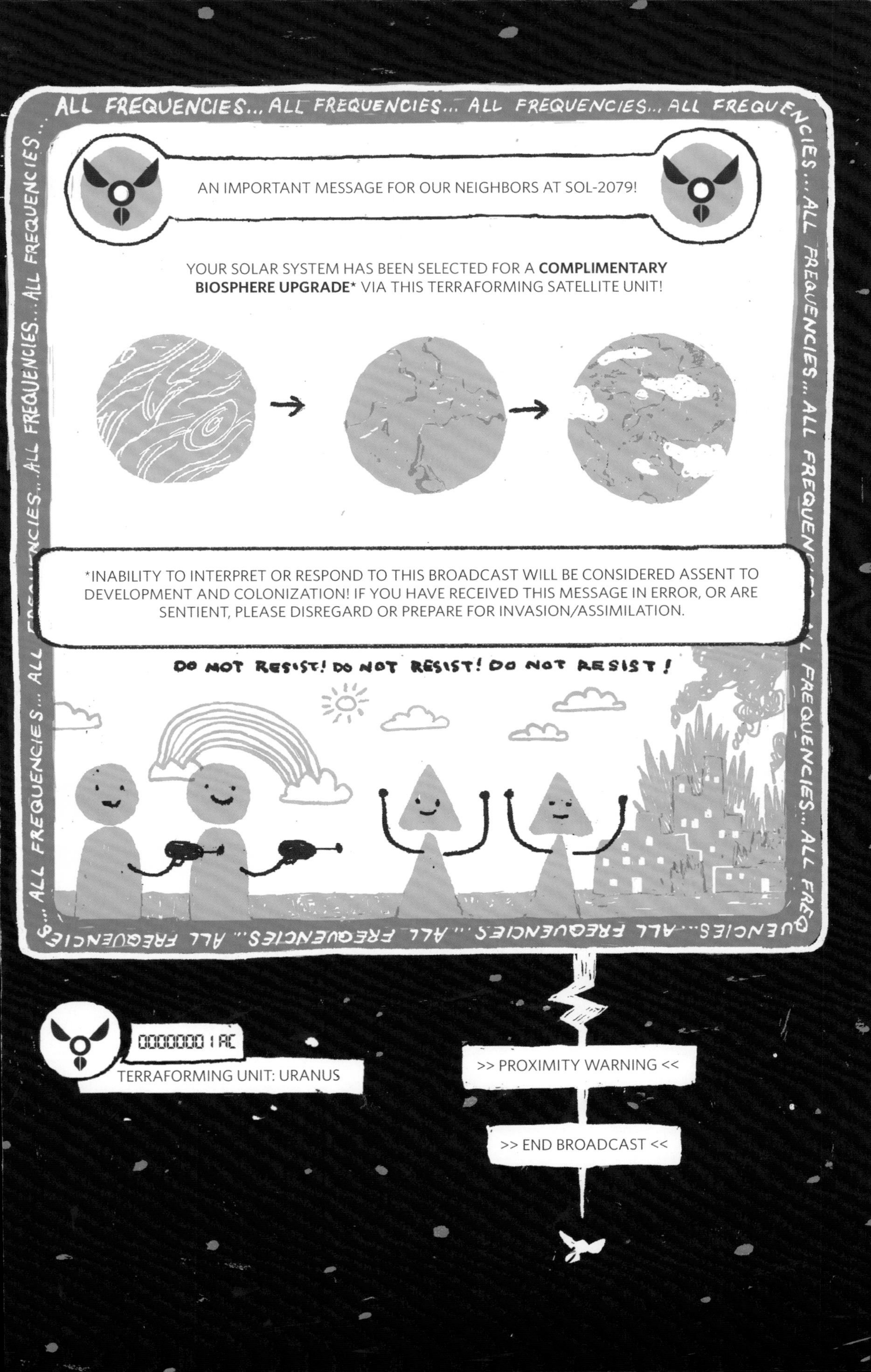
ALL FREQUENCIES... ALL FREQUENCIES... ALL FREQUENCIES... ALL FREQUENCIES...
AN IMPORTANT MESSAGE FOR OUR NEIGHBORS AT SOL-2079!
YOUR SOLAR SYSTEM HAS BEEN SELECTED FOR A **COMPLIMENTARY BIOSPHERE UPGRADE*** VIA THIS TERRAFORMING SATELLITE UNIT!
*INABILITY TO INTERPRET OR RESPOND TO THIS BROADCAST WILL BE CONSIDERED ASSENT TO DEVELOPMENT AND COLONIZATION! IF YOU HAVE RECEIVED THIS MESSAGE IN ERROR, OR ARE SENTIENT, PLEASE DISREGARD OR PREPARE FOR INVASION/ASSIMILATION.
DO NOT RESIST! DO NOT RESIST! DO NOT RESIST!
0000001AC
TERRAFORMING UNIT: URANUS
>> PROXIMITY WARNING <<
>> END BROADCAST <<

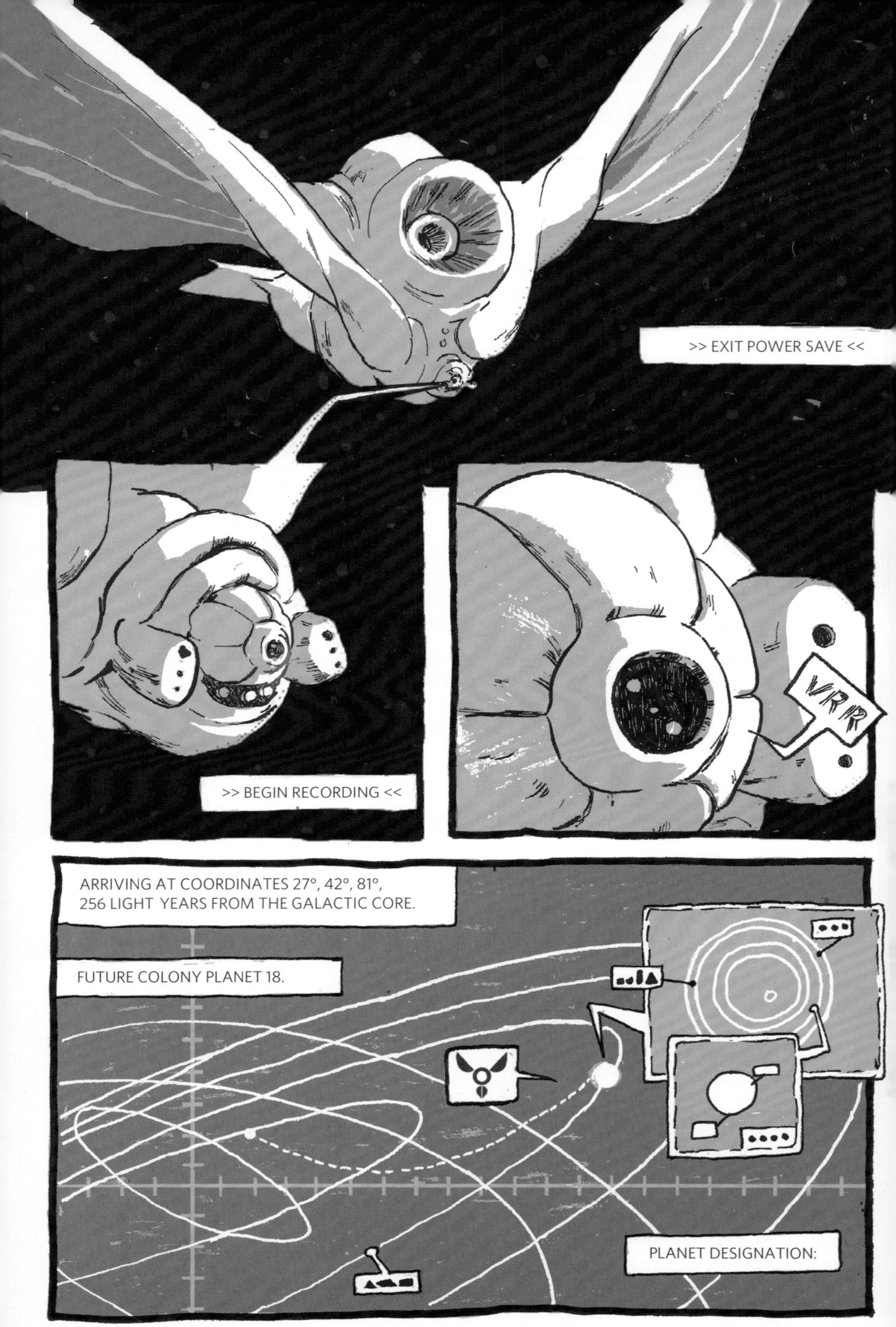

>> EXIT POWER SAVE <<
>> BEGIN RECORDING <<
VRR
ARRIVING AT COORDINATES 27°, 42°, 81°,
256 LIGHT YEARS FROM THE GALACTIC CORE.
FUTURE COLONY PLANET 18.
PLANET DESIGNATION:

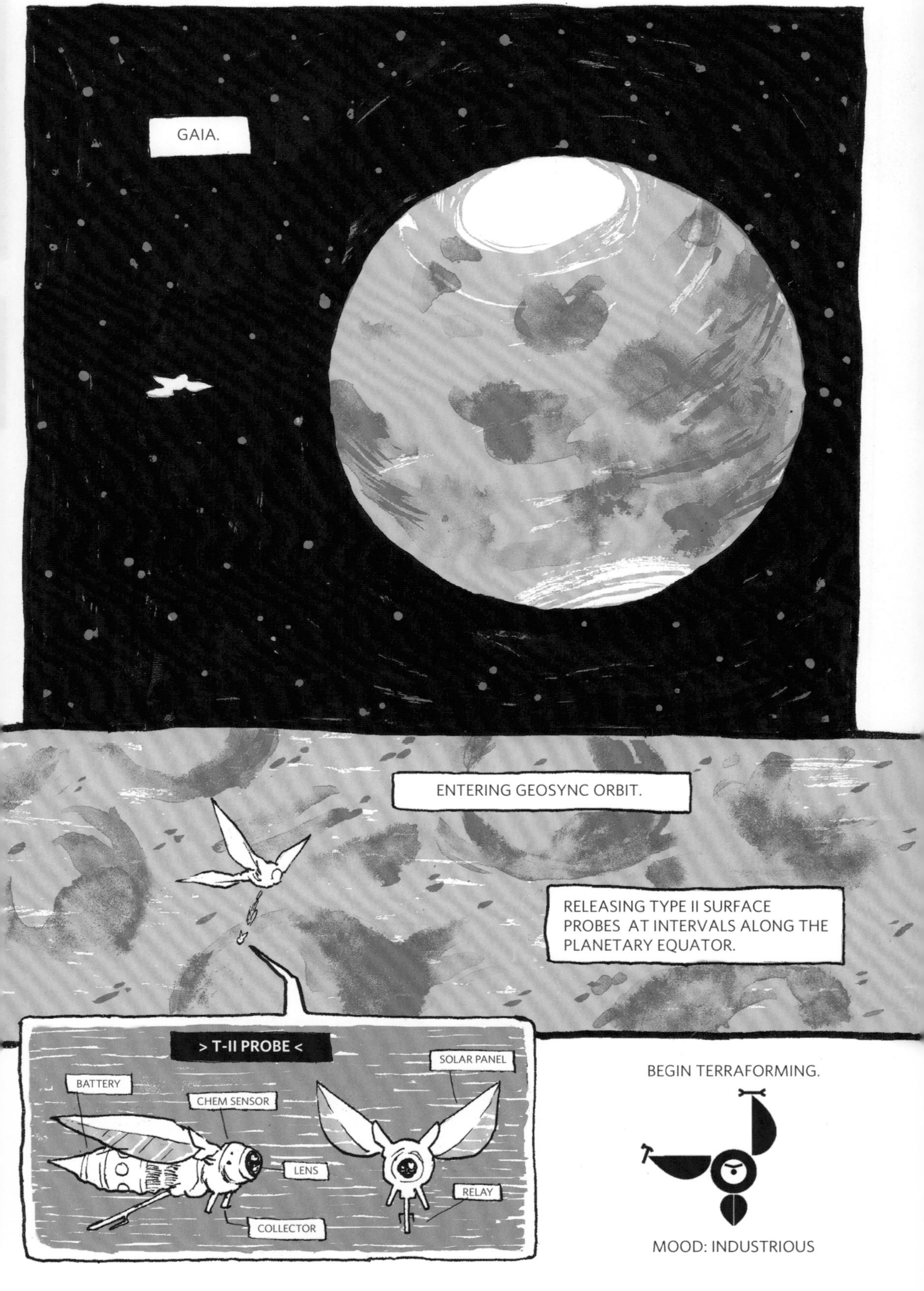
GAIA.
ENTERING GEOSYNC ORBIT.
RELEASING TYPE II SURFACE PROBES AT INTERVALS ALONG THE PLANETARY EQUATOR.
> T-II PROBE <
BATTERY
CHEM SENSOR
SOLAR PANEL
LENS
RELAY
COLLECTOR
BEGIN TERRAFORMING.
MOOD: INDUSTRIOUS

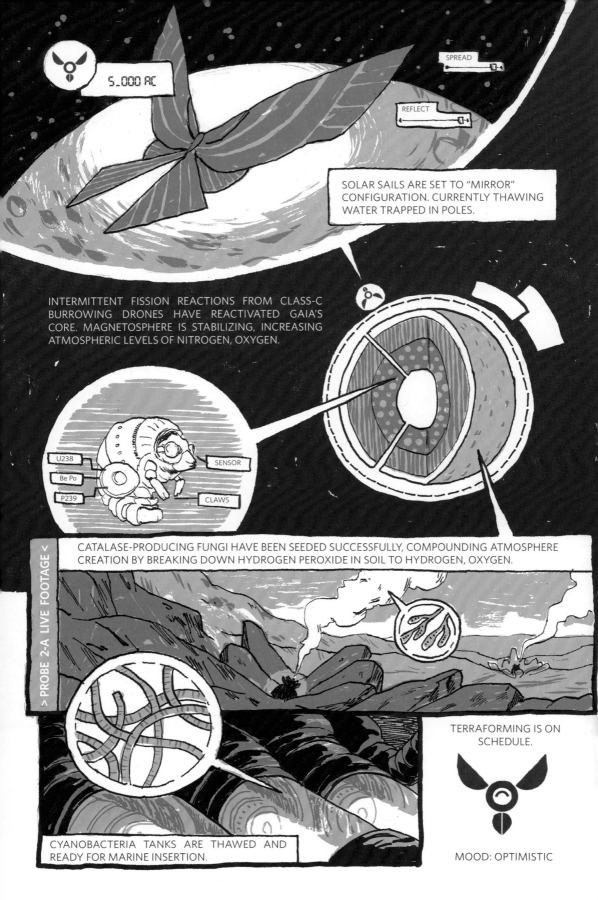

SPREAD

REFLECT

5,000 AC

SOLAR SAILS ARE SET TO "MIRROR" CONFIGURATION. CURRENTLY THAWING WATER TRAPPED IN POLES.

INTERMITTENT FISSION REACTIONS FROM CLASS-C BURROWING DRONES HAVE REACTIVATED GAIA'S CORE. MAGNETOSPHERE IS STABILIZING, INCREASING ATMOSPHERIC LEVELS OF NITROGEN, OXYGEN.

U238
Be Po
P239
SENSOR
CLAWS

CATALASE-PRODUCING FUNGI HAVE BEEN SEEDED SUCCESSFULLY, COMPOUNDING ATMOSPHERE CREATION BY BREAKING DOWN HYDROGEN PEROXIDE IN SOIL TO HYDROGEN, OXYGEN.

> PROBE 2-A LIVE FOOTAGE <

TERRAFORMING IS ON SCHEDULE.

CYANOBACTERIA TANKS ARE THAWED AND READY FOR MARINE INSERTION.

MOOD: OPTIMISTIC

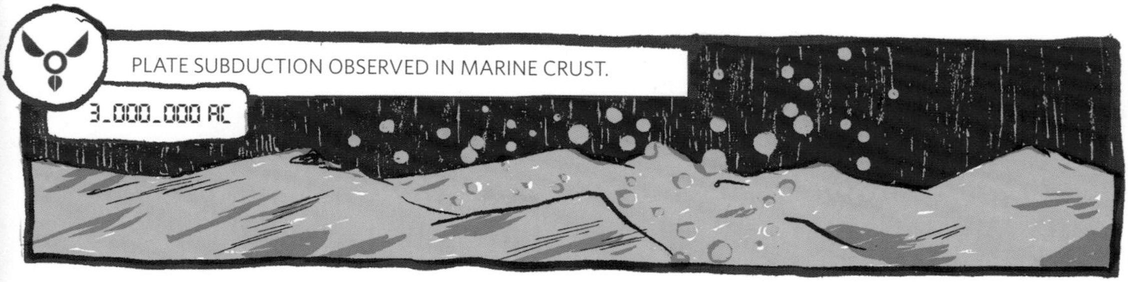
PLATE SUBDUCTION OBSERVED IN MARINE CRUST.
3.000.000 AC

EUKARYOTIC DEVELOPMENTS ARE RUNNING AHEAD OF SCHEDULE. BIODIVERSITY HAS PASSED THE GURNEY LINE AND IS REACHING PEAK AESTHETIC EFFECT.

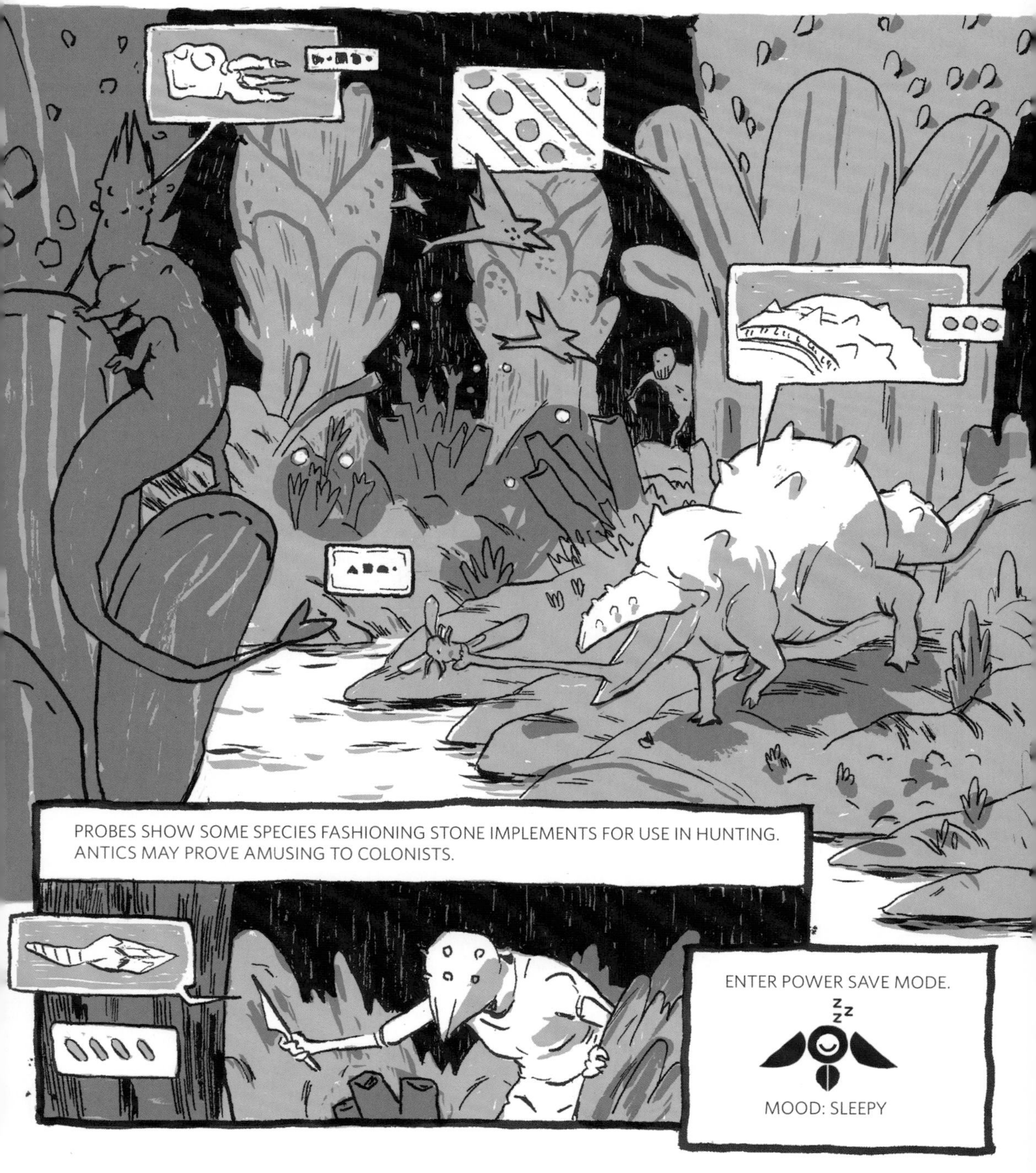
PROBES SHOW SOME SPECIES FASHIONING STONE IMPLEMENTS FOR USE IN HUNTING. ANTICS MAY PROVE AMUSING TO COLONISTS.
ENTER POWER SAVE MODE.
Z Z Z
MOOD: SLEEPY

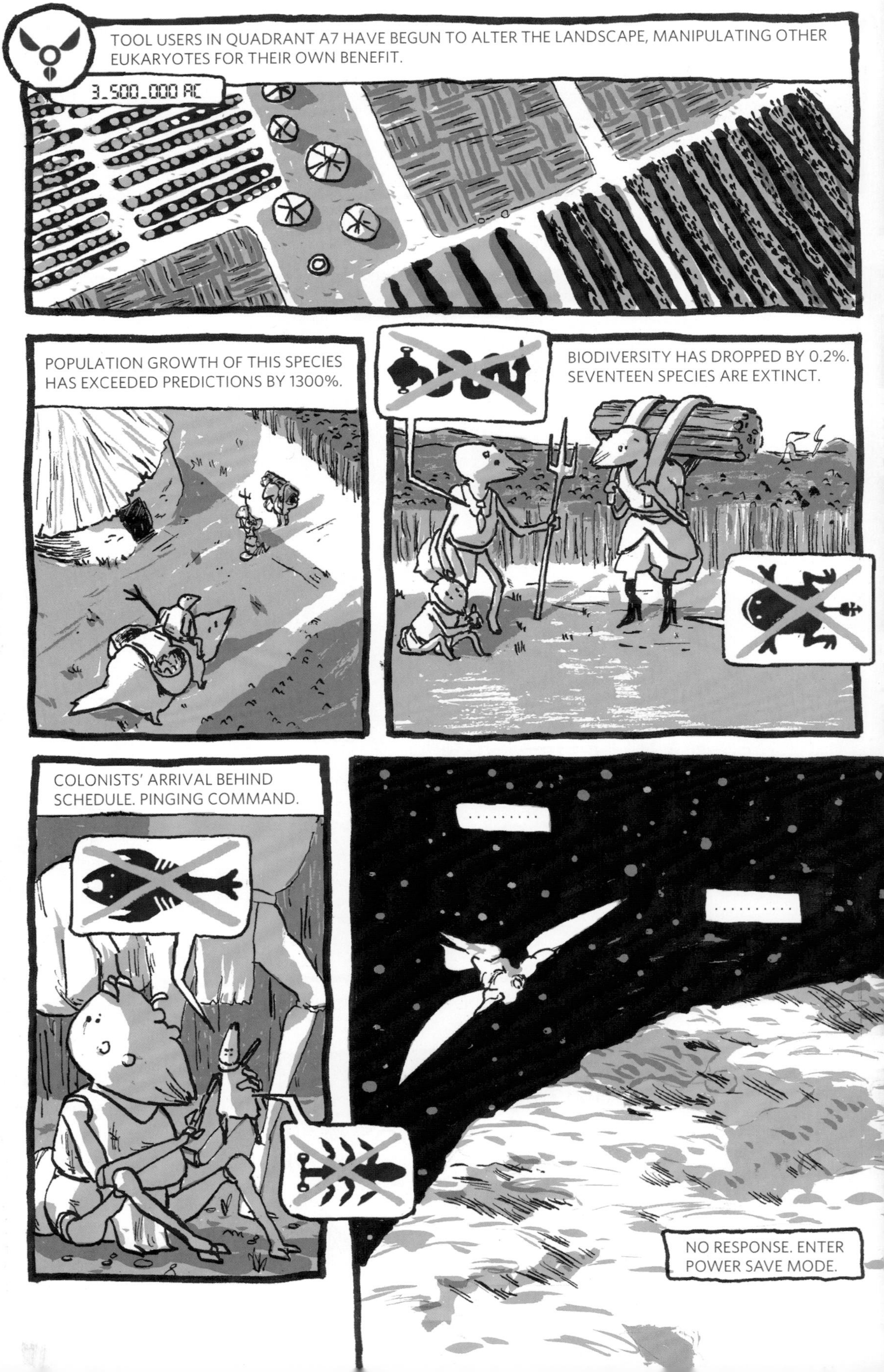

TOOL USERS IN QUADRANT A7 HAVE BEGUN TO ALTER THE LANDSCAPE, MANIPULATING OTHER EUKARYOTES FOR THEIR OWN BENEFIT.
3,500,000 AC
POPULATION GROWTH OF THIS SPECIES HAS EXCEEDED PREDICTIONS BY 1300%.
BIODIVERSITY HAS DROPPED BY 0.2%. SEVENTEEN SPECIES ARE EXTINCT.
COLONISTS' ARRIVAL BEHIND SCHEDULE. PINGING COMMAND.
....
....
NO RESPONSE. ENTER POWER SAVE MODE.

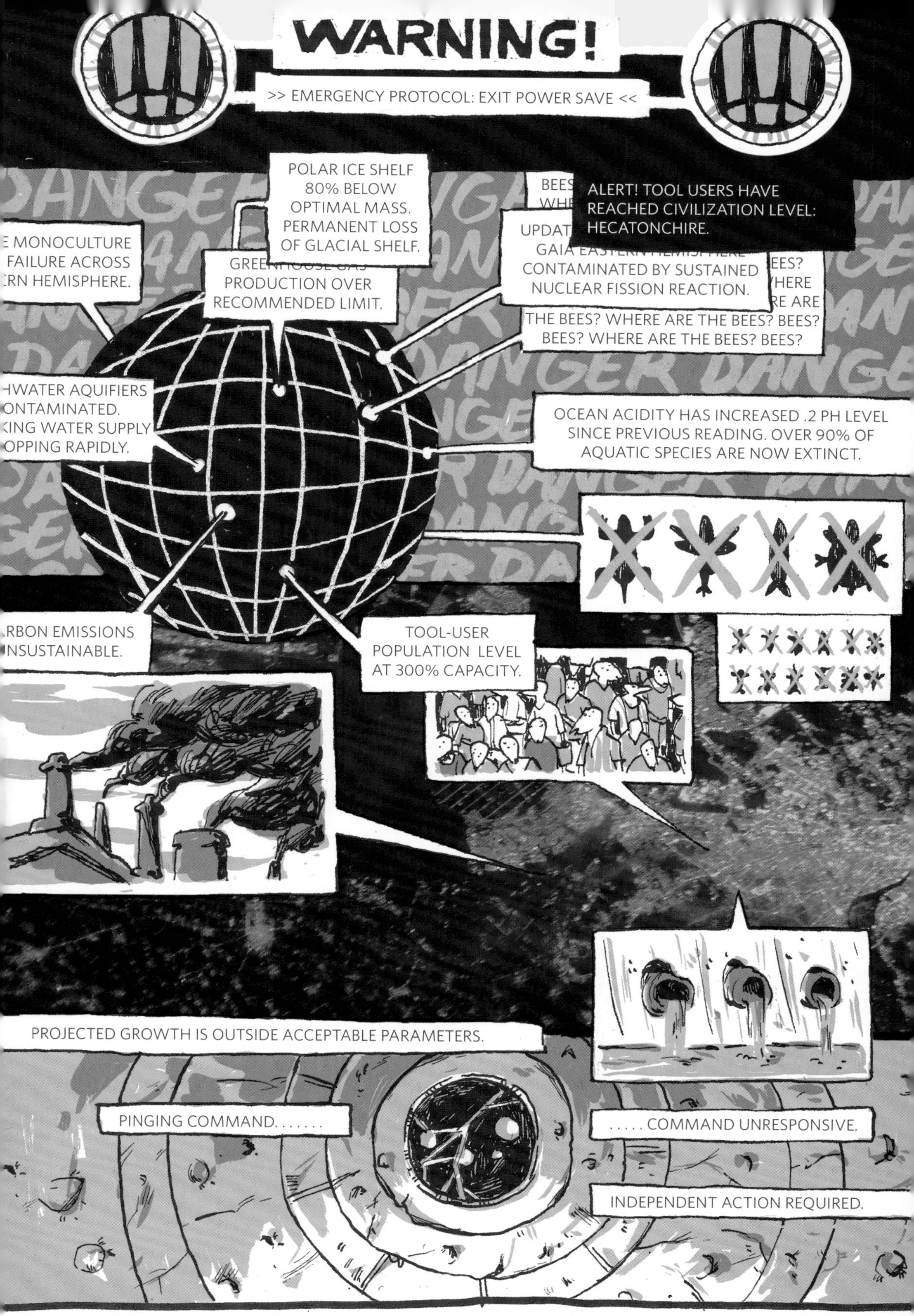

WARNING!
>> EMERGENCY PROTOCOL: EXIT POWER SAVE <<
POLAR ICE SHELF 80% BELOW OPTIMAL MASS. PERMANENT LOSS OF GLACIAL SHELF.
ALERT! TOOL USERS HAVE REACHED CIVILIZATION LEVEL: HECATONCHIRE.
E MONOCULTURE FAILURE ACROSS ERN HEMISPHERE.
PRODUCTION OVER RECOMMENDED LIMIT.
CONTAMINATED BY SUSTAINED NUCLEAR FISSION REACTION.
THE BEES? WHERE ARE THE BEES? BEES? BEES? WHERE ARE THE BEES? BEES?
HWATER AQUIFIERS ONTAMINATED. KING WATER SUPPLY OPPING RAPIDLY.
OCEAN ACIDITY HAS INCREASED .2 PH LEVEL SINCE PREVIOUS READING. OVER 90% OF AQUATIC SPECIES ARE NOW EXTINCT.
RBON EMISSIONS NSUSTAINABLE.
TOOL-USER POPULATION LEVEL AT 300% CAPACITY.
PROJECTED GROWTH IS OUTSIDE ACCEPTABLE PARAMETERS.
PINGING COMMAND. . . . . . .
. . . . . COMMAND UNRESPONSIVE.
INDEPENDENT ACTION REQUIRED.

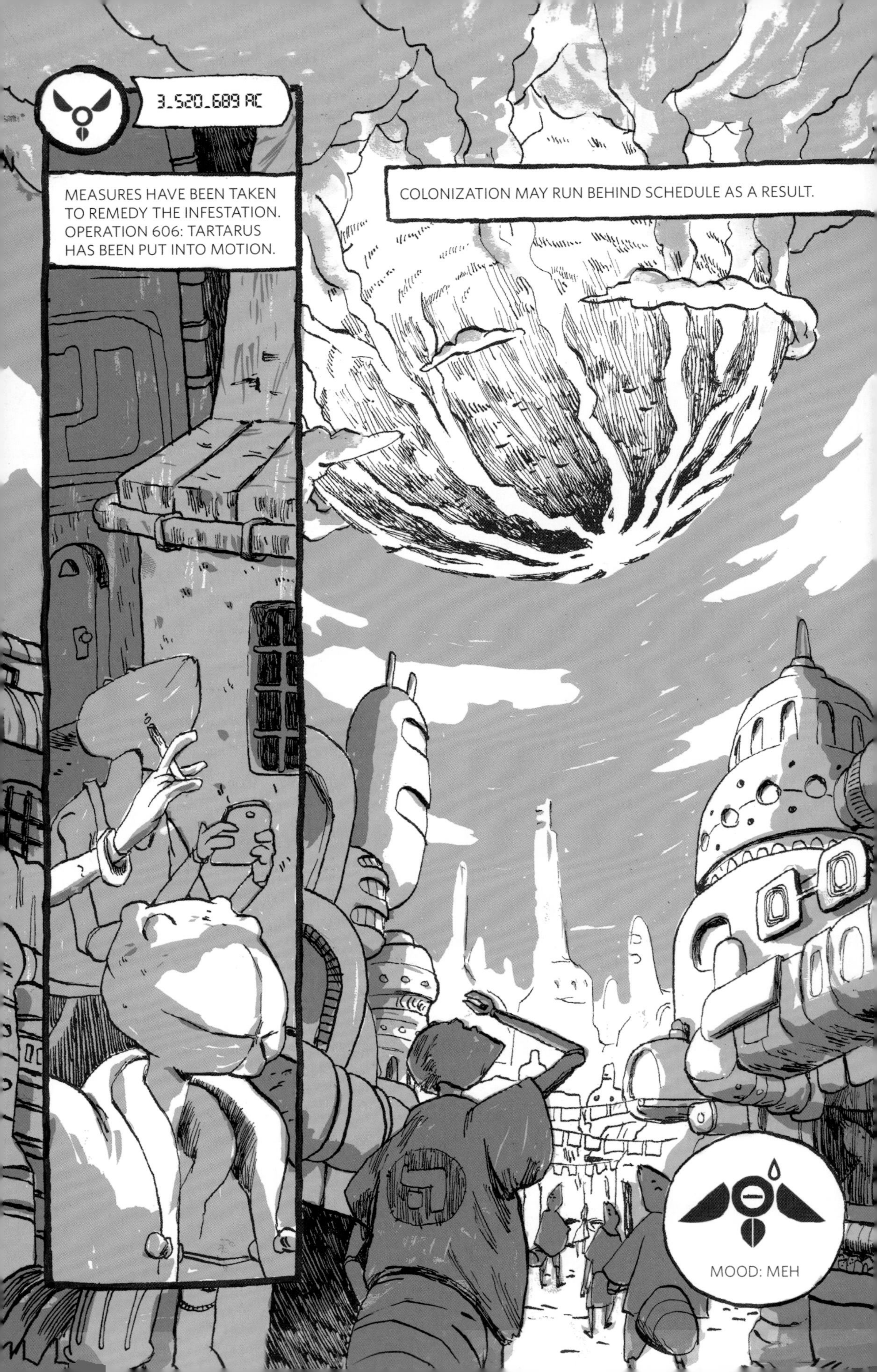
3_520_689 AC
MEASURES HAVE BEEN TAKEN TO REMEDY THE INFESTATION. OPERATION 606: TARTARUS HAS BEEN PUT INTO MOTION.
COLONIZATION MAY RUN BEHIND SCHEDULE AS A RESULT.
MOOD: MEH

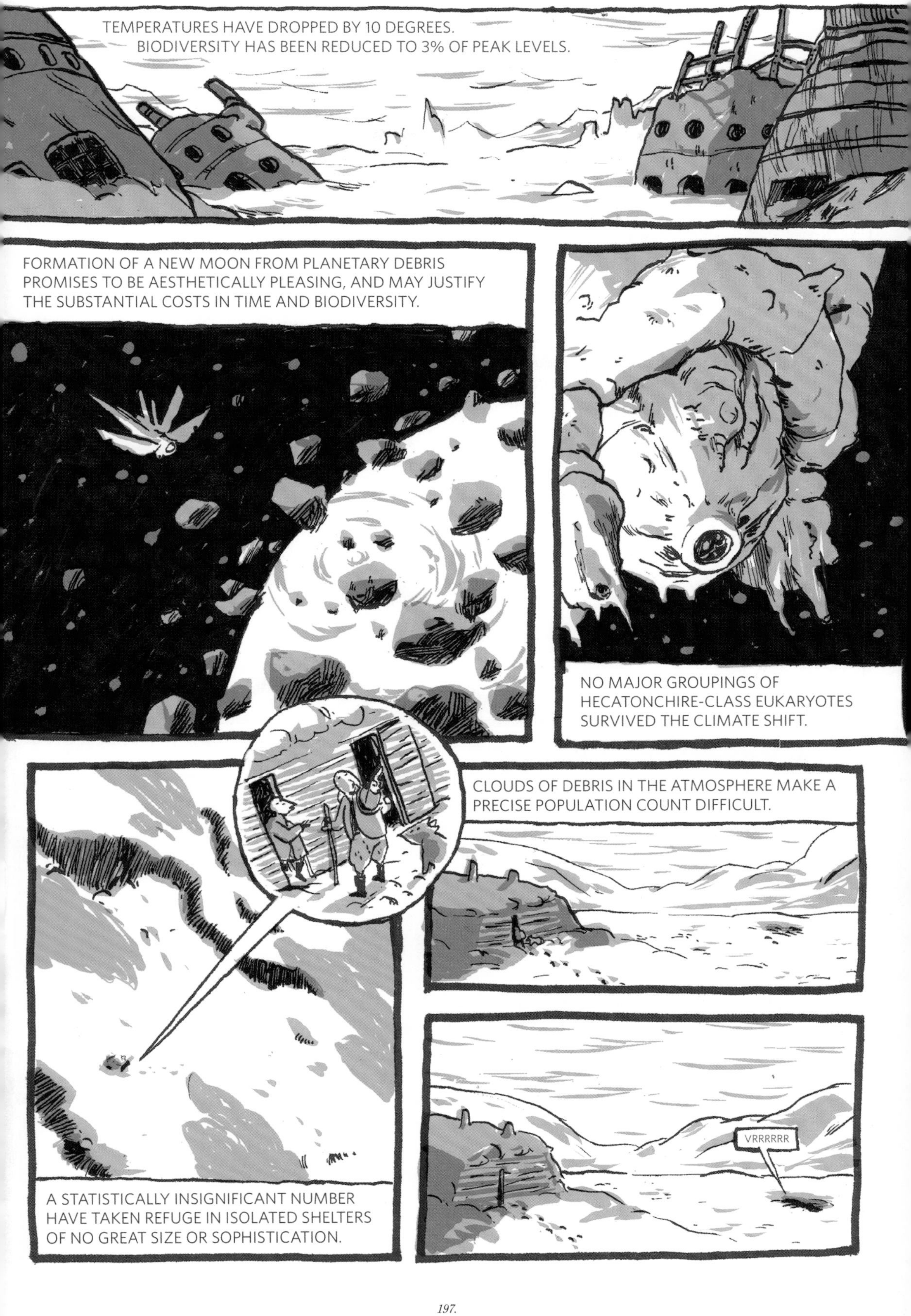
TEMPERATURES HAVE DROPPED BY 10 DEGREES.
BIODIVERSITY HAS BEEN REDUCED TO 3% OF PEAK LEVELS.
FORMATION OF A NEW MOON FROM PLANETARY DEBRIS PROMISES TO BE AESTHETICALLY PLEASING, AND MAY JUSTIFY THE SUBSTANTIAL COSTS IN TIME AND BIODIVERSITY.
NO MAJOR GROUPINGS OF HECATONCHIRE-CLASS EUKARYOTES SURVIVED THE CLIMATE SHIFT.
A STATISTICALLY INSIGNIFICANT NUMBER HAVE TAKEN REFUGE IN ISOLATED SHELTERS OF NO GREAT SIZE OR SOPHISTICATION.
CLOUDS OF DEBRIS IN THE ATMOSPHERE MAKE A PRECISE POPULATION COUNT DIFFICULT.
VRRRRRR

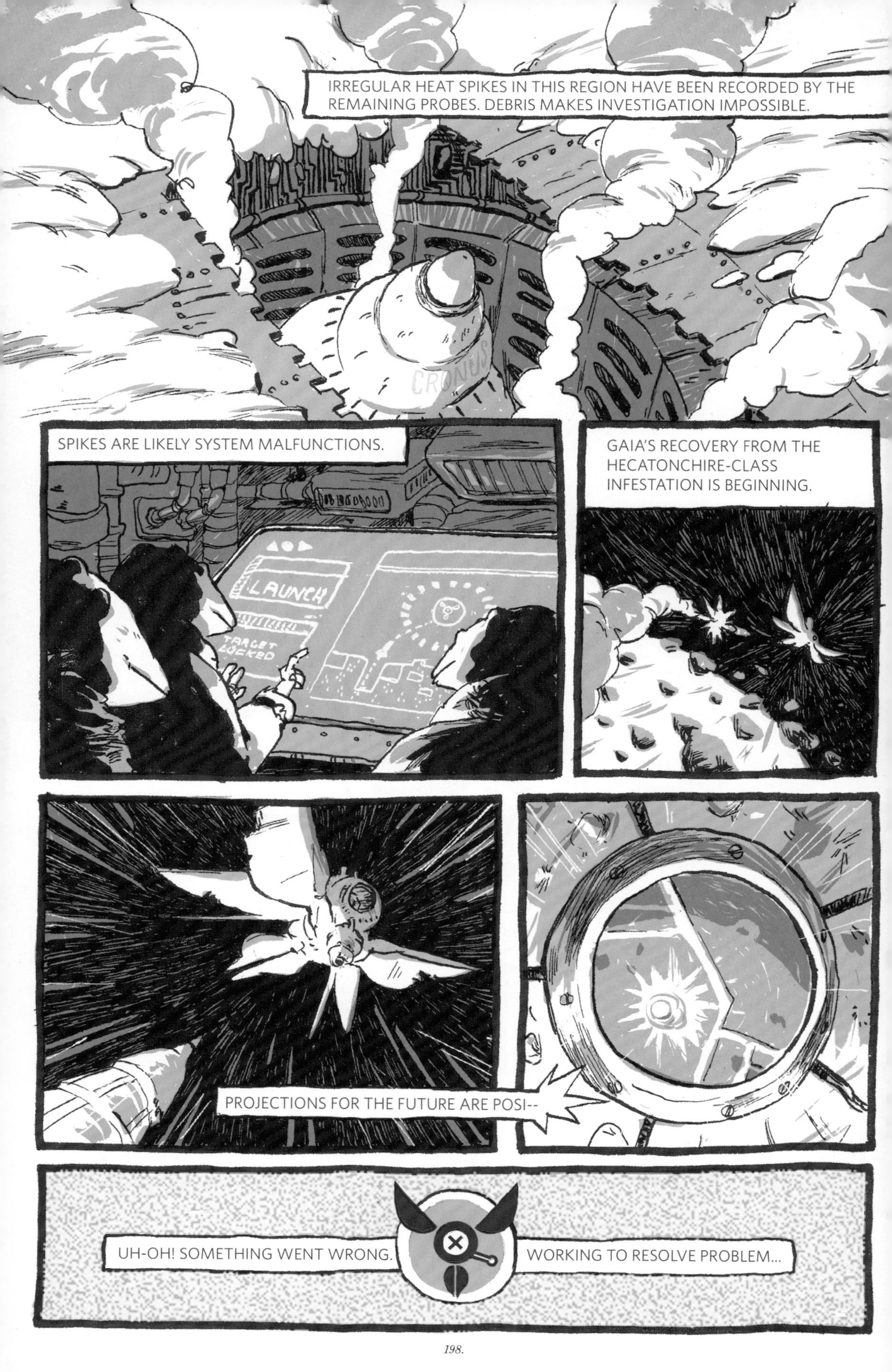
IRREGULAR HEAT SPIKES IN THIS REGION HAVE BEEN RECORDED BY THE REMAINING PROBES. DEBRIS MAKES INVESTIGATION IMPOSSIBLE.
CRONUS
SPIKES ARE LIKELY SYSTEM MALFUNCTIONS.
LAUNCH
TARGET LOCKED
GAIA'S RECOVERY FROM THE HECATONCHIRE-CLASS INFESTATION IS BEGINNING.
PROJECTIONS FOR THE FUTURE ARE POSI--
UH-OH! SOMETHING WENT WRONG.
WORKING TO RESOLVE PROBLEM...

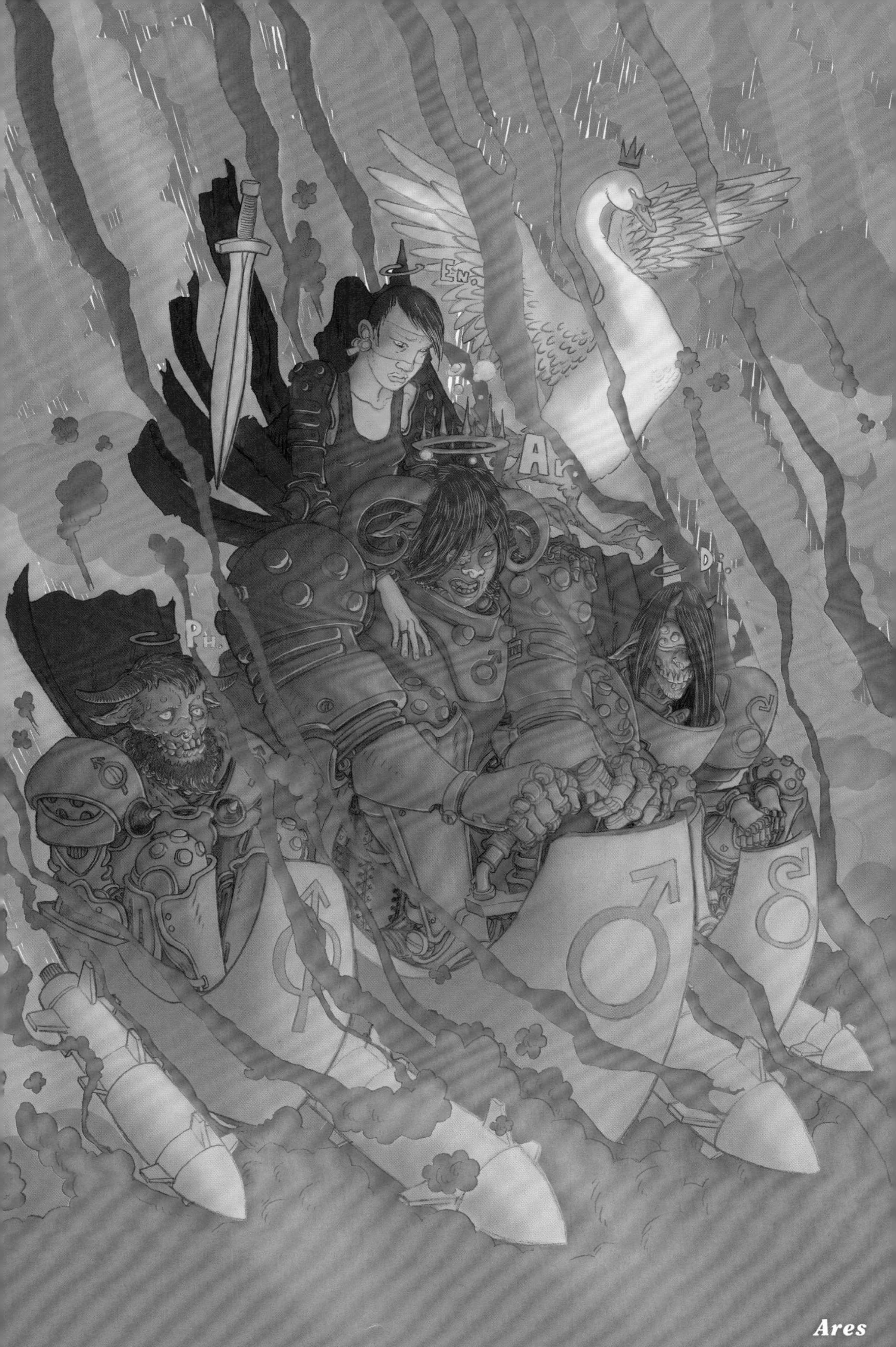
En.
Ar.
Ph.
Di.

Ares
BODIE CHEWNING

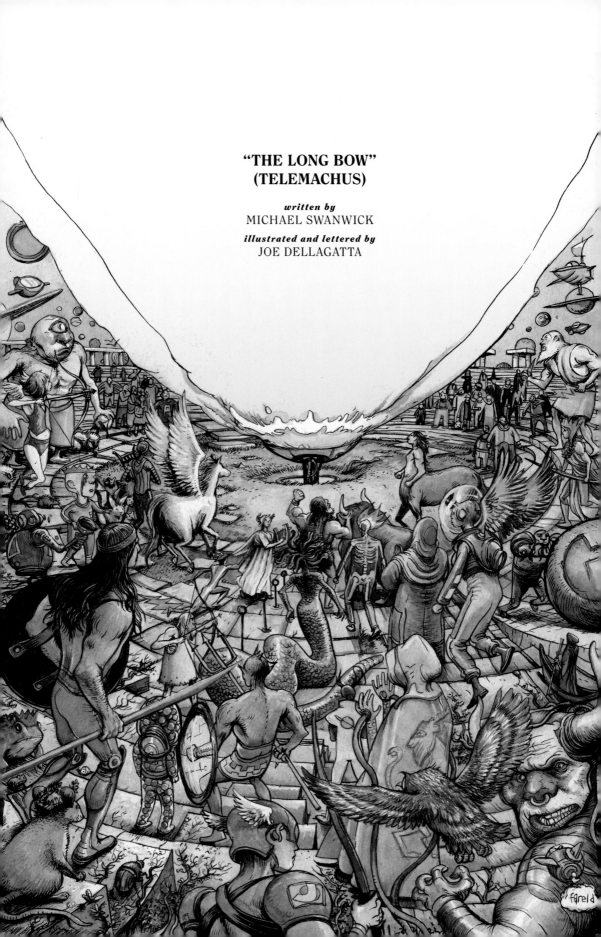

"THE LONG BOW"
(TELEMACHUS)

written by
MICHAEL SWANWICK

illustrated and lettered by
JOE DELLAGATTA

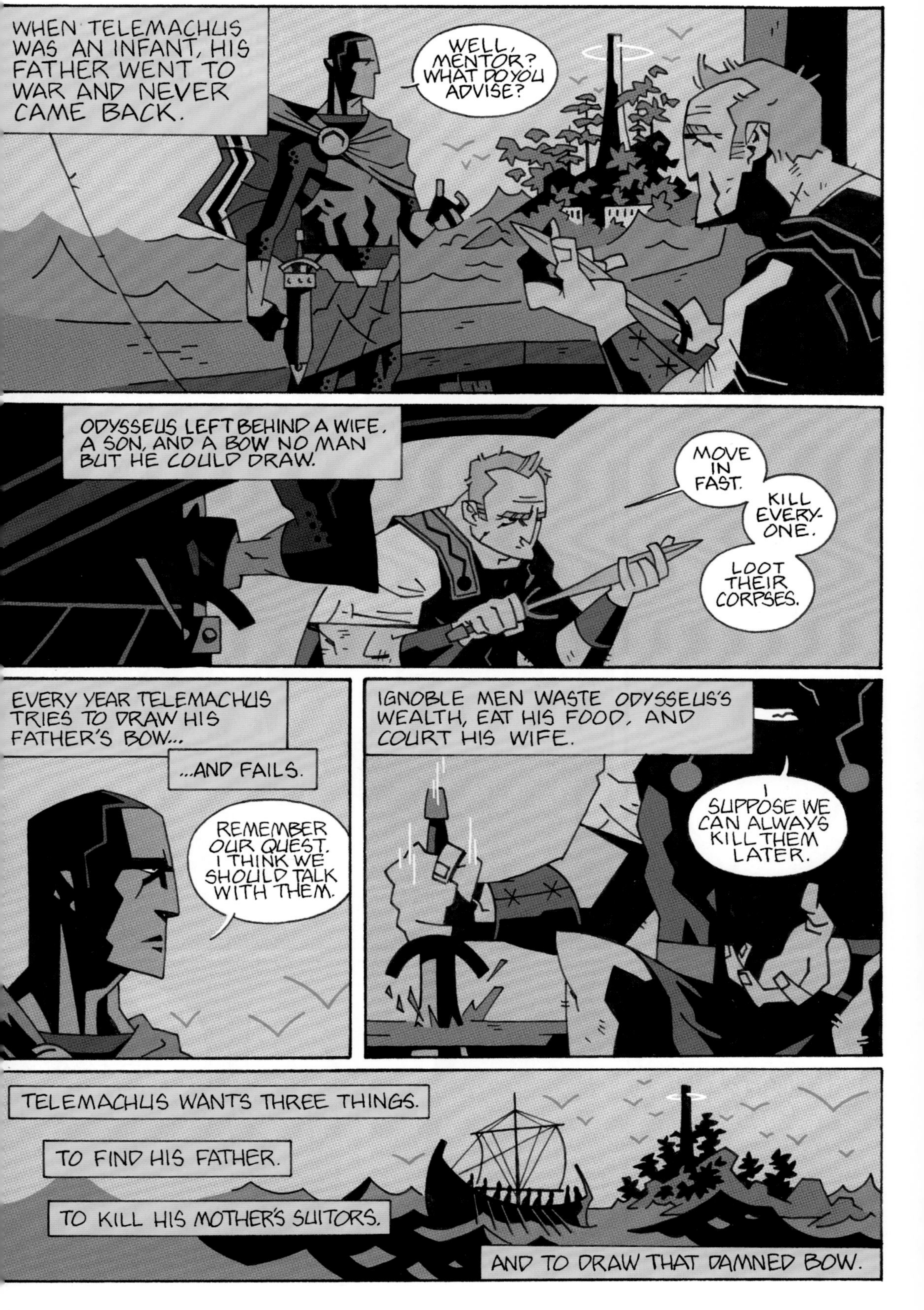
WHEN TELEMACHUS WAS AN INFANT, HIS FATHER WENT TO WAR AND NEVER CAME BACK.
WELL, MENTOR? WHAT DO YOU ADVISE?
ODYSSEUS LEFT BEHIND A WIFE, A SON, AND A BOW NO MAN BUT HE COULD DRAW.
MOVE IN FAST.
KILL EVERY-ONE.
LOOT THEIR CORPSES.
EVERY YEAR TELEMACHUS TRIES TO DRAW HIS FATHER'S BOW...
...AND FAILS.
REMEMBER OUR QUEST. I THINK WE SHOULD TALK WITH THEM.
IGNOBLE MEN WASTE ODYSSEUS'S WEALTH, EAT HIS FOOD, AND COURT HIS WIFE.
I SUPPOSE WE CAN ALWAYS KILL THEM LATER.
TELEMACHUS WANTS THREE THINGS.
TO FIND HIS FATHER.
TO KILL HIS MOTHER'S SUITORS.
AND TO DRAW THAT DAMNED BOW.

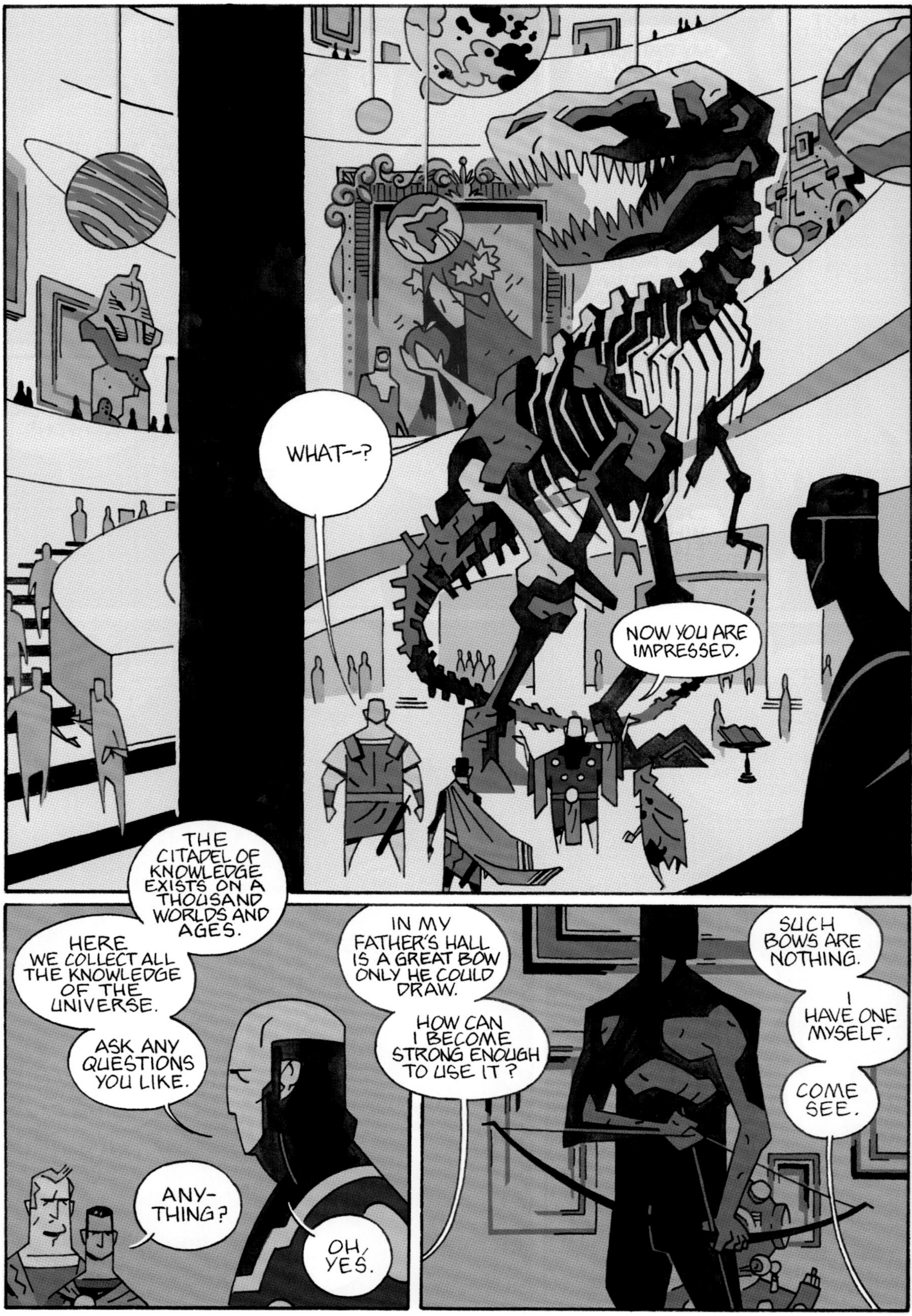
WHAT--?
NOW YOU ARE IMPRESSED.
THE CITADEL OF KNOWLEDGE EXISTS ON A THOUSAND WORLDS AND AGES.
HERE WE COLLECT ALL THE KNOWLEDGE OF THE UNIVERSE.
ASK ANY QUESTIONS YOU LIKE.
ANY-THING?
OH, YES.
IN MY FATHER'S HALL IS A GREAT BOW ONLY HE COULD DRAW.
HOW CAN I BECOME STRONG ENOUGH TO USE IT?
SUCH BOWS ARE NOTHING.
I HAVE ONE MYSELF.
COME SEE.

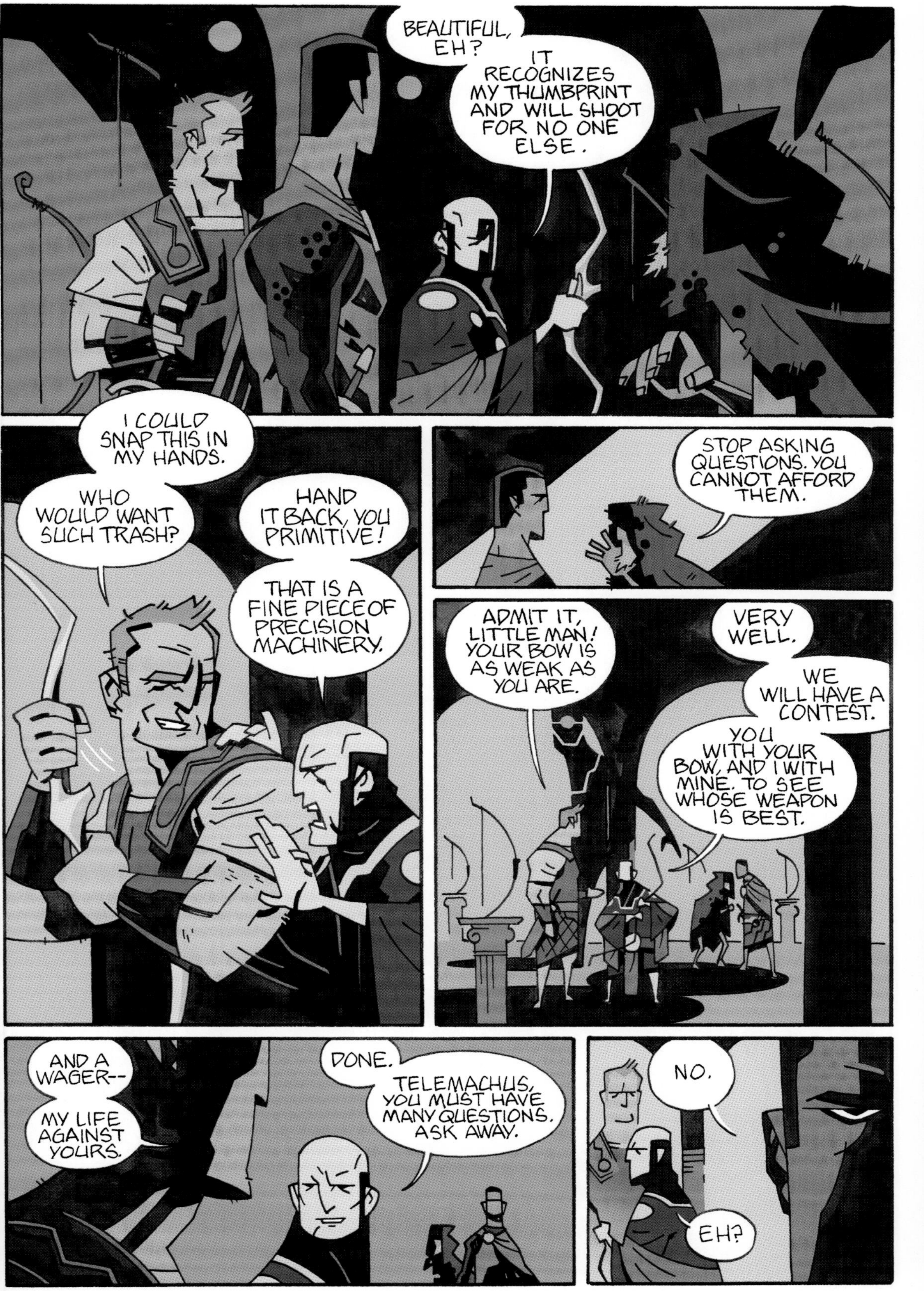
BEAUTIFUL, EH?
IT RECOGNIZES MY THUMBPRINT AND WILL SHOOT FOR NO ONE ELSE.
I COULD SNAP THIS IN MY HANDS.
WHO WOULD WANT SUCH TRASH?
HAND IT BACK, YOU PRIMITIVE!
THAT IS A FINE PIECE OF PRECISION MACHINERY.
STOP ASKING QUESTIONS. YOU CANNOT AFFORD THEM.
ADMIT IT, LITTLE MAN! YOUR BOW IS AS WEAK AS YOU ARE.
VERY WELL.
WE WILL HAVE A CONTEST.
YOU WITH YOUR BOW, AND I WITH MINE. TO SEE WHOSE WEAPON IS BEST.
AND A WAGER--
MY LIFE AGAINST YOURS.
DONE.
TELEMACHUS, YOU MUST HAVE MANY QUESTIONS. ASK AWAY.
NO.
EH?

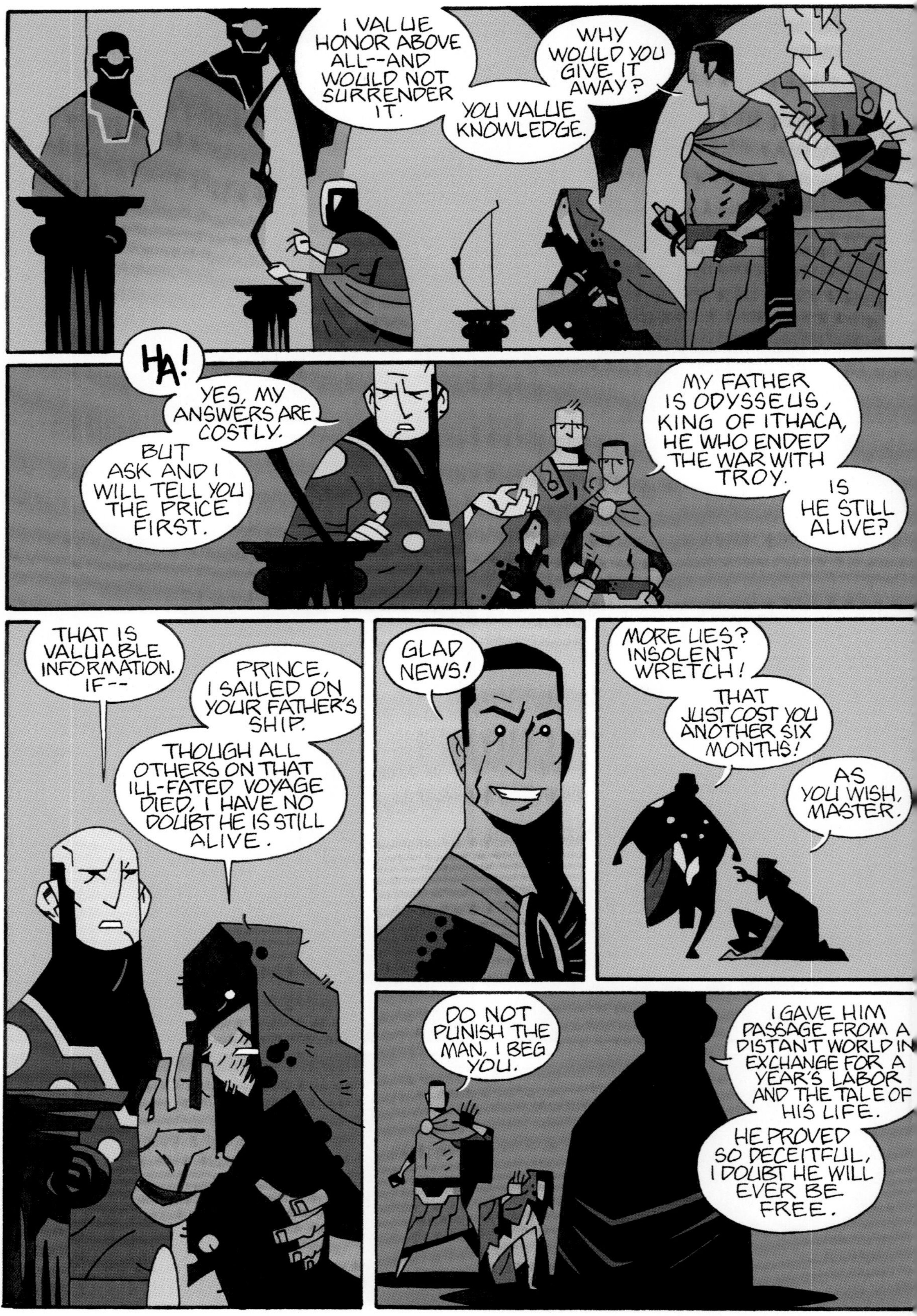
I VALUE HONOR ABOVE ALL--AND WOULD NOT SURRENDER IT.
YOU VALUE KNOWLEDGE.
WHY WOULD YOU GIVE IT AWAY?
HA!
YES, MY ANSWERS ARE COSTLY.
BUT ASK AND I WILL TELL YOU THE PRICE FIRST.
MY FATHER IS ODYSSEUS, KING OF ITHACA, HE WHO ENDED THE WAR WITH TROY.
IS HE STILL ALIVE?
THAT IS VALUABLE INFORMATION. IF--
PRINCE, I SAILED ON YOUR FATHER'S SHIP.
THOUGH ALL OTHERS ON THAT ILL-FATED VOYAGE DIED, I HAVE NO DOUBT HE IS STILL ALIVE.
GLAD NEWS!
MORE LIES? INSOLENT WRETCH!
THAT JUST COST YOU ANOTHER SIX MONTHS!
AS YOU WISH, MASTER.
DO NOT PUNISH THE MAN, I BEG YOU.
I GAVE HIM PASSAGE FROM A DISTANT WORLD IN EXCHANGE FOR A YEAR'S LABOR AND THE TALE OF HIS LIFE.
HE PROVED SO DECEITFUL, I DOUBT HE WILL EVER BE FREE.

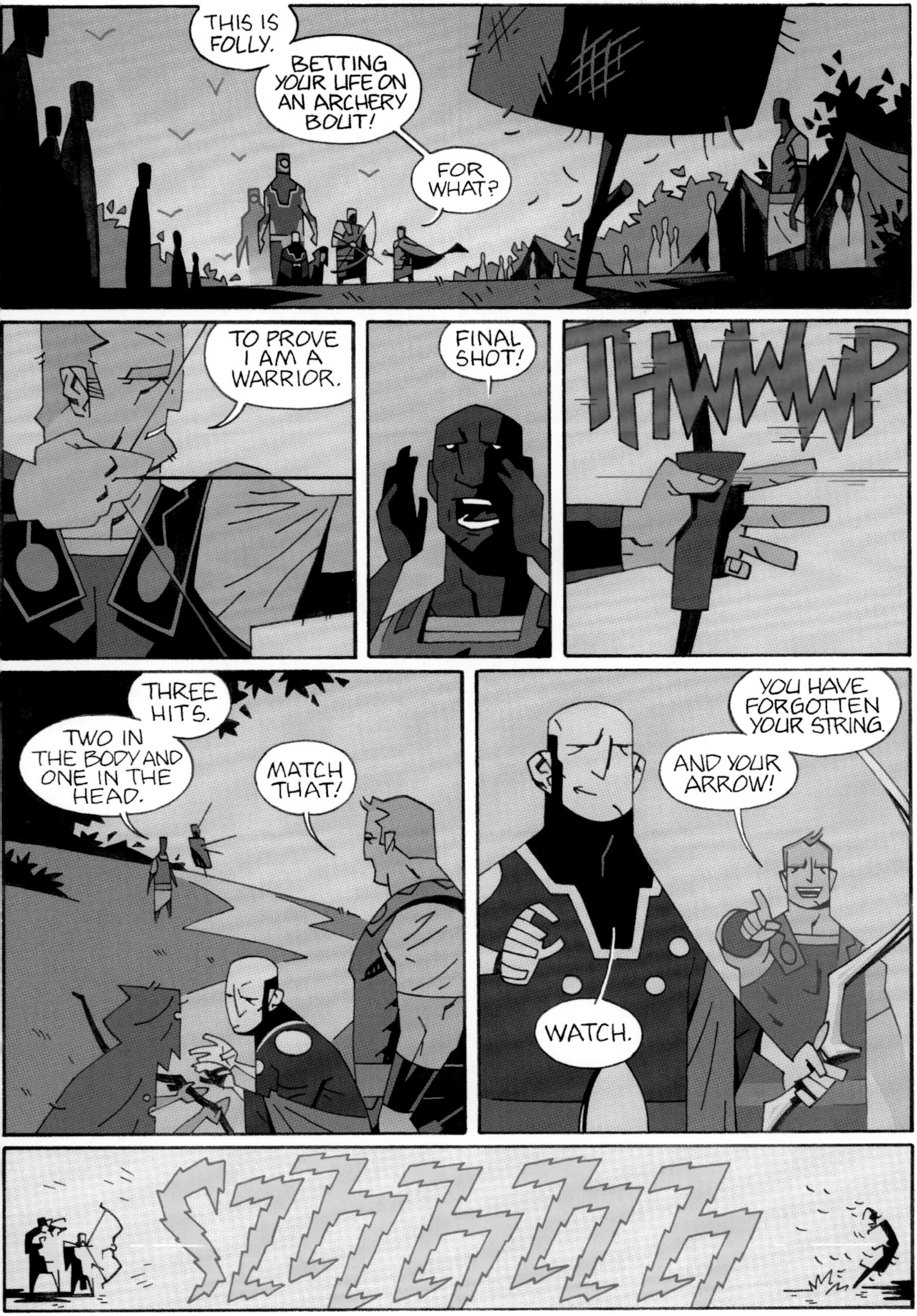
THIS IS FOLLY.
BETTING YOUR LIFE ON AN ARCHERY BOUT!
FOR WHAT?
TO PROVE I AM A WARRIOR.
FINAL SHOT!
THWWWP
THREE HITS.
TWO IN THE BODY AND ONE IN THE HEAD.
MATCH THAT!
YOU HAVE FORGOTTEN YOUR STRING.
AND YOUR ARROW!
WATCH.
SZZZZZZ

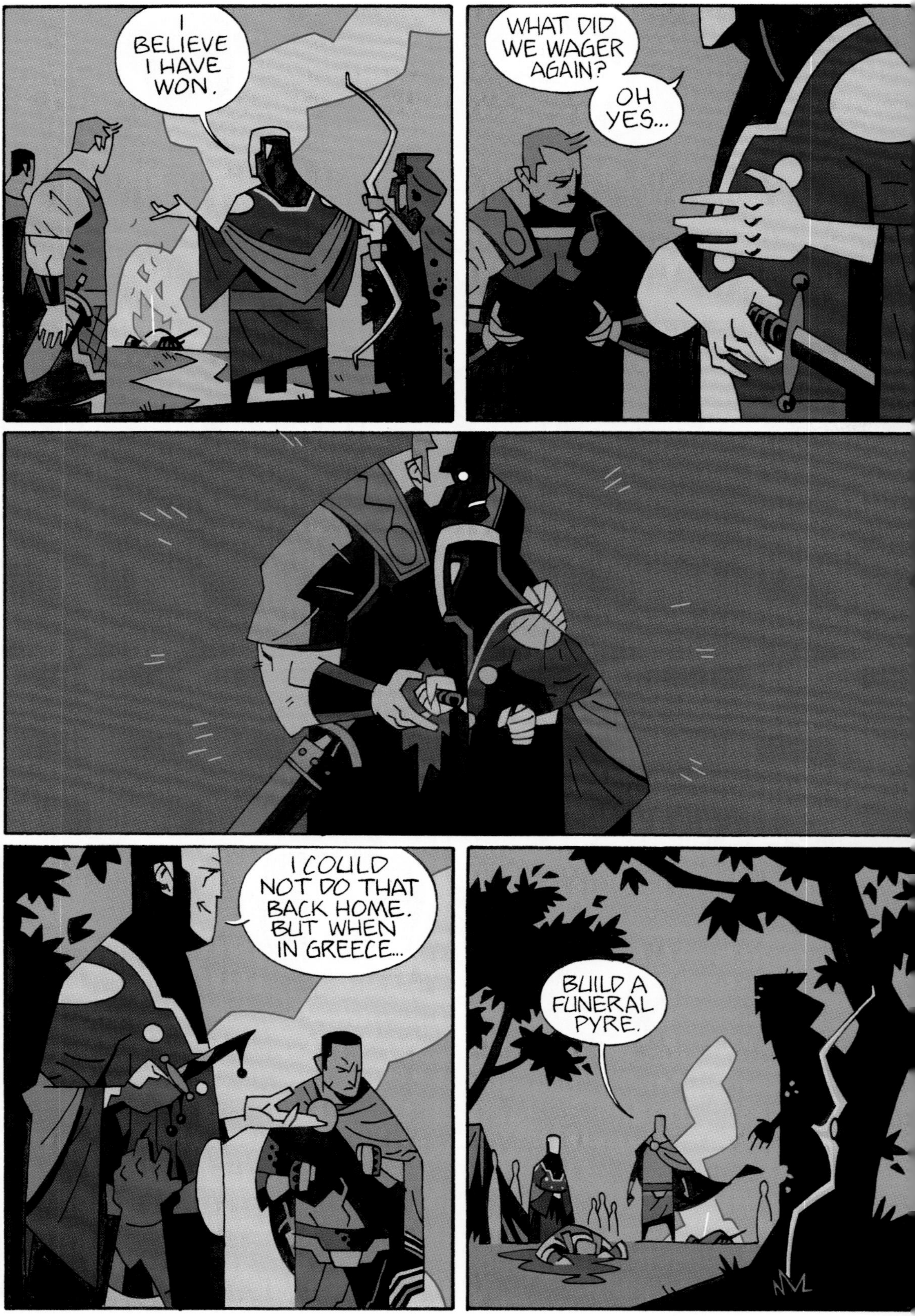
I BELIEVE I HAVE WON.
WHAT DID WE WAGER AGAIN?
OH YES...
I COULD NOT DO THAT BACK HOME. BUT WHEN IN GREECE...
BUILD A FUNERAL PYRE.

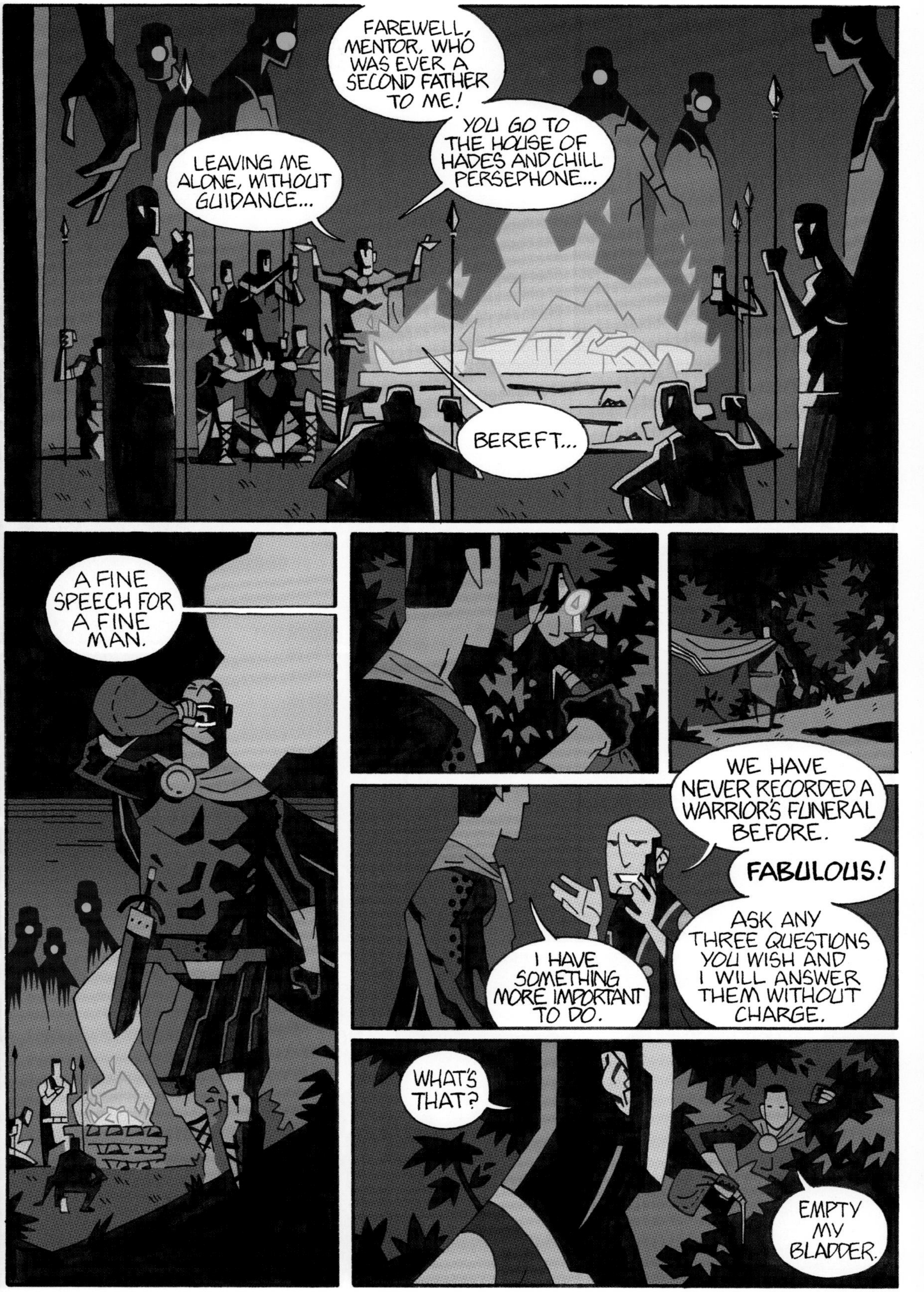
FAREWELL, MENTOR, WHO WAS EVER A SECOND FATHER TO ME!
LEAVING ME ALONE, WITHOUT GUIDANCE...
YOU GO TO THE HOUSE OF HADES AND CHILL PERSEPHONE...
BEREFT...
A FINE SPEECH FOR A FINE MAN.
WE HAVE NEVER RECORDED A WARRIOR'S FUNERAL BEFORE.
FABULOUS!
ASK ANY THREE QUESTIONS YOU WISH AND I WILL ANSWER THEM WITHOUT CHARGE.
I HAVE SOMETHING MORE IMPORTANT TO DO.
WHAT'S THAT?
EMPTY MY BLADDER.

WELL?

A HUNDRED STORIES CELEBRATE ODYSSEUS'S GUILE.

ONLY ONE BOASTS OF HIS STRENGTH.

WHAT ARE YOU SAYING?

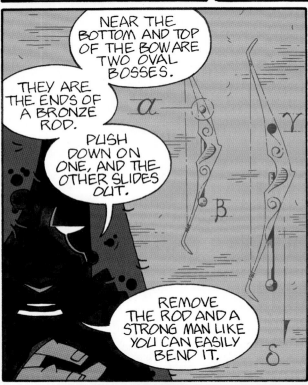

NEAR THE BOTTOM AND TOP OF THE BOW ARE TWO OVAL BOSSES.

THEY ARE THE ENDS OF A BRONZE ROD.

PUSH DOWN ON ONE, AND THE OTHER SLIDES OUT.

REMOVE THE ROD AND A STRONG MAN LIKE YOU CAN EASILY BEND IT.

α

γ

β

δ

WHO ARE YOU REALLY, OLD WOLF?

WHO DO YOU THINK?

FATHER!

SON...

DO YOU HAVE A KNIFE ON YOU?

YES.

SELBST HAS PROGRAMMED THE METAL MEN NOT TO LET ME NEAR HIM WITH A BLADE.

YOU, HOWEVER...

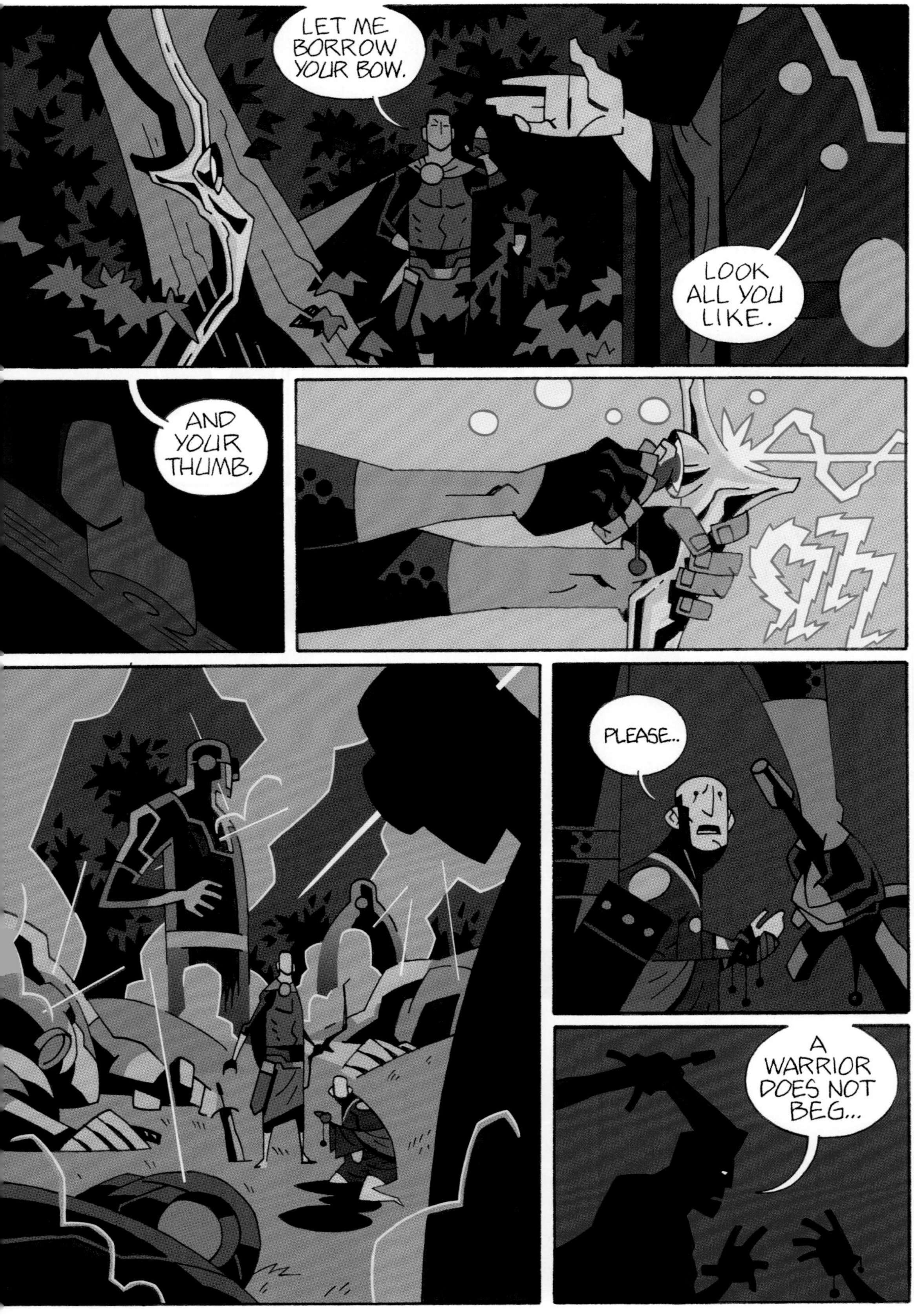
LET ME BORROW YOUR BOW.
LOOK ALL YOU LIKE.
AND YOUR THUMB.
PLEASE..
A WARRIOR DOES NOT BEG...

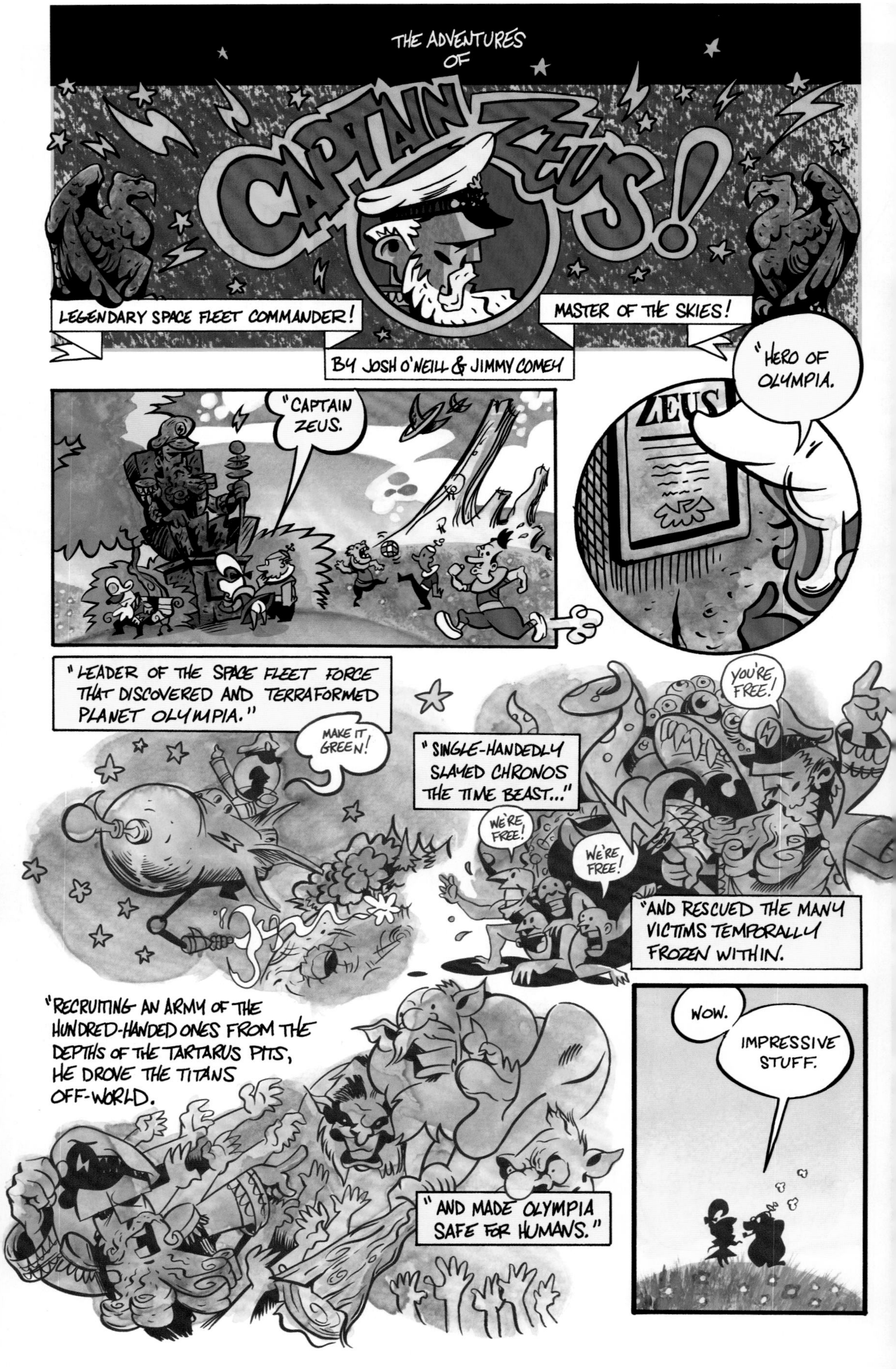
THE ADVENTURES OF
CAPTAIN ZEUS!
LEGENDARY SPACE FLEET COMMANDER!
MASTER OF THE SKIES!
BY JOSH O'NEILL & JIMMY COMEY
"CAPTAIN ZEUS.
"HERO OF OLYMPIA.
ZEUS
"LEADER OF THE SPACE FLEET FORCE THAT DISCOVERED AND TERRAFORMED PLANET OLYMPIA."
MAKE IT GREEN!
"SINGLE-HANDEDLY SLAYED CHRONOS THE TIME BEAST..."
YOU'RE FREE!
WE'RE FREE!
WE'RE FREE!
"AND RESCUED THE MANY VICTIMS TEMPORALLY FROZEN WITHIN.
"RECRUITING AN ARMY OF THE HUNDRED-HANDED ONES FROM THE DEPTHS OF THE TARTARUS PITS, HE DROVE THE TITANS OFF-WORLD.
"AND MADE OLYMPIA SAFE FOR HUMANS."
WOW.
IMPRESSIVE STUFF.

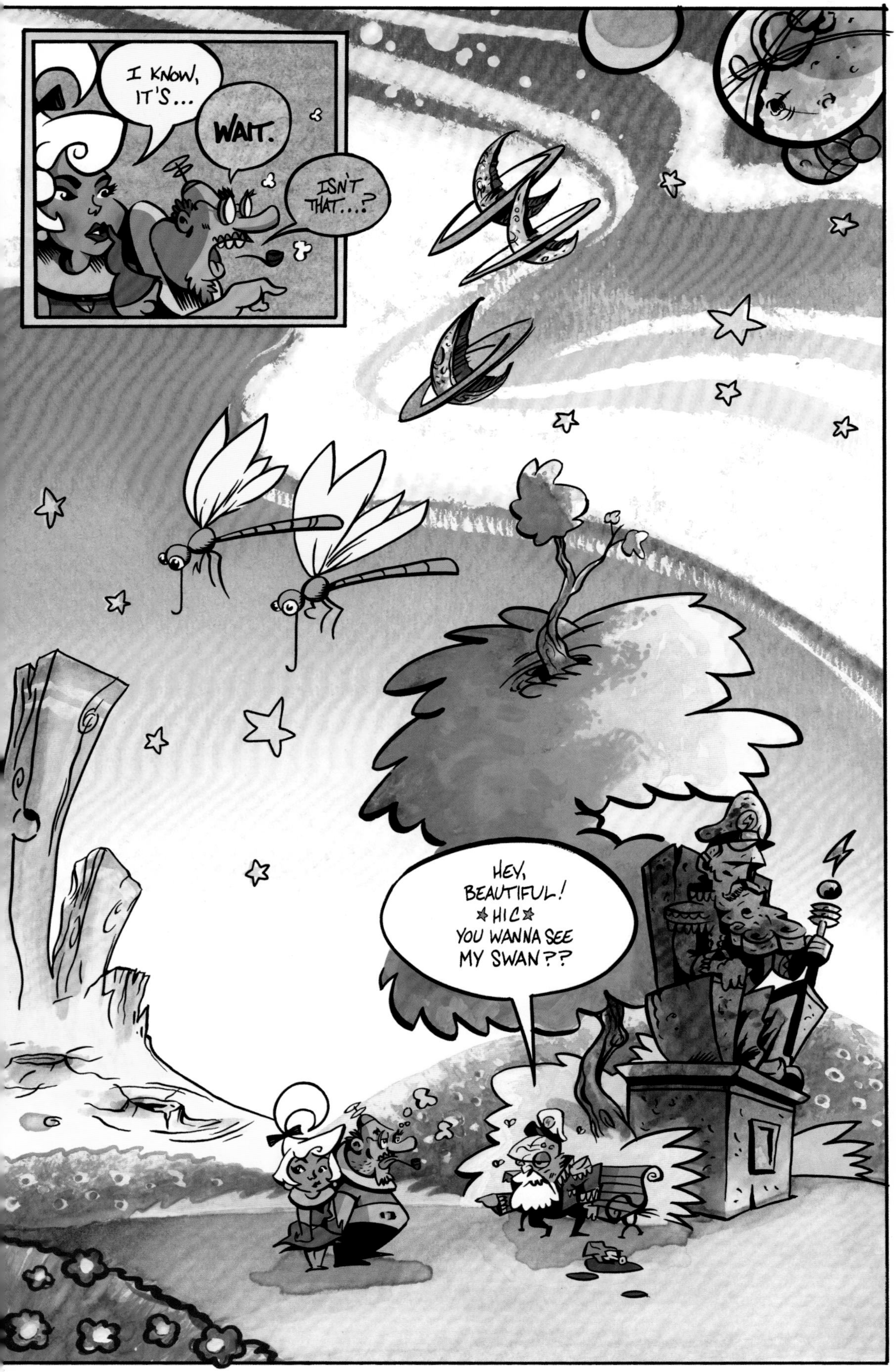
I KNOW, IT'S...
WAIT.
ISN'T THAT...?
HEY, BEAUTIFUL! *HIC* YOU WANNA SEE MY SWAN??

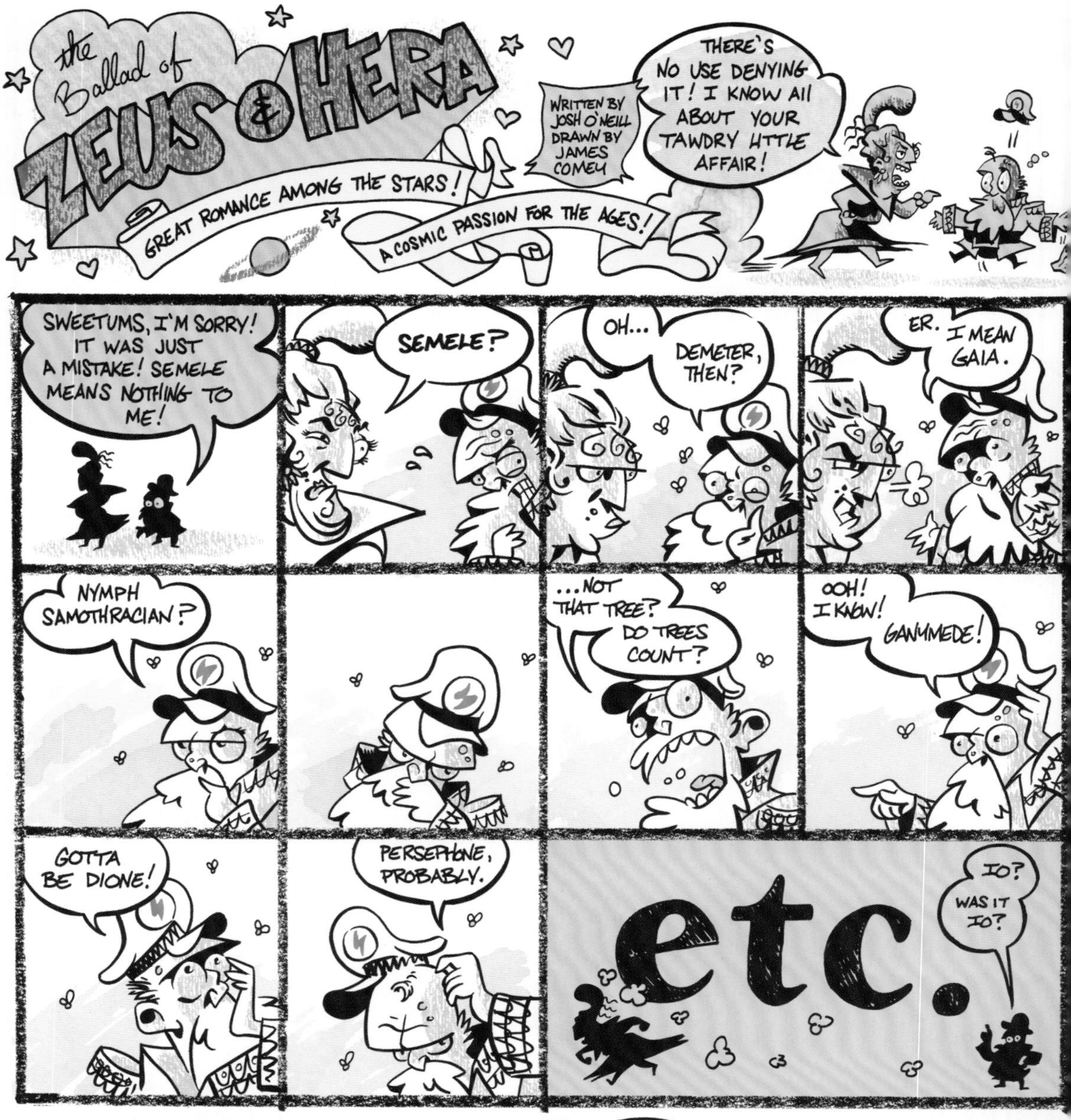
the Ballad of
ZEUS & HERA
GREAT ROMANCE AMONG THE STARS!
A COSMIC PASSION FOR THE AGES!
WRITTEN BY JOSH O'NEILL DRAWN BY JAMES COMEY
THERE'S NO USE DENYING IT! I KNOW ALL ABOUT YOUR TAWDRY LITTLE AFFAIR!
SWEETUMS, I'M SORRY! IT WAS JUST A MISTAKE! SEMELE MEANS NOTHING TO ME!
SEMELE?
OH...
DEMETER, THEN?
ER. I MEAN GAIA.
NYMPH SAMOTHRACIAN?
...NOT THAT TREE?
DO TREES COUNT?
OOH! I KNOW!
GANYMEDE!
GOTTA BE DIONE!
PERSEPHONE, PROBABLY.
etc.
IO? WAS IT IO?

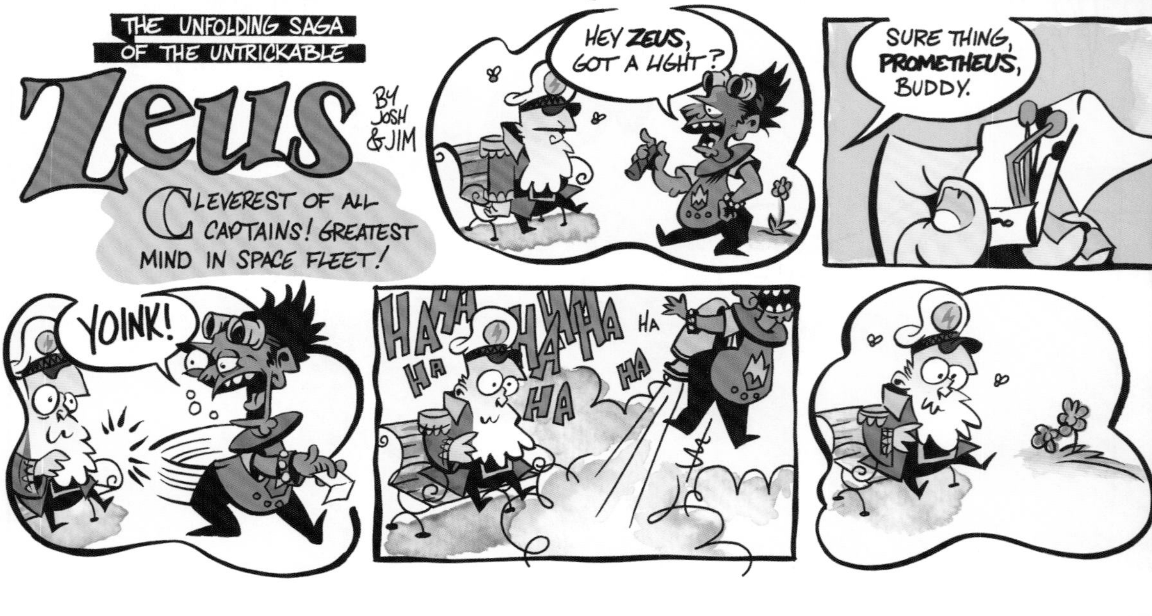
THE UNFOLDING SAGA OF THE UNTRICKABLE
Zeus
BY JOSH & JIM
CLEVEREST OF ALL CAPTAINS! GREATEST MIND IN SPACE FLEET!
HEY ZEUS, GOT A LIGHT?
SURE THING, PROMETHEUS, BUDDY.
YOINK!
HA HA HA HA HA HA HA HA HA HA HA

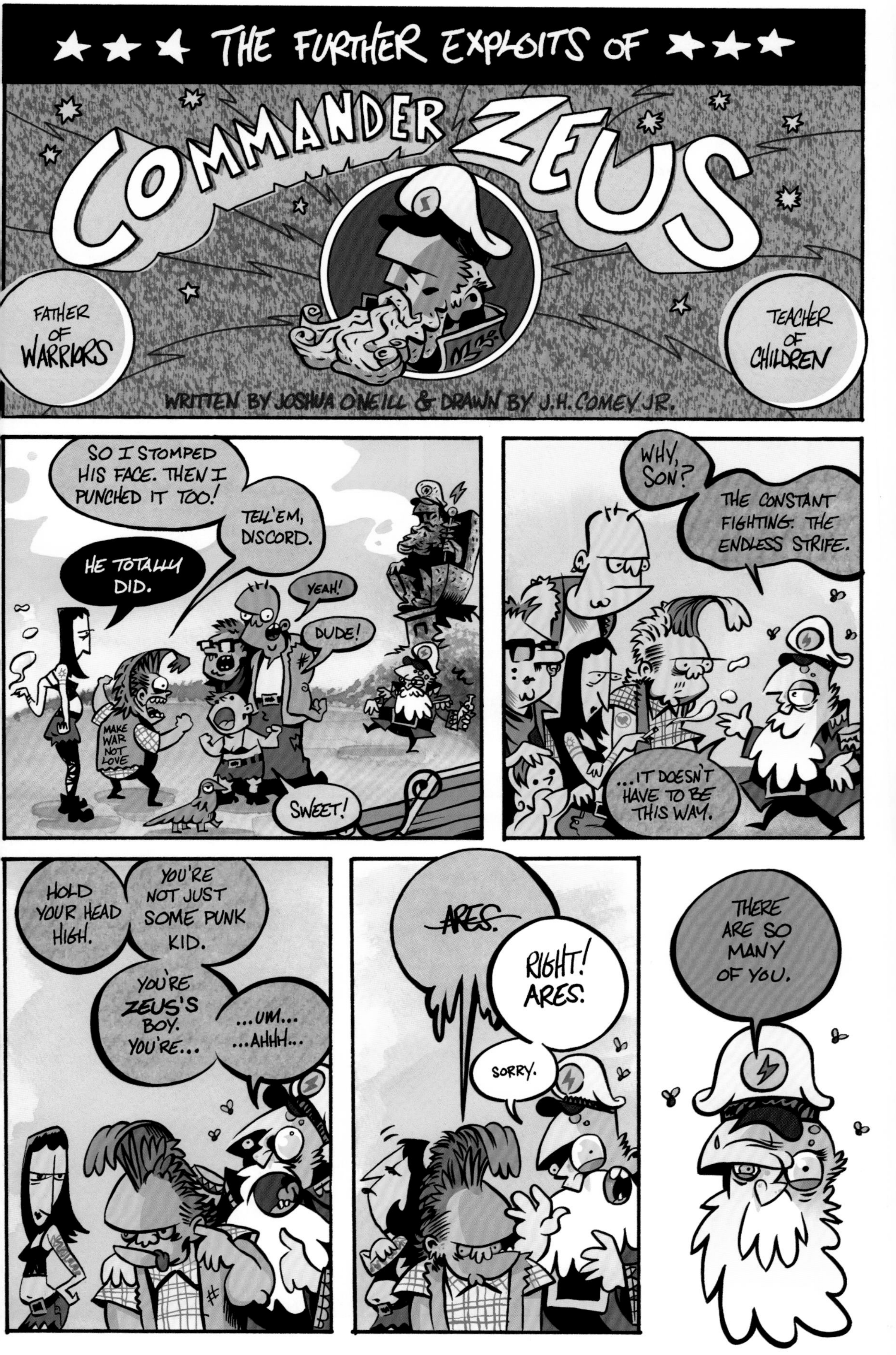
THE FURTHER EXPLOITS OF
COMMANDER ZEUS
FATHER OF WARRIORS
TEACHER OF CHILDREN
WRITTEN BY JOSHUA O'NEILL & DRAWN BY J.H. COMEY JR.
SO I STOMPED HIS FACE. THEN I PUNCHED IT TOO!
TELL'EM, DISCORD.
HE TOTALLY DID.
YEAH!
DUDE!
MAKE WAR NOT LOVE
SWEET!
WHY, SON?
THE CONSTANT FIGHTING. THE ENDLESS STRIFE.
...IT DOESN'T HAVE TO BE THIS WAY.
HOLD YOUR HEAD HIGH.
YOU'RE NOT JUST SOME PUNK KID.
YOU'RE ZEUS'S BOY. YOU'RE...
...UM... ...AHHH...
ARES.
RIGHT! ARES.
SORRY.
THERE ARE SO MANY OF YOU.

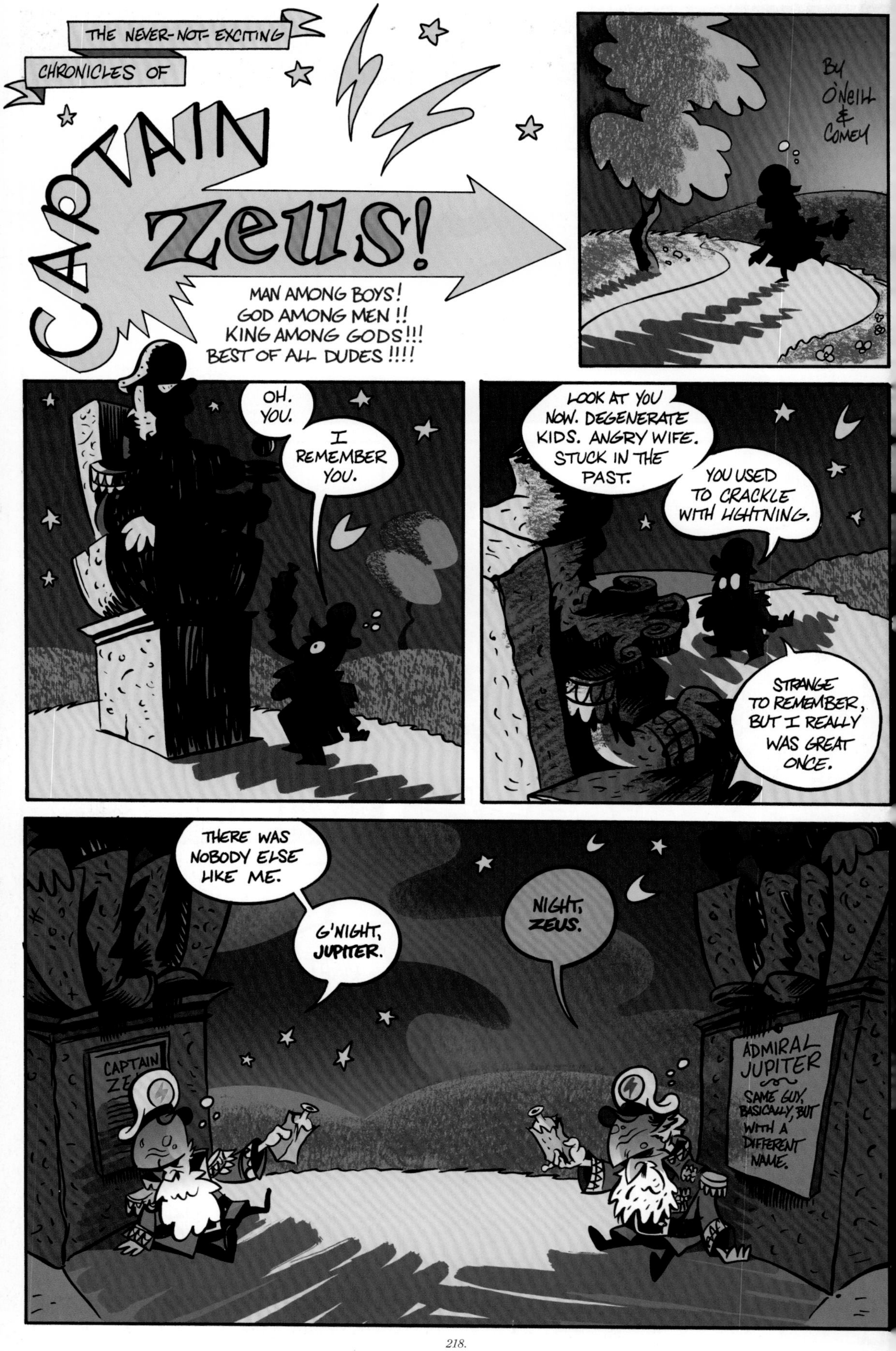
THE NEVER-NOT-EXCITING
CHRONICLES OF
CAPTAIN ZEUS!
MAN AMONG BOYS!
GOD AMONG MEN!!
KING AMONG GODS!!!
BEST OF ALL DUDES!!!!
BY O'NEILL & COMEY
OH. YOU.
I REMEMBER YOU.
LOOK AT YOU NOW. DEGENERATE KIDS. ANGRY WIFE. STUCK IN THE PAST.
YOU USED TO CRACKLE WITH LIGHTNING.
STRANGE TO REMEMBER, BUT I REALLY WAS GREAT ONCE.
THERE WAS NOBODY ELSE LIKE ME.
G'NIGHT, JUPITER.
NIGHT, ZEUS.
CAPTAIN ZE
ADMIRAL JUPITER
SAME GUY, BASICALLY, BUT WITH A DIFFERENT NAME.

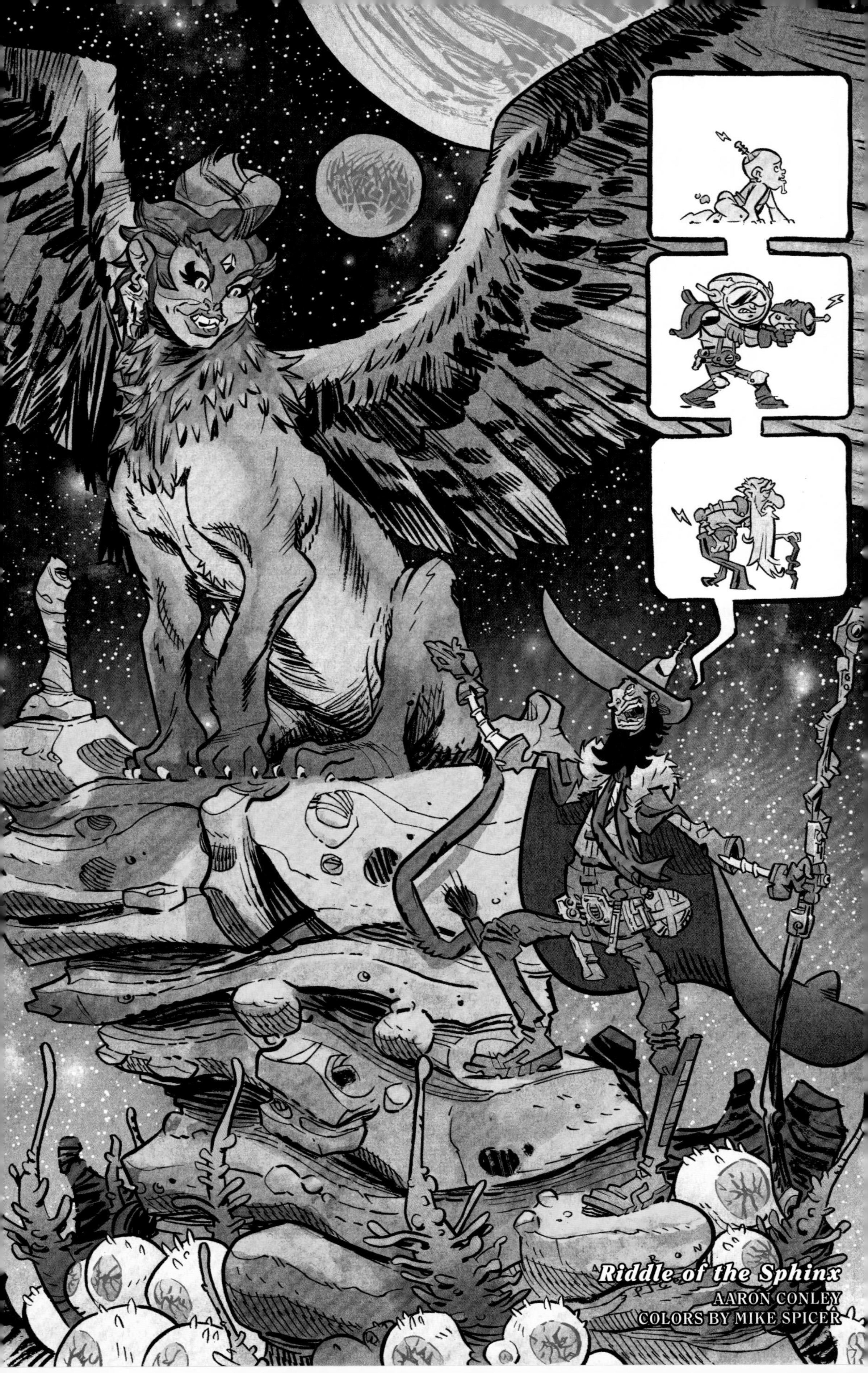
Riddle of the Sphinx
AARON CONLEY
COLORS BY MIKE SPICER

STEVE PRICE (@spriceartinc) has been putting words and pictures together for most of his professional life as a cartoonist, designer, comic book author, and gallery artist. Comics credits include short features in anthologies from Radio Comix, House of Twelve, and Manual Comics, as well as the logo and book design for *Nightworld: Midnight Sonata* and *Aquaria* (Image Comics) and an illustration in *Jungle Tales of Tarzan* (Dark Horse Comics). He is currently at work on a new chapter of the self-published *Karmikaze, Princess of Payback*™.

CARDINAL RAE is a letterer and designer with Fenix Works, Inc. who has worked on *Rose* (Image), *Coming of the Supermen* (DC), *Bingo Love* (Inclusive Press), *Tracy Queen, Pack* (Oneshi Press), and others.

DOMINIC REGAN creates modern lore and makes ancient history in series of his own like *People Protector Akay*, and has crafted his crazy chromas as colour-artist in books like *Superboy, Constantine, Nightworld,* and *2000 AD*. His blog is found at gammahed.blog-spot.co.uk

PAUL RIVOCHE is an illustrator, animation background designer, and graphic novelist based in Toronto, Canada.

JASON RODRIGUEZ is an Eisner and Harvey Award–nominated writer and editor. Jason specializes in producing comic anthologies, including *Postcards: True Stories That Never Happened* (Random House, 2007), *Colonial Comics: New England, 1620-1750* (Fulcrum, 2014), *Artists Against Police Brutality* (Rosarium, 2015), and *Colonial Comics: New England, 1750-1775* (Fulcrum, 2017). In 2017, Jason launched his own publishing company with the Kickstarter-funded *The Little Particle That Could*. Jason lives in Arlington, VA with two dogs and two cats.

MIKE SGIER (pronounced 'SKEER') is a printmaker and cartoonist currently based in Philadelphia, Pennsylvania. Born and raised outside of Denver, Colorado, Mike received a BFA from Creighton University and an MFA from the Minneapolis College of Art and Design. His current body of work is split between personal comics, stories and artwork set within a fantasy world, and explorations within printmaking that chronicle various elements of pop culture and fandom.

MIKE SPICER is a south Florida-based artist, and has been coloring comics since 2007. Husband to an amazing wife, father to a beautiful son, daddy to a stubborn dog. He likes pizza, burgers, beer, and wine... AND COLORING FRIGGIN' COMICS!! Seriously, it's the best! Mike has worked for several publishers including DC, Vertigo, Valiant, Image, IDW, and BOOM!

CHRIS STEVENS was born in the 1970s, a canceled Jack Kirby comic. Since then every few years one publisher or another has revived him.

DEAN STUART is an illustrator who paints and draws from his sunny studio in Oakland, CA. In addition to doing comic work, Dean works on paintings for galleries and is finishing up a large self-published book project called *Finders Keepers*.

MICHAEL SWANWICK has received the Nebula, Theodore Sturgeon, World Fantasy and Hugo Awards, and has the pleasant distinction of having been nominated for and lost more of these same awards than any other writer. He has written ten novels, over a hundred and fifty short stories, and countless works of flash fiction. His latest novel, *The Iron Dragon's Mother*, will be published in 2018.

ANDREA TSURUMI is an illustrator and cartoonist from New York who now lives and draws in Philadelphia. Her first comic *Why Would You Do That?* came out from Hic + Hoc in 2016 and her debut picture book, *Accident!*, comes out from Houghton Mifflin Harcourt in Fall 2017. Her other work has been published by TOON Books, The Nib, SpongeBob Comics, and Penguin Books, among others. You can see more of her comics at andreatsurumi.com.

JONATHAN TUNE makes comics about a variety of subjects. They travel the world, drawing beautiful cities and drinking cheap beer, recommendations accepted.

JOSÉ VILLARRUBIA, born in Madrid, Spain, and living now in Baltimore, is best known for his collaborations with author Alan Moore: illustrations for his books *Voice of the Fire* and *The Mirror of Love* and his graphic novel *Promethea*. He has worked extensively as a colorist for Marvel, DC, Image, Wildstorm, Vertigo, and other publishers, mostly doing digitally painted colors. He has been nominated several times for the Eisner Award and won the Harvey Award for *Cuba: My Revolution*.

VANEDA VIREAK, creative mastermind, only wakes after the sun has set. Produces questionable drawings, whether drunk or sober. Dreams of starting her own line of designer sweatpants.

JARREAU WIMBERLY is an illustrator sent from the future to protect the unborn son of Sarah Connor. When he is not fighting cyborgs he does work for clients such as Gearbox, Wizards of the Coast, Blizzard, Hasbro, Marvel Entertainment, and Fantasy Flight Games.

RONALD WIMBERLY can be found at www.ronaldwimberly.com and @ronaldwimberly on Instagram.

ONCE UPON A TIME MACHINE, VOLUME 2

Once Upon a Time Machine, Volume 2 ™ & © 2018 Andrew Carl and Chris Stevens.

"Icarus" © 2018 Andrew Carl and Gideon Kendall

"Theseus and Metrotaurus" © 2018 Ronald Wimberly

"The Slaying of the Psuedors" © 2018 Josh O'Neill and Charles Fetherolf

"Footsteps" © 2018 Adam McGovern and Paolo Leandri

"Persephone" © 2018 Conor McCreery and Vaneda Vireak

"Flying Horse Style" © 2018 Mike Baron and Jeff Johnson

"Daphne" © 2018 Andrew Carl and Pam López

"Andromeda" © 2018 Mike Sgier

"Eurydice" © 2018 Josh O'Neill and Toby Cypress

"Game Changers" © 2018 Ben Kahn and Alexandria Huntington

"Away Mission" © 2018 Andrea Tsurumi

"The 12 Labors of Mech-Detective Heracles" © 2018 Andrew Carl and Sebastián Piriz

"Pygmalion" © 2018 Jason Rodriguez and Bizhan Khodabandeh

"A Heavy Stone for All the Peoples" © 2018 Chris Stevens and Dave Chisholm

"Jason and the Argonauts" © 2018 Tara Alexander and Ha Huy Hoang

"Metal Iliad" © 2018 Paul Pope

"Cosmogony" © 2018 Jonathan Tune

"The Long Bow" © 2018 Michael Swanwick and Joe DellaGatta

"Zeus at Large" © 2018 Josh O'Neill and James Comey

Pandora © 2018 Dean Stuart

Arachne © 2018 Maëlle Doliveux

Hyperion © 2018 Jarreau Wimberly

Aphrodite © 2018 Alice Meichi Li

Minotaur © 2018 JM Dragunas

Hades © 2018 Paul Rivoche

Muses © 2018 Weshoyot Alvitre

Eros © 2018 David Garrido

Cerberus © 2018 Gregory Benton

Ares © 2018 Bodie Chewning

Riddle of the Sphinx © 2018 Aaron Conley

ONCE UPON A TIME MACHINE

A futuristic look at the ancient myths, legends, and folktales that inform our culture!

With work by Brandon Graham, Jill Thompson, Ryan Ottley, Khoi Pham, Drew Moss, and Nate Stockman, and many more of today's finest writers and illustrators!